BILLY'S PLACE

By
James Alden Dykes

Dedication

Billy's Place is dedicated to my remarkable grandchildren, Violet, Bowie, Harrison, Imogen and Olive, with gratitude to my extraordinary parents, my wonderful wife Carmen, for all her support and to R. Bennet Coles and Michelle Balfour of Cascadia Author Services for all their insightful advice and guidance.

CONTENTS

Dedication ii

About the Author v

Prologue vii

Book 1 – Straw Angels 1

Chapter 1 – The Farm 2

Chapter 2 – The Spring Storm 4

Chapter 3 – The Spring Storm 13

Chapter 4 – The Children's Aid Society 19

Chapter 5 – The Match Boxes 27

Chapter 6 – The Christmas Tree 35

Book 2 – The Flashlight 44

Chapter 1 – The House 45

Chapter 2 – The Radio 51

Chapter 3 – The Magic Shoebox 55

Chapter 4 – Bedtime Stories 59

Chapter 5 – Harvest 65

Chapter 6 – The Coal Chute 72

Chapter 7 – The Old Man 77

Chapter 8 – Trust 86

Book 3 – The Football 91

Chapter 1 – Home at Last 92

Chapter 2 – The Cat-In-The-Box 97

Chapter 3 - The Quarterback Club 116

Chapter 4 - The Christmas Present 130

Book 4 – The Guitar 137

Chapter 1 – The Two B's 138

Chapter 2 – The Sadie Hawkins/Valentines Dance 146

Chapter 3 – The Party 151

Chapter 4 – Hockey Camp 161

Chapter 5 – Chocolate Therapy 167

Chapter 6 – The Big Game 173

Chapter 7 – Uncle Walter 177

Chapter 8 – Return To The House 186

Chapter 9 – Mr. Melnyk's Surprise 199

Book 5 – The Cameras 202

Chapter 1 – Changing Places 203

Chapter 2 – Easter Baskets 207

Chapter 3 – The Circus 210

Chapter 4 – The Heist 220

Chapter 5 – The Album 230

Chapter 6 – The Escape 237

Chapter 7 – The Chase 242

Book 6 – The Play 252

Chapter 1 – Leonard's Room 253

Chapter 2 – Adversity 261

Chapter 3 – Good Grief 263

Chapter 4 – Bittersweet 266

Chapter 5 – Alone Together 270

Chapter 6 – Melanie 276

Chapter 7 – The Rise And Fall Of Ebenezer Scrooge 280

Chapter 8 – The Memorial 287

Epilogue 288

About the Author

James was born and grew up in Winnipeg, Manitoba. He earned his Bachelor of Architecture at the University of Manitoba and was awarded a Shimizu Fellowship for postgraduate studies at the University of Waseda in Tokyo, Japan. During his 46-year career as an architect, he spent the first half in the private sector, where he worked on many notable projects, including as a senior design architect on Calgary's Olympic Stadium and as the project architect for both the Alberta Research Council's headquarters in Edmonton and the Brain Injury Unit at Alberta Hospital Ponoka.

During the latter half of his career, he served in the public sector, first as the Director of Planning and Development at the University of Alberta, then as the Western Regional Manager of Architectural and Engineering services with Public Works and Government Services Canada (PWGSC). He retired from PWGSC as the National Advisor for laboratories.

James is a Fellow of both the Royal Architectural Institute of Canada (RAIC) and Sustainable Labs Canada (SLCan). He is also the founding president of SLCan.

Page Blank Intentionally

Prologue

With winter always fast on the heels of fall, weather-dependent Thanksgiving BBQs have long been popular in Winnipeg. In 1960, the sun was cooperating as friends and family gathered at the MacDonald's home on Kildonan Drive to celebrate the day. BJ MacDonald, a large man in his late sixties with snow-white curly hair, was checking the progress of the turkeys on his dual BBQs while his wife Carolyn, a strikingly stylish senior with a pixie-cut, welcomed guests onto their immaculately manicured backyard. In the middle of the expanse of lawn that extended down to the Red River stood Kathleen Melnyk, the sun highlighting strands of red amidst her long, silver hair. She held a commanding presence over the bustling activity of her catering staff as they completed setting out the buffet tables.

BJ and Kathleen immediately joined new arrivals: Egil and Dr. Amanda Amundson. Amanda evoked an image of royalty with her perfectly coiffured salt-and-pepper hair and her stunning black-and-white outfit. Her distinguished-looking husband, a retired deputy chief of police, was still slim and fit, sporting a perfectly trimmed mustache.

The couples greeted each other with smiles and hugs, as life-long friends do. Laughter and animated banter quickly infused the air. Thanksgiving was a good reason for this happy gathering, but the real reason was to inform family and friends of the progress of their pet project: a new youth center for disadvantaged children.

Amongst the guests were several former residents of Assiniboine House (BJ and Kathleen included), which had been home to many orphaned children after the Second World War. When the flood of 1950 rendered 'The House' uninhabitable, the children were all dispersed to foster care homes across the city. While a few managed to maintain a connection over the years, they never forgot their challenging childhood past.

After overcoming their difficult start to life, some managed to become quite successful, including BJ (CEO of MacDonald Construction Ltd.) and Kathleen (owner of Melnyk's Bakery and Catering), and they were determined to do something for today's underprivileged kids. With that ambition, they embarked on a journey that led to the final stage of construction of the William F. Johnson Youth Centre.

Upon arrival of all the friends and family, including children and grandchildren, dinner was served and thoroughly appreciated by all. Everyone in attendance had, by now, been fully apprised of every detail of this cherished project, but surprisingly, not everyone appeared to be familiar with Billy (William F. Johnson). Following dessert, Dr. Amundson addressed the gathering as Chair of the fundraising committee and began by explaining that Billy had once been a resident at Assiniboine House. She announced that, to fill in the history behind the naming of the building, six short stories were being printed that would introduce Billy to those who had not heard of him, including their own grandchildren. She advised that copies of the stories were available on a table by the back door to be picked up before leaving.

"However," she apologized, "Only five stories are included in the current edition, as the sixth, which I'm still working on, is not quite finished."

She assured everyone that it would be made available shortly.

Next on the agenda was the upcoming opening ceremonies, which was expected, but what was not expected was that it was being planned to coincide with a children's Christmas party on Christmas Eve. This new information received mixed reactions, especially from Amanda's sixteen-year-old granddaughter, Stacy, and BJ's fifteen-year-old granddaughter, Katie. They both expressed their reluctance to forgo their precious Christmas Eve for a building-opening ceremony, even one attended by Santa Claus.

In response to their concerns, Dr. Amundson suggested that they first read the stories and then make their decision. She clarified that as long as the girls read the stories, Santa would not disappoint, even if they chose not to attend. The girls both agreed, and everyone left happy with copies of the five stories about Billy.

Book 1
Straw Angels

By Egil Amundson

Chapter 1
The Farm

In 1938, my father learned that he had inherited his Uncle Ole's farm in Manitoba, Canada. I was only two years old, and so I wasn't consulted on whether the family should leave Norway for a place even colder in winter than Starheim, so without my consent, we moved to Canada.

The farm was located about twenty miles north of Winnipeg, near Lockport, a flyspeck of a town. For my parents, especially for my Papa, learning English was hell. Lucky for them, they became fast friends with their neighbors, the Johnsons, who owned the farm kitty-corner to ours. The Johnsons were happy to help my parents learn English, the language of our adopted homeland, and they enjoyed each other's company.

Mrs. Johnson often visited Momma for tea and to help with her English; they also read stories to my sister Bridget and me. She especially loved the traditional fairy tales, while I preferred Little Engine That Could by Charles S. Wing. The Johnsons had only one child, a fifteen-year-old son named Bill. I remember him only vaguely from the time or two he babysat us when my parents drove to Selkirk or Winnipeg for supplies and shopping. I do remember one time when we played cops and robbers, and the robber (Bill) tied me to the attic ladder while I waited to be rescued by the cops. Meanwhile, Billy parked his curly blond head on the couch and napped until my parents returned.

In 1942, Bill enlisted in the army. Not long after that, his unit, the Queen's Own Cameron Highlanders, was shipped overseas, leaving behind his fretful parents and a tearful girlfriend. After that, we never saw Bill again. He was but one of the over 900 Canadian soldiers who never returned from the beaches of Dieppe in occupied France.

We saw the Johnsons regularly until February 1943. Then, the visits stopped. We didn't see them again until one day in the middle of March when Momma packed us up in our winter snowsuits and told us we were going to see the Johnsons' new baby. It was several years later that I learned the real story. Before Bill was shipped overseas, he'd secretly married his girlfriend, René, without her parent's approval. René was already pregnant when Bill was shipped out. Her parents were furious when they found out about it, and not just because René was only seventeen, but because they were also devout Catholics, and Bill was not. Abortion was out of the question. And, of course, a baby born out of wedlock was born in sin. René cried and flooded the house with tears, but her mother wasn't having it. Poor René. Only sixteen. Having no choice, she agreed to give up the baby for adoption before returning to Montréal with her family.

Even though René's mother had sworn her daughter to secrecy, it turns out that Rene had confided in Mrs. Johnson just after Bill was shipped out for England. Then came the day the official telegraph arrived:

MINISTER OF DEFENCE DEEPLY REGRETS TO INFORM YOU THAT PRIVATE WILLIAM JOHNSON OFFICIALLY REPORTED KILLED IN ACTION IN DIEPPE ON 19 AUGUST 1943. STOP IF ANY FURTHER INFORMATION BECOMES AVAILABLE; IT WILL BE FORWARDED AS SOON AS RECEIVED.

That was when the Johnsons met with René's parents and pleaded with them for permission to adopt the baby. He was their grandchild, after all, and was the only link left to their son. And so it was that, in March 1943, a new baby named Billy became our neighbor.

Chapter 2
The Spring Storm

For the next five years leading up to that fateful day in the spring of 1948, our families, like most farm neighbors, made regular visits back and forth, assisting each other with chores, sharing meals together, etc., and Billy soon became more like a younger brother than a neighbor.

Spring snowstorms were common in Winnipeg. We kids were often happy when they came. One more round of snow angels, snow forts, and snowball fights. But this snowstorm was different– treacherous, blinding, slicking the roads with ice in the days before snow tires were common.

Billy's grandparents had driven to Selkirk to do some shopping, and Billy was staying with us. When we sat down to dinner, the sky was already dark outside. I remember Momma saying she wasn't surprised they hadn't returned to pick Billy up yet, what with all that snow.

When the clock chimed eight o'clock, Momma began to worry. We had no telephone, so Momma told me to listen to the radio for any announcements about road closures. I listened attentively with my ear a hair from the speaker, but… nothing. When bedtime came, Momma put on a cheerful smile that even I could tell was forced. She told us Billy would be sleeping in the loft with us overnight.

In the morning, we woke to the sound of adult voices downstairs. I heard Momma crying softly. As the first one down the ladder, I was surprised to see two RCMP officers in the front room. Papa hurried to the ladder and ushered us all, except Billy, into their bedroom. He asked us to wait quietly, and then he closed the door and headed back to the kitchen without any explanation.

When the Mounties left, Papa led us out to find Momma sitting in the kitchen with her eyes red and full of tears. She was holding Billy tightly on her knees, rocking him gently, while Papa paced the kitchen floor. Suddenly, Papa stopped and fixed his pale blue eyes on us, a perplexed expression on his drawn face. He had difficulty enough expressing himself in Norwegian, let alone in English, and it was clear he had something serious to say. He chose English for my younger siblings' sake because their English was better than their Norwegian.

"What's wrong, Papa?" Bridget asked, twisting her hands.

"Come here," he said, leading us to the table and gesturing for us to sit with Momma and Billy.

He began slowly, "We have a very unhappy…unhappy…"

"Situation!" Momma completed his sentence without her eyes off Billy.

"Yah! Yah! The situation," Papa said. "Thank you, Momma." Papa continued, "The situation is that…Mr. and Mrs. Johnson have met a serious disaster."

"It was an accident," Momma corrected him, still rocking Billy slowly.

"A serious accident," Papa continued, "Billy's grandparents, they are taken to heaven."

"Will they be coming back soon?" Ingar asked.

"I'm afraid not, my little ones," Momma replied, with her eyes still fixed on Billy.

Since the Children's Aid Society couldn't track down Billy's mother and Billy had no other relatives, they allowed him to stay with us temporarily. For the next few days, numerous official-looking people came and went from our house, and Momma and Papa made several trips over to Johnson's house. On the first trip, they brought back Billy's clothes, a toothbrush, and a small teddy bear from beside his bed, which Momma thought would comfort him. To her surprise, it had just the opposite effect. He started to whimper and couldn't be consoled.

With considerable patience and coaxing, Momma managed to decipher something about a shoebox. After supper, Billy and I put our boots and coats on and trudged through the deep snow back to his grandparent's home to find his precious box. As soon as we entered the house, Billy pulled off his boots and raced to retrieve it from under his bed.

When we returned, he showed us the contents of his special shoebox. There was a straw angel Christmas tree decoration, a strange L-shaped khaki flashlight, a leather pilot, a small army knife, and three children's books: *Little Toot*, *Winnie-the-Pooh*, and *Little Black Sambo*. We were all interested in Billy's books, and Momma promised that if we all helped to clean up, she would read to us before bedtime. She told us to let Billy choose his favorite book.

Bridget and I cleared the table while Billy, Lars, and Ingar sat in the corner of the living room floor, going through the contents of Billy's magic shoebox. Bridget wanted Winnie-the-Pooh, but Ingar insisted on *Little Black Sambo*. Billy nodded his approval.

As Momma took hold of the book, Billy pulled it tight to his chest and said, "I can read it!"

Momma's surprise shifted to a smile.

"Really? You can read?" she asked.

"Uh huh!" Billy replied.

"That's wonderful, Billy," Momma said.

"Come sit beside me then, and let's get started."

Billy scampered up onto the Chesterfield and cuddled up beside Momma. He opened his book and flipped the pages with great excitement.

Finding the right spot, he began, *"Once upon a time, there was a little black boy, and his name was Little Black Sambo."*

He paused as we looked at the picture of Little Black Sambo, and when Momma turned to the next page, Billy started again, "And his mother was called Black Mumbo."

Bridget and I could both read, and we were quite impressed as we crowded behind Billy, but Lars was suspicious that Billy was not reading it correctly. Momma seemed equally surprised. Billy was barely five years old and hadn't started school yet.

She turned the page once more, and Billy continued, "And his father was called Black Jumbo."

While we focused on the picture of Black Jumbo, Billy continued without a pause, "And Black Mumbo made him a beautiful Little Red Coat and a pair of beautiful Little Blue Trousers."

When Momma turned to the next page, she started to chuckle quietly. Although it was not apparent to us, Momma realized that Billy had memorized the words and was reciting from pages we hadn't even reached yet. Apparently, Billy's grandmother had read this story to him so many times that he knew it by heart without knowing how to read at all. This book has been banned in many places today as it uses stereotypes, but it never occurred to us, and that was hurtful.

Without revealing Billy's trick, she let him finish the story, which we all enjoyed very much. Not wanting to discourage his interest in books, Momma complimented him on his ability to read while glancing at us sternly and shaking her head to warn us not to show we knew he couldn't.

After that, Momma began working with him to 'improve' his reading skills, and in a few months, he started reading at the same level as Bridget.

I'd never been to a funeral before, so the double funeral for Billy's grandparents is pretty much seared into my memory. We all had to stuff into the old pickup truck, which meant that the older kids had to sit in the open back. Billy, wearing his father's pilot hat, squeezed in with Ingar and Liv beside Momma in the front seat. I swept out all the bits of snow, and Momma brought a pile of blankets to keep us cozy. Then, just as we were leaving, Tess, our border collie, jumped into the back. Papa had said she couldn't come, but she had a mind of her own, so we made room and headed off, the wind blowing in our faces.

I'd been expecting gloomy weather, as befitting a funeral, but it was a lovely, sunny spring day at Little Britain Church, there on the west bank of the Red River, just north of the Lockport Bridge, with rushing water flowing freely through the open locks below. The last time I'd been to Lockport was when Papa took us to Skinners Drive-in to try their famous hot dogs. Alas, that happy place with its red booths and cheerful waitresses was not our destination.

The church was a lovely old Tyndall stone structure built in 1874. It had seating for about 120 people, but there were many more crammed into the hall on that sad day, and there wasn't a dry eye in the room. After the funeral ceremony, everyone reconvened in the reception hall on the other side of the parking lot.

Momma and Papa both looked very tired, and Bridget, who was always the thoughtful one, hinted at me, "I'll bet they'd love some coffee."

Taking the hint, I brought them coffee before I filled up my own plate with dainty afternoon tea-style crustless sandwiches. My thoughtfulness with the coffee surprised and pleased Momma. She asked me if I'd watch Billy and Ingar while they mingled with the grown-ups.

I must have agreed; I don't recall, only that I got distracted by all the food until Momma patted me on the shoulder and asked, "Are the boys okay, Egil?"

I was soon frantically searching for them. I hurried over to where Bridget was serving coffee and asked her if she knew where the boys were.

She glared at me, "Jeez, don't you know? You're supposed to be looking after them."

I gave her a dirty look as she smugly asked, "Are their coats and boots still by the door?"

I rushed over to the door. Billy's coat and boots were gone, as were Lars' and Ingars', so I felt some relief, believing Billy must be with them. I also realized that Bridget probably saw them go outside and was just waiting for me to figure it out.

With all the snow from the recent storm, combined with the warm sun, conditions were perfect for making snowballs and snowmen, which, I deduced, would seem like a great idea to the boys. I quickly put on my coat and boots and rushed outside, looking for footprints in the snow to follow. Unfortunately, there were footprints everywhere, so I ran around the building to see if there was any sign of them.

The church was near the main street, but the cemetery, with its grey, weathered tombstones, extended all the way down to the west bank of the Red River. As I came around the building, I heard Tess barking and saw her running around the top of the riverbank. Then, I caught sight of a boy standing beside her, looking down at the river.

"Ingar?"

I called out his name but got no answer; I raced toward the river as fast as I could.

When I skidded to a stop at the embankment, I found Ingar staring intently down at the edge of the river. I grabbed his arm and peered over the edge. To my horror, I saw Lars standing on the lower bank of the river, extending a branch out to Billy, who was kneeling on a raft of ice about five feet wide. He was holding his pilot hat in one hand and desperately trying to grab onto the branch with the other.

Standing beside Lars were three boys, all bigger than him, pointing at Billy with great amusement. When I called out to Lars, the three boys looked up at me and scampered off like scared rabbits. The tall, red-headed one dropped his toque as they ran off and disappeared.

I looked back down at Billy. I was instantly aware of the danger, so I slid down the embankment as fast as I could, tearing my pants and scratching my hands on rocks. Now, I was at the river's edge beside Lars. His branch wasn't quite long enough, so I broke off a longer one. The current was strong, and the ice Billy was kneeling on was slowly drifting away from the bank. Unfortunately, my branch wasn't long enough either. I nearly panicked. Then I remember ordering myself: Think, you idiot! That's when I noticed that the current was starting to rotate Billy's little ice raft so that the end that Billy was kneeling on was moving closer to where Lars was standing. I couldn't reach

Billy with my stick, but I could, just barely, reach the other end of the ice with my branch, just enough to push it and the rotation and move Billy closer to Lars.

It worked. Billy was now close enough to grab hold of Lars' branch. Lars started to pull the piece of ice closer to the shore. As Billy reached the shore, he stretched out his free arm so Lars could grab him. When Lars pulled him onto the shore, Billy's feet slipped backward, sending the ice away from the shore. I nearly cheered aloud that Billy was safe, but then he loosened his grip and lost his balance.

The scene unfolded in slow motion while I watched in dread as Billy tried to stand up, dropped his pilot hat on the ground, and then tilted backward into the river. As he splashed into the freezing water, the strong river current pulled him out about two feet from shore. He lifted his head up for a breath of air, but his soaking winter clothes were dragging him under, and he struggled to stay afloat.

As he flailed around in the water, he ended up next to the ice flow. He grabbed for it, and–I still don't know how he did it–but he miraculously managed to pull his upper body onto the ice until he was on his tummy with his legs still in the water. As he splashed about, the piece of ice wobbled around, and he slipped back into the water a little but managed to pull himself back up on the ice. Throughout this whole scene, which probably only lasted a few seconds, I stood helplessly frozen on the bank.

I yelled at Billy to hold on and stay absolutely still, then told Lars to get Papa quickly. He– along with Tess, who was still holding Billy's hat in her mouth– raced up the riverbank and back toward the reception hall. With the branch still in my hand, I began to wade out to Billy, but the bank dropped off too quickly. There was no way I could reach him.

Since the water was freezing and I couldn't swim, I just stood there watching Billy. He was now lying quietly on his stomach on the edge of his ice raft. By lying motionless, he'd managed to stop the ice from wobbling, but it was still slowly drifting further away from shore.

I heard voices approaching the top of the riverbank, along with Lars yelling, "Hurry! Hurry!"

I couldn't see anyone from the bottom of the bank, but I joined Lars in yelling for help. After what seemed an eternity, I glanced up and saw Papa staring down and sizing up the situation.

He, too, slid down the bank, and in a blink, he was standing right beside me. He handed me his coat, kicked off his shoes, and fearlessly dove into the freezing water, swimming his way through the loose, treacherous ice to reach

Billy. Papa managed to swim behind Billy's ice raft, and with his feet kicking furiously, he pushed it toward the shore.

By the time he reached the bank, some of the other men were standing beside me. One of them had brought a hoe, and he used it to reach out and grab onto the ice. Once it was close to the edge, two of the other men stepped into the water. One helped Papa, and the other lifted Billy's limp frame off the ice and carried him up the embankment.

Tess, being the loyal puppy that she was, dropped Billy's hat beside me and stepped into the water.

To help, she then leaped right back out of the freezing water and shook herself off all over me.

I picked up Billy's pilot hat as two men helped Papa climb up the bank. I followed them with Tess clambering up in front of me, slipping back on top of me several times and scratching me. Once we got to the top of the embankment, Tess raced straight to the hall, but by the time I got there, Papa and Billy were already huddled in front of the wood stove in the corner of the room, surrounded by concerned people with blankets and hot drinks.

Poor Tess was not allowed in and was left howling at the door, so Lars escorted her to the back of the truck. Shivering, my teeth chattering, I pulled off my shoes, wrung out my socks at the door, and rolled up my pants, thinking no one would notice, especially with everyone gathered around the wood stove. No one did, which was a huge relief for me because I fully expected to be blamed for everything.

I tiptoed over to the stove with my shoes in my hands and my socks in my back pocket. Papa was wrapped in blankets, and when he noticed me approaching, I feared he might scold me for not watching the boys closer, but instead, he came over and wrapped his blanket around me as he grabbed my shoes and moved me close to the stove to get warm. Then he pulled up a chair for me beside Momma and set my shoes by the stove to dry. Momma put her arms around me to help me stop shivering. With Momma's arms around me and the warmth of the stove, a welcome calmness swept over me.

Fortunately, Dr. Bell, who was Johnson's physician, was at the funeral with his wife and two grown sons, Don and Doug. He attended to Billy, who was sitting motionless, wrapped in blankets on a chair in front of the stove.

"We need to get Billy to a hospital immediately," Dr. Bell announced.

"He's suffering from shock and hypothermia."

"I'll take him, Dad," Don answered, as Dr. Bell was attending, "I'm on duty soon anyway."

"Someone should go with him," Dr. Bell replied, "and Mrs. Amundson needs to stay here with her husband."

"Bridget can go with you," Momma said, and then, looking at me to see if I was okay, she added, "And you too, Egil, if you're feeling better?"

Dr. Bell added, "Thanks, Don. There are some socks and boots in my car. I'll stay here with Mr. Amundson and drop by the hospital later."

Doug then gently picked up Billy and carried him to Don's car. Bridget followed them to fetch the dry socks and boots for me. They were about five sizes too big, but at least they were dry. When I reached Don's car, I found Bridget and Billy already neatly tucked in the back seat. Don suggested that I get in the front seat beside him, and he put a blanket over my legs to keep me warm.

On our way to the Winnipeg General Hospital, Don told us he was a police officer and that he enjoyed his job. It sounded so interesting that I started thinking about my own future. I knew that Papa wanted me to work on the farm with him, but I was finding farm work boring, to be honest, and I already knew I wanted something different.

The hospital provided Don with a wheelchair, and he wheeled Billy into the examination room.

He had to go to report for duty, so he left shortly after Billy was checked in. Bridget and I were shown into a waiting area by the admissions nurse in her starched cap and uniform.

Her name was Mrs. Melnyk, and she was very kind. She brought us some refreshments and magazines and stayed with us until Dr. Bell arrived to check on Billy. After a short wait, he emerged with Nurse Melnyk and told us that Billy had pneumonia and would have to stay in the hospital for a while. Nurse Melnyk handed Dr. Bell a note as we were leaving, and he passed it to me.

"Please give this to your father when you get home," he said.

"What is it?" I asked.

"Mrs. Melnyk's brother-in-law is a chiropractor who can help relieve the pain in your father's," he replied.

"This is his name and phone number."

"What's the problem with his back?" Bridget asked.

"I'm afraid he has a herniated disk again," Dr. Bell said as he led us to his car and drove us home.

While Bridget went to the kitchen to help fix supper, Momma suggested that I join Papa in the living room, where he was settled in his favorite chair. Lars soon joined, and I noticed that he was holding something in his hand.

"What's that?" I asked.

"The tall kid with the red hair dropped it when he ran away," Lars replied, handing me a worn-out red toque.

"Who were those kids anyway?" I asked.

I held up the toque and noticed a big red letter, 'R.'

Lars shrugged, "I don't know. I've never seen them before."

"Why were they laughing and not helping?" I asked.

Lars frowned and shook his head.

"First, they made fun of Billy's hat, and then that tall, red-headed kid grabbed it and threw it on the ice. Billy stepped on the ice to get his hat back, and the tall kid stomped on the ice at the edge of the bank. That's when we heard this loud crack."

"What cracked?" Papa asked.

"The ice," Lars replied.

"And the next thing I knew, Billy was kneeling on that hunk of ice, and it was spinning away from the edge."

"And they thought that was funny?" Papa asked.

"I guess," Lars mumbled.

"Because they laughed really loud."

"Dumb jerks," I mumbled back.

Billy stayed in the hospital for over two weeks. When he came home, it was with a big jar of green powder called Belladonna Asthmador. The doctor had diagnosed him with asthma, and it was the beginning of Billy's life-long struggle. It was as if, after that terrifying day of struggling in the icy water, he could never catch his breath again.

Chapter 3
The Spring Storm

In the fall, after we returned to school, we learned that Tess was going to have puppies, and everyone was thrilled. At supper, Billy asked when the puppies would be ready, and Momma said they should be here around Thanksgiving.

"Are we going to keep them, Momma?" Ingar asked.

"Maybe one," Momma replied. "And we'll find good homes for the rest, but they'll have to stay with Tess for two months."

A few days before Thanksgiving, I got home from school and was surprised that Tess hadn't bounded out to greet me. Momma was making supper, and when I walked in the door, she asked me to put Tess's dinner out on the porch. I did and called her, but she didn't come. No sign of her at all. I poked my head back in the door and told Momma, and she suggested that Billy and I check on her *valpepenn* in the barn.

"What's *a valpepenn*, Momma?" Billy asked.

"It's a quiet, secluded place for Tess in the empty stall at the far end of the barn where she can give birth to her puppies."

Momma had put down a layer of hay with some blankets on top and set out a bowl of water. She had shown it to Tess a couple of times, and Tess didn't seem very interested, but Momma just smiled and said, "She will when she's ready."

Billy and I checked out the barn, and it was then that I realized what Momma meant. Tess was stretched out in her *valpepenn*.

We ran back to Momma, and Billy called to her breathlessly, "I think she's ready, Momma!"

"Who's ready?" Bridget asked.

"Tess!" I answered.

"Come and see," Billy called out.

He wheezed and tried to catch his breath.

Momma thunked down a jug, and the cutlery jumped.

"Not now! Sit down and finish supper first. Tess will still be there after you've eaten."

"Were there any puppies yet? Were there?" Bridget asked, her eyes nearly shining with excitement.

"Not that we could see," I replied, as we all began shoveling our dinner down as fast as we could.

Just then, Papa came in for supper and stopped as he approached the table.

"What's going on here?" he asked curiously.

"Tess is having her puppies," I replied.

"Eating quickly won't make any difference to when the puppies will be born, and they'll still be there after dinner," Papa said.

Without quite finishing our supper, we excused ourselves from the table.

Momma, without even looking up, simply said one word, "Dishes!"

We all stopped in our tracks and returned to the table to clean up. When we finally finished the dishes, which took forever, we raced back to the barn and stared at Tess over the stall gate. She looked like she was sleeping.

"Is she doing anything?" Billy asked.

"Not yet," Bridget said.

We stood there silent and still, in excited anticipation, for the longest time.

"It doesn't look like she's doing anything," Billy observed.

"That's because she's not," Bridget agreed. "False alarm."

We turned around despondently and began slowly filing out of the barn. All except Billy, who was still standing at the gate and staring at Tess.

"Hey, we didn't have any dessert," Ingar said.

"Is there any?" Lars asked, perking up.

"There's *a riskrem* with raspberries in the ice box," Bridget declared.

"Hmm, my favorite," Lars said.

Then we heard Billy say softly, "She moved."

This was just as Momma entered the barn. We whirled and raced back to the stall while Momma stood in the barn doorway, wondering what she'd done to frighten us. We were gazing over the stall gate again to see what Tess was doing when Momma came up to check for herself. She gently opened the stall gate, with Billy and Ingar still hanging on to the top rail and staring down at Tess.

"Here comes the first one," Bridget announced.

Momma gently knelt down beside Tess as we all tried to get in the stall for a closer look, but she shooed us away and told us to give Tess some space. The first puppy arrived. Momma gently picked it up to check if the membrane was covering the puppy's face. It was, so Momma gently held the puppy up to Tess.

"Tess has to lick the membrane of her baby's face so it can breathe," she smiled.

Tess licked the membrane off and nipped through the umbilical cord so the placenta dropped on the blanket. Meanwhile, the next puppy was emerging, keeping Momma busy.

Billy snuck into the stall to examine the placenta on the blanket.

"Look," he said with surprise. "She dropped one."

Momma and the rest of us were too busy watching the next puppy emerge to pay any attention to Billy.

"It's not breathing," Billy said sadly, picking it up and holding it up to Tess. "Here, Tess, lick the puppy's face so it can breathe."

Poor Billy was shocked when Tess snatched the placenta in her teeth and ate it.

"She just ate her puppy!" Billy shrieked and started to cry.

He looked bewildered and confused when we all laughed. Momma knelt beside him, giving him a big hug and shielding him from our laughing faces. His crying launched him into another coughing and wheezing fit.

"It's all right, Billy, it wasn't a puppy," Momma said tenderly. "That was just the afterbirth, which is the membrane sac that feeds the puppy while it's inside mommy's tummy,"

She picked up the placenta from the second puppy to show him, then gave him another hug and looked at us as she gestured her hand across her throat. We understood, and we stopped laughing, although it wasn't easy.

Mamma gave us her best, *you-should-be-ashamed* look, "The Johnson farm didn't have many animals, and their dog was a boy, so this is the first time Billy has ever witnessed the miracle of birth."

"Here comes the third one!" Bridget cried out.

We turned our attention back to Tess to see one more beautiful puppy. Before long, Tess had five new puppies attached to her tummy.

"I think that was the last one," Momma said as she petted Tess gently and slowly stood up, "I think we need to give her some private time with her new babies."

"Is it *Riskrem* time, Momma?" Lars asked hopefully.

Bridget rolled her eyes, "As if you didn't know!"

"Don't forget to wash your hands," Momma said with a smile as we raced to the kitchen.

"How many?" Papa asked.

"Five, Papa!" Lars pronounced proudly. "Two girls and three boys."

"Can we keep some Papa? Can we?" Ingar pleaded.

"Just one," Papa said as he sipped his coffee. "You can choose."

"What about the white one with the black patch over his one eye?" Billy suggested.

"I like the black girl puppy with the white mark on her forehead. She looks like an angel," Bridget added.

"I like Patch too, Papa," Ingar added.

"Patch, that's a good name," I said, and Billy nodded.

"Pick one and only one," Papa said as he picked up his coffee and headed for his favorite chair in the living room.

"What'll happen to the other ones?" I asked.

"Mr MacLeod asked for one," Papa replied as he sat down. "And my chiropractor, Dr. Melnyk, asked if he could have a girl dog for his brother's friend Mr. Reilly."

Billy was counting on his fingers and said, "That still leaves two with no homes."

"We'll find homes for all of them," Momma added. "Now it's time to get ready for bed."

"Okay, Momma," Bridget said with a yawn. "Just watching Tess give birth was so exhausting."

"It certainly was," Momma said and sighed as she peered over the top of her glasses at Papa.

Papa lifted up his paper to pretend he didn't notice.

"This will be the last time, Momma," he said softly.

Bridget had her eyes glued on Momma and Papa. "What's going on, Momma?" she asked.

I watched in complete confusion, but Bridget jumped in excitement, understanding something that went way over my head.

"Is it really true, Momma?" she asked, running over to give Momma a big hug.

Momma smiled and nodded gently while Papa put his paper down slowly. He also smiled at Momma.

"I hope it's a girl this time," Bridget yelled as she hugged Papa next.

"Me too," Momma said, "I think we have enough boys."

Papa just cocked his head; I sat there quietly.

Bridget came over to me, delighting in my obvious confusion, and pinched my cheek.

"You're going to have another sister, stupid," she jeered.

I felt like an idiot. But then I grinned and looked over at Billy. "It's going to get crowded around here!"

Chapter 4
The Children's Aid Society

At the end of November, Papa announced that we could join him on his annual pre-Christmas pilgrimage to Eaton's department store. During the days leading up to that special Saturday morning, we behaved like angels, giving our Momma a welcome break from the usual mayhem.

All of us except Bridget and Ingar rode in the open back of a pickup truck. In December. In Manitoba. It was the only vehicle we had. Papa tossed an old mattress in the back, and Momma gave us a heap of blankets to keep us warm and pillows to protect us in case Papa had to slam on the brakes. This was likely safer than being in the front seat. There were no seat belts back then. It's a miracle that any of us survived.

"Papa!" Momma called as we climbed into the back of the truck. "Don't forget that the Children's Aid lady will be here at four o'clock sharp."

"I remember Momma," Papa called back as we drove away.

Billy brought his trusty flashlight to use under the blankets, but we braved the cold instead and sat with our backs against the pillows, peeking out over the blankets to see all the buildings along Main Street and Portage Avenue.

Eaton's store was an eight-story building full of so many magical things, including a whole toy department. Papa found a parking spot about two blocks down from Eaton's, away from the crowds. That way, we could slip out of the back of the truck without anyone noticing us packed in the back of a freezing old pickup.

As we passed by the Eaton's *Once Upon a Christmas* windows, all full of seasonal scenes and figures. We were treated to animated and still figures, with the magical sound of Christmas music piped over the busy sidewalk. Each window was set up with a different Christmas display where figures bobbed, nodded, tumbled, and twirled with the music. One was Santa's workshop full of elves making toys; in another, a skater circled a gazebo in front of a two-story log cabin set on a snowy hill with children playing everywhere; in yet another, animated carollers sang songs of the season. But the corner window at Portage Avenue was my favorite. In that window, a full-sized animated Santa sat in the middle of a room, with toys of every kind surrounding him; the toys were spread out on a table, on the floor, and they filled all the shelves on the wall behind him. I could have stayed there all day, but Papa reminded us of our mission, so we headed inside.

He told me to make sure that all of us stayed together and to meet in two hours, in front of the Timothy Eaton statue on the main floor. Then he loaned me Uncle Ole's sold watch to make sure we wouldn't be late. Bridget agreed to watch Ingar, and I dragged Lars and Billy along, carrying our coats, on our quest for the perfect presents.

We pooled our Christmas funds and savings from our monthly allowances to buy something nice for Momma and Papa for five dollars each. We decided on a new sweater for Momma and a new pipe for Papa. Bridget and Ingar went off to the ladies' department to search for the perfect sweater, and I took the boys with me up to find a pipe.

Papa was still using the same old pipe he'd brought with him from Norway, so it was older than me and covered with teeth marks where he often chewed on it when he wasn't actually smoking it. At the counter, the salesman—a middle-aged man with thin hair, a small mustache, and wire glasses—looked at us with suspicion. I dug out the five dollars in change and spilled it on the counter.

The man eyed it, "Where are your parents, young man?" he asked.

"Our Papa's here in the store somewhere," I answered. "But he can't tell us what we're getting because it's a Christmas surprise."

The man now smiled gently and asked what we were looking for.

Billy pushed toward the counter, breathless with excitement, "Papa needs a new pipe!"

"Well, you've come to the right place." The man smiled again, "How much do you have there?"

"Five whole dollars," I said proudly.

"Well, today is your lucky day, boys," he said as he checked to see if we really had five dollars.

"Most of our best pipes usually cost much more than five dollars. But we just happen to have an excellent Brigham pipe on sale today."

The man explained that these pipes had something called rock maple inserts so that tars and moisture could be absorbed, and that would allow Papa to enjoy the pure tobacco flavor. I had no idea what that meant, but it sounded good. The pipe was a beauty, and it was only four dollars and ninety-nine cents. The man even wrapped it for us.

We were thrilled at our success as we headed back to the statue. Bridget was already waiting for us.

"Look what we got, Momma!" she whispered as she pulled a beautiful blue and green print dress from her shopping bag. "It's a knee-length rayon print," she said, sounding like a saleslady.

"What's rayon?" I asked. "I thought you were going to get her a sweater?"

"We were," Bridget replied. "But none of the sweaters was as good as the ones Momma makes, and they had this lovely dress on sale for half price. It was only four dollars and ninety-eight cents, and I just knew it would be perfect for Momma."

"How do you know it'll fit?" I asked.

"Well," she said. "One of the sales ladies was just about the same size as Momma, and she assured me it would fit perfectly."

"Can we look at toys now?" Ingar asked impatiently, pulling on my jacket.

I checked Uncle Ole's watch.

"Okay, let's go," I said.

The remaining hour and twenty-two minutes seemed to race by as we searched through all the wonderful toys for sale. In one way, it was good that I only had a bit of money, as it would have made choosing five toys impossible. Liv wasn't even two yet, so it was easy to find a cute cuddly toy for her. Ingar liked toy cars, and Lars loved those wooden puzzles, so they were easy, too.

Bridget was too old for dolls, but she liked sewing and knitting. I noticed a fun-looking thing called a spool knitting kit, which was really only an empty thread spool with four little nails on top that you wrapped wool around to make a wool rope that pulled through the bottom of the spool.

The rope could be used to make coasters and other things. It came with eight small balls of colored wool. The whole kit was a dollar, but I realized that I could easily put some nails in one of Mamma's empty spools and just buy eight big balls of wool for only fifty cents.

With that problem solved, I looked around for something for Billy. There! A box of magic card tricks for forty-nine cents. With my search over, I paid up for everything and began the fun job of herding cats again. Ingar and Bridget were easy, but Billy and Lars? Not so much. Lars had found everything he wanted, but I couldn't drag him away from the model train display. It was really wonderful, so I let him stay there until Billy was ready. Bridget and Ingar joined Lars, but Billy was still searching for something, although he wouldn't tell me what.

I kept telling him we were running out of time. Twice, I pulled him over to the cashier station, and both times, he ran back to the toys, shouting, "I've changed my mind."

With only two minutes left before we had to meet Papa at the statue, I dragged Billy back to the cashier station.

"Egil! Please! I'm still not finished," he cried as he pulled away from me again.

"If you're not back here before I count to ten, Billy," I yelled. "We're leaving without you."

"Just one second," he replied, looking desperate as he went into another one of his coughing fits.

"I mean it. I'm counting."

When I reached right, he ran back, still trying to catch his breath. He put his items on the counter so I couldn't see them and took his money out of his pocket. I told him to stay there, and I began prying the others away from the trains. When I finally had everyone gathered together, we hustled down the escalators to the main floor and found Papa patiently waiting by the statue. He looked at his watch and stretched out his hand as a reminder to return Uncle Ole's watch.

"Are we late?" I asked, glancing at the watch as I handed it back to him.

"Don't you know?" he asked.

"Only four minutes," I replied sheepishly. "It was impossible to get them to leave."

"That's why I asked you to do it," he said with a smile. "But it'll be your turn to wait for me on the way home."

"How come, Papa?" Lars asked.

"I have to make a quick stop at hardware and pick up something," Papa said. "Let's go now."

"Can't we go inside with you, Papa?" I asked.

"Sorry. We don't have time."

We all put our coats on and headed back to the truck. Ashdown was a six-story building with all the hardware items that anyone could ever want and much more. Papa returned after only about ten minutes, so we tucked ourselves under our blankets and headed home.

On the way home, Papa made a quick stop at Weinberg's Grocery store to pick up some items for Momma. He let us all come in with him to warm up a bit, but I didn't have any money left. Billy, Lars, and Bridget somehow had enough left to buy some candy. I helped Papa load the vegetables in the back of the truck, and we were soon on our way home.

We were still breathlessly talking about our adventures, sorting out our presents, and enjoying the cookies Mamma made for us when there came a hard rap on the front door.

Momma opened it, wiping her hands on her apron and smiling nervously. I don't recall her ever smiling that way before. It was the lady from the Children's Aid Society, and she was here to interview Momma and Papa to decide if they'd make fit parents for Billy and if our house was suitable. She was dressed in a drab grey suit, wearing thick glasses, with her hair in a tight bun at the back of her head. She had a clipboard with one of those new-fangled ball-point pens. Her eyes reminded me of bird's eyes, and she spoke in this clipped superior way. I thought her snooty as all get out. Who was this lady to examine our home and our Momma and Papa? Our home and our parents are the best; I wanted to shout at her!

But I didn't say anything, as I knew I had to be polite. I gave her a tight smile and left to hide in the loft while Momma served her tea in the living room. I couldn't hear much of their discussion until they came near the ladder, so I peeked down to see what they were doing, with Billy and Lars leaning on my back.

"And this is our bedroom," Momma said.

"I'm not interested in your bedroom," the lady said. I could hear the clicking of her. "Show me where the children sleep."

"Over here is the girl's bedroom," I heard Momma say as I heard her open our bedroom door.

Silence.

Then.

"You already have two girls and three boys, with another on the way. Is that correct? Yes? Now, where do the boys sleep?"

"Upstairs in the loft," Momma replied, showing her the ladder.

I pulled my head back out of sight, my heart thudding, as Billy and Lars slipped off my back.

"But where are the stairs?" the lady asked loudly, masking the sound of Billy and Lars landing on the floor.

"Papa is going to build some stairs soon, very soon, but for now, we use this ladder," Momma said. "Would you like to go up and see the room?"

"I certainly would not," I heard the lady say. "This ladder is not safe for anyone, let alone little children. You don't seem to understand the importance of safety for children, Mrs. Amundson. It's no wonder that Billy almost drowned."

"It's quite a large and comfortable space," Momma replied.

She was twisting her apron and looked as if she might want to drop through the floor.

Oh, I wanted to throw my shoe at that lady then.

"Thank you, Mrs. Amundson," the lady said and clicked her pen. "I believe I have all the information I require."

Papa came out of the living room and put his arm around Momma as they watched the lady put on her coat and boots.

"Can I–?" Momma began to ask.

"I can see myself out," she interrupted so rudely it made my blood boil. "Thank you for your time."

"When will–?" Papa started to ask, but she stepped out the door and slammed it shut behind her.

Momma and Papa just stood there looking at the door. Bridget had come out of her room just in time to witness the lady's rude behavior.

"Why don't I make some fresh tea, Momma," she offered.

"Could you make coffee instead, please?" Papa asked as Momma covered her eyes and began to cry.

Papa, with his arm still around her, led Momma into the living room and gently sat her down while I went into the kitchen to help Bridget. After coffee, Momma pulled herself together, as she always did when there was a crisis.

"We won't let this spoil our Christmas," she said with a forced smile, wiping her eyes gently with her apron.

"We don't have a formal letter yet," Papa smiled. "So, there's still hope."

We didn't understand why Billy couldn't stay with us. He was part of our family. We loved him like a brother. We may not have had a mansion, but it was a good, safe home. Even today, I still cherish my recollections of that home and my parents and grow angry at that sanctimonious lady with her glasses, drab suit, and clicking pen.

Chapter 5
The Match Boxes

We were all itching to know what Papa bought Ashdown's, but we were so caught up trying to find places to hide our own treasures that we soon forgot all about it. Once we were sure that our hiding places were as secure as Fort Knox, Bridget helped Momma in the kitchen while I set the table.

"Where'd Papa go?" Momma asked.

"I think he took his package out to the tool shed," Bridget said.

"Egil," Momma called. "Go and tell Papa it's suppertime."

"Okay," I replied as I put my coat and boots on and headed to the barn.

On my way, I noticed that the barn door was open, so I went in, and I was surprised to see Billy peeking around a post, looking down at the far end of the barn. I crept up behind him softly so he couldn't hear.

"What are you looking at, Billy?" I blurted.

Billy jumped and yelped in shock. I tried not to laugh.

"Oh, I'm just wondering what Papa's doing," he whispered.

Down at the far end of the barn, I saw Papa. He was busy raking straw in an empty stall.

"He brought his Ashdown's bag out here," Billy answered without taking his eyes off Papa.

"Did you see what was in it?"

"Not really," he whispered again.

"Never mind. It's time for supper."

"Aren't you curious?" he asked, turning to me.

"Not really," I lied. "It's probably just some tools he needed, so he brought them out there to stash them away."

"Don't tools go in the tool shed?" he asked.

I called out to Papa to tell him supper was ready, and he answered with a simple 'okay' as we headed back to the house.

After dinner, Momma set out her work table in their bedroom and hauled out with her big bag of quilting fabric scraps, five rolls of ribbons, a tin of safety pins, and one pair of big scissors. While Momma was helping Ingar and Liv wrap their presents, Lars, Billy, and I climbed up to the loft to wait our turn. Lars and Billy were sitting in the corner showing each other what they'd bought, except, of course, the presents for each other.

I was reading a book and wasn't really listening closely until Lars asked, "Where'd you get those?"

"At the grocery store," Billy replied.

"You got two?" Lars asked.

"They were two for a nickel. Do you want one?"

"You sure?" Lars asked.

"It's okay," Billy said, handing Lars one of whatever they were.

"Geez, thanks a ton!" Lars replied.

I just assumed it was some kind of candy and lost interest. Then we heard Momma call out, "Billy, it's your turn."

Billy asked me to hold his shopping bag while he climbed down the ladder. Once he was near the bottom, I handed down his shopping bag. As he reached up for it, he dropped something.

Momma picked it up for him and looked at it curiously.

"Why do you have a box of wooden matches?" she asked, looking at him puzzled.

"I, I, well, I bought them at the grocery store," he answered nervously.

"Why in heavens do you need matches?" Momma asked.

"I still have some firecrackers left over from bonfire night," he replied.

"You're much too young to play with matches, Billy," Momma said. "I'll put them up in the kitchen cupboard, and you can have them when you are a bit older, okay?"

Billy didn't say anything as he watched Momma stand on the kitchen step stool and put the matches on the top shelf.

"Come along," Momma said, stepping down from the stool and smiling at him. "Let's go and wrap some presents."

"Are you mad at me?" he asked, looking woeful.

"No, Billy," she replied, gently taking hold of his hand, "I'm just worried about your safety, that's all."

As the oldest, I was last to wrap presents, and when we finished, we gently placed them in our shopping bags until Papa cut a tree down and set it up in the house.

On the following Monday, Billy and Lars stayed late after school to help decorate the classroom, so Papa picked them up at school as he was running errands anyway. When he arrived, I was a bit surprised to see that Lars had brought his best friend Mark Weinberg home with him. His family was from Germany, but they'd been forced to move to Canada in the 1930s to escape the Nazi regime's persecution of the Jews.

"Is it okay if Mark stays for supper, Momma?" Lars blurted out as he charged through the door, "Papa said it was okay."

"Then it's okay," Momma replied and turned to Papa. "Will you give Mark a ride home later?"

"No need," Papa answered. "Mel was at the school to pick up Mark's sister, and he said he would pick Mark up on his way home from curling."

"Can we play in the barn for a while, Momma?" Lars asked.

"Supper will be ready in half an hour."

Mark was a regular visitor during the summer when he could ride his bicycle here, but it was difficult to ride through the snow in winter.

I joined Papa in the living room, listened to the radio, and read comics in the newspaper until Momma asked me to call Lars and Mark for supper. I put my coat and boots on and dragged myself out to the barn. As I opened the door, I heard them laughing at the far end of the barn. I could see that they'd switched the light on in the back stall, so I could see them clear as day, but they couldn't see me at all.

I was about to call them when I noticed something strange. A big puff of smoke. I stood still to see what they were doing. Smoking cigarettes.

My first thought was to tell Papa, but then I realized that if I told on him, Lars would have a miserable Christmas, and, as annoying as he could be sometimes, he was still my brother. I slipped out of the barn and came back in, slamming the door behind me. I yelled for them to come for supper, interrupting their smoking shenanigans.

"We're coming!" Lars yelled back.

I walked inside so they could see me and asked, "So, what are you two up to?"

"Nothing, nothing at all," Lars replied, looking around as guilty as if he'd robbed a bank.

This was revenge enough, and I smiled at myself as I went back to the house.

After supper, Lars and Mark went back out to the barn to play, but I knew what they were up to. Still, I said nothing. Bridget and I helped Momma clean up the kitchen, and then I went to the living room to finish my homework. When Mark's father arrived to pick him up, Papa answered the door and invited him in.

Momma said, "I'm just making some tea. Would you like to have some?"

"Maybe you'd prefer a glass of port, Mel?" Papa asked.

"That'd be very nice," he replied. "Thank you."

While Papa and Mr. Weinberg went into the living room, Momma poured two glasses of port and set some shortbread on a plate.

"Egil," she called, "Can you please take these to the living room and tell Mark that his father's here?"

I'd had it with covering for those two, so I replied, "I have homework to finish, Momma. Can't Bridget go?"

"She has homework too," Momma replied, "I guess I'll ask Billy."

When Mr. Weinberg was ready to leave, Momma asked Billy to tell Mark that his father was there. Billy got out his trusty flashlight, put on his boots and coat, and went to the barn.

A few minutes later, Lars and Mark bustled into the house.

"Don't take your coat off, Mark," Mr. Weinberg said. "We have to leave."

Mr. Weinberg bid us good night, and Mark thanked Momma for supper.

Lars took his coat and boots off as the rest of us went back to what we were doing without another thought.

Then, Momma turned around and looked puzzled at Lars as he was headed to the ladder, "Where's Billy," she asked.

"I don't know," Lars replied, looking around, "I thought he was right behind us."

"You go up to the loft and do your homework," Momma said, "Egil, can you go and see where Billy is, please."

"Okay, okay," I said, and grumbling away, I put on my coat and boots and headed back to the barn.

I was expecting to meet Billy walking back to the house, but there was no sign of him, so I trod off to the barn. I opened the door. Did those two leave a light on the far end of the barn? I thought. And then I smelled smoke. That light. It was coming from a fire. I rushed down to the end of the barn. There was Billy whacking the fire with one of the small horse blankets, desperately trying to put out the flames that crackled in the stall- the stall where Lars and Mark had been smoking.

"Billy! What are you doing?" I yelled.

"Trying to put out the fire," he yelled back.

"Stand back! Go get Papa! I'll put it out."

Billy dropped the small blanket and raced back to the house. I grabbed one of the big blankets, ran to the rain barrel beside the door, dumped the blanket in, rushed back to the fire, and hurled the wet blanket on the blaze. Smoke billowed up in a choking cloud. I'd slowed the fire down, but it was like the fire was alive and trying to outsmart me. Right away, it flared up again in another part of the stall. I grabbed another horse blanket and soaked it in the barrel. Once more, I tried to put out the fire. Once more, it only slowed the fire down.

Papa and Momma came running in. No coats on in that freezing weather. Papa grabbed another blanket, dunked it in the rain barrel, and came running down to the fire. While he smothered the flames with the wet blanket, he told me to soak the other blanket and bring it back. Throwing the wet blankets over the fire created even more smoke, and our only horse, Uncle Nicky, was banging around in his stall and making a lot of noise. I ran back with my blanket as Momma ran past me with another wet blanket. By the time I got back to the fire, the flames were out, and it was dark inside the barn. Papa threw the blanket that Momma brought over the smoldering fire while Momma found the switch to turn on the light. I gave Papa my wet blanket, and he tossed it on the pile, smothering any sign of flames.

"I think it's out, Momma," Papa said, staring at the pile of smoldering blankets, "but the blankets are kaput. Go back to the house right now, Momma. You can't get cold in your condition."

Momma looked at Billy, coughing and wheezing beside Lars, over by the stall gate, and asked gently, "Are you okay, Billy?"

Billy didn't say anything. He just kept coughing, his eyes fixed on the smoking blankets.

Momma knelt down and put her arms around him. "It must have been so scary for you, Billy, but you were so very brave."

"What happened here?" Papa asked as he peeled the blankets off the fire. "Lars, go and get Momma's coat before she freezes to death."

"Yes, Papa," he answered, running back to the house.

"Egil, get a bucket of water," Papa called to me, "We must make sure the fire is out."

I ran back to the barrel, picked up two buckets, and filled them with water. I hauled the buckets back to the site of the fire; Papa told me to put them down and go find the rake.

I brought the rake, and Papa began pulling back the burned straw, a little at a time, and throwing water from a bucket wherever he thought the fire might flare up again. Then, to my surprise, Papa pulled out a large, mostly burned-up shopping bag from the bottom of the fire.

"What's that?" Momma asked as Lars returned with her coat and put it over her shoulders. I looked at Lars, but he avoided my eyes.

Papa squatted down and tried to open the bag, but it just fell apart. He didn't answer. He just shook his head. He used the rake to pull out the contents of the destroyed bag, but we couldn't make out what they were.

Finally, Papa stood up straight and let out a long sigh. "That, Momma, was our Christmas tree decorations and lights."

We all looked down at the charred remains of something, but it was impossible to make out what anything was except for some strands of black wires.

"Oh, no!" Momma cried, coming over to see for herself. "That was supposed to be a wonderful surprise."

"How'd this fire start?" Papa asked, eyeing us all suspiciously as he kept raking to be sure the fire was out. I picked up a hoe from the next stall and began helping him when I spied a cigarette butt in the hay beside a small box. I reached down to pick them up.

"What have you found there, Egil?" he asked.

It'd be hell for Lars if Papa saw a cigarette butt, so I palmed the butt and picked up the box to hand to Papa.

"That looks like the matches Billy bought," Momma said, taking them from Papa's hand. "The ones I put up on the top shelf."

"Are these your matches, Billy?" Papa asked as Momma showed them to him.

Billy began to cry, and Momma put her arms around him again, but he was coughing too hard to answer.

"It's okay," Momma said softly, "But you see, this is why you shouldn't play with matches."

"Egil!" Papa called. "Open the barn door wide to let all the smoke out and check Uncle Nicky."

Papa dumped the rest of the water over the brunt of black hay to make sure the fire was truly dead.

"Everyone back in the house now," Momma said. "Or you'll all catch your death."

I'll come back later to double-check on the fire," Papa said. "And I'll clean it up in the morning."

We all returned to the house feeling miserable. We were mourning something we didn't even know we had.

"I'm putting the water on the stove," Momma announced to Billy, me, and Lars. "Put your clothes in the laundry, take a bath, and wash your hair before bed to get rid of the smoke smell."

We only had one bathtub, so we had to take turns and share the water. As the oldest, I had to go last. That meant that the water was well used by the time I got in. Momma always made sure I had plenty of fresh warm water, though, to rinse off with before I got out.

We also had to dry our hair before we went to bed, but we didn't have hair dryers back then, so we used the electric fireplace. I can still remember the smell of burning hair when it fell into the hot grate.

I'll never forget that evening, that feeling of our whole life nearly going up in flames. At least we found out what Papa had bought at Ashdown's. Too bad we never got to see it. We were all glum and quiet at breakfast the next morning. Papa was silent.

"Are we still going to have a Christmas tree, Papa?" Ingar asked, his eyes darting around the table.

"Yes, but a poorly decorated one," Papa replied glumly.

"We still have some decorations from last year," Momma said with a smile of encouragement.

"Some," Papa agreed. "But we gave away the ones I replaced, and now we have no lights."

Billy quietly slipped away and disappeared into the loft without a word.

"Should I go up and check on him?" Bridget asked Momma.

Momma shook her head, but she looked worried.

"I'll go up and see how he's doing as soon as we clean up here," Momma replied.

Bridget and I helped clear up. But before we finished, Billy was back. He stood beside Papa, still as a mouse, holding up the straw angel from his shoebox.

"You can have my angel, Papa," Billy whispered.

Papa stared at him, not knowing what to say. At that moment, Momma dried her hands, bent down to Billy, and accepted the angel.

"Thank you, Billy," she said. "Your angel will look lovely on the top of the tree."

A big smile lit up Billy's face as he handed the angel to Momma.

"We could make more. I know how. My grandmother showed me."

"That's a wonderful idea," Papa said. His blank stare gave way like magic to a big smile. It was the first time I'd seen a smile on my face all morning.

Chapter 6
The Christmas Tree

The school day passed slowly as molasses. I couldn't wait to make up decorations for our tree. A spruce that Papa had chosen from the grove was already set up in the living room when we tumbled through the door. It was the most beautiful tree you had ever seen. As we stood agape in admiration, Papa asked Momma to bring out Billy's straw angel. He handed it to Billy and then hefted him high so he could set his angel on the top of the tree. It looked perfect as if it were meant to be there.

Momma set up her work table in the kitchen with everything we needed to make straw decorations and a lot more. We dropped long pieces of straw in a pot of warm water, joking about how it looked like spaghetti. From an old cookie tin, Momma pulled out baling wire of all different lengths as well as a pair of needle nose pliers to make hooks for the decorations and for holding the straws together. She brought out two calligraphy pens, each with different-sized nibs, some paint brushes, a stack of white letter paper, and a muffin tin with different colors of ink that Momma had made with food coloring. Papa donated his old newspapers and Momma her sewing scissors. There was popcorn for us to paint, as well as a bowl of flour, a pitcher of water, and a big mixing bowl for making paper mache. We also had balls of brightly colored wool, a whole slew of ribbons, and a roll of scotch tape. Then I noticed a little box of chocolate bar wrappers.

"What are these for?" I asked Momma, picking up one of the wrappers.

"For the tin foil, of course!" Momma answered.

"What do we do with them?" Bridget asked.

"If you separate the cover layer from the foil liner," Momma said and smiled. "You have sheets of shiny tin foil that we can wrap over the paper mache shapes to make our decorations shiny."

Momma showed us how to make paper mache balls, wrapping them first with tin foil and then different colored strands of wool, but sparsely wound so we could see the foil shining through. Oh, those were beautiful Christmas balls! Better than anything from Eaton's.

At school, Bridget must have paid attention to art as she made these intricate paper snowflakes by folding and notching paper. But, of course, what we were jumping to make were straw angels.

We'd barely started when Momma called us for supper. We were so busy that we hadn't helped set the table or anything.

"Sorry, Momma," Bridget apologized. "We forgot—"

"Oh, never mind, it's nice to see you all so busy and not arguing. Now come for supper."

Over the next few evenings, we made bucket-loads of straw decorations, including angels, stars, Christmas trees, birds, and small animals. The decorations ranged from 'not bad' to really bad, but they improved a bit by the third night. We added a lot of wool, ribbon, and paint to make them colorful, and it didn't really matter if they weren't professional; after all, we were just kids.

On the third night, we used the whole roll of Momma's scotch tape.

"Is there any more?" Bridget asked cautiously, knowing that Momma guarded her tape as if it were made of gold.

"I've one more," she said. "And if you promise to be careful and not be wasteful, I'll let you use it."

"Thank you, Momma," Bridget replied gravely as she clutched the tape. "I'll guard it with my life."

"Egil?" Momma asked. "Can you get the step stool and reach the tape? It's on the top shelf."

I was only eleven, but I was nearly as tall as Momma, so I knew I could reach it with the step stool. I got up on the stool and looked around the world on the top shelf. There was the tape. And beside it? The box of matches that Momma had taken from Billy. I reached for the tape and glanced again at the box of matches. How could Billy have reached it? I wondered then. He was way shorter than me. Papa had kept the box from the fire and locked it in his tobacco drawer.

Just as I was pondering all this, I heard Lar's whining voice; "Hurry up, Egil, we're all waiting."

I jumped down from the stool, handed the tape over to Bridget, and sat down, but I couldn't concentrate on making any more decorations. The box of matches kept turning around in my head. For the next while, I just sat there, but everyone was too busy to notice my silence. Soon, Momma announced that it was time for the little ones to get ready for bed. For me, that was a half-hour notice, so I decided to find out if Papa still had the matches from the barn, but the question was how?

He was sitting in his chair in the living room doing a crossword puzzle. I asked him if he'd like a cup of tea.

"Yes, please, Egil," he said. "Momma would probably like some too."

"Okay, Papa," I replied.

Momma had already put Liv to bed and was helping Ingar and Billy, but I knew she wouldn't be long. I made some toast and cut some cheese to go with the tea so I could sit in the living room with them. When everything was ready, I called Momma and brought it into the living room.

As I was hoping, once Papa had finished his toast and cheese, he unlocked his tobacco drawer and took out his pipe. This was my chance to see if the matches were still there. They were.

As I watched Papa light up his old pipe, I got distracted thinking about the new pipe we'd bought at Eaton's for his Christmas present. I sure hoped he'd like it. But I was still confused about the matches, and my mind kept drifting back to the night of the fire. I thought about it a lot that night.

Billy must have had two boxes of matches; I thought as I tossed and turned in my bed. Either that or the other box must have belonged to someone else.

Then I remembered the conversation between Billy and Lars. *They were two for a nickel,* Billy had said. I'd thought he was talking about candy, but what if he'd been talking about matches?

Then, I also remembered that he gave one to Lars and that he and Mark had been smoking earlier that evening. Was it possible that Billy *didn't* start the fire?

I didn't sleep much that night thinking about it. I was a big fan of those radio detective shows, like *The Whistler* and *Sherlock Holmes,* and so the next morning, after breakfast, while Lars and I were getting ready for school in our little cloakroom, I decided to interrogate him properly.

"What really happened on the night of fire, Lars?" I demanded, staring right at him like I could see his brain working away.

"Whaddya mean?" He looked away from me and tied his shoes like he was just learning how.

"You know what I mean!"

"Nope, nope, I don't," he shot back.

I bent my head close to his. "Look, Lars," I whispered. "I saw you and Mark smoking out there."

"You saw? Saw what?" He straightened up abruptly, banging his head on a hook. "What's with your voice?"

"Don't change the subject," I said, as I gave up on the hard-boiled detective voice I'd put on. "I didn't you out. I didn't want to get you in trouble."

He rubbed his head and looked around to make sure no one else was in earshot. "Really? Why not?'

I set my hand on his shoulder and gave a grown-up sigh. "You're my brother, but if Billy didn't start that fire, is it fair that he should take the blame?"

"What makes you think he didn't start it?" Lars asked, eyeing me now.

"Well … you see, Lars, when I was looking for the tape in the cupboard, I saw the box of matches that Momma took from Billy."

"So what?" Lars asked. I noted that he bit his lip, which was a sign of nerves.

"So," I said, pacing the little cloakroom, my hands behind my back. "The matches that Papa found in the barn weren't Billy's.

"Maybe he put them back," Lars replied.

I stopped pacing. This was the dramatic moment. The twist. "No! Papa still has them! In his tobacco drawer."

"It's time to go to school," Lars said, grabbing his books and heading for the ladder. "It's our last day before Christmas."

I didn't try to stop him. I just collected my stuff, and we left for school. When we returned home later in the day, Lars avoided me, and I didn't say anything more about our earlier discussion. The worktable was cleared off, and all our decorations were carefully laid out, ready to decorate the tree. Momma had strung our colored popcorn to make a garland for the tree.

We were all excited to decorate the tree, but we had to keep a lid on our enthusiasm until after supper. When supper was over, and the dishes were cleared, we all rushed to the table to choose some decorations. All except Lars. He hung back, listless, his guilty conscience nailing him to his chair. I looked at him with knowing, narrowed eyes. If only I had a toothpick to chew.

We started with the popcorn strings and then we took turns each hanging a decoration on the tree. Momma then looked over at Lars, puzzled.

"Are you feeling all right, Lars?" Momma asked, as she put her hand on his forehead checking for a temperature.

"I think I'm, ah, just a bit tired," he replied.

"Do you want to lie down for a while, sweetheart?" Momma asked.

"Maybe," Lars replied and walked slowly over to the ladder.

The rest of us kept piling decorations on the tree until Ingar hung the last one near the bottom.

"What do you think, Papa," Momma asked proudly.

"Beautiful!" He smiled and clapped his hands. "You've done a wonderful job."

"Yes, you certainly have," Momma praised. "Thank you for all your hard work. It is a most magnificent tree."

We all stood in front of our tree, admiring our achievement.

"I think maybe it's time to put some presents under our beautiful tree," Momma said with a big smile.

"But it's not Christmas yet," Papa noted.

Momma cocked her head and peered at him over the top of her glasses. Papa cleared his throat.

"You are right, Momma. Get the presents."

Momma looked at me. "Egil. Go see how Lars is feeling and tell him to bring his presents down."

I climbed up the ladder and found Lars sitting on his bed, his head in his hands. He looked up at me imploringly.

"Are you going to tell on me? Are you?"

I sat down beside him. I didn't feel like a radio detective anymore. I felt bad for him, even if he had lied.

"No, I won't tell on you, cross my heart. But if Billy didn't start the fire, you're the only one who can say anything."

"What should I do, Egil? Oh, I'm the worst!"

"It's up to you to decide what to do. Billy hasn't told you either. Looks like you have to decide."

"I can't decide," he said with tears in his eyes.

I put my arm around him and patted his shoulder then and told him we were putting our presents under the tree.

"Come on, Lars. Get your presents and come and see our beautiful tree."

He took a big sniff and dried his eyes with his shirt sleeve.

"It'll all be fine," I said, "Tell you what. You just go down, and I'll get your presents for you."

"Thanks," he said, sniffing one more time, "I'm okay now. I can do it."

I grabbed the bags of presents from the 'hideout,' as we called the low storage space below the descending roof in our attic bedroom. I picked up Billy's and mine while Lars took his and Ingar's, and we slowly worked our way down the ladder.

"How are you feeling, Lars?" Momma asked, looking quite concerned.

"A bit better," Lars murmured.

"Come and see our amazing tree. It's the best we've ever had," she said.

When Lars entered the living room, his eyes lit up like electric bulbs.

"It's beautiful," he whispered, staring at the tree.

We all placed our presents carefully around the base of it, arranging them to the best effect like museum curators of ancient treasures.

"Since there's no school tomorrow," Momma announced, "you can all stay up a bit longer, and we can toast our beautiful tree with hot chocolate. What do you say?"

We all nearly shouted 'yes,' and then Lars astounded us all.

"I have something to say first," he said, standing tall.

All eyes focused on him. We went quiet. Papa looked up at him from his armchair.

"The matches you found in the barn weren't Billy's, Papa," he said in a rush.

"What are you trying to say?" Papa asked.

"Billy's matches are still in the cupboard where Momma put them," Lars declared, his courage beginning to weaken.

"Who do they belong to then?" Momma asked.

"Me," he sputtered, lips quivering as his tears filled his eyes.

"And what were you doing with matches?" Momma asked, frowning. Oh, it wasn't often Momma frowned like that, and I admit I felt bad for Lars then.

"Smoking," he answered, his lips still quivering. "With Mark."

"You were smoking? In the barn?" Papa stood up from his chair and loomed over Lars.

"W-w-with Mark," Lars stuttered. "And when Billy came to tell us that Father was here for him, he caught us by surprise."

All of a sudden Billy rushed over to Lars and gave him a big hug, at that Lars' courage failed him and he buried his face in his hands and broke down in tears.

Billy held on tight to Lars, "Thank you, Lars, thank you," he said.

Momma flung her arms around them both and ushered them over to the Chesterfield to sit down.

"I-I'm so sorry," Lars blubbered.

"Shush now," Momma said as Lars leaned his head on her shoulder. "Everything's okay now."

Billy held Lars' hand tightly as Papa crouched down beside Lars.

"How did the fire start?" Papa asked in a quiet voice.

"M-M-Mark dropped his cigarette," Lars stuttered. "We panicked, I guess, because Billy had seen us."

"Billy," Papa said. "Did you see them smoking?"

Billy nodded meekly.

"And you didn't say anything?" Momma asked.

Billy just shook his head.

"Then what happened?" Papa asked.

"I don't remember exactly," Lars began again. "But while Mark was stamping out his cigarette, I put mine out and tried to grab all my stuff together."

"Is that when you dropped the matches?" Papa asked.

"I don't know," Lars mumbled. "Maybe."

"So, you gathered up your things and came back to the house?" Momma asked.

"Uh-huh," he murmured.

"Was the fire out when you left?" Papa asked.

"I thought it was. I really did."

"And then you left the barn with Mark?" Momma asked.

"Yes."

"Why didn't Billy come with you?" Papa asked.

"I don't know. I really don't."

"Billy?" Momma asked.

Billy looked from Momma to Papa. He looked very small, I thought, in his too-big shirt, his blonde hair sticking every which way.

"I was going to go with them, but they rushed past me so fast I dropped my flashlight. I picked it up, but when I looked at the back of the barn, I saw that the light was still on.

"Did you turn it off?" Papa asked.

"Uh-huh," he replied.

"But when I turned the light off, it didn't go out. I mean, it did, but—"

"Because of the fire?" I guessed.

Billy nodded.

"Oh, so that's when I found you trying to put the fire out?" I asked.

He nodded again.

"I'm sorry I did a bad thing," Lars said and sniveled.

Papa stood beside him and placed his hand on Lars' shoulder, and he smiled down at him.

"Yes, it was not good," he said and then paused. "But you just did something much better by telling the truth, and we're very proud of you, Lars. Aren't we, Momma?"

Momma looked up at Papa, urged Lars, and gave him a big hug.

"Yes, we are very proud."

I stepped behind him, patted him on the head, smiled, and said, "Me too, little brother."

Momma looked up at me curiously and asked, "You knew, too?"

I just smiled and shrugged. A detective never gives his methods away, after all.

"Am I still in trouble?" Lars asked.

"It's almost Christmas," Papa said. "A time to forgive. And just look at this marvelous tree we have here, all because someone made a little mistake."

"No, you are not in trouble, my dear one," Momma smiled. "And thanks to you, neither is Billy."

Momma beckoned Billy to come over and sit beside her. She hugged him and kissed him on the forehead. Bridget, could you please get my Brownie camera? I would like a picture of all the wonderful men in my life. Bridget hurried into our parent's bedroom and grabbed Momma's Brownie camera. She ran back and led Ingar to a spot in front of Momma and urged him to sit down.

"Papa. You stand behind Momma. This'll be a wonderful picture, Momma."

Lars hugged Momma on one side; Billy hugged her on the other; Then Momma put one hand on Ingar's shoulder; her other hand one mine. As for Papa, he wrapped his arm around Momma's waist, proud as I've ever seen him.

"This'll make the best Christmas photograph ever!" Bridget said with a gleeful smile.

"But Christmas is still two days away," I pointed out.

"It feels like Christmas is here already," Momma said.

"I think you're right, Momma, and I think I see tears in someone's eyes," Papa said. He smiled.

Momma beamed. "But they're happy tears, Papa."

My detective work made everything turn out all right, and I knew right then and there what I wanted to do with my life.

The End.

Book 2
The Flashlight

By Kathleen Melnyk-Lang (née McKenzie)

Chapter 1
The House

It was a steaming hot August afternoon in 1949, and with my blouse clinging to my perspiring back, I was sitting alone on the front entrance steps of Assiniboine House, or as I called it; 'my beloved prison.' I was fascinated by ants in those days, and as the ants crisscrossed the stone steps in front of my beloved prison, I became mesmerized by their wonderful little world, and the strange assortment of things that were carrying, pushing, and pulling: leaves, clumps of dirt, and the tiniest of flower petals.

At least for a short time, watching the ants' curious behavior distracted me from my self-pity. I knew it was wrong, feeling sorry for myself all the time, but my parents had died in a horrendous boating accident on Lake Winnipeg last year. It had been the worst year of my entire life. I'd been deprived of the love of my parents, and I resented having to live in this horrible place. Assiniboine House. What a silly name. It wasn't even on the Assiniboine River. It was on the Red River, which was also misnamed since it wasn't red but a muddy, grungy brown. Just then, I felt an almost irresistible urge to stomp on those stupid ants.

Fortunately for the ants, the sound of an approaching vehicle distracted me. I stood up, hoping it was the postman. Every day I prayed for a letter from my grandmother–she lived in a town somewhere in Scotland called Darvel. I imagined Darvel as a cozy, sweet little town and often prayed that she had found a way to rescue me from my incarceration! Alas, my hope for a postman was dashed. It was just a dirty old farm truck entering the circular gravel driveway that led to the front entrance of my beloved prison.

Kneeling on the front seat of the truck, with his head staring out the open passenger window, was a small boy with blonde hair sticking out every which way. Beside the boy was a beautiful white dog with a black patch over its left eye. With the sound of squealing brakes, the truck stopped at the base of the stone steps that led to the daunting front doors. The dust settled, and the driver–a tall, slender middle-aged man–stepped out from the driver's side. The old truck had long since seen its best years, yet somehow the man had managed to keep it running. The man looked up, grim-faced, at the brick façade, then, without a word to the little boy, he put his head down and strode up the steps, climbing them two steps at a time. He brushed right past me as if I were indistinguishable from the shrubbery and disappeared behind our large, dark-oak prison doors. I was beginning to feel invisible. Nobody seemed to notice me, not even the ants.

I glanced back at the truck to see if the boy was following him, but he remained silent and still, staring out the window with one arm around his dog and the other gripping the top of the glass. He seemed transfixed by the size of the building, and he was still oblivious to my presence. He appeared to be staring at one of the fourth-floor windows. I turned to face the windows, but I couldn't see anyone, just the red bricks of our prison walls. I turned back to observe the strange boy in the truck with his dog, and I wondered, just then, if the tall man had glued the boy's tiny hand to the top of the window so he wouldn't run away. That's a dumb idea, I told myself and strained to see if the boy was in some sort of a trance.

He was obviously not impressed by the charm of our beloved prison. The red brick of Assiniboine House dominated an expanse of well-kept lawn that stretched from a row of mature elm trees that lined Churchill Drive down to the north bank of the Red River. It's not there today, but the land is now part of Churchill Drive Park.

When it was originally constructed as the Assiniboine Hospital, well before the turn of the century, it had neither electricity nor elevators. However, with numerous modifications and upgrades, it has managed to serve several different functions over eight decades. When it was converted into a recovery care center for war veterans after the First World War, it was renamed Assiniboine House. When it was turned over to the Association of Children's Aid Societies in 1943, it became the Assiniboine Foster Care Centre. We simply called it The House, or our Beloved Prison.

I wanted to go over and warn the little boy about our prison, but an image of our house warden, Mrs. Jankowski popped into my head, telling me in her thick Polish accent, "Not to be telling people is prison, Kathleen. Is good home for nice children who needing help, and please to remember how we are all love you each one and taking good care for you."

I clambered to the top of the stone wall beside the steps and, as I sat in my new spot, I realized that I had a lot in common with both this dilapidated building and the old truck. Oh, I was feeling so sorry for myself that day, aged only seven, waiting to be rescued by my sick grandmother, who was too poor to send for me. So, the truck, the building, and I were all waiting patiently, I imagined, wondering what would become of us.

Most of the other kids were in the playground on the west side of the building down by the riverbank, but it was 93° Fahrenheit in the sun, so I preferred to be by myself in the shade at the front of the building. For those who grew up with the metric system, 93° Fahrenheit is 39° Celsius. Curiously, at 40° below zero, they are both the same, which occurs a bit too frequently during a normal Winnipeg winter!

Eventually, the man returned, accompanied by Mrs. Jankowski. She was a large elderly woman, whose long white hair was always wrapped up in a tight bun. I imagined that her hair had probably been blond when she and her husband Jerzy emigrated from their native Poland in 1932. She had a curious disposition, being both strict and fair with a quick temper, which was balanced by a soft and gentle motherly nature. As much as I revered her, she often terrified the daylights out of me.

With considerable persistence, the tall man and Mrs. Jankowski managed to peel the little boy's tiny fingers from the truck window and coax him out. I remember vividly how, as he stepped out of the truck, he was clutching an old shoebox tightly to his chest with one arm and clinging to his dog with the other. The man grabbed a small, brown suitcase from the back of the truck, returned to where the boy was standing, and gently pulled the dog away. He put the dog back in the truck, closed the door, and was escorting the boy toward the steps when Mrs. Jankowski suddenly spotted me.

Now, I wished I really was invisible. Surely, she was going to yell at me and tell me to go and play with the other kids. To my surprise, she smiled and motioned to me gently to come.

She softly asked in her thick Polish accent, "Kathleen, please come here to help?"

I cautiously approached her as she added, "Please say hello to Mr. Amundson and welcome to Billy. As you do not seem to be playing with swings, please come help to show the House to Billy?"

Turning to Billy, she said tenderly, "Billy…is new friend Kathleen."

With her smiling eyes fixed on Billy, she stretched out an arm and beckoned me, her fingers flicking impatiently, "Come, come, and show now."

Mr. Amundson stopped at the base of the steps, knelt down, and gave Billy a big hug. Billy dropped his shoebox and clung tightly to Mr. Amundson for what seemed a long time. Although tears dripped down Billy's face, somehow, he held back from crying out loud. Mr. Amundson promised that he and the rest of the family would soon be back to visit, but Billy remained un-consoled. He stood motionless, his swollen eyes fixed on Mr. Amundson as he climbed into his truck, put it into gear, and drove from sight.

Mrs. Jankowski picked up the suitcase along with the shoebox, turned the two of us around, and marshaled us up the steps.

Once we were through the inside vestibule doors and in the main hall, she instructed me; "Number six bed in young boy's ward is make ready for him. Please show and don't forget to show the bathroom."

"But, Mrs. Jankowski," I protested, "girls aren't allowed—"

"Go now," she interrupted sternly, "there are no boys there now. They outside to play where you should be…and Billy, when finished."

She handed the suitcase to me and the shoebox to Billy, who then turned and disappeared into the toddler's ward on the east side of the building. Meanwhile, Billy stared in fascination at the beautiful wooden staircase with its large, round, brass handrail that divided it in the middle. The center stair was as wide as it was long. On either side of the center stairs that led upward, there was a flight of stairs leading down, but they were both roped off to remind us that downstairs was off-limits.

Billy followed me as I headed up on the right-hand side of the center staircase, which led to a large landing midway between floors. I told him that we always go up on this side of the stairs and down on the other.

As I turned to the right at the landing and continued up the next flight to the second floor, I checked behind me and noticed that Billy had stopped on the mid-landing and was staring curiously at the other flight of stairs on the left side of the landing.

"C'mon," I yelled. "Your place is up here."

Out of habit, I turned right at the top stair and was racing toward the girl's wing when I remembered that I had to show Billy to his room, which was on the other side of the floor. I whirled around and rushed back to the stairs, only to find Billy still musing as he slowly approached the top of the stairs.

"Keep up, okay?" I said as we headed toward the boy's wing.

Soon we stood before the door leading to the boy's ward. I looked up at the sign, which read *'Ward Two – Boys Aged Four to Seven'* and realized that I'd never been on this side of the floor before. It was off-limits to girls and, even though Mrs. Jankowski had said it was okay, I was still wary about entering this forbidden space.

Billy finally made it up the stairs. When he stopped behind me, I heard him say very slowly, "Ward Two, Boys Aged Four to Seven."

I turned back curiously and asked, "How old are you?"

"Six," he replied.

I crossed my arms and eyed him, "What grade are you in?"

"I don't go to school yet, but I'm going to start soon."

"How come you can read then, eh?"

"Mrs. Amundson taught me," he replied as I opened the door and we stepped into the young boy's ward.

Billy shrank back and clutched his shoebox even tighter, "Where's my place?"

I led him in with some trepidation but soon realized that the boy's ward was simply the reverse of the girl's ward, with the same rough blankets covering the same iron beds all spaced out equally in regimental order down the room. Surely, I could find bed number six easily. The only difference was that the washrooms were on the left side of the entrance door instead of the right side. Since it was just like our ward, with a row of six beds along each side, I knew that number six would be one of the beds at the very end.

"It's this way, and that's the bathroom," I said, pointing at the bathroom door while leading Billy quickly toward the end of the room.

Before we reached the second bed, a familiar voice startled me and stopped me in my tracks.

"No girls allowed," yelled BJ Dafoe.

I looked over. There he was on the other side of the room, hiding behind his bed, revealing only a mussed head of dark hair.

"Mrs. Jankowski told me to bring Billy up here. And anyway, you're supposed to be outside!" I said.

I was trembling inside and shocked at myself, but also proud. I had just stood up to the Ward Two bully.

BJ jumped up from behind his bed and shoved the comic book he was reading under his pillow.

"Who's Billy?" he asked.

He gave a disdainful once-over to the little boy, who stood frozen behind me.

"He's new," I said, my bravery wavering.

Keeping my eyes on BJ, I reached behind and pulled Billy to my side.

Pointing to the bed opposite BJ's, I said, "That's your bed at the end."

I handed him his suitcase and added, "Just put your things on the bed and we'll go outside."

I pushed Billy toward his bed with my eyes still locked on BJ. He was big for a seven-year-old, and he had a really bad temper. Fearing that BJ might do something to hurt Billy, I lied.

"Mrs. Jankowski will be up in a minute."

Billy hastened down to the end of the room. He threw his suitcase on the bed opposite BJ's, slid his precious shoebox under the covers, and ran back toward me.

We ran off as quickly as we could, with BJ's question fading behind us, "Hey, what's in the box?"

"You better not touch it!" I shouted back at him without turning around, "And Mrs. J. is on her way up."

Billy followed close at my heels and began coughing as he ran, and so we charged noisily down the staircase. Mrs. Jankowski's voice collided with us just as we reached the main floor.

"What's so much making noise up there?"

We both froze as she loomed over us. Recognizing the fear in my eyes and hearing Billy coughing and wheezing, she calmly dried her hands on her apron and asked, "So...there is fire upstairs?"

I looked awkwardly back up the stairs and barely managed a terribly slow reply, "There's someone up there..."

"Is nobody–" she started to profess but stopped short when she glimpsed BJ peeking over the rail just before he ducked back into the room.

She then checked on Billy, whose wheezing was easing, and turned to me, "Billy will be fine now. Outside, please."

She urged us gently toward the door, with her eyes glued to the upstairs rail. She then stomped up the stairs as Billy and I scampered outside and headed for the playground.

Chapter 2
The Radio

Once outside, Billy's coughing eased, and I asked him if he was feeling all right.

"It's just my asthma." Billy coughed. "I'm okay now."

He then fired a barrage of questions at me starting with; "What kind of name is BJ?"

"They're his initials. His real name is Bernard Jean."

"So, why don't they call him - Bernie or Jean?"

"He doesn't like those names because they sound too French."

Of course, that didn't really answer Billy's question, so I filled him in as best as I could about BJ, based only on stories I had heard.

"BJ showed up just after last Christmas," I began. "He had foster parents. The LeBlancs? I think that was their name. Anyways, he did something in their garage. An accident is what I heard."

"What kind of accident?" Billy asked, wide-eyed.

"Something caught fire. BJ said it was the cat, but they didn't believe him. I mean, who would?"

"Is that why they sent him here?"

"I guess, but the LeBlancs are French, from St. Boniface, and BJ doesn't speak French at all. His last name's Dafoe. That's a French name, so maybe they thought he was French too. He failed grade one at the French school, so he had to repeat grade one all over again in English."

I told him that BJ often got into trouble and that all of us were afraid of him. Billy was quiet. I realized I hadn't learned anything about him yet.

"Was that your dog in the truck?" I asked. "He's really cute."

"Nah. Patch is the Amundson family's dog." He scuffed the ground and sniffed sadly. "But it feels like he's really my dog."

"What kind of dog is he?"

"Mostly border collie."

"Why can't you stay with the Amundson's?"

"Cause they don't have enough room for me anymore since Mrs. Amundson is going to have another baby soon."

He sighed, "That's what the adoption lady said."

"Oh!" I said, still not really understanding.

"My grandparents died, and that's why they took me in."

He looked back at our four-story beloved prison and said it was pretty huge compared to a tiny farmhouse. After that, I could never get Billy to talk much about his past. Whenever I asked him a question about his grandparents or the farm, he'd just shrug. I soon stopped asking, after all, I understood exactly how he felt.

When we reached the playground, I introduced Billy to Miss Lowry–the toddler ward guardian and playground supervisor. I then took Billy over to meet the rest of the gang. Four of my friends came running over to see who the new boy was. The first to greet us was Joe Ferrara. He was one of five orphaned children from Italy. They came to Canada in 1944. His real name was Giuseppe, but none of us could say it properly, so he told us to just call him Joe. I thought he was kind of small for a six-year-old, but he had a big heart, a beaming smile, dark curly hair and I remember thinking he was rather cute.

The next two were my two best girlfriends, Daria Levinski and Sandra Curtis. Sandra was the same age as me. Daria was from Poland and a year younger, but she was very bright. I never did learn what happened to her, but I assume it was something awful because Mrs. Jankowski told us not to pry. She was especially protective of Daria and often spoke very quietly to her in Polish when Daria was feeling down.

On the other hand, Sandra seemed quite happy most of the time, but I quickly learned that it was best not to pry about our past lives as we'd all had some tough times.

The last to wander over was Murray (he was also in my class). Murray and his older brother, Dudley came from England before the war; he wouldn't talk about what happened to his parents.

By today's standards, our playground wasn't much; two swings, two teeter-totters, a small merry-go-round, and a sandbox, but we all thought it was special. All that is, except BJ, who showed up a few minutes later and sat on the grass all by himself against the south wall of the building. He quickly disappeared behind the stack of comic books he'd lugged with him. BJ had turned his milk money into a big collection of comic books. I can't even imagine what they'd be worth if they existed today.

Rebecca Lowry, or Miss Becky as we called her, was a pretty brunette in her late twenties. She'd stationed herself with her book at the solitary picnic table under the shade of the large elm trees.

From there, she could keep an eye on the entire playground and all the kids.

Miss Becky shook the bell and the clanging sound forced BJ out from behind his comic. This was the 4:25 bell that gave a five-minute warning to the kids on kitchen duty and alerted radio fans about the 4:30 show. Billy watched curiously as BJ jumped up and ran around to the west entrance doors. I started to laugh and explained to him that BJ's favorite show *The Cisco Kid* was coming on and this was the only thing he liked better than comic books.

"C'mon," I said, "I don't have dining room duty till five o'clock, so I still got some time to show you the big room."

We followed BJ through the west entrance and past a set of double doors.

"This is the Servery where we pick up our meals," I said, showing Billy where to pick up his tray, plate, cutlery, and glass of milk, juice, or water, "The kitchen is back there, behind that counter."

Once past the Servery, I showed Billy the dining room, which still had a lingering, but feint aroma of burnt coffee. It had five long, pitted, and initially carved wooden tables on each side of the room. There were benches at each table that could seat six kids on either side. It wasn't particularly cozy, but it worked. Except for the scrambled eggs, which made me gag, I remember that the food was quite good.

"Mr. Benoit is the cook," I told Billy. "He makes really interesting food, and it's usually good, except when it's the Polish food Mrs. Jankowski tells him to make."

"What's wrong with Polish food?" Billy asked.

"Nothing really," I said. "It's just that she asks for it a lot. So, we get cabbage rolls and perogies every week. Sometimes twice a week."

"What are perogies?" Billy asked.

"If you don't know, you'll find out soon enough. I hope you like mashed potatoes and cheese."

Beyond the dining room, at the far west end, was a large open space with windows on three sides. We called it the big room. Scattered around it were four old Chesterfields, all different sizes and colors, and six worn-out armchairs. There were two old tables in the middle with mismatched, hard chairs at each. One table always had a puzzle in progress, and the other was usually set up with a crokinole board.

Since nothing matched, I assumed that the furniture had been salvaged from somewhere, but we appreciated it, especially if we were lucky enough to get a soft chair. There was an old wooden fireplace on the right side of the room, badly painted to make it look like brick. It had one of those electric heaters for a grate with some fake coal and bits of red glass covering two small lightbulbs, with a fan beneath. The lights made the imitation coal glow in a feeble attempt to make it appear like a real coal fire. It was only turned on when we had really cold days, but a place beside it was coveted when the thermometer was nearing forty below. With the hot temperature outside, I remember thinking that it couldn't possibly be cold again in less than five or six months.

On the other side of the room, sitting on a table in the far-left corner, was the object of our quest: the wooden radio. It was perched on an old side table that was badly in need of a coat of paint.

Beside the table was a low oak bookshelf with only two shelves and wide slots at each end. The top shelf held books for the older kids. The bottom shelf was for us. The slots at each end were used for the story books. The right end was for the boys and the left for the girls. Each ward guardian read their kids a story every night and the current storybooks were always kept in their appropriate slots until they were finished.

There were already about a dozen kids gathered around the radio with BJ right up front on the floor. The story of *Cisco Kid and the Black Kerchief* was just starting.

"Go join them," I said to Billy, nudging him toward the radio.

Billy did. Over the next few weeks, I watched as he adjusted to his new home and made friends with everyone. Everyone except for BJ, that is.

Chapter 3
The Magic Shoebox

By October, Billy had learned the ropes and was carrying out his chores like everyone else. The hardest part for him was going to bed at eight o'clock, knowing that the big kids could stay up an hour later than us.

Our ward guardian was the cook's daughter, Miss Marie Benoit. She may have seemed elderly to us, but at the ripe old age of twenty-seven, she made Mrs. Vincent and Mrs. Jankowski seem positively ancient. Mrs. Vincent was the boys' ward guardian, and for someone born before the turn of the century, she had an amazing amount of energy. On the one hand, she was firm with her charges—boys being difficult to manage; on the other hand, she was often a softie. She was like Mrs. Jankowski in that way.

As a means of controlling her boys, being a softie often proved more effective than strict discipline. One technique she used was to read to her boys before bedtime as a reward for good behavior during the day. Miss Marie followed suit, and soon we all enjoyed a chapter from a popular children's book almost every night. To the young boys and girls, Miss. Benoit would read books like The *Boxcar Children* by Gertrude Chandler Warner, and to the big kids, Mrs. Vincent would read books like *The Adventures of Tom Sawyer by* Mark Twain.

Once Billy learned that reading was a major part of the daily curriculum at the House, he was anxious to show us his prized shoebox possessions. When Joe and I had finished our chores, we grabbed hold of Billy and ran outside, filled with excitement and inquisitiveness. We weren't disappointed.

We found an empty bench under the elm trees and sat down, captivated by the contents of Billy's shoebox. Murray, Daria, and Sandra came running over to see what we were doing. Billy took the lid off when they arrived and then held up a vintage leather aviator hat, just like the ones pilots wore in biplanes. It had wool-lined flaps on each side with small holes in them for headphones. It had a soft sheepskin cap turned up at the front with leather straps hanging down from the flaps.

Billy put it on, and his head disappeared. With the hat covering most of his nose, he cranked his head back and tried to peer from below the cap how we laughed at that! When that didn't work, he flipped the hat off and reached back into the shoebox.

Just then, BJ appeared. Sure enough, he couldn't resist making a snide remark.

"You looked better with it on."

"What do you want, BJ?" Murray asked.

"None of your business, dork," BJ replied.

He sneered like one of the villains in his comic books.

Billy gathered his arms around the shoebox if to protect it from any more mean comments. Shoeing mosquitoes away, BJ abruptly turned and left, while we crowded around the shoebox. Next, Billy took out a khaki-colored flashlight. Because the end where the light shone out was bent at ninety degrees, it looked like a small periscope.

Holding it up, he added, "When you push this button in and out like this," showing us how it worked, "It sends Morse code signals."

"What's Morse code?" asked one.

I tried to explain to Joe that it was a previous method of sending messages. There were radios. They used it for sending telegraph messages, using a combination of short and long sounds to spell out words that make up the message.

"Why don't they just use the telephone?" Joe asked.

"Oh, never mind," I answered, realizing that he wasn't really listening.

"Can I see? Can I?" Murray asked, nearly jumping with excitement.

"Sure," Billy replied, handing the flashlight to Murray while reaching back into the box and pulling out a small army knife, the same color as the flashlight. He explained that it had two knife blades and an awl.

"What's an awl?" Joe asked.

Joe was learning a lot today, I thought.

"Here, I'll show you," Billy said, his eyes wide with excitement.

Opening each of the blades, he added, "This is the little one. This is the big one. And this is the awl. The awl can make holes in things like cans and leather."

"Where'd you get all these neat things?" Murray asked.

"They were my dad's during the war," Billy replied.

The knife was not as sophisticated as today's Swiss Army knives, but it impressed us no end back then. After the knife, he pulled out a home-made Christmas tree decoration in the shape of an angel. It was made of straw. I remember thinking how both beautiful that straw angel was and how delicate.

Finally, Billy showed us the treasures that I most wanted to see; four books.

"Why do you have two *Winnie-the-Pooh* books?" I asked.

"My gran gave me the first one. Mrs. Amundson gave me the second one for Christmas because it's about Winnipeg, and I really like that," Billy replied.

"*Winnie-the-Pooh* is an English book, silly. It's not about Winnipeg," I said with an air of superiority that I often put on back in the day.

"It is so!" Billy said. "There was a real bear named Winnipeg. He lived in a zoo in England. My grandpa told me he was called Winnie cuz it's a nickname for Winnipeg, and that's cuz his owners were these soldiers from here."

"That's just ridiculous," I said.

For years, I never believed that story, but uncharacteristically for me, I was wrong. Apparently, Winnie, the real bear, was the mascot of the 2nd Canadian Infantry Brigade. His owner, Captain Harry Colebourn, really *was* from Winnipeg, and he loaned Winnie to the London Zoo while the brigade was posted in France during the First World War. A. A. Milne's son, Christopher Robin became so fond of Winnie after numerous visits to the zoo that he named his own teddy bear *Winnie*. Who knew?

Daria, Sandra, and I looked through each of Billy's books while Joe and Murray played with the flashlight, blinking at some imaginary boat on the river. Meanwhile, BJ had returned to his favorite spot: holding up the west wall of The House, burying his nose in another comic book.

From time to time, he peeked over the top page to keep an eye on us as we delved through the treasures of Billy's shoebox. Then, before we knew it, Mrs. Vincent was ringing the hand bell, and it was time to go in.

We put the books back in Billy's shoebox and I said, "C'mon you guys. I can't wait to hear the next *Boxcar Children* book. Miss Benoit is going to start reading us *The Hurricane Mystery*."

Daria, Sandra, and I hurried inside, but Billy, Joe, and Murray followed at a dawdling pace. BJ came up behind Billy and knocked his shoebox to the ground. I whirled around just in time to see BJ pick up Billy's box, yank out all his treasures, and throw them on the ground.

"This stuff is all junk," he called out as he headed inside.

"What's his problem?" Sandra asked as we stopped to help Billy pick his things up.

"He's just angry," I answered.

"But why?" Sandra asked.

"Maybe because his foster parents didn't want him," Joe suggested.

"But we're all orphans here, so what makes him special?" Murray asked.

"Or, possibly because his mother didn't want him," I replied. "I lost my parents too, but not because they didn't want me."

"My mother didn't want me either," Billy put in.

"But at least your grandparents did," I said. "So, you had *someone* who wanted you."

"And the Amundson's as well," Billy added quietly.

Whenever I think back on that day, I have such mixed feelings of sympathy for BJ, grateful appreciation for the love of my parents and a curious sense of guilt.

Chapter 4
Bedtime Stories

Billy's arrival marked a turning point for many of us at Assiniboine House. With Billy on the scene, BJ had found someone new to torment, so he tended to leave the rest of us alone. For some reason, he seemed determined to take any opportunity to get Billy into trouble. He made several attempts over the next few weeks, but his first near success came with our renewed interest in reading books. Most of the young kids preferred comic books simply because they liked the pictures, and most couldn't read. However, except for BJ's collection, comics were quite rare at The House, and since BJ didn't share his with anyone, comic books and reading in general was not a particularly popular activity. Billy's influence soon changed all that.

Joe told me at breakfast that on his very first night, after all the boys were in bed and the lights had been turned out, Billy quietly slid his flashlight and the *House at Pooh Corner* book out of his shoebox, crawled under his covers, and started reading.

"I saw the light through his covers cuz his bed is beside mine," Joe told me.

He then explained how he snuck out of bed, crawled over to Billy's bed, lifted the covers up, and saw Billy huddled on his knees, shining his flashlight on his book. When Billy noticed Joe, he just shuffled over and whispered for him to come on under. Joe did, and Billy started the book over at the beginning.

"He read really softly," Joe added in a kind of awe. "So not to wake the other kids."

"He did this after lights out?" I asked with surprise.

"Yeah," he grinned at me, "And we're going to do some more tonight. I betcha he's gonna have to start all over again, though, 'cuz some of the other kids want in, too."

Thus, Billy started a new tradition. Within a few days, all the kids in his ward, except Murray and BJ, would crowd around the flashlight on the floor behind Billy's bed and listen to *Winnie*. Murray could already read on his own, so he didn't need a younger kid to read to him, but by the end of the week, he, too, joined in and shared the reading with Billy. Sometimes, I borrowed *Little Toot* and read it to the girls in my ward during the day, but never after lights out. I didn't want to get in trouble, I told the other girls, but the truth was I didn't have a flashlight.

I don't know why reading suddenly seemed so exciting. Perhaps it was something that bonded the kids. Or maybe it was just because it was against the rules. Whatever the reason, it wasn't long after that first night that all the kids started to learn to read, even if they weren't in school yet.

As the end of August approached, we began to prepare for school. I was going into grade two, so I knew what to expect, but for Billy and Joe, it was a brand-new experience. Lord Roberts School was only a few blocks away, so it wasn't too far, except on really cold days. We were among the first wave of baby boomers, and I guess they weren't prepared for us, because the schools were crowded and cramped, and the teachers always seemed overwhelmed.

It took years to get funding to build new schools, so in the meantime, they put us on staggered hours. That meant that one class was attended in the mornings from 7:00 am to 11:30 am, and another class used the same room in the afternoon from noon to 4:30. The classes reversed mornings and afternoons every month. I didn't like mornings because we had to go to bed an hour earlier and leave for school so early that it was still dark by the time we got there. That September, we started with mornings, but at least we were all on the same time schedule.

This didn't stop Billy from reading after lights out, and it didn't stop BJ from teasing or yelling at someone, especially Billy. One evening, after our story time, Mrs. Vincent went to the bookshelf to get *Tom Sawyer*. She was just about finished reading it to the big kids, who were clamoring to hear the ending. To her surprise, it was gone. One of the big kids told Mrs. Jankowski about Billy reading in bed and said that he might have borrowed it. Mrs. Jankowski headed straight upstairs to the Young Boy's Ward. We all went to bed, with our curiosity still burning.

When morning finally came, Daria, Sandra, and I searched for Joe to find out what happened.

We found him in the big room with Billy and Murray.

Daria asked Joe, "What happened last night?"

Joe looked around for anyone in earshot and confided that they hadn't heard Mrs. Jankowski coming up the stairs so they weren't even ready for bed when she barged into the ward.

Joe did a pretty good imitation of Mrs. J's loud voice, "What happens in here?"

Then he told us how she spotted Billy tucking something in his covers and how she marched towards him with her arm outstretched and–

"Give me what is hiding there," Murray interrupted, imitating Mrs. Jankowski.

"You should have seen her move," Joe added. "Like lightning, right over to Billy's bed."

"Come, come … give me now," said Murray, again imitating Mrs. J.

Joe said, "So she yanks back his blankets, grabs the book, and then she turns around, slow, slow, Murray was shaking and—"

"Was not!" Murray hissed.

Joe grinned and continued, "And she looks at us, with eyes like, like..."

"Daggers?" I suggested.

"That's it!" Joe said.

Murray put his hands on his hips, imitating Mrs. J again, "Chop! Chop! Back in bed now. All of you."

"Then she turned to Billy," Joe continued. "He's all shaking in his bed and coughing and wheezing, so she starts whispering—"

"So, reading, when should you be sleeping?" Murray interrupted, now in a whispery Mrs. J's voice.

"That's right, and Billy here, he didn't say a peep," Joe said.

Billy nodded.

"So, then what happened?" Sandra asked who, until then, had listened in wide-eyed horror.

Joe shook his head in sorrow, taking time (oh, Joe was quite the ham).

"Mrs. J. looks at *Winnie-the-Pooh,* like this," he mimed leafing disapprovingly through a book.

Murray continued imitating Mrs. J, "Where did you get this? You have more books?"

"Joe stood up for me," Billy now put in. "He was so brave. He told Mrs. J that he didn't steal any books. That he had his own books in his own shoebox."

"So, then what happened?" Daria asked.

"Mrs. Jankowski glared at me," said Joe softly. "Right through to my grave. Then she says, Where is the shoebox?"

"Gosh, what did you do, Joe?" asked Sandra.

Joe bowed his head in contrition and pointed under Billy's bed.

"That's what I did," he said. "And then we all watched like hawks as Mrs. J reached under Billy's bed, grabbed his shoebox and shook it first, like maybe it was dangerous, and then popped open the lid."

"*Tom Sawyer* is your book?" Murray now added, still doing his Mrs. J accent.

"My turn!" Billy said.

He'd been mostly sitting quietly and listening as the story unfolded but now this was his shoebox being opened and I guess he had to speak up.

"I said, 'nope,' that's not my book. I got *Winnie-the-Pooh* books. I got *Little Toot*. And I got *Little Blacks Sambo*. That's it!"

Murray stood over Billy and tapped his feet as if he were Mrs. J herself.

"So, young man, what is going on with this *Tom Sawyer book* in your box?"

"Billy turned to me, Sandra, and Daria as if we were some kind of jury," Joe said and told Mrs. J that he didn't know.

Billy now piped in, "I told her I didn't know and said, '*Tom Sawyer's* not mine!'"

"But I don't think she believed him," Murray added. "Oh, the way she was squinting at Billy and trying to figure out if he was telling the truth! I nearly busted a gut trying not to laugh."

It became a true who-does-a-better-Mrs. J-accent competition by this point, and Joe wasn't going to be outdone. He jumped up on Billy's bed, looked as tall as Mrs. J, and glared down.

"Only two weeks at school, and you are reading already, *Tom Sawyer*," Joe said.

He tried hard not to laugh.

"It's not my book," Billy said, looking ready to cry.

Poor Billy. He was so smart for his age, but he was still only six and at this point he seemed to think Joe and Murray really *were* channeling Mrs. J.

Then Billy wiped his nose and straightened up, "And I told her, 'It's not my book, but I can read it back to you if you want.'"

Murray took over. He told how, up until then, BJ had just been watching all the action from his bed and how he had a big fat grin on his face the whole time. How Mrs. J didn't miss a thing and asked him what he was grinning about, how BJ ducked under the covers fast as a jackrabbit, and how Mrs. J gave Billy the once over, then handed him back the Tom Sawyer book and told him to read it aloud.

"My turn," Joe said and jumped off Billy's bed.

Sandra, Daria, and I had been clumped together the whole time as we listened, and I only realized then that Murray and Joe were competing for our attention.

"So, Billy finally gets to the part where Tom Sawyer is playing hooky, and that is when she says good reading, Billy, and she takes the book from Billy very slowly, like this," I giggled since it looked more like he was plucking a flower than anything else.

Joe winked and continued, "And then Mrs. J turned to BJ, who was still under the covers, and said, *BJ - please take book to Mrs. Vincent. Now.*"

And BJ says, "Why do I gotta take the book? And what do I tell her?"

Murray put in his face all surly in imitation now of BJ.

"I think you know, Bernard Jean," Joe said in his Mrs. J. voice.

And then we learned how BJ went all red in the face and how Mrs. Jankowski just glowered at him over the top of her glasses, and BJ just squirmed.

"And then Mrs. J told BJ that *sorry would be good*," Murray said and laughed.

"And BJ tries to say something, but Mrs. J just looks at him like so," Joe said and raised his eyebrows as high as he could, "And tells him, 'You go, quickly, now.'"

Sandra sat on the bed beside Billy, who was now laughing, "My goodness, what happened to you, Billy?"

"Nothing happened to Billy then," Joe answered, "But she sure had a long talk with him this morning."

"I don't read in bed after lights out anymore," Billy said and frowned.

"But who took the book then?" Daria asked, looking around, confused.

"BJ, of course," Joe replied. "And somehow Mrs. J. knew."

We all knew that Mrs. J has seven brothers and four sons. She knew everything that went on with boys. There was nothing that got past her. She could see through a lie ten miles away. She even knew what you dreamt about, or so the stories went, but I never believed that part.

Chapter 5
Harvest

For the first few weeks after Billy's arrival, on most Sunday afternoons the Amundson's truck was a familiar fixture in the front driveway. Ove and his wife Birgitta usually brought along some of their six children. Occasionally, they even brought their dog Patch.

I always enjoyed their visits, especially when their daughter Bridget, with her beaming smile and flaxen hair, came with them to brighten up my day. She was a bit older than me, but she didn't seem to mind, and I loved spending time with her. Lars was my age and he and Billy appeared to be quite close. Their little brother Ingar never missed a trip to The House and Billy was always so happy to see them.

In October, just before Thanksgiving, the Amundson suddenly stopped visiting. I'd looked forward to their visits almost as much as Billy did, and so it was a terrible disappointment when they didn't show up. Then great news. Mrs. Jankowski announced we'd be visiting the Amundson farm that next Saturday to see Tess's litter of six-week-old puppies.

Mr. Jankowski's boss loaned him one of the company's two-ton trucks to drive us to the farm. His boss had a contract with the post office to deliver parcels, so the back was full of empty canvas mailbags. The back was open, with wooden rails around it, similar to Mr. Amundson's truck, but about five times bigger. The truck was large enough to hold all of the younger kids. Packing eighteen youngsters in the back of a two-ton truck without seats or seat belts would certainly not be allowed today, but back then, no one gave it a thought, and so we rearranged the mailbags to make ourselves as comfortable as possible, and off we went.

Mrs. Jankowski knew that BJ suffered from car sickness, so she confiscated his comics and gave him a teaspoon of some of her special travel sickness medicine. She said it was an old Polish remedy. I noticed the name on the bottle and for the longest time, I thought that cognac was the Polish word for Gravol.

In any event, it seemed to work this time because BJ slept most of the way there. When we arrived, Lars tore out of the house to greet us with Ingar close on his heels. Mrs. Jankowski unloaded a huge pot from the front seat and headed toward the house. It was a beehive of activity with people everywhere. We scrambled out of the back of the truck and followed her, but Mr. Amundson told us not to go inside just yet. We didn't mind, as long as we got to see the puppies.

Bridget gathered everyone together and escorted us to the barn, except for BJ. He was still sleeping.

"What are all these other people doing here?" I asked Bridget. "Are they here to see the puppies, too?"

She laughed at that and explained that it was harvest time and that all the neighbors worked together to help each other. She pointed to the fields.

"My dad and five neighbors bought a threshing machine and now they can finish a whole farm up lickety-split when it used to take weeks and weeks. My mom and all the other moms are in the house, making a huge lunch for everybody."

"How many men are there?" I asked.

"I dunno. Counting the big kids, like my brother Egil. He's thirteen. There's about fifteen neighbors and other helpers, I guess."

"Can we watch them?" Joe asked.

"Maybe later," Bridget replied, like a proper guide. "But right now, we're going to see the puppies."

We ran to the barn and Lars opened the door beside the chicken coop. The chickens squawked and scattered in all directions at the sound of all these kids descending on them. Inside the barn, it was dark and smelly, but we were so anxious to see the puppies, we didn't mind. The Amundson's had Tess and two other border collies.

"The puppies are over here," yelled Lars, leading us to a stall behind the door we had just come through, "In the old pigsty."

The smell was even stronger behind the door, and there we saw the source; a wheelbarrow filled with manure from the stalls sat right beside the pigsty.

"Where are the pigs?" asked Murray.

"We don't have pigs anymore," Lars replied.

"Why not?" I asked.

"Us kids used to give the piglets names, and we'd play with them and all that, and so Papa couldn't stand all the crying when he carted the pigs off to market," Lars said.

He shook his head and laughed.

"Didn't they like the market?" I asked innocently.

Lars laughed even louder.

"He means the abattoir, dummy!" Murray said.

"What's that?" I asked.

Oh, I regretted displaying my ignorance.

"It's where pigs are turned into bacon and pork chops," Murray clarified with a superior smirk.

"Well, how would I know that?" I cried, "I've never been on a farm before!"

Bridget put her arm around me and said, "Ignore them; they're just being jerks."

When Lars turned around, he looked a bit shocked at how many kids were now gathered around the old pigsty.

"Wait! Wait!" he shouted, "Only a few at a time. The rest of you gotta wait your turn."

Bridget followed us into the stall and closed the gate. The puppies were so adorable. I couldn't wait to pick one up. Tess had five puppies and they were all different mixtures of black and white.

As I picked up an adorable white puppy, I asked Bridget, "Did you give them names yet?"

She replied, "Not really. We just call them by their color."

Lars leaned over the rail and added, "That's Snowball you're holding."

The gate had only been closed for a minute when it suddenly opened from the other side. Lars started to say, 'Shut the door,' but then he noticed that it was his older brother Egil. At the sight of him. Billy jumped up and ran over to give Egil a big hug.

"Momma's real keen to see you, Billy," Egil said with a grin, "But she's to her neck with lunch."

Just then, Bridget grabbed me, "Kathleen! Over here."

She was holding two puppies in her arms as she stood up, "C'mon Lars, show the puppies to everyone," she said, taking her pups out of the stall gate to the mob outside.

"I was gonna just let them in here a few at a time," Lars protested.

"Don't be silly!" Bridget said. "We'll be here all day. Bring them out where everyone can see them."

"It's okay, Lars," Egil said. "I'll take responsibility for letting them out."

Lars gave a sigh of relief.

"Thanks, Egil," he said.

For the next half hour, most of us were preoccupied with the puppies. A few explored the barn and were fascinated by the hayloft. All of the stalls were empty, except for one with a solitary, old grey horse who seemed content to stay inside. In the early morning, the other fifteen stalls would normally be filled with dairy cows, but at this time of day the herd was out grazing in the pasture under the careful watch of the other dogs, Patch and his brother Skinner.

Billy's eyes grew large with excitement at the sudden appearance of one of the ladies in the doorway. With the bright sunshine behind her, she was all in the shade, and although we couldn't tell who it was, Billy knew instantly.

He jumped up and ran to her.

"Momma!" he cried out.

Birgitta Amundson's smile beamed through the shadow as she knelt down to greet him with a big hug.

"Billy, let me look at you," she said, "My, you get bigger every time I see you."

I smiled too when I heard her Scandinavian lilt.

After a quiet moment with Billy, she stood and asked us, "What are you doing in this dark barn on such a beautiful day? Outside, all of you."

She then turned to Egil, "Have the men returned from the field?" she asked him.

"Yes, Momma," he replied. "They should all be in now."

"You should go inside too, Egil," Mrs. Amundson replied, "Your dinner will get cold."

Then she turned to Lars and instructed him to put the puppies back and take the kids to the cornfield.

"Billy," she added, smiling down, "Please help Lars gather up all the puppies and put them back in the stall. Don't forget to latch the gate. We don't want them getting out with the chickens again."

As Lars and Billy collected the puppies from the other kids, the rest of us followed Bridget to the cornfield. All, but one! Unnoticed by the others, BJ had slipped in through the side door and was lost in the dark shadows of the barn, observing from the background.

He knew that Billy was responsible for locking the gate, and he must have been unable to resist this golden opportunity to get Billy into trouble, so he stayed hidden in the barn.

Bridget guided us through the cornfield where the stalks were as tall as adults. Most of the corn had already been picked, so we were allowed to run around and play hide-and-seek. Billy and Lars joined us after locking the gate.

We had only been playing for about five minutes when we heard some strange sounds coming from the barn. We weren't sure what it was at first, but soon realized it was a combination of dogs barking, chickens squawking, and a child's voice yelling to beat the band.

By the time we reached the barn, the noise had diminished, but there remained evidence of some sort of skirmish. First, there was BJ on his back, covered in manure, and holding Snowball, with Tess standing over him, still barking. Next, there were a few chickens hopping about in different directions with two puppies following them, while the other chickens ignored them and simply clucked and pecked at the seeds on the ground. Then, there was a rooster strutting around in front of the chicken coop, appearing to be on guard, and finally, there was Egil, leaning on the doorway, shaking his head and quietly chuckling to himself.

We all arrived just as the dust was settling. In only a few seconds, Ove Amundson's large stride closed the distance from the house to the barn. He helped BJ sit up, brushing off some of the manure and the dirt. BJ gently placed Snowball on the ground as he tried desperately not to cry.

Mrs. Amundson and Mrs. Jankowski were right behind him.

"What's been going on out here?" Ove asked.

As BJ tried to explain, the tears began to flow. Between the sobs, he blurted, "I-I was tr-trying to get the-the puppies back in their room!"

"How did they get out?" Ove asked sternly.

BJ replied, "The gate. It was…it was unlocked."

"But Papa," Lars protested, "We locked the gate before we went to the cornfield."

BJ stopped crying when Mrs. Amundson gently helped him to his feet.

Then he mumbled, "It-it came open!"

"Gather up the puppies Lars. Bridget, please take care of the chickens," Ove directed, looking down at BJ suspiciously.

Egil's burst of laughter from the doorway broke the tense silence.

"Egil?" Ove asked, "You know something about this?"

Trying to control his laughter, Egil took a breath and, pointing back to the barn, he began to explain, "Well, I didn't see how the gate came open but…"

"I'm sure we latched it," Lars repeated.

"Lars!" Ove snapped, "Just take care of the puppies."

"I made sure all the kids were out of the barn and checked the gate before I started back to the house," Egil continued, finally getting his laughter under control, "I was holding Tess by her leash and sat down in the yard with her to calm her down before I went in for lunch, but she was so anxious to check on her puppies that when she heard the puppies barking again, she got away from me and raced back to the barn. I chased her, but when I got there, the gate was wide open again, and our young friend here was backing out of the stall, holding two puppies over his head. Tess was already jumping all over him and barking her head off. I guess he didn't see the wheelbarrow."

We all glanced at BJ, who was being gently tended to by two caring ladies.

"Well," Egil continued again, "Somehow, he managed to get up, still holding the puppies. He ran right past me as if I was invisible and headed over to the chicken coop. I watched him dump one puppy in front of the entrance and shoo it up the ramp. I guess he thought it'd just go inside by itself, but it didn't. While he was running around trying to catch it, the chickens got all riled up, which brought the rooster out. And the rooster, along with Tess, kept chasing him."

"Enough of this, Egil," Ove said. "Go and have your dinner before it gets cold."

"Bridget," Mrs. Amundson called. "Could you please help us over here?"

Then, turning to the rest of us, she called, "Lars, did you bring any cows to the barn?"

"No, Momma," he replied. "They wouldn't come."

She sighed and wiped her hands on her apron.

"Never mind then. Can take the kids back to the cornfield until lunch is ready?"

The rest of the day was not quite as exciting, but it was a lot of fun playing in the cornfield, which we pretended was some mysterious castle garden maze.

When we returned for lunch, we were directed to the side of the house where several picnic tables had been set up. To our surprise, BJ was all cleaned up and sitting at one of the tables with Mrs. Amundson and Mrs. Jankowski. He was devouring a large piece of strawberry shortcake, with a big smile on his face. Egil was sitting beside him teaching him how to play checkers.

Billy stopped in his tracks and stared at them. He began one of his coughing and wheezing fits again. Mrs. Jankowski rushed over, put her arm around him, gently coaxed him over to the table, and sat him down beside BJ.

BJ just smiled at Billy and said, "Try this. It's delicious. Best thing ever!"

Billy looked confused, but when Mrs. Amundson set a piece of cake in front of him and urged him to try it, he soon stopped coughing and dug into his cake. Meanwhile, we all found seats at the other tables. I watched BJ and Billy closely during lunch and before long I was both surprised and pleased when I saw them laughing together at something Egil said.

After lunch, we learned how to milk a cow and then watched the men operating the threshing machine before we were once again packed into the back of the truck. On the way home, Billy sat beside BJ. They're finally becoming friends! I thought. But then BJ pushed Billy away, got up, and moved to the other side of the truck. I didn't hear what was said, but it looked like a very short friendship had just ended.

Chapter 6
The Coal Chute

Halloween was an exciting time for all of us at The House, even though we had no money to buy costumes. Making costumes for almost fifty kids wasn't feasible, but I soon learned there was another option waiting for us downstairs. The basement was normally off-limits for all of us–except at Halloween when we could rifle through the boxes and racks of old military and medical uniforms, caps, gloves, and all kinds of interesting things to use for a costume. Of course, everything was adultized and didn't fit, but that just added to the charm.

While Miss Becky and Miss Marie were helping us sort through these fascinating choices, Billy and BJ disagreed about one of the uniforms. Billy left in a huff; I didn't see him for a while as I was so focused on cobbling together some sort of nurse's costume. I lost track of time and had no idea how long Billy had been gone, but as I was trying on nursing caps in front of a mirror, I was shocked by Billy's frightened image rushing up from behind me. I spun around to confront ashen-faced Billy. He was panting with fear, coughing, and wheezing.

"Billy? What's the matter with you?" I whispered, not wanting to attract attention to us.

"Th-th-there's a monster back there, in the–" Billy sputtered.

"Shhhh!" I interrupted, putting my hand over his mouth, and checking around to see if anyone was watching us. Fortunately, everyone around us was caught up in finding a costume.

"Calm down!" I urged him, still whispering.

He kept checking behind to see if he was being followed, so I grabbed him by the arm and pulled him behind a rack of winter coats. He sat on the floor with his back against the wall and tried to catch his breath.

"Now!" I asked sternly, "Where have you been?"

His eyes grew wide once more. I realized he was focused on something behind me. I whirled around and glimpsed Joe. On his head was an old-fashioned head mirror.

"Joe! Come here," I whispered loudly.

"It's okay," I said, turning back to Billy. "It's only Joe."

Joe emerged from behind the coats; Billy's panting and wheezing slowed down, but he was still looking around suspiciously as if expecting someone to jump out of the coat rack.

I sighed with impatience, "Billy! For gosh sakes, what is it?"

He stammered out his story, "Well, you see… I wanted to explore some of the other parts of the basement, so I took my flashlight and went to see what else was down there. At first, it wasn't very interesting, cause most of the rooms were empty. Some had chairs and old beds and stuff, but nothing interesting. Then I heard a strange noise in the furnace room. The noise sounded like a dog growling softly, so I thought there might be puppies inside. I opened the door, but there was no light, so I looked around with my flashlight. No puppies! The growling noise came from a big pile of blankets on the floor. When I shone my light on the blankets, they were all covered with fur, and then they started to move. It was really scary, and I figured it might be a monster or a bear or something. It started to move again, so I ran back here."

I put on my best grown-up face, "Why, that's just silly! There's no monsters or bears in here."

"Well, there's something there!" Billy stated. "Maybe it was a pig… a furry pig."

I rolled my eyes, "Oh, now you're being ridiculous," I said.

Our conversation was interrupted by Miss Becky's voice ordering us to collect our costumes and take them upstairs.

"C'mon," I said as I gathered up my nurse's outfit.

"Billy, you better find something fast or you won't have a costume."

Billy ran around quickly and found a sailor's white hat and suit that someone else had tossed aside. With our costumes in hand, we were ushered back upstairs. After lunch, Billy vowed that he was going back downstairs after lights out to find the monster. Joe and I laughed and reminded him that there were no such things.

He challenged us to come with him, "If there's no such thing as monsters, then how come you're afraid?"

"You can't go downstairs after lights out! You'll get caught for sure," I replied. "Anyway, I'm not going to get into trouble because of your stupid imagination."

"I'll go by myself then!" he said with a defiant nod.

He left sulking and we didn't discuss it again until after supper. After cleaning up, I noticed Billy sitting on the floor over by the south window. As I approached him, he put his finger to his lips to shush me before I could speak.

I plonked down beside him and whispered, "What are you doing there?"

"Listen!" he whispered, pointing to the floor register.

I looked down at the floor grate and then back at Billy, "Listen to what?" I asked.

Billy pressed his ear to the grate, "There. Hear that?"

I leaned down to the grate, "I can't hear anything."

"Listen carefully," he urged.

I tried again. This time I thought I heard a faint noise, like something rattling.

"What is it?" he put his ear back to the grate.

That's when BJ showed up and asked what we were doing.

"Oh, nothing, nothing," Billy answered.

"Is it a secret?" BJ asked, but Billy ignored the question.

BJ scowled, "You're such a jerk, Billy."

He then looked at me and Joe, "You two are just as dumb if you listen to him."

Just then, a pair of lady's shoes tap-tapped behind him. I didn't have to look up to know who the shoes belonged to. Billy's ear seemed glued to the grate. He waved at me to join him. He was totally oblivious to the shoes behind him. I stayed stuck still as one of the shoes began to tap again. Now Billy heard it. He blinked and looked at me. With my head still lowered, I risked an upward glance and realized that BJ had bolted.

Billy looked up, then froze at the sight of Mrs. Jankowski. He looked at me in panic as if pleading for help to make her disappear.

"So? What is happening here?" she asked in her familiar Polish accent.

"I-I dropped something," Billy replied in a faint voice.

"And you were looking for it with your ear?" she inquired. "Something is not working with your eyes, maybe? Out of the dining room now! It's almost time for a story."

When we reached the big room, I saw BJ shooting one of the smaller kids from a soft chair to take it for himself. We found an empty Chesterfield and plunked ourselves down, feeling relieved that we'd somehow avoided the wrath of Mrs. J.

Billy seemed more resolved than ever. He told us that he was for sure going downstairs right after he heard Mrs. Jankowski leave for the night. Both Miss Becky and Miss Marie had rooms on the main floor, as they stayed in The House every night. But Mrs. Jankowski lived with her husband in their own home, and he usually showed up at about 9:30 every evening to pick her up.

Billy said he had a plan, but I still didn't want any part of it. That night, after lights out, I couldn't sleep. Part of me wanted to go with Billy, but the other part was terrified. I kept thinking about the expression 'curiosity killed the cat.' When I heard Mr. Jankowski's truck approaching, I decided to get ready. Because it was cool downstairs, I put my dressing gown on over my pajamas. These were old hospital gowns that we simply tied at the front instead of the back, and they were very thin, but we were glad to have them. I got dressed quietly and waited by the door until the Jankowskis left for the night.

I opened the door just wide enough to peek out, and it wasn't long before I saw a faint light peeking out from under the boy's ward door down the hall. When the door opened, I recognized the shadowy figures of Billy and Joe tiptoeing into the hallway.

They didn't hear the door close softly behind me and were startled when I went, "Pssst."

Billy snapped his flashlight off and froze.

"It's just me!" I whispered.

"You shouldn't sneak up on us like that!" Joe hissed.

"If you're scared of me, how are you going to stand up to a monster?" I hissed back.

Billy signaled to move, "Shhhh! C'mon, let's go!"

The hallway was dimly lit, but it was enough to see our way without the flashlight. As we crept slowly down the stairs, we could hear Miss Becky and Miss Marie faintly down the hall. We crawled under the rope at the top of the basement stairs. As we continued down it got darker and darker. Billy turned on his flashlight when we reached the bottom of the stairs and stood still for a few moments pretending that we were listening while we built up enough courage to carry on.

"Okay," said Billy softly. "This way."

We followed Billy down the hall leading to where he saw the monster earlier.

Suddenly he stopped, "Shhhh! Listen!" he whispered.

At first, I didn't hear anything, but just as I was about to protest, a strange sound came from a room down the hall. Joe thought it sounded like a bear, but to me, it was more like a grunting pig. We moved with great trepidation toward the source of this curious noise which seemed to fluctuate between a soft breeze and a low growl.

We stopped in front of the door and listened intently. Billy was hesitant to open the door, so he decided to turn his light on me to see if I was scared. He was surprised by the smile on my face. I pushed the door open gently and peeked inside. Reaching back, I grabbed Billy's flashlight and focused it on a big pile of blankets on the floor in the corner of the room.

Chapter 7
The Old Man

"It's just a man snoring," I proclaimed softly, having recognized the sounds my father used to make. "He's gotta be sleeping under those blankets."

There was a stale, unpleasant odor in the room, and it grew stronger as we moved closer to the shape on the floor. A huge metal tank with giant pipes springing from all sides, like a mechanical octopus, filled the other side of the room.

"Is he dead?" Joe asked.

"Don't be silly! You can't snore if you're dead," I said.

Just then, the pile of clothes moved, and a snorting erupted from the heap of old army coats. We turned and clumsily tried to escape. As Billy and I reached the hall, we heard a thump behind us. We both stopped and waited for Joe to come out. He didn't. Something was wrong. I just knew it.

"Who's there?" asked a gravelly voice from under the coats.

Joe had still not come out of the room. I shone the light on Billy. Neither of us had any idea what to do next. A quiet moan. It came from inside the room. Joe needed our help.

Billy and I crept back to the room. The flashlight captured an old man kneeling beside Joe. Poor Joe! He was lying on the floor rubbing his forehead. Turns out, he'd run straight into the door while trying to escape.

"Yuh, okay, there, little fellow?" the old man asked. He had a gravelly voice, slurred but gentle.

He covered his eyes against the flashlight's glare.

"Do you mind, young lady?" he asked, his soft voice easing my fears. "That's a bit hard on these old eyes."

I handed the flashlight back to Billy and the old man and I hefted Joe up between us.

The old man asked again, "How're yuh feeling my little man?"

As the old man fussed over the bump on Joe's head, I noted that he had long grey hair poking out from under a red and black plaid cap with big ear flaps. He also had a full white beard. He may have looked a bit scruffy and dirty, but he had kind eyes.

"Could yuh hand me that light, please?" he asked, as he examined the bump closer.

"Looks like yuh'll have a nice lump there tomorrow, but you'll be fine."

For a few seconds, we stared at him. He sized us up, one at a time.

Then he broke the silence, "Excuse my manners, my young friends," he said, removing his cap. "My name is Sam Grady. And you are?"

"I'm Billy, and these are my friends Kathleen and Joe," Billy replied. "We thought you were a monster."

"A monster, eh?" Sam laughed, "What kind—?"

"What are you doing down here?" I said, arms crossed.

Sam took a deep breath and sighed, "Yuh know, it's getting cold out there and no one seemed to be using this room, so…"

"How'd you get in here?" Billy asked.

"Coal chute!" he replied, slowly getting to his feet.

He still had the flashlight, and now he pointed it at an old metal coal chute on the wall. A beat-up wooden ladder beside it led to a small, flap door near the ceiling.

"That that's a furnace used to run on coal. Must have been converted to oil a while back," Sam told us, "So, this coal bin ain't used much anymore."

"Is there a bathroom down here?" Billy asked.

"Washroom's down the hall, but ain't no bath," Sam replied.

Clambering to his feet and rubbing his forehead slowly, Joe asked, "Is that why you smell?"

"S'pose it could be," Sam replied slowly,

"It smells like booze!" I said.

"Come now, young lady, what would a little angel like you know about such things?"

"From my dad! Why do you drink that stuff?"

Sam sighed, "Well, there's not really much to eat down here."

"You hungry?" Joe blurted out.

"Maybe, just a bit," Sam said smiled, and put his thumb and index finger close together.

"There's lots and lots of food upstairs!" Billy said.

"Psst. Billy. What are you doing?" I asked. "You trying to get us all in hot water?"

"But there's no one in the kitchen," Billy replied as if this were the most obvious thing in the world. "And Mr. Benoit sure won't miss a few perogies."

"Perogies?" Sam asked, "My, my, I haven't had perogies for some time."

"C'mon then. Who's coming with me?" Billy asked.

I tried to protest, but Billy was resolute.

"Maybe Joe should stay here until he feels better," Billy said as he grabbed my hand and pulled me toward the door.

"There's gotta be light in here somewhere," Sam remarked, reaching and fumbling around to find the chain above his head.

The brightness of the bare bulb startled me, but Billy was so intent on his quest for food that he dragged me out of the room before my eyes had a chance to adjust.

Billy and I crept upstairs and invaded the kitchen like commandos on a mission. I found the roll of brown wax paper that Mr. Benoit used to wrap our lunches. I ripped off a big piece as quietly as I could while Billy scrounged through the new electric refrigerator. There were lots of perogies as well as a big can of Klik. Billy found some egg salad and a few odds and ends, and we wrapped it all up in the wax paper. Tucking the spoils under our arms, we then stealthily returned to the basement. We forgot to bring cutlery, but Sam didn't mind. He sat right down on the floor and ate that simple food like it was the world's finest feast. We might have disappeared the way he was so intent on eating every morsel, and we watched him mesmerized. Watching Sam that night taught me a valuable lesson: never take food for granted.

Sam soon opened up and began volunteering his life story.

"I was born in England, yuh know, back in '94. Came to Canada before the Great War," Sam explained in between bites.

"Is that why you got such a strange accent?" I asked.

"I don't have an accent," he replied with a big grin. "It's you lot that do."

"What's an accent?" Joe asked.

"It's how you talk, silly," I said.

"You mean like Sam's growly voice?" Billy asked.

Sam gave a surprisingly pleasant and jovial laugh and said, "No, lad, an accent is the way words are pronounced and has nothing to do with the type of voice you have."

"So why do you have a growly voice?" Billy asked curiously.

"Well, lad," he said solemnly, "That's a long sad story."

Billy sat down beside Sam and said softly, "I like stories. Even sad ones sometimes."

"I suppose you're all a bit too young to know anything about the Great War," Sam began. "Which happened long before you were born. I joined the Army to defend us from the Huns, and while I was in France, I was exposed to mustard gas."

"I like mustard on my hot dogs. Will I get a growly voice, too?" Joe asked.

"No, son," Sam said with a chuckle, "And I certainly hope that none of you ever have to go through another war."

"What's a Hun?" asked Joe.

"The enemy," Sam explained. "But I think you're all too young to listen to war stories. Lost many good friends back then."

"My dad died in the war," Billy said sadly.

"I'm so sorry, laddie," Sam said, putting his arm gently around Billy.

"I was one of the lucky ones," Sam continued. "Had a few close calls and let's just say that I have some problems today that make it tough for me to keep a job."

"That seems so unfair," I said, tucking my skirt over my knees so I could sit down beside him.

Joe plunked down on the floor beside us, and we peppered Sam with more questions. We learned that when he returned after the war, he suffered from 'shell shock' and spent several months right here in our beloved prison back when it was a veteran's care center.

"No kidding?" Billy said, wide-eyed.

Joe and I echoed that. We couldn't imagine it as anything other than our beloved prison, after all. That's why Sam was so familiar with this place and why he could find his way in and out without anyone seeing him. The breathing and lung problems made him cough a lot, and that, in turn, damaged his vocal cords. That's why he had such a gravelly voice, we learned.

"Billy coughs a lot," Joe said. "Will he get a gravelly voice?"

"I hope not. It'd sound darn strange on a kid," Sam said with a laugh.

Over the next few nights, the three of us repeated our goodwill mission. But then Joe and I grew antsy about visiting Sam after lights out, and so we stopped going. Billy, though, was undaunted by the risk of getting caught and he kept bringing Sam food night every night.

On the following Saturday, just two days before Halloween, we once more headed to the basement to search through the pile of artifacts for the final pieces for our costumes. We were all so excited about going trick or treating. Billy once again slipped away for a few minutes to visit Sam, unaware that this time he was being followed. By BJ.

Luckily, Joe warned Billy that we had to head back up pronto. As he started down the hall, he noticed a shadowy form peering into the furnace room through the crack of a door. He recognized BJ straight away and ducked into the washroom for fear of alerting him. A few seconds later BJ tiptoed quickly past the washroom, back to the storage room, oblivious to Joe's presence.

Now that BJ knew about Sam, the question was: what would he do? The rest of the day, we bit our nails, wondering if Sam's secret would be revealed. Billy didn't care. Once again, he snuck down to the basement after lights out, but that morning he told me that he'd sensed he was being watched.

"When I got back to the ward," he said, "BJ was sitting up in bed and staring right at me. He saw me looking and then ducked under the covers and pretended like he was asleep."

"Did he say anything?" I asked, chewing on my braid.

"Not a word," Billy answered.

Sunday, I was so full of anxiety and anticipation that I could barely eat. Would BJ spill the beans to Mrs. Jankowski about Sam? We couldn't stop worrying about it while we got ready for Halloween. BJ didn't join in any of the Halloween fun, and it didn't seem like he'd said anything, either. After supper, Mrs. Jankowski brought out four huge pumpkins, one for each ward to carve. Cleaning them was really messy as we had to separate the seeds from the pulp. However, we were rewarded with both pumpkin pie and roasted pumpkin seeds, so it was certainly worthwhile. Our carving efforts were not brilliant, but still, the pumpkins, with their off-kilter triangle eyes, looked scary when we put the candles inside and set them out on Halloween.

Finally, it was Monday, and still no sign that BJ had betrayed our secret. Supper was early on Halloween so we could finish trick or treating before it got too dark. Once I was dressed in my authentic nurse's costume, I joined the others at the front entrance. BJ showed up in an army uniform. Billy went over and asked him to join us.

"No thanks," he replied curtly, "I'd rather go with friends who share."

"Jeez, okay, just trying to be friendly," Billy replied.

"Friends don't keep secrets," BJ said as he stomped away.

As soon as we finished our trick-or-treating, we headed to a dining room full of games and events including a big wooden tub filled with water and apples for bobbing, and a pot of warm caramel alongside a big bowl of popcorn for making popcorn balls. Mr. Jankowski had set up the room for playing darts, shuffleboard, crokinole, and ping-pong. BJ didn't join in, which worried Billy, but otherwise, it was a magical evening.

I'm ashamed to admit it, but Sam had completely slipped my mind until after lights out. We were allowed to stay up a bit late that night, and I'm sure I wasn't the only one who had trouble getting to sleep with all the candy and excitement. It was after ten o'clock when I heard Mrs. Jankowski leave. I lay in bed for some time, feeling guilty, wondering if Billy had gone downstairs with some food for Sam.

Suddenly, I thought I heard the Jankowski's truck returning. A moment later, the faint sound of both doors closing proved my fears. But why's she coming back? I wondered.

Billy and Sam! I thought. I leaped out of bed to race to the stairs. I had to warn Billy. Too late! As I peeked through the stair rail, I saw Mrs. Jankowski already starting down the stairs. I couldn't see the basement, so I knelt and listened.

First, there were just footsteps, and then I heard Mrs. Jankowski ask, "Billy? That is you?"

Silence from Billy.

"What you are doing down here?" she added, anger creeping into her voice.

Still no answer from Billy.

"Gerzy!" she shouted to her husband, followed by something Polish.

Again, I heard Mrs. Jankowski's voice, this time asking sternly, "Why are you being downstairs and out of bed after lights out?"

"It's not his fault, ma'am!" came the sound of Sam's voice from the bottom of the stairs.

Billy shouted, "Sam, get back!"

"Don't mean to intrude, ma'am, but Billy was just helping out an old man down on his luck."

"Who are you, and how are you getting in here?" I heard Mrs. Jankowski ask crossly.

Mr. Jankowski cut in with a barrage of Polish.

When he was finished, I heard Mrs. Jankowski ask point blank, "You are bum?"

"I-I guess that's about right, ma'am."

"You are sleeping in the basement?" she asked, but this time with a hint of compassion.

"I-I'm sorry, ma'am!" Sam replied, "Yuh see, it's a bit cold out there and—"

"I think maybe that is you smelling bad?" Mrs. Jankowski interrupted.

"S'pose it is."

His sigh traveled all the way up to where I was crouched.

"You are hungry?" she asked, her tone soft now.

"Well, thanks to my young friend here," Sam replied, "I've had a little something, thanks."

"What you have had?" she asked.

"Some delicious pirogies, ma'am," Sam replied. "Best ones I've ever had in my life, and I've lived a while."

I guess that was the right answer as Mrs. Jankowski then said, "Come, come upstairs you both, standing on stairs is not a place for talking."

Worried that I might get spotted, I scooted back to my bed.

In the morning, I learned that Sam had been treated to a hot bath, given some clean clothes, and had been allowed to sleep in the spare bedroom on the main floor in exchange for helping out around The House. Billy was lucky too. Mrs. Jankowski let him off with just a mild scolding.

After Halloween, each day got shorter, and Billy's flashlight was a welcome companion on our morning walks to school.

One Thursday morning, Billy's flashlight was missing on our morning trek.

When I asked him where it was, he studied the snow at our feet, then said quietly, "Someone borrowed it."

"You mean someone stole it?" Joe asked.

"Who would do that?" I asked angrily.

"Bet I know," Joe added.

It was a dark week without Billy's flashlight. When we returned home from school on Friday afternoon, Sam shuffled over to us in the living room with both arms hidden behind his back.

He asked Billy to pick a hand. Billy peered at him, pondered his decision, and said, "That one!"

Pointing to Sam's right hand.

Sam slowly pulled his right arm from behind him, revealing… nothing. His left hand, however, held Billy's lost flashlight.

"Gosh, thank you! Where'd you find it?" Billy asked.

"In the storage room."

"But I never used it in the storage room," Billy said.

He looked at his flashlight, confused, as if it might have walked there on its own.

"No! Yuh didn't," Sam assured him.

"So, how'd it get there then?" Billy asked.

"Your friend over there!" Sam replied, nodding toward BJ, who was buried behind another comic book.

We all stared at BJ, but he was oblivious to anything but his precious comic.

Sam explained, "There I was in the washroom on Wednesday before dinner when I heard footsteps, and I thought, here comes Billy. But when I came out, I saw someone slip out of the storage room and hurry upstairs. He was too big to be any of you, but when I heard someone had nicked Billy's flashlight, I figured it might've been BJ and that maybe he'd hidden it there. Took me until this afternoon to find it."

"Why would he do that?" I asked.

"I think he was mad I didn't trust him with our secret," Billy said, and shook his head sadly. "I should have told him about Sam, I guess."

"Should we tell Mrs. Jankowski he nicked the flashlight?" Joe asked.

"No," Billy insisted, "I got my flashlight back, thanks to Sam."

Chapter 8
Trust

Christmas was drawing nearer, but for us at Assiniboine House, it was not quite the same as for other kids with families, even though the staff pulled out all the stops to make it as special as they could. Other kids at school could expect many presents because, in addition to their parents, they had brothers, sisters, aunts, uncles and especially grandparents. Besides our stockings, each of us could expect only a couple of presents. Everyone received one from Santa and possibly two or three from our gift exchange.

The gift exchange was started by Mrs. Jankowski to add more fun and excitement at Christmas. She brought in armfuls of craft supplies for us to make presents. They weren't much, but we also had old Christmas cards, wrapping paper, and ribbon to work with, and we made the most of it.

Each of us would make and wrap a few presents for our closest friends, which meant that we would have more than just one present from Santa to unwrap. The real excitement was in the giving and unwrapping anyway, so we had a lot to look forward to. Everyone joined in except BJ. He wasn't even talking to us anymore.

The real sad part for BJ? Because he didn't make presents for anyone, no one made anything for him. The craft tables were bustling during the last two weeks before Christmas. We tried to work at different tables from our friends so they couldn't see what we were making. As soon as we had made something, we would wrap it up quickly and put it in the big box beside where the Christmas tree would soon stand.

Every year, the Shriners donated a big tree, complete with lights. With Christmas being on a Sunday, the tree was delivered a week before Christmas, and when we added all the decorations. Most of us made a decoration for the tree from the craft supplies we had to make our presents. Mine was a snowflake, made by folding paper multiple times and clipping out notches and circles on the folds. When the paper was opened, it magically resembled a large snowflake. Oh, but it truly was a magnificent tree!

As Christmas approached, BJ became more and more withdrawn. He didn't join in any of the activities and I'm ashamed to say that we didn't really encourage him to participate. I'm sure that I wasn't the only one to wonder if there were any presents for BJ, but no one said anything. He would at least get one present from Santa.

At long last, Christmas Eve arrived. After supper, Miss Marie read us the story of Christmas before we were treated to a special surprise. Mrs. Jankowski had arranged for a magician to perform for us. He was more of a comedian than a magician, but we all enjoyed him. Then Mrs. Vincent finished reading the last few chapters of *A Christmas Carol by* Charles Dickens, which was part of our Christmas tradition.

Finally, Christmas morning arrived. Before breakfast, we gathered around the tree, and all the presents were placed neatly under it. Then Miss Marie came in, followed by Sam, wearing a Santa Claus hat. With his white hair and beard, he did look a lot like Santa. He took his place in a soft seat beside the tree, and Miss Marie stood beside the tree to pick up presents to hand to Sam. It was only then that I noticed BJ sitting by himself in the dining room. My heart sank to see him so sad and lonely on this special morning.

The first present, neatly wrapped in colored comics from the newspaper, handed to Sam was for Billy. It was a present from Joe. It was a little model cabin made from popsicle sticks. We all waited, full of expectation, as Miss Marie called out names and Sam handed out presents. I was a little surprised to feel a knot in my stomach, but I was really surprised to realize that it grew tighter each time I glanced over at BJ, still sitting by himself.

I became so worried about him that I would have missed my own name being called had Billy not nudged me and whispered, "That's you, Kath!"

I ran to Sam, took my present, gave him a kiss on the cheek, and plunked back into my seat, all in a flash. It was beautifully wrapped in red-and-white checkered cloth, cut from an old shirt from Sandra; I already knew what it was. She had been making bracelets out of long strands of braided wool.

I was in the midst of opening it when I heard Sam calling, "BJ? BJ? Where are you?"

"He's in the dining room," Murray piped up.

I put my present down and followed Sam, adding to his plea with a curious sense of relief, "BJ! C'mon!"

We found BJ all alone in the dining room at the end of the long table. What a lonesome sight. He lifted his head from his comic book and stared at Sam. Some other kids had traipsed along with us and chorused additional encouragement.

"C'mon, BJ! C'mon!"

BJ slowly eased his grip on the comic and approached Sam but with the scared look of someone who was knowingly walking into a trap. Sam held out a present. It was nicely wrapped in brown paper with a green ribbon. It looked like a box about the same size as Billy's shoebox.

"Come along, BJ," Sam encouraged, now with a hint of impatience.

Sam tried to read the card but couldn't quite make it out.

"Whose name is that?" he asked Miss Marie, showing her the tag.

"It says: From your friend," Miss Marie read aloud.

Silence fell over the room. All eyes focused on BJ as he walked up to get his present. It seemed to take forever, but it must have felt even longer for BJ, what with everyone staring at him. When he finally reached Sam, he took the present and scooted off toward to his place at the end of the long table.

"Whoa! Whoa, there laddie. Not so fast!" Sam called out.

BJ stopped, turned back, and mumbled sheepishly, "Thank you!"

"Yer welcome," replied Sam with a smile. "C'mon now, have a look inside."

The tension was unbearable as BJ alternated between examining the present and looking at everyone watching him.

He slowly removed the ribbon. He carefully pulled off the paper. A box. He cautiously took off the lid. Then he slowly reached inside and pulled out — a flashlight!

The box, paper, and ribbon fell to the floor as BJ stood there holding the flashlight. It looked exactly like Billy's flashlight.

"Turn it on!" yelled Billy.

BJ pressed the button and started flashing the light on and off.

"C'mon over here and shine it inside my popsicle house," Billy asked.

BJ shuffled over to Billy and said thanks. Then he whispered to him, and they both slipped into the next room. I was curious, so I followed them but stopped when they sat down on a bench just inside the doorway. I turned my back so they wouldn't think I was spying and stood perfectly still as I watched the other kids receive their presents.

They spoke softly but, to my surprise, I could hear them clearly.

"You found it then," BJ said.

"Nope, Sam found it," Billy replied.

"Why didn't you snitch on me?" BJ asked.

"Friends don't snitch on each other," Billy replied, "And you didn't snitch on me."

I couldn't see them, so I didn't know what they were doing, but there was a long silence that Billy finally broke with, "No, no, it's a gift. And I'm really sorry I didn't tell you about Sam. Friends should trust each other. Friends shouldn't keep secrets."

"But I thought this was your most important treasure," BJ said.

"Friends are more important," Billy replied, "Besides, I know I can trust you with it."

Then they spoke softly, but I heard the word "Trust" three times.

"Do you wanna see the tiny cabin Joe made?" Billy asked as they both got up and returned to watch the rest of the gifts get handed out.

As BJ walked into the room, I noticed he was smiling, and it was a lovely smile. Had I ever seen him smile before? I mean, a real, true smile and not a sneer? With the rest of the presents being handed out, I didn't realize that BJ had slipped away, not until I noticed him return with a rolled-up newspaper tied with a red ribbon. He quietly slipped it to Sam, and Sam then called out Billy's name.

"What's this, Sam?" Billy asked.

"It's a gift from a friend," Sam said softly.

The newspaper was just the wrapping. It had no card. When Billy tugged on the ribbon and the newspaper fell off, his mouth dropped. It was a Lone Ranger comic book.

He looked up at BJ. And BJ? He was now grinning from ear to ear with that big, new smile of his.

"But-but, this is your most favorite one!" Billy protested.

"Friends are more valuable," BJ replied, "And I trust you with it."

Just then, Murray turned to me, "You crying like a girl, Kath?"

I wiped my eyes, "I am a girl, you idiot,"

Well, I wasn't the only one, as I recall. Sam was sniffling, and so was half the room. Even Mrs. Jankowski was dabbing the happy tears in her eyes.

The End.

Book 3
The Football

By BJ MacDonald

Chapter 1
Home at Last

I'll always remember the devastating flood of 1950 and the impact it had on everyone who lived along the banks of the Red River. I was repeating grade one, in English this time, because I'd done so badly at that wretched French school that I failed grade one last year. I was living at Assiniboine House when the ravaging waters forced us to leave and be dispersed across the city into the hands of whatever foster parents offered to take us in. In a minute, it seemed, we were torn from the only family we'd ever really known. It was a difficult time for everyone, and foster kids like us were shuffled around from one home to another. I lived with four different foster parents over the next two years. Then, in the late summer of 1952, the miracle happened.

It was one of those picture-perfect August afternoons, and I was parked in the backyard of my foster home in St. Vital, quietly reading my comic books. Being the oldest of the four foster kids who lived there meant that I was expected to watch the younger kids, but all I could do was watch. None of them listened to me when I told them to stop screaming or hitting each other. There was no playground equipment - just enough room to run around, so that's what they did. They just ran all over the yard, trampling what was left of the grass and screeching.

As usual, I cringed when my foster mom yelled, "BJ! You out there?"

"Uh-huh," I grunted.

"Tell those kids to shut up. Then come inside."

I pushed open the back door. My foster mother worked up a smile and spoke all genteel now.

"Come into the living room, please, BJ. There's someone here to see you."

She was doing her darndest to impress someone, and so I cheered up a little, hoping that it might be someone here to rescue me. My hope quickly soured, though, when there, facing me, was my Children's Aid case worker,

Miss Dorthy Stone, or Miss Dire Straits as I called her. She was a dour, mousy looking lady, and never the bearer of good news. Whenever she showed up, it usually meant I was being moved to another foster care family.

She smiled, "Don't look so glum, young man. I have good news for a change."

Turned out she looked quite pretty when she smiled, but I was still a grumpy kid, and it'd take more than a pretty smile to charm me.

"Ah, don't worry, I'm not here to take you to another foster home. I think we may have found you a permanent home."

I eyed her, "Really?"

"I'm here to take you to meet them," she smiled again. "They've invited you for dinner. What do you think of that?"

At this point, the other three foster kids clattered into the kitchen, straining to hear the conversation.

"They don't even know me. What if they don't like me?"

I thought about the kids then at Assiniboine House. Lots of them didn't like me. Not that they didn't have good reasons.

"Don't worry about that. They've already made up their minds to like you."

What a weird thing to say, I thought then. I looked down at my old shoes. One of the laces was untied. I sure hoped she didn't notice.

"Well, what if I don't like them."

"You will, BJ. Trust me."

Angela, one of the other foster kids, who was now standing behind me listening, asked Miss Stone, "Are they going to adopt BJ?"

"We hope so."

The smile was still on her face like it was permanently etched. I felt a glimmer of hope.

"Can Jenny and I have BJ's room?" Angela asked our foster mom, but she ignored her and fussed with the tea for Miss Stone.

That question spurred me into action. I looked up at Miss Stone.

"Let's go," I said, as if this was my idea and she led me to her car.

I was thrilled to have any kind of break from my nutty foster family. All during that drive to East Kildonan I choked back questions, even though I was burning with curiosity.

When I finally did work up a question, "Who are they?"

Miss Stone held me in suspense with, "It's a surprise."

The car turned into a long driveway. I'd expected another shabby house with a dirt yard, and garbage burning in some home-made incinerator, but the house at the end of that driveway wasn't like that at all. My jaw dropped in astonishment. I thought she'd made a mistake and took a wrong turn. It was a big two-story home with a double car garage and a large side yard with shady trees and rose bushes everywhere. As we drove up the driveway, I saw a man and a lady standing at the front door, watching us intently. Miss Stone walked with me to the door, and the couple invited me into the front hall.

Once in the hall, I spied two younger girls standing bashfully behind the lady who Miss Stone introduced to me as Mrs. MacDonald and the man beside her as Mr. MacDonald. Miss Stone then excused herself abruptly, saying something about having to get things ready but assuring the MacDonald's that she'd be back after dinner. I stood there awkwardly as the lady crouched down in front of me, studying me with her kind, soft eyes welling up with tears. She pulled me close and held me tight. I remember that, at first, it felt strange, but then it felt very comforting. Had I ever been hugged like that? I wondered. As if in answer, she held me tighter. She smelled so nice, like roses. This hugging isn't so bad, I decided. Finally, she slowly pulled away and looked me over with tears now rolling down her cheeks.

"Our beautiful, handsome Bernie," she said softly.

Our? Handsome?

"It's BJ," I corrected her.

"I'm sorry. BJ," she replied, sighing tenderly.

I was even more confused when Mr. MacDonald crouched down beside me and explained, "This is your Aunt Michelle, BJ," he said. "Your *real* mother's sister, and we've been looking for you for some time now."

"My real mother?" I asked, still confused. "Where's my mother?"

"Unfortunately, she's no longer with us," he explained. "But she was Michelle's older sister Marie, and we'd almost given up hope of finding you."

"Are you… are you, my father?" I asked softly, barely getting the words out.

"No, BJ," he smiled and shook his head. "But I'd like to try to be if you'd let me."

My aunt called the two girls to come over, "Ellen and Maria, this is your cousin BJ."

The two girls approached me slowly and the older one reached out her hand, "I'm Ellen. Are you really my cousin?"

"Yes, he is, sweetie," Mrs. MacDonald explained. "He's my sister Marie's son. But he may soon be your brother."

Then I noticed Maria looking at me, probably as confused as I was.

"Are you really going to be my brother?"

"We hope so," Mrs. MacDonald said with a tentative smile.

"Will you be a good brother?" Maria asked sweetly.

I'll never forget that moment; the way the confusion all turned to smiles. The bright sun. My new sisters. The start of my new and wonderful life. I threw my arms around my aunt and this time it was me holding on to her for dear life, hoping never to wake from this incredible dream.

After a wonderful dinner, Miss Stone returned to check on how things were going.

"Would you like to live here BJ?" she asked, as Aunt Michelle smiled optimistically.

Everyone stared at me. It was like a spotlight glaring down. I managed a nod and an awkward smile.

"Does that mean you're my big brother, BJ?" Maria asked curiously.

"If you want me to be? I mean, do you? Is that okay? I'll do my best to be a good big brother," I said.

Both girls nodded. They smiled, too. And with that, the decision was made.

"Okay," I replied with what I was sure was a big, stupid grin.

Aunt Michelle came over and gave me a big hug, "Welcome to your new home, BJ."

Maria and Ellen both joined our hug, while Mr. MacDonald watched with a big smile on his face, putting his arm around me in a fatherly way once I let go. And Miss Stone? She just stood in the front hall beaming. She seemed quite satisfied that one of her charges had found a real home.

"Can I bring his things in now?" she asked.

"Of course! Let me give you a hand," Mr. MacDonald said.

"Do I call you Aunt Michelle?" I asked as they headed to the car.

"Or you can call me *Mom* if you like?" she smiled. "And I know that Mr. MacDonald would be very pleased if you called him *Dad*."

Chapter 2
The Cat-In-The-Box

Soon enough I was settled in my new home and had even made a new friend, Terry Mitchel, who was also eleven, but a grade above me, in grade six and lived just across the street. As we'd be going to the same school, we started chumming around together. Even though I missed my old friends from Assiniboine House. I was adapting to my new life like a duck to water.

On my first day at Lord Wolsey School, I learned that it, like my last school, had staggered hours. The morning shift was from 7:00 AM to 11:45AM. Terry and I were both on afternoon shifts, from noon to 4:45. We switched every two weeks, and this went on until the new Agnus McKay School opened in 1953. I think it was harder for parents than for kids to keep track of our school hours.

Grade five flew by. Nothing particularly unusual happened. My new life was blissfully boring sometimes.

In grade six, however, something changed. We were still on staggered hours, but Terry and I were at the same time now.

On the first day of school, I started on the morning shift again. When we were finished, the afternoon shift was just arriving. I was talking to Terry when I felt a tap on my shoulder. I looked around. The kid wore a blue sweater that was just a bit too big and had a hole in one sleeve. He had blonde, unruly hair that somehow seemed familiar. He grinned at me.

"Billy?" I asked with astonishment. "Gees! Is it really you? You've grown!"

"Yup. It's me." He gave me a hug then, right there in the playground.

I patted his back a bit awkwardly. He drew back, and I punched him playfully in the arm.

"So, what the heck are you doing here?" I asked.

"This is my new school now. I bet you thought you'd seen the last of me!"

That was life as a foster kid. You couldn't get too close to anyone.

"This is great. You coming or going, Billy?"

"Just finished class," he replied.

Terry had to go to his class, so I invited Billy to come home with me for lunch. On the way home, I learned that his new foster home was only about a half hour walk from here, but he wasn't happy there. Like some of my old foster parents, they were only taking kids in for the money.

His foster parents had two kids of their own, he explained, and yet they took in four foster kids. The foster kids shared the basement, while the family lived on the main floor with three bedrooms and two bathrooms. The other foster kids were all younger than Billy, so he spent a lot of time looking after them as well as babysitting the other two kids upstairs. He was what you'd call philosophical, but the two kids upstairs sounded like brats to me, and the parents seemed lousy, too.

Billy wanted to explore the rest of the neighborhood, so I grabbed my football and we wandered along some of the back lanes. In between flipping the ball back and forth, Billy would peek over the fences.

"What you looking for?" I asked.

"Oh, just curious about what's in people's backyards. The Jenkins' backyard is a mess. I sure wish I could get adopted by nice people like you did."

"I was lucky. My aunt was looking for me; otherwise, I wouldn't have been adopted either. Your turn will come. You'll see."

"I'm too old," he said and kicked at the grass.

"Don't say that."

"It's true. People wanna adopt cute babies, not me."

I'd never seen him pout and it kinda worried me. But he was right.

As we walked past Doug Bell's place, Billy spied a big gap in the fence from the lane to the garage giving a perfect sightline on his spiffy bright-green lawn. Just as I was throwing the ball to Billy, he swerved up the driveway, announcing he was checking to see if there was a garden in the back. The ball bounced off his shoulder and onto the perfect grass, right under the water arcing out from what I guessed was a sprinkler.

Billy eyed the ball getting soaked by the sprinkler and decided to rescue it. He raced onto the lawn under the sprinkler, grabbed the ball, and raced back. The sprinkler followed him. I peered around the garage. It wasn't a sprinkler but a man watering his lawn. He set the water full onto Billy as he ran back to the driveway, soaking his blue sweater.

"I warned you kids this morning, to stay off my lawn!" he yelled, drenching Billy until he was behind the garage and out of the line of fire.

As Billy stood there soaking wet, Doug turned the hose off and walked around to where Billy stood, dripping wet.

He crossed his arms and glared at us, "Why are you kids back here again?"

I stood in front of Billy, "It couldn't have been us, Mr. Bell. We were at school this morning."

"Who were those other kids, then?" Mr. Bell asked.

I shrugged, "Coulda been some afternoon kids."

"What's an afternoon kid?" Mr. Bell asked.

"The kids who go to school only in the afternoon," I said, wondering how anyone couldn't know that.

"We have staggered hours," Billy added. "The school is stuffed to the gills, so they gotta break us up."

"I see. Hmm, it looks like I really soaked you there, son," Doug said, looking more sympathetic at Billy.

"You have good aim," Billy said and laughed.

"He should," I said. "He's a firefighter."

"And I'm sorry to soak you like that," Mr. Bell smiled. "C'mon over and sit down on the deck while I get you a towel."

"Thanks," Billy replied, coughing and wheezing softly.

"Here," Doug said, bringing a towel from the house. "Let's get you dried off."

As Doug was drying Billy off, he asked, "What are you kids up to anyway?"

"Just playing with the football while we were walking home," Billy replied, "I got distracted by your beautiful lawn and missed the ball."

"Do you know *why* it's a beautiful lawn?" he asked, pointing at the grass.

I said I hadn't a clue. I can't say I was all that interested, but Billy was all ears.

"Because it's not just ordinary grass," Doug continued. "This is brand-new fresh sod and, just like a baby, it needs to be treated with tender loving care. Running all over it is not good for it until it's strong and healthy."

"I'm really sorry, Mr. Bell," Billy said as his coughing and wheezing worsened.

"You okay there? That cough sounds bad."

"It's just asthma. That's all. I'll be fine."

"I'm sure the drenching didn't help much," Doug smiled apologetically, "Can I give you a ride home and explain it all to your parents?"

"No thanks, sir," Billy replied politely, still coughing. "My foster mom isn't home anyway."

"What's your name, son?" Doug asked softly.

"Billy Johnson, sir," Billy replied, trying to hold back from his coughing. "You mind if I ask what happened to your real parents?"

"My father died in the war, and I was raised by my grandparents, but they died in a car accident."

"Johnson?" Doug asked, surprised. "Did they live near Lockport?"

Billy nodded while continuing to cough.

"Are you the Billy Johnson who fell in the river at their funeral?"

Billy looked up at him and slowly nodded again.

Doug shifted over beside Billy, put his arm around his shoulder, and looked down at him, all solemn and speaking very softly, he said, "I'm really sorry, Billy. I was there you know… at the funeral. My father was your grandparent's doctor. Do you remember?"

Billy stopped coughing as he looked intently at Doug.

"I carried you out to my brother's car?" Doug prompted.

Still focused on Doug, Billy finally asked, "Is your brother a policeman?"

"Yes!" Doug smiled. "My brother Don is the policeman who drove you to the hospital."

I had no idea what they were talking about, and didn't have time to ask, as Doug now shooed Billy into the house, saying he had to get Billy into some dry clothes immediately. I waited outside and a few minutes later, Billy came out wearing a huge pair of shorts and a shirt that almost reached his knees. Doug followed right behind him and said he was just going to hang Billy's clothes in the sun so they'd be dry shortly.

He then explained that he'd just finished rolling the front yard topsoil smooth that morning and had gone in for coffee when he heard kids yelling in the back yard. He saw six or seven kids running all over his perfectly smooth topsoil and that's why he thought we were them.

"Now look at it," he said sadly as he gestured to the back yard.

Now we understood why he'd been so upset with us.

"What a mess," I said.

"And it sure wasn't very nice," Billy added. "Can we help?"

I nodded.

"Well," Doug explained. "If you could load some of those pieces of sod into the wheelbarrow while I roll the topsoil all over again, that would be very helpful."

After about an hour, more than half of the front yard was neatly covered in sod, and Billy's clothes were dry, so Doug said, "It's root beer time, boys."

After that, went back to finishing laying the rest of the sod and we continued down the back lane on our way home, carrying the football this time.

Billy stopped once more.

"Who lives here?" he asked as he poked his head over a fence to peek into another backyard.

"Mrs. Musgrove," I replied. "You wanna stay away from that yard."

"Why?" he asked. "It looks like a super nice garden."

"Yeah, but it's a real challenge for garden raiders."

"Garden raiders?"

"Yeah," I chuckled. "Haven't you ever gone on a garden raid?"

"Nope," he replied.

"You mean, you've never ever snuck into a backyard and grabbed some carrots or peas or something?"

"Why would I do that?"

"For fun. It's like raiding crab-apple trees, except it's a garden."

"But you said your new mom has a great garden, and you can have anything you want, right?"

"Well, yeah!" I said, "I suppose so, but it's not the same. It's the challenge of not getting busted."

"Really?" he asked uncertainly. "So, why is this one such a challenge?"

"She's a widow," I explained. "And she loves gardening, so she's either in the garden or watching it."

Billy tapped his chin in thought, "She can't watch it all the time. I mean, she's gotta eat, sleep, or go to the bathroom, doesn't she?"

"Sure, but she's also got a yappy little dog," I explained. "Who'll squeal on you when she isn't watching?"

"What kind of dog?"

"It's a furry little thing with big ears. I think it's called a Papillon?"

"Sounds like a real challenge, all right," he said, peeking over the fence again.

"Why don't you come with us sometime?" I asked, "Maybe you could stay over on Friday night, since we can stay up late. It'll be all kinds of fun."

"I don't think Mrs. Jenkins would let me," Billy replied with a sigh. "She always makes me babysit on Friday nights."

"I can ask my mom to call her," I suggested.

"Really? That'd be terrific. I hate babysitting those brats."

I said that we probably should be heading back as it was getting close to suppertime. Before he walked home, I asked Mom if she would talk to Mrs. Jenkins. Mrs. Jenkins was quite reluctant at first to let Billy stay over, but Mom could be very persuasive.

For Friday night, Dad set up some cots for us in the basement so we could pretend we were camping. Billy came home with me after school on Friday, and Terry came over after supper, as we had agreed to take Billy out on his first garden raid.

Once it started to get dark, we picked up our cloth bags and did a couple of easy yards, bagging a few carrots.

After we washed the carrots off with the garden hose and finished eating them, Billy commented that it wasn't much of a challenge.

He asked, "What about Mrs. Musgrove's Garden?"

"Are you nuts?" Terry contested. "We'd get caught for sure."

"But her garden's the best," Billy pointed out.

"No way," Terry said.

"Chicken?" Billy asked.

"You first, then!" Terry dared.

"Okay," Billy said. "Let's go."

We headed off to Mrs. Musgrove's and peered over the back fence. No sign of her or her little dog, but the lights were on, so we knew she was home.

"Okay, Billy, this was your idea," Terry reminded him.

Billy peered over the fence and couldn't see anything, so he slowly and quietly opened the back gate. Nothing.

We peeked through the gate as he crawled along the ground toward the long rows of carrots and then stopped to listen. Still nothing. He pulled out a few carrots and stuffed them in his bag. Then we saw another small figure creeping up behind him - meow. Billy turned and stroked the cat until he felt the coast was clear. He stopped crawling and walked while crouching toward the sweet peas with the cat right on his heels. As he snapped off some peas and shoved them into his bag, everything went smoothly until the sound of barking pierced the quiet evening, and a light flicked on, illuminating the yard, porch, and backyard.

Terry and I peered through the cracks in the fence, dead still. The back door opened, and the yappy little dog charged out toward Billy. Billy jumped up and started to run toward the gate, but yappy puppy beat him to it, so he turned around and headed to the other gate leading to the front yard, with yappy puppy right on his heels.

When he reached the gate and pulled it open, he stood poised to race to the street but froze in his tracks, finding himself face-to-face with Mrs. Musgrove. She stood before him with her arms crossed, blocking his way like an impenetrable wall. The side door was still open behind her. So that was how she'd so quickly intercepted him. He stood there stone-faced as if he'd just gazed at Medusa, and then the yappy puppy grabbed onto his pant leg and started pulling.

"Hush, Bunny," she shouted at the puppy, who ignored her and kept on growling and tugging at the same time. The puppy only stopped and ran away when the cat whacked him on his back. Now, the cat rubbed up against Billy's leg. He certainly could make friends, that kid.

We shifted away from the gate and sat with our backs frozen to the fence in absolute silence. We knew we couldn't be seen, but we couldn't see or hear anything either. So, we waited and finally heard Mrs. Musgrove.

"I think Stephanie likes you," Mrs. Musgrove said softly.

More silence!

"What do you have in that bag, young man?" she asked gently.

"Carrots, ma'am," Billy replied softly.

Still more silence.

"Are those my carrots?" she demanded.

"Yes, ma'am," Billy said, now with a quaver in his voice.

"Didn't your mother ever tell you it's wrong to steal?"

"I don't have a mother," Billy whispered.

We could barely hear him now.

"What about your father?" she asked.

"I don't have a father either."

At that, Billy poured it on, playing the poor little orphan card.

"Where do you live?" she asked in an even softer tone.

"I live in a foster home with five other kids and sometimes get hungry. I'm really sorry I stole your carrots, but they're the most beautiful carrots, I've ever seen," Billy said, playing it up.

"I'm very proud of my garden and especially my carrots," Mrs. Musgrove replied.

"They're like, impossible to resist," Billy said, laying it on even thicker.

Terry stuck his finger in his mouth and made a gagging face. We smirked but didn't make a sound.

"What else do you have in your bag?" she asked, "I see peas, but no beets. Don't you like beets?"

"Yes, ma'am," he replied politely, "I love beets."

"What's your name, dear?"

"Billy, ma'am," he replied even more graciously.

"Let's get you some beets then, and some tomatoes too," she added, now speaking in a very kindly manner.

"Thank you so much," Billy said with exaggerated appreciation.

"I also have some lovely crab apples at the front if you like?" she suggested. "You know, Billy, it's not always a bad thing to take vegetables from gardens. I used to tell my children not to do that when they were little, but we mothers knew that our children often did just the opposite of what their parents told them. It was a good way to get our kids to eat vegetables."

She laughed and added, "I suppose that mothers still do that today."

Terry and I looked at each other, wondering if that was true.

"Let's go inside and get those carrots washed," she said. "Would you like a glass of milk?"

"Yes, please," we heard Billy say as the door closed behind him.

We sat there stunned, wondering what had just happened. A few minutes later, we heard the dog bark and the door open again.

"Thanks so much for your kindness and understanding, Mrs. Musgrove," Billy called out. "And you do have the best garden in town."

"Thank you, Billy," she replied as he knelt down and petted Bunny. "Now, be careful walking home in the dark and comeback and visit me again sometime."

Billy quickly came through the gate with both his cloth bag full and another shopping bag full of crab-apples. He closed the gate and we started to head back to my place.

"I think that's cheating," Terry complained.

"Why's that?" Billy asked. "Our objective was to get carrots and other garden stuff, and we did, right?"

"The objective was to do it without getting caught," Terry stated. "So, it's cheating."

"Okay," Billy agreed. "You don't have to eat any then."

"Who's Stephanie?" I asked as we began walking away.

"Her cat," Billy answered.

That was enough garden raiding for us, so we went back to my place to play some ball hockey downstairs. Billy suggested we give most of the stuff to my mom, but I wasn't sure how to explain how we got it, so Billy said he'd do that.

We dumped all the vegetables on the kitchen table; Mom looked at it suspiciously.

"Have you boys been garden raiding?" she asked.

"Mrs. Musgrove gave us a bunch of stuff from her garden," Billy replied.

"Why in heavens would she do that?" Mom asked.

"She's really nice," Billy said. "She even washed the carrots for us."

Mom picked up some carrots to check, "Hmm, but why would she give it to you at night?"

"We saw her earlier today," he clarified.

"How is it you saw her at this time of night then?" Mom asked.

"I was petting Stephanie when she came outside." Billy smiled.

"That's very curious," Mom replied. "Her cat usually doesn't usually like strangers."

"That's what Mrs. Musgrove said, too," Billy agreed. "And then Bunny wanted some attention, so I had to pet her too."

"That's strange indeed," Mom said. "Mrs. Musgrove's pets aren't usually friendly."

"That's probably why she asked me so many questions," Billy replied, almost sincerely. "And then I gave her lots of compliments on her beautiful garden."

"Of course," Mom replied, nearly chuckling. "That would explain it."

"She's really great and looks like she could make anything grow," Billy said.

"She is a good person," Mom agreed. "Sometimes, she babysits the girls for me."

"She did say something very strange about garden raiding, though," Billy remarked.

"What was that?" Mom asked.

"She told me that she used to tell her kids not to raid gardens, knowing that if they were told not to do something, they'd do just the opposite."

"Really?"

"Yeah," he continued. "She said it was a way to get them to eat their vegetables. Is that true?"

Mom looked at me, watching her and waiting for an answer.

"Oh, I don't think so, Billy," Mom replied.

"She sounded really serious, Mrs. MacDonald," Billy replied.

Mom just smiled, "I think it's getting close to bedtime, boys."

The best thing about sleepovers was breakfast because she always made bacon, eggs, and pancakes, something Billy never had at the Jenkins' house.

Then, one Saturday, Mom asked me to take a jar of crab-apple jelly that she had made over to Mrs. Musgroveas a thank you. I couldn't refuse, but how would I explain that the crab-apples she gave to Billy ended up at our place?

"Easy," Billy said, "I'll just tell her how nice your mom has been to me."

We rang the doorbell. Inside Bunny started yapping. Mrs. Musgrove came to the door holding Stephanie in her arms. She was crying, we noticed.

"What's the matter, Mrs. Musgrove?" Billy asked sympathetically.

"It's my Stephanie," she replied. "She's been very sick. Come in, boys."

"We brought you some crab-apple jelly. Mom made it from the apples. The ones you gave Billy?"

"You two are friends then?" she asked, looking from me to Billy.

"We go to school together," Billy replied. "And sometimes Mrs. MacDonald lets me stay over."

"That's nice, dear," she replied.

"What's wrong with Stephanie?" Billy asked. "Can I hold her?"

"Of course! Stephanie would like that."

She passed Stephanie over, and Billy gently took Stephanie in his arms.

"Would you like some milk and cookies, boys?" she asked.

"Yes, please!" I answered.

As she went to the kitchen, Billy gave me a very strange look.

As soon as Mrs. Musgrove was out of hearing range, he whispered, "I think Stephanie may be dead."

I reached over to check.

"She's looking at you," I whispered back. "Feel her," Billy whispered again.

I did and then yanked my hand back. She felt cold. We stared at each other.

"Do you think she knows?" I whispered.

"I don't know," Billy whispered back.

"Why are you whispering?" Mrs. Musgrove asked as she brought us our milk and cookies.

"We don't want to wake up, Stephanie," Billy replied.

"Don't worry, dear, you won't wake her up."

"Are you sure?" I asked.

"Of course," she replied, "Stephanie's gone to heaven. She had cancer."

"Really?" I said, feigning surprise.

"Couldn't you tell?" she asked. "She passed away a few hours ago, but I just had to hold on to her. It's so hard to let go of someone you love."

At that moment, I felt so sad for her.

"So, what will you do with her?" Billy asked hesitantly.

"What I should do," she replied. "Is take her to the vet in Elmwood. He has a pet cemetery in the back, and I've purchased plots for her and Bunny, but I was up all night with her, and I don't think I can face the trip."

"Would you like us to do it for you, Mrs. Musgrove?" Billy volunteered, "I'd be happy to. You've been so good to me."

"Could you really?" she asked, dabbing her eyes.

"I'll go with him!" I added, not wanting to be left out of the do-gooding.

"But I've nothing to carry her in," she said, looking around. "You can't just carry her in a blanket."

"We got lots of boxes at home," I volunteered. "And I'm sure I can find one that'd be perfect."

"That'd be very kind of you, boys," she said. "And I'll give you some streetcar tokens and a quarter each for your trouble."

"We don't need any money," Billy piped up.

I glared at him.

"I insist," she said. "But don't forget your milk and cookies."

Her oatmeal cookies had a date filling. They became my favorite cookie. After I wolfed down two cookies, I raced home for a box. I explained to Mom what had happened, and she helped me. Most were either too big or too small. Then I glanced over to Dad's collection of boxes.

There it was. A box fit for a cat, just the right length, height, and width and it even had a handle.

It had some writing on it and a number 50, but it didn't mean anything to me.

"This one's perfect, Mom!" I shouted.

She looked at it and cocked her head, "I don't know if that's quite right, dear."

"What's wrong with it?" I challenged. "It's strong too."

I picked it up and raced out the door before she had a chance to object. When I returned to Mrs. Musgrove's house, she had wrapped Stephanie in a white towel. I put the box down and opened it up. She gently placed Stephanie inside. It was a perfect fit.

"The address, a note to the vet, tokens, and money are in this envelope," she said. "And do thank your mother, BJ."

Billy picked up the box in his arms, not trusting the handles, while Mrs. Musgrove watched us intently as we whisked her baby away. We walked swiftly up to Henderson Highway to catch the streetcar to Elmwood. The vet's office was two stops past the Roxy Theatre. We normally liked to sit at the back of the streetcar, but all the seats were taken by high school students wearing East St. Paul's jackets, so we sat on the bench seat with our backs to the window. Billy set the box on the seat between us.

As the streetcar trundled near the Roxy, the high-school students stood up, getting ready to leave.

That's when a tall, red-haired kid stood in front of us, eyeing the box. Suddenly, he snatched it and held it up.

"Look what we have here, guys," he called out. "It's party time."

"Put that back," Billy protested.

He stood up and reached for the box. The red-haired kid pushed Billy back in his seat.

"Back off, twerp," he yelled at Billy. "This stuff ain't for babies."

The other students were all laughing as I grabbed for the box.

"You can't take that!" I cried. "Give it back!"

"Who's going to stop me, creep?" he jeered, grabbing me by the collar.

"You're not old enough to have this, so I guess I'm going to have to confiscate it."

He shoved me back in my seat, handed the box to one of his mates, and pointed at us, saying, "Don't even think about getting up."

The streetcar stopped and they all got off laughing away and passing the box around. None of them opened it. I don't know what they thought was inside it, but they appeared to be pleased with their ill-gotten spoils as they scampered away.

As the streetcar began to move again, Billy rushed toward the back exit.

"BJ! We gotta find it," Billy said as he waited for the streetcar to stop.

"How the heck are we going to do that?" I asked, catching up to him.

"We gotta get back to the Roxy Theatre," he said. "They'll probably be really mad when they find out there's no beer in the box."

"Why would they think there's beer in the box?" I asked.

Sometimes, I could be thick as a brick.

"Because it's a beer box. Labatt's 50!" he replied.

"How do you know that?" I asked.

"Mr. Jenkins has got lots of those boxes. Full of empty bottles."

He jumped off the streetcar, and I followed him as he walked quickly, coughing away, toward the Roxy Theatre.

"It's gotta be somewhere near the theatre," he said, slowing down and wheezing.

"When they discover what's in it, they'll probably just throw it away."

"Right. Good deduction," I said, feeling like we were in some radio drama now.

We walked all around the theatre, and down some back lanes but found nothing, so I suggested we just go home.

Billy looked at me and sighed, "Yeah, but what do we tell Mrs. Musgrove?"

"Oh," I said softly, "I hadn't thought about that."

At the Roxy streetcar stop we sat on the bench and waited. A few minutes later, we heard a familiar voice behind us.

"Why so glum fellows?" Doug Bell asked.

"Hi, Mr. Bell," Billy replied. "Were you at the theatre?"

"Nope, just coming home from work."

Billy explained what had happened, and he smiled, but only briefly, as he began to appreciate our dilemma.

"I see," he said sympathetically. "Did the cat have a collar?"

"Yes," I said, "A bright pink one."

"Listen, boys. I'll talk to my brother and see it gets reported to the police. They can identify the cat by the collar and maybe put out an alert for Stephanie."

"Oh, that'd be great!" Billy replied, all shiny-eyed with hope. "Thanks."

Just then the streetcar arrived, and we all got on, as we were heading to the same street. Doug sat with us and gave us a lot of encouragement and when the streetcar was approaching Hazel Dell Avenue, he looked down sympathetically at us.

"You two might want to get off here," he smiled as he handed us a two-dollar bill and added, "I think you could both do with a nice milkshake at the drugstore to cheer you up."

"Really? Thanks, Mr. Bell," I said as I took the money, and we got off the streetcar.

After we finished our shakes, Billy had to go and deliver his papers, so I headed back to my place. I reminded him that Mom had invited him for dinner. Dad was in the garage fixing up one of his old cars, so I went to help him until Billy showed up. I still hadn't told Mom what happened to Stephanie.

When Billy arrived, we were throwing a football around in the backyard when we noticed a police car pull up in front of the house. A police officer got out of the car and approached the house. Dad spotted him from the open garage door and came over to see what the problem was. After a few minutes, I heard the dreaded word.

"BJ!" dad called.

Billy handed me the ball and we walked over to the car.

"This is Corporal Bell, Doug Bell's brother."

"I hear you had quite a story to tell Doug today," Corporal Bell said kindly.

"Yeah, and he bought us milkshakes," I said.

"And that was really nice of him and——" I was going to blabber all when Billy nudged me.

He was a cop, after all, and was making us nervous just standing there.

"We found Mrs. Musgrove's cat," Corporal Bell cut in. "But there's a slight problem."

"With Stephanie?" Billy asked.

"No, not with Stephanie," Corporal Bell replied. "It's with the owner of the restaurant where she was found."

"What's wrong with Mrs. Musgrove's cat?" Dad asked.

"She passed away," Mom answered, as she, drying her hands on her apron, came up to see what was going on.

"Is Stephanie okay?" I asked.

Corporal Bell scratched his head under his cap.

"Well, she's still dead, of course, but otherwise intact."

"I'm glad," I said. "Not that she's still dead, but that you found her. We haven't told Mrs. Musgrove yet that we lost her."

Mom looked at me sternly, "And it seems you forgot to tell us, too, didn't you?"

"Sorry," I replied, feeling my face turning red. "I didn't know what to say."

Corporal Bell repeated the story that Doug had relayed to him while I kept glancing at Dad and Mom to try and read their reactions.

"Did you recognize any of the boys who got off the streetcar?" Constable Bell asked.

"They were all wearing East St. Paul's jackets, but I don't know any of their names," I answered.

I explained what happened on the streetcar, and Dad then asked, "Where did you find the box Constable?"

"We received a call from Mr. Bing Lee. He's the owner of the Golden Dragon restaurant. He reported that someone had left the open box beside the entrance door to his restaurant, and he was pretty upset, so we went to see him."

"We know that restaurant," Mom said. "We've been there a few times, and their food is very good."

"I'm sure he'd appreciate hearing that Mrs. MacDonald," Corporal Bell smiled.

He was hopping mad.

He kept saying, "I don't cook cats. Why do people think I cook cats?"

"I guess he had every reason to be upset," Dad added.

"The box was wide open, right beside the door," Constable Bell said, "So it was visible to anyone who entered the restaurant."

"Why would anyone put the box there in the first place?" Mom asked.

"Probably as a prank," Constable Bell said. "They were probably a tad disappointed to find out that the beer box they'd just taken from the boys had a dead cat instead of beer."

"That would do it!" Dad said, and I could see he was trying not to smile.

"That's terrible," Mom said. "Poor Mr. Lee."

"Where is box now?" Dad asked.

"I have it in the car," Corporal Bell said.

"Could we possibly take it to the veterinarian's office?" Mom asked.

"We haven't informed Mrs. Musgrove yet," Corporal Bell replied, "As Doug suggested I should chat with you first."

"Thank you, officer," Mom added. "Poor Mrs. Musgrove."

"If you wouldn't mind?" Constable Bell replied. "It'd probably be easier on Mrs. Musgrove if she didn't know all the details of what happened."

"I could take the cat to the vets now before they close," Dad said, as he followed Constable Bell to his car.

"I think I'll take some flowers to Mrs. Musgrove while you're gone," Mom said.

"Don't cook dinner tonight, dear," Dad suggested.

"Let's go out for Chinese."

"Thank you for taking care of this," Constable Bell said as Dad picked up the box and took it to his car.

"I'll drop by Doug's place and let him know."

Then he turned to Billy.

"You probably don't remember me driving you to the hospital several years ago, but Egil remembers," he said.

"Egil? Gosh, how do you know Egil?" Billy asked, eyes wide.

"The first time I met him was when I drove you to the hospital, but now that he's a police officer, I see him almost every day. He says he hasn't seen you for a long time, and his mother has been very worried about you."

"I didn't know he became a policeman," Billy replied, surprised. "That's amazing!"

"If you want to write him a note with your address where he can get a hold of you. I can wait," Constable Bell said.

While Billy was writing his note, Dad left to take Stephanie to the vet's office, and I explained to Mom about Billy's connection with the Amundson family. With Billy's note, Corporal Bell left while Mom put some flowers in a vase to take to Mrs. Musgrove.

Shortly after Dad returned, Doug dropped by and, following a quick discussion with my parents, they all went to see Mrs. Musgrove. When they returned, we learned that all of us, including Mrs. Musgrove, Doug, and his wife were going to the Golden Dragon for dinner.

At the restaurant we were seated at a big round table for nine. The adults sat on one side of the table, with all the kids on the other. Mom was sitting beside Mrs. Musgrove when the owners, Mr. and Mrs. Lee, came to our table to greet us. Then Mom, forgetting that Mrs. Musgrove knew nothing about what happened to her Stephanie, offered the Lee's condolences for their unfortunate experience earlier in the day.

"I'm so sorry to hear about all your trouble with the cat today," Mom said sympathetically.

"What do you know about cats?" Mr. Lee asked.

"We no cook cat here."

"No, of course not," Mom replied, shocked.

"We no cook cat here," Mr. Lee repeated in a louder voice.

"I certainly hope not," Mrs. Musgrove said, "I loved my Stephanie."

Just then a very attractive young Asian lady, about twenty years old, rushed out from the back.

"Dad, Dad," she said and switched to Chinese and ushered her father into the kitchen.

When Mrs. Lee followed them, Dad got up to join them all in the kitchen. I couldn't tell what they were saying, but I soon heard the young lady saying thank you before Dad returned to our table.

"What's going on?" Mrs. Musgrove asked.

Dad leaned over and whispered to her, "It's supposed to be a surprise."

"What is?" Mrs. Musgrove asked.

Suddenly, Mr. Lee appeared followed by his wife and daughter. He carried a tray that held the figure of a smiling, eight-inch-high ceramic cat, and he placed it on the table in front of Mrs. Musgrove.

"So sorry for loss of special cat," he said and made a slight bow.

"How thoughtful," Mrs. Musgrove replied.

"Not for eating," Mrs. Lee clarified. "For taking home to remember loving friend."

Mrs. Musgrove looked very pleased.

The young lady brought out a tray of tea pots and set them on the circular lazy Susan in the middle of the table. That lazy Susan fascinated me no end.

I don't know how many dishes were brought out to spin around on the lazy Susan, but I tried a lot of new flavors that day. At the end of the evening, Dad raised his teacup to make a toast to Stephanie and to Mr. and Mrs. Lee.

From the expression on Mrs. Musgrove's face, I could tell she was delighted, as were the Lees.

Chapter 3
The Quarterback Club

It was a Saturday in September when David Neuman first entered our lives. He was the eight- year-old son of Mom's nursing school friend, Wendy Newman. She was a head nurse at the Shriner's Hospital and sometimes she needed someone to take care of David. She and her husband, Dr. Albert Neuman had two children, David, and Rachael.

Today, David would be called a special needs student, but they didn't have much in the way of such programs for kids like David back then. He was slight and small for eight but not skinny. He had a narrow face, brown eyes, and straight brown hair, that was cut short but not like a crew cut. I'm not sure what his condition was called, but when I came home for lunch, he was sitting at the kitchen table with a bowl of spaghetti and a toy gun beside his plate. I didn't even have time to say hello when he stood up and pointed his toy gun at me.

"You're a suspect and you're under arrest," he said, squinting at me, all serious.

"I have to put you in jail."

With that, he brought out his toy handcuffs and clapped them on my one hand; I yanked my other hand away and scowled at him. You'd think he'd take the hint.

"I'm Sergeant Friday, and you're a prisoner," he insisted.

Luckily for me, Mom, my get-out-of-jail-free card, came to my rescue.

"This is David, BJ," Mom said, gently pulling David's hand away from mine,

"I'm looking after him while his mother is on day shift."

Being the sensitive young man that I was, I blurted out, "What's his problem, anyway?"

"He has a bit of an overactive imagination," Mom explained.

I snorted, "Really? Can you make him imagine that he's invisible?"

The toy gun stuck hard in my ribs again, "I have to take this suspect to jail. Now."

I rolled my eyes, "Mom, Mom. Can you call him off, please?"

Mom gently guided David back to the table, "Let's finish your lunch, David. Spaghetti's your favorite, isn't it?"

"Yup," he said, handing his gun to Mom.

"Keep an eye on my suspect, and if he moves, shoot him."

"Right. Somebody shoot me, please. Put me out of my misery with this kid.

"BJ! Be nice!"

"All right. All right," I grumbled, then asked if there was any spaghetti left.

"It's on the stove," she said. "Help yourself."

I waited until Mom was fusing over David again, then high-tailed it upstairs with my spaghetti.

We weren't supposed to eat in our room but something about that kid just bugged me. I could faintly hear my sister Maria having some weird conversation with David. Poor Maria, I thought.

"When you're finished lunch, BJ,"

Mom called up, "Can you please come down and help out?"

"Uh, With what?"

"David needs help with his puzzle," Mom said as I came down and saw her sitting beside him at the table.

"You like puzzles, and I know you're good with them."

I studied the puzzle on the table, intrigued. The pieces were all differently colored, geometric shapes: squares, rectangles, triangles, circles, and L-shapes. The board had indented areas to match the shape of each space. David had to put each piece in the space on the board where it would fit. How difficult could that be?

I sat down and soon learned the answer: pretty difficult for David. I was beginning to soften up about him just a little.

"David could use a little help with this," Mom said and gave me a pleading look.

I sighed and said, "Sure," as I sat down beside David.

This time, he didn't try to arrest me. His obsession with *Dragnet* is forgotten.

I held up a triangle and asked him, "Can you show me where to put this?"

He took the piece and stuck it in the space meant for the circle. Then he started banging it with his fist to make it fit.

I looked up at Mom, this time with my own pleading look, and she nodded toward the board. I took David's hand as gently as I could, moved it above where the triangle space was, and stopped there.

"How about this place?" I asked.

I pushed his hand down and the piece gently slipped into place. He then smiled at me and clapped, just as the doorbell rang. It was Billy. As soon as he entered the room, he was arrested as a suspect.

"He thinks he's Joe Friday from *Dragnet*," I explained.

"I'm innocent, Joe, honestly," Billy pleaded with David. "You've got the wrong guy."

"You're a suspect, and I've got to take you to jail," David said, doing his best imitation of Joe Friday.

"Okay, Sarge, I'll go quietly," Billy said, playing along and raising his hands.

"Hi Billy," Mom said. "Have you had lunch?"

"Yes, thank you. What's our new friend's name?"

"David," Mom said, looking at him kindly. "This is Billy and I think he likes puzzles too."

"He's a suspect and he's under arrest," David said keeping his eyes fixed on Billy.

"Can you show me your puzzle before you shoot me?" Billy asked.

"Okay," David replied, "But don't try to escape."

"Of course not," Billy replied, taking David's hand and leading him to the puzzle.

Now it was Billy's turn. I was impressed. He had a whole lot more patience than I did. Billy managed to coax David into setting down six more pieces correctly. He clapped eagerly after each triumph.

Mom had been watching as Billy helped.

"Thank you, Billy. He needs that kind of reassurance."

"What's the problem?" Billy asked.

"He has some learning challenges," she said and smiled. "He goes to a special school in the mornings, but when his mother works in the afternoons, I look after him. He really is a sweet boy."

"Just a bit confused, you could say," I added.

"That's enough, BJ," Mom said and glowered at me.

"Why don't you two go out and play now?"

"Great idea!" I replied.

Billy looked at David and asked, "Would it be okay if I got out of jail for a while?"

David looked at Billy and didn't say anything.

"I'll be right back," Billy said, "I promise."

"OKAY," David said, sulking, "If you promise?"

When we came back, tuckered out from running outside, Mrs. Neuman had arrived to take David home.

"I'm back, just like I promised," Billy said and grinned at David.

"I have to leave now," David said sadly.

"So, you'll have to stay here in jail until I get back, OKAY?"

"OKAY," Billy replied as we watched them leave.

On the next Saturday, Billy came over and shortly after he arrived, Mrs. Neuman dropped David off again, carrying a new puzzle.

"Can you please let me out of jail, Sergeant Friday?" Billy asked.

David just stared at him. I hoped he'd forgotten who we were, but nope.

He replied firmly, "No you're suspects."

Mrs. Neuman smiled and said, "Don't you want to show BJ and Billy your new puzzle?"

"OKAY," David replied slowly.

"But don't try to escape."

David plunked his new puzzle on the table and Billy joined him while I just watched. This board was similar, but the pieces had numbers on them. There were about thirty or forty pieces with numbers from 0 to 9.

"This is my favorite," David said as he dumped the numbers on the table. Billy grabbed a handful of them and spread them out.

"What do we do with these?" Billy asked.

"Thirty-one," David said, picking some pieces up to examine.

"What?" Billy asked.

"Thirty-one, thirty-one," David said, looking at the table.

"What's he talking about?" I asked.

"Do you have thirty-one suspects?" Billy asked.

David just kept repeating thirty-one in a whisper, so Billy picked up a few more pieces and put them on the table as well.

"Fifty," David said.

"What's fifty?" Billy asked patiently.

"Fifty, fifty," David kept saying.

"Fifty what?" I asked, exasperated.

"Wait a minute!" Billy said, pointing at the numbers on the table. He quickly took away a number seven, a nine, and a four.

"Thirty," David said, seemingly focused on the piece in his hand, "Thirty, thirty."

"That's right, David," Billy said as he put the nine back on the table.

"What's right?" I asked. "What are you talking?"

"Thirty-nine," David said.

"That's amazing, David," Billy practically shouted.

"What's amazing? I asked.

I was getting peeved. I couldn't see what he was talking about.

"He can add," Billy said. "He can add numbers and subtract, too."

Just then, Mom popped into the kitchen.

"What's going on?" she asked.

"David can add and subtract numbers," Billy stated, still excited.

"Really?" Mom asked. "How do you know?"

"Well," Billy said, "I put two threes, a five, an eight, a four, a seven, and a one on the table, and then he said 'thirty-one,' but we didn't know what he was talking about."

"What, exactly, are *you* talking about, Billy?" Mom asked.

"Those numbers add up to thirty-one," Billy said. "So, I put four more numbers down, a five, a nine, a three, and a two, and right away, David said fifty."

"My, my, that's most interesting," Mom said.

"And then," Billy began again, "I took away the seven, the nine, and the four, and David said thirty."

"That doesn't really prove anything, though. Does it?" I asked.

"Let's try it again," Mom suggested.

We all put a few numbers on the table and pulled our hands away. David instantly added the numbers and said the answer. As for us, we had to diligently add them up. Each time David was right, but he always seemed to be focused on something else when he spoke the answers. Billy would take away a few and David would say another correct answer.

"This is amazing," I said.

"We could sell tickets and make a ton of money."

Mom gave me a sharp glance.

"BJ don't get too excited yet. He must be tested by professionals first."

"Do you think this could be a breakthrough?" Billy asked.

"I'm not sure, Billy," Mom said with a smile.

"But it is certainly interesting."

We spent about a half hour more with David and each time he placed a number correctly in its proper place he would get excited and clap, but never when we congratulated him on his correct answers for adding or subtracting. It was like that part was not interesting at all. David would sometimes shift back to his Dragnet persona and arrest some suspects and then just as quickly loose interest and return to the tablet play with the numbers.

Over the next two weeks, Billy spent a lot of time working with David. He was fascinated with David's gift for numbers and got a kick out of helping him progress. That was Billy for you.

The next Saturday, I phoned Billy before breakfast and told him that I had some tickets for the Quarterback Club at ten o'clock and asked if he could make it.

"What's that?" he asked.

I quickly explained that it was the Winnipeg Blue Bombers Quarterback Club, which was for kids who couldn't go to the football games in person. They made movies of all the games and played them for club members on Saturday mornings at the Civic Auditorium.

"But it's already eight o'clock, and I haven't even started breakfast."

I twirled the phone cord around my fingers.

"That's two hours. What's the problem? Just eat fast."

"Okay, be there soon. Bye," he said and hung up.

David was already here when Billy arrived and, of course, he was really looking forward to Billy helping him with his special puzzles. Billy bee-lined it for the table and sat down beside David.

"Hey, what are you doing? We gotta go."

Billy looked up at me, "When?"

"When? Ten minutes!"

"Where are you going, Billy?" David asked.

"We have to go out," Billy replied softly.

"Can I come?" David asked.

Billy looked at me for an answer, and I just shook my head.

"I don't think you'd like it much, David. It's football."

"I like football," he said.

"Do you know what football is?" I asked.

"My dad likes football," David replied, without looking up.

"Have you ever been to a football game?" Billy asked.

"No," David answered, again without looking up.

"You probably wouldn't like it," I said.

"My dad likes it," he repeated.

"What does he like about it?" Billy asked.

"He likes Indian Jack Jacobs," he replied, talking to the table.

Billy looked at me, and I shook my head again.

Billy pulled me aside.

"It might be fun for him," he suggested.

"Yeah, maybe for him, but not for us," I whispered.

Mom came in and picked up her coffee cup.

"What are you plotting in there?" she asked.

"Nothing Mom," I said.

"We were just wondering if we could take David with us," Billy said.

"No, we weren't," I said.

"To where?" Mom asked.

"Just to see a football movie," Billy answered.

"How long will you be?" Mom asked while I glared at Billy.

"Only a couple of hours," Billy replied. "Right, BJ?"

"Maybe longer. But, you know, I really don't think David is gonna like football very much."

"Would you make sure he'll be okay?" Mom asked.

"Don't worry, Mrs. M," Billy said. "I'll look after him."

I just glowered at Billy as Mom said, "You're so kind, Billy. And I trust you both."

I wanted to protest more, but David grinned at Billy and asked if it was time to go. We quickly got ourselves ready while Mom put David's coat on.

"Shouldn't you ask his mother if it's okay," I asked in one last attempt to get Mom to change her mind.

"She trusts my judgment,"

Mom replied, "And I'm trusting you to bring him home safely."

These were not the words I wanted to hear, but Billy was anxious to get going with David in tow. He was actually pretty good on the streetcar and stayed with us, holding Billy's hand all the way.

David didn't say a word from the time we left home. We got in line with the other kids, waiting to trade our passes in for three green tickets. I handed Billy and David their tickets and we headed into the auditorium, thinking that the numbers on our tickets were seat numbers, but they weren't. We could sit anywhere we wanted, so I just followed Billy until he found a row with several empty seats.

When everyone was settled in, the MC walked out on stage to make some announcements.

Before the movie started, he introduced Tom 'Citation' Casey to come out and say a few words of welcome. Everyone cheered except David, who didn't know who Tom Casey was. When he was finished, the MC announced that today's game was the one played against the Edmonton Eskimos last week, and he cautioned those who knew the outcome not to spoil it for the rest who didn't.

The lights dimmed and the film began, in black and white of course. David sat quietly through the whole game. He didn't say one word. He seemed to be focused on the screen, but it was hard to tell, because even when the crowd cheered at something, he didn't react.

When it was half time, they stopped the film and the MC made a few more announcements before he said,

"Now it's that time you've all been waiting for. The autographed football."

"What's that?" Billy asked.

I nearly jumped out of my seat with excitement.

"I think it's the draw for a football autographed by the whole team. Get your ticket out."

"What ticket?" he asked.

"The green one! The one I handed you when we came in."

Billy and I looked at each other and fumbled around to find our tickets.

The MC started calling out numbers and after each number, I heard Billy say, "So far, so good."

I looked at mine, and I also had the first five numbers. Then when they called the final number, we both went,

"Ahhhh!"

"One number off," Billy said.

"Me too," I said.

"Just one number off."

Billy and I compared tickets, and the last number on his list was seven. The last one on mine was five. We looked at each other and then looked at David, who was sitting there not paying attention to anything.

"David! David! Where's your ticket?" Billy asked as the MC read the number out one more time.

David had no idea what Billy was talking about.

"Ticket, David?" I asked raising my voice and flashing my ticket across David's eyes.

"Does anyone have the winning ticket?" the MC asked again.

Billy then spied the green ticket poking through the top of David's shirt pocket.

"Okay, then," the MC said. "Looks like we'll have to draw again."

Billy snatched the ticket from David's shirt, read the last number, jumped up, and yelled, "Wait!

"Wait! Here it is!"

"C'mon up, son," the MC called out and Billy grabbed David by the hand and literally dragged him up to the stage.

"It's his ticket," Billy announced as he reached the stage, pointing at poor David, who was looking pretty confused.

The MC, realizing that David was reluctant to come up the steps to the stage, took the mic off the stand and came down the steps to greet him. I handed the ticket to the usher, and he confirmed to the MC that it was the winning ticket.

"What's your name, young man?" he asked David.

David gave me a pleading look.

"It's okay, David," I said softly. "Just tell the nice man your name."

David stayed silent, but the MC had a few tricks up his sleeve.

"I'll bet I can guess your name. Is it… David?"

"Uh huh," David answered slowly.

"If you were telling Santa what you want for Christmas, who would you tell him to give it to?"

"David Neuman," he answered this time.

"Fantastic," he replied loudly,

"David Neuman is our winner of this week's treasured football, autographed by all the players of our favorite team."

The crowd applauded, and David smiled.

"How old are you, David?" the MC asked.

"Eight," David responded, feeling a little more at ease.

"You're a pretty smart young man. I can tell just by looking at you," David smiled, just a bit.

"Who's your favorite quarterback, David?"

"Indian Jack Jacobs," David replied without any hesitation.

"Well," the MC said proudly, "That's certainly a great choice. Now who's your favorite halfback?"

"Indian Jack Jacobs," David repeated.

"Well, he does play halfback sometimes. I don't suppose that Jack is your favorite fullback, too, is he?"

"Yes," David said proudly as the audience laughed.

"Well, folks," the MC said, handing David the football, "Looks like Indian Jack Jacobs is the entire Bomber team, so on behalf of Indian Jack, I'm proud to present you this autographed football."

Lights flashed as photographers took his pictures, accepting the prized football. When things settled down, Billy shepherded David back to his seat, and I was anxious to see the football. David clung to it for dear life, but he let me look at it as long as I didn't touch it. He was like that all through the rest of the film and all the way home.

We made it home safely, without any incidents, which thrilled Mom. David still clung tightly to his football and wouldn't let Mom touch it either. He wouldn't even let his dad touch it when he arrived to pick him up. Every time David came for a visit over the next few weeks, he brought his football with him, but still wouldn't let anyone touch it, not even Billy.

Finally, during the third week, he let Billy hold it for a few minutes as Billy read to him all the names of the players who signed it.

When he read out Jack Jacobs, David asked, "Where does it say that?"

"Right here," he said, pointing to Jack Jacobs's signature.

"Here?" David asked, putting his finger on the spot that Billy was pointing to.

"Right," Billy said, "that's a 'J' and 'a', this is a 'c' and that's a 'k.' Together, that spells Jack."

David didn't say anything at first. He just kept looking at the football and finally said, "That's right."

"Can he really read?" I asked.

"Sure, he can," Billy said assuredly, looking at David.

"Can't you?"

"Yup," David said.

Billy looked at me and shook his head, "Guess he's not as good with letters as he is with numbers."

"Do you want to play catch?" I asked him.

"No," David said, clutching his ball again.

We tried hard to get him to play ball with us, but he just wasn't interested. He put the ball in his lap and went back to playing with his numbers. That went on for a week or so and then one Saturday when Billy and David were both here, Billy mentioned that the Roxy was playing a *Lone Ranger* movie.

"I remember how much you liked *The Lone Ranger*," Billy said, looking up at me from the table where he was working with David.

"Still do," I replied.

"Do you want to go?"

"Let's do it," Billy replied.

"You leaving, Billy?" David asked, looking up at Billy with his pleading blue eyes.

I saw my chance and answered for Billy, "Looks like it. Unless you got a better idea?"

"Like what?" David asked.

"Like, hmm, like playing football," I suggested.

Billy rolled his eyes, knowing what I was up to.

David had left his football on the kitchen chair so I picked it up to have a close look at it for the first time. To my surprise, David didn't react. I'd expected him to get mad, but he just walked over and pointed to a place on the ball.

"This says Jack Jacobs," he said.

"What's this one?" I asked.

"Tom Casey," David said.

"He knows them all," Billy said with a grin.

"Would you like to play catch with me, David?" I asked, all formal.

"With Billy, too?" he asked.

"Of course," I said.

"So… you're not leaving me and going out?" he asked.

"Not if you want to play football?" I asked, encouraging him to get his coat on, "C'mon outside and we'll show you how."

"Stay away from the road, all of you," Mom called out.

"I think those dump trucks are driving far too fast for a residential street."

"What dump trucks?" I asked.

"There's some construction down the street, and the dump trucks are going back and forth."

"We'll go around to the side yard then," I said.

"You coming with us, Billy?"

"And don't stay out too long," Mom reminded us. "It's chilly out there."

With our jackets on, we followed David, who was clinging to his ball. We started off slowly, with underhand pitches at a close distance. David had trouble catching the ball because his hands were so small. When he threw the ball at me, it went far to the right, and I chased after it. I quickly picked up the bouncing ball, held it in my hand, imitating a quarterback, and threw it to Billy. Billy easily caught it and threw it underhand back to me. Surprisingly, I caught it, too, and threw a long pass back to him. He ran for it and made a great catch. He was clearly on a roll, and then he did something both unexpectedly and unfortunately. He kicked the ball. Hard.

We watched in horror as the ball sailed up in the air right overtop a dump truck trundling down the road. We yelled helplessly as it dropped right into the back of the truck.

Billy, without a thought for safety, raced after the truck. He tore through a ditch beside the road as I yelled for him to stop. Too late. He tripped on the edge of the sidewalk, pitched head-forward into the ditch, twisting his leg and landing on his shoulder.

It all seemed to happen in a matter of seconds, this calm day turning into an absolute disaster. David's prized football was gone, and Billy was sprawled out in a ditch in agony. I stood there looking back and forth between the truck disappearing down the road and Billy lying in the ditch.

Meanwhile, Billy made enough noise to drown out an ambulance. Mom came running out to see what was happening and ran over to Billy who was still lying in the ditch and holding his knee with one hand. I followed her and looked back to see how David was doing. He was still frozen, staring at the truck as it disappeared up the road, not paying any attention to Billy's cries for help.

He simply looked at me and asked, "Where's my ball?"

Chapter 4
The Christmas Present

Dad had come around from the garage after hearing all the commotion. While he and Mom helped Billy up and practically carried him into the house, David followed silently behind.

"Where's my ball?" he kept asking with a desperate, pleading look.

As they were easing Billy onto the Chesterfield, Mom asked me to call an ambulance, but before I even reached the phone, through the open door that I forgot to close, I spotted Dr. Neuman, turning into our driveway to pick up David. So, instead of making the phone call, I ran outside to tell him to hurry because Billy was hurt.

He grabbed his bag and rushed into the house to find Mom kneeling beside Billy. The next little while was hectic, with Billy moaning, and Mom and Dad running around getting Dr. Neuman some things he needed.

Meanwhile, I just stood beside David, listening to him say over and over, "Where's my football? Where's my football?"

It was a nightmare.

The next thing I remembered was Dr. Neuman saying, "Hold him tight and still while I set his shoulder."

I heard a thump and then a Blood-curdling scream as Dr. Neuman reset Billy's dislocated shoulder.

Dr. Neuman asked Mom if he could use the phone because he couldn't do anything about Billy's knee until it could be x-rayed.

After his call, he said, "Dr. Gensler, can you see Billy at five o'clock? Can you take him?"

"Certainly," Dad replied.

Mom seemed relieved, so things settled down a bit. Billy soon stopped moaning and was resting quietly, so Dr. Neuman had some time to spend with David.

"Where's my ball, Daddy?"

Then came the hard part. Dr. Neuman knew nothing about us, losing David's ball, and since Billy couldn't tell him anything, I simply hummed and stammered my way through a very clumsy explanation so that Dr. Neuman understood that the ball was gone. He told David that he was very sorry, and he promised to get him a new one, but to no avail.

The sound of David crying was much worse than Billy's moaning, and even Dr. Neuman couldn't calm him down. Mom came over to see if she could do something, but nothing worked.

"His mother is the only one who can calm him down when he gets like this," Dr. Neuman sighed.

"I'll call Wendy now and let her know, shall I?" Mom said.

"Thanks, Michelle," he replied. "I need to get David home right away."

"Maybe Michelle should go with you and sit with him until you get him home?" Dad suggested.

"Could you please?" Dr. Neuman asked with a look of relief.

"I'll be happy to," Mom replied, "I'll ask Mrs. Musgrove to look after the girls. I'd like to spend some time with Wendy anyway."

Mom and David got in the car with Dr. Neuman while David continued crying.

Dad said to me, "Help me get Billy in the back seat of our car."

"Are we going to the hospital?" I asked.

"No, BJ," Dad replied. "We're taking Billy to Dr. Gensler's clinic. He's an orthopedic surgeon who specializes in sports injuries. He's a close friend of Dr. Neuman's, and he agreed to see Billy as a favor."

"I thought he needed an x-ray?"

"Dr. Gensler has an X-ray machine in his office," Dad replied.

When we got there, Dad took Billy into an examining room. Billy was in there for about an hour.

When he finally came out, he was walking with a crutch under his right arm and his left arm in a sling.

Dr. Gensler followed Billy out and said, "He's very lucky. His knee is not dislocated but he's twisted it quite badly, so he's going to have to stay off it for a while. His shoulder is still a bit tender, but it'll be right as rain in a few weeks."

"I guess I can't deliver papers for a while," Billy said with a wan smile.

"Or play football," Dr. Gensler added. "I'll let you know as soon as I hear back."

"Thanks, Dr. Gensler," Billy said. "I really appreciate it."

"What was that all about?" I asked.

"I'll tell you later," Billy whispered mysteriously.

Dad helped Billy in the car and asked if Billy was still living with the Jenkins.

"Unfortunately," Billy groaned.

"Can they look after you properly?"

"They don't look after him now, Dad," I said, "So I doubt it."

"We'll have to check it out then."

When we reached the Jenkins' house, Dad went in alone to see the house and talk to the Jenkins. He was only in there for about ten minutes when he came storming out of the house, got in the car, and slammed the door.

He didn't say a word for about another ten minutes, and I didn't dare ask what happened.

Finally, he blurted out, "Lord, love a duck."

That was his angry expression, which was followed by, "Billy will stay with us for now and I'll be talking to the Children's Aid people for sure."

I helped Dad set up a bed for Billy in my room and he stayed with us until after Christmas, when the Children's Aid found him and all the other foster kids at the Jenkin's house a new foster home. Fortunately, his new home was even closer to us than the Jenkins.

Over the next two weeks, Billy improved. One day, I joined them when Dad drove us to his check-up. As Billy limped from the examining room, I heard Dr. Gensler giving him some instructions.

"Really, Dr. Gensler?" Billy said. "Really! That's fantastic. See you soon."

"What was that all about?" I asked.

"You remember after David's football got lost," Billy began, his words tumbling out with excitement.

"I told Dr. Gensler about it and learned that David is his godson. I also found out that he was the orthopedic consultant for the Bombers when their players got injured, and he said he could help us."

"His godson?" I asked.

"Yeah," Billy answered. "Then he told me that he knew how upset David was feeling and that worried him."

"So now what?" I asked, crossing my arms.

This whole thing was trying my patience.

"He asked the manager if he could get another signed football," Billy beamed, "And he agreed!"

I laughed at that.

"No kidding. Well, David's gonna be thrilled."

"Me, too," Billy sighed. "I still feel terrible about what happened."

"When can we pick it up?" I asked.

"When I return my crutches on Saturday," Billy said.

"David will be at our place on Saturday," Dad mentioned. "Maybe he can come with us?"

On Saturday morning we all loaded up in the car, with David repeatedly asking, "Where are we going? Where are we going?"

When we reached Dr. Gensler's office, David asked, "Why are we visiting Uncle Karl?"

I guessed that he'd been here before, so we had no problem coaxing him inside. We sat down in the waiting room, and when Dr. Gensler came out to greet us, David ran to him and gave him a big hug.

"I've never seen him hug anyone but his parents before," Dad remarked.

"I have a special privilege," Dr. Gensler smiled, as he knelt down to hug David back.

"How's my special boy?"

"Good," David replied quietly.

"And how are you, Billy?" Dr. Gensler asked.

"Much better," Billy replied. "Thanks to you."

When Billy came out of the office, minus his crutches, Dr. Gensler followed him and announced that he had a surprise for David. He was holding a large box, beautifully wrapped in blue-and-white paper with a big gold bow.

"David!" he said softly, smiling, "We have a present for you."

"A Christmas present?" David asked.

"It's like a Christmas present," Dr. Gensler said.

"I like Christmas presents!" David said.

"You're going to love this one," Dr. Gensler smiled.

David frowned, "Can't open a Christmas present until Christmas."

"Don't you want to see what's inside?" Billy asked. "It's real special."

"Is it from you, Billy?" David asked.

"Yes, it is," Dr. Gensler replied.

This all seemed to be taking a while, so I said, "Come on, why don't you open it?"

"Can't open a Christmas present until Christmas," David said firmly.

"I guess you'll just have to wait, boys," Dr. Gensler said with a smile. "Once he gets something in his head, it's very difficult to change his mind. But you two already know what it is."

"Christmas is only a month away, boys," Dad reminded us.

David clung tightly to his present all the way home.

When his father came to pick him up, he also encouraged David to open it, but again we heard, "Can't open a Christmas present until Christmas."

Christmas finally arrived. Billy stayed over on Christmas Eve since he was almost part of the family now. We were invited to the Neuman's for Christmas brunch and when we arrived at the Neuman's home in Tuxedo. I was amazed at how big their foyer was. We all fit in easily and still had enough room to remove our coats, hats, and boots.

Dr. and Mrs. Neuman greeted us and showed us into the living room. A huge Christmas tree by the front window dominated the plushy furniture and there was David on the floor next to the tree playing with a train set beside his unopened blue-and-white present with the gold bow. David barely acknowledged us until Billy came into the room and then his eyes lit up.

"Merry Christmas, David," Billy smiled as he knelt down and picked up a loose train car.

"What have you got here?"

"It's a train," David replied.

"And what's this?" Billy asked, picking up the unopened present and showing it to David.

"You know," David said, accepting the present from Billy.

"It's Christmas, so why haven't you opened it yet?" Billy asked quietly.

"He's been waiting for you," Mrs. Neuman replied for him.

David looked up at his Mom and Dr. Gensler and they both nodded their approval.

"Can I help?" Billy asked.

"Okay, but don't tear the paper," David requested politely.

"Right," Billy replied, as he gently untied the bow.

He then pulled out his trusty pocketknife and delicately slit the tape so the paper just fell off without tearing.

David lifted the lid off carefully and took a deep breath when he looked inside.

Then he gave an excited gasp, "My football."

He eagerly pulled out the ball to examine it and then to everyone's surprise his smile slowly transformed into a frown. All eyes were focused on David.

"That's not my ball," he said.

Billy sprang into action, "No, it's not, because it's an even better very special football."

He turned the ball around in David's hands and pointed to some writing on the ball.

"Whose name is this?" Billy asked.

"That's Jack Jacobs's name," David said, still sulking.

"And whose name is this?" Billy asked, moving his finger up above the previous spot.

David looked at it carefully and slowly read, "D… A …V… I …D."

"And what does that spell?" Billy asked again.

"David," he said, looking up at Billy curiously.

"Right!" Billy replied excitedly.

"It says, *to my very special friend David Neuman*, and it's signed Jack Jacobs."

David looked over towards Dr. Gensler.

"Is that right, Uncle Karl?"

"It sure is," Dr. Gensler confirmed. "Your other ball was just a regular one that the team had signed, but this one was personally selected by Jack just for you."

"Really?" David asked.

"Truly. I swear it," Dr. Gensler replied with a big smile. "I was there and watched him sign this ball, especially for you."

"What do you think of that, David?" Billy asked affectionately.

David just stared at Billy for long enough to keep us in suspense and then he jumped up and gave Billy a giant hug.

David's mom gasped, and she covered her mouth in astonishment.

Dr. Gensler reached over to Billy, tenderly placed his hand on Billy's shoulder, and whispered, "Welcome to the Privileged Club, Billy."

I glanced up at Mrs. Neuman just as her husband gently grasped her hand. Tears were welling up in her eyes, but I knew they were happy tears.

Patience, kindness, and empathy all came more easily to Billy than to me and whenever I get impatient, I think of Billy and that football and David's happy face.

The End.

Book 4
The Guitar

By Carolyn MacDonald (née Reilly)

Chapter 1
The Two B's

During the summer of 1957, my parents bought a larger house in East Kildonan which was closer to my parents' best friends, the Melnyk's, with whom we regularly exchanged visits and shared holiday dinners. The Melnyk's were always very attentive to me and my sister Sharron since they had no children of their own.

When they learned that they could never have children, they decided to adopt and chose a little girl named Kathleen, who was eight when I was seven. Even with the slight age difference, we had a lot in common and I always enjoyed our visits even before we moved, but I only saw her a few times a year.

Following the move, I was thirteen, starting grade eight, and she was fourteen. Since we were both attending Melrose Junior High, we walked to school every day. On one such day, she asked me if I remembered her telling me about Assiniboine House, where she'd lived before she was adopted. The reason she asked was because she'd bumped into one of the boys from the house, named BJ MacDonald, who was in grade eight. I told her I'd heard his name, but he wasn't in my class.

"Were you good friends back then?" I asked.

"Not at first," she replied. "He was kind of a loner."

"And now?" I asked, worried I had asked too much.

"He seems to have changed a lot since then, probably because he was adopted too," Kathleen replied. "Anyway, he's asked us if we want to join him for a soda at the Hazel Dell Drugstore after school tomorrow."

"Us? Us?" I asked with surprise. "Why me? We don't know each other."

"Not yet, maybe," she said and smiled. "But I think he'd like to."

"Really?" I replied. I chewed my lip.

She nudged me, "Don't be such a Modest Molly, Carolyn."

"What does that mean?" I asked. I could be so naïve at times back then.

"It means we're going for a soda tomorrow."

The next day Kathleen introduced me to BJ MacDonald. He was sitting on a stool talking to a blond guy who was working the soda spigots behind the counter. We called these guys' soda jerks,' which sounds odd nowadays, but wasn't meant as an insult then.

BJ greeted Kathleen with a big hug and said, "Glad you could make it, ladies."

"This is BJ, Carolyn," Kathleen said. "And that jerk behind the counter is Billy."

Billy chuckled, "That's Soda Jerk to you if you don't mind!"

I recognized BJ with his dark, curly hair. I'd seen him a few times in the school corridor, but I'd assumed that he was in grade nine because he was quite tall. I also recognized the soda jerk as the boy who delivered my mom's prescriptions, but I didn't know him very well, so I simply smiled and wiggled my fingers. The names, though, rang a bell with something else Kathleen had told me about her experiences at the House, and I looked at her curiously.

"Billy and BJ - from the house?" I asked quietly.

"The same," Kathleen confirmed.

She made a sweeping gesture towards the two, like a queen introducing minions.

"Oh, Oh," Billy groaned. "We've been busted, BJ."

Kathleen laughed and said, "Oh, you bet I've warned her all about you two."

"Why, thanks, Kath," Billy said and grinned. "But Angel knows it's not true."

"Who's Angel?" BJ asked.

"Carolyn's puppy," Billy replied.

"You know Carolyn's dog?" Kathleen asked, giving him her side-eye look.

"It was kinda unusual," I explained. "You know Angel takes a while to warm up to strangers. But, when Billy showed up with Mom's prescriptions, she barked at first, just like normal, until I opened the door…"

"And? Go on," Kathleen said.

"Because," Billy answered for me, "Angel jumped up on me instead, her tail all wagging."

"He got a good face wash," I said and giggled a bit.

I'd been feeling pretty shy, but Billy and BJ were so friendly.

"You said she didn't warm up to strangers quickly," Kathleen said.

"That's because we aren't strangers," Billy added. "I was there when she was born, and you saw her, too, Kathleen, at the Amundson's farm when she was just a puppy."

"You mean Angel is one of Tess's puppies?" Kathleen asked, eyes wide.

"Yup," Billy answered, "And I picked out her name too."

"Good choice, Billy," I smiled. "She's an Angel."

"Sometimes," Kathleen said and chuckled.

"Did your dad get his new guitar?" Billy asked, looking at me.

"He did," I replied. "And now he's working out the chords for that new song you like."

"I really like *Peggy Sue*," Billy replied. "So, Carolyn's Dad said he'd figure out the chords and teach them to me next week."

"You're learning guitar, Billy?" BJ asked. "This is news."

"Yup," Billy replied. "Now, can I get you girls something?"

"Give us each a soda on me," BJ offered.

We gave Billy our orders and headed over to a booth by the window.

"Is Billy going to join us?" I asked.

"When Sandy gets here," BJ replied. "Her father owns this place. Billy's just filling in for her until she gets back from volleyball practice. He can't stay long, though. He's got papers to deliver."

"He has two jobs? Gee whiz, that's a lot," I said.

"More like six jobs," BJ replied, explaining that in addition to Billy's job at the pharmacy and his paper route, he worked part-time at some electronic store, shoveled snow in winter, cut lawns in summer, and sometimes helped out in the pro shop at the Rossmere Golf Course during the summer.

"Why?" I asked and sipped my lemon-lime soda.

BJ fiddled with his napkin, "Well, he has to work to pay for room and board."

"He lives on his own?" I asked.

He was just a kid like us. It didn't seem right.

"Billy never did get adopted," BJ explained. "And he was bounced around from one foster home to another for years until he decided he'd had enough of foster homes. An old friend of ours, Sam Grady, found him a room in Mrs. Gregg's boarding house last year, and he really likes it there,"

Just then, we heard Billy say, "Hi, Sandy, it's all yours."

Billy swept off his uniformed jacket and hat and joined us at our booth.

"Anyone going to the dance next month?" BJ asked.

"You mean the Sadie Hawkins dance?" Kathleen asked.

"Yup," BJ confirmed, smiling at me with a wink.

I wanted to shrink into the shiny red seats.

Billy nudged BJ, "You asking Carolyn?"

"I would, but I can't," he replied with what looked like a pretty fake pout.

"Why not?" Kathleen asked.

Oh, I wanted her to shut up just then!

"Because…" he replied slowly, "It's a Sadie Hawkins Dance."

"What does that mean?" I asked.

"You know," Kathleen replied, looking at me with that don't-you-know-anything look.

"Where the girls ask the boys to the dance?"

"I've never heard of it," I muttered, feeling my cheeks get hot.

"Don't you read *L'll Abner*?" Billy asked.

"Not really," I admitted. "Should I?"

"You're kidding, right?" Kathleen asked, looking at me in disbelief.

"How are you going to learn anything if you don't read the comics?" Billy asked.

"I leave the comics to my sister," I protested, getting flustered.

What did comics have to do with anything?

"Well, you just have to read *L'll Abner* if you want to learn proper social etiquette," Kathleen added, as she opened her schoolbag and pulled out a copy of a *L'll Abner* comic strip, penned by Al Capp.

"See!" she said, pointing to a cartoon sketch of a rather homely hillbilly girl. "This is Sadie Hawkins."

"Really?" I said, "Mr. Capp must have had an off day when he created her, poor thing."

"That's exactly the point," Kathleen said, poking the cartoon with her finger.

"She was the homeliest girl in Dogpatch, and her father, Hekzebiah Hawkins, was worried no one would ever ask her to get married, which meant that he'd be stuck with her forever."

"Being the most influential man in Dogpatch," Billy interjected in an old man's voice, "He decreed the first annual Sadie Hawkins Day, a footrace where the unmarried girls chased the town's bachelors. If any girl managed to catch one of the bachelors before the end of the race, he had to marry her."

"So now, to celebrate this tradition," Kathleen added. "We throw a dance in November. The girls invite the boys,"

"That's not a real tradition. It's just a stupid cartoon!" I protested.

"And why do you have a copy of a cartoon in your bag anyway?"

"I volunteered to be on the dance committee," she smiled. "And Amanda gave it to me."

"Who's she?" Billy asked.

"Amanda Page," Kathleen replied. She's a grade twelve student in Miles Macdonell who's taken over as the new chair of the dance committee."

"Why is a Miles Mac student chairing our dance committee?" Billy asked.

"Because," Kathleen explained, "It's a joint Melrose and Miles Macdonell dance."

"Is that because both schools are physically connected and share the same gym?" I asked.

"That's right, and we can't both hold a dance on the same night," Kathleen clarified.

"Does that mean you're not going, Carolyn?" Billy nodded, smiling at BJ.

"Unfortunately, it's not going to be held this November," Kathleen said.

BJ gave an exaggerated sigh, "That's a real shame. Just when Carolyn was going to ask me."

"Don't you worry, BJ," Kathleen smiled. "It's just being postponed until February."

"Why's that?" Billy asked.

"Because the Miles Mac kids who were in charge of organizing it couldn't agree on anything, so nothing was arranged," Kathleen replied. "It's now the Sadie Hawkins / Valentines Dance."

Just then, Sandy approached with her piercing eyes framed by a messy head of dark curly hair.

"Is there anything else I can get for the newest members of the 2B fan club?"

"What?" I whispered, confused.

BJ chewed on his straw, "Very funny, Sandy. I think your dad's looking for you."

Looking at our bewildered faces, Sandy said, "BJ and Billy. Two B names! Get it?"

"Gosh, do they really have a fan club?" I asked naively.

I might have asked if they had a rocket ship, the way she looked at me.

Sandy gave a sarcastic smile, "All superheroes have fan clubs, sweetie."

"Thanks, Sandy," BJ said abruptly.

"You haven't told them about your superpowers, have you?" she asked BJ, shaking her head at him as if he were a naughty little boy.

"Don't you have some work to do, Sandy?" BJ said.

"Somebody needs to warn these innocent ladies about who they're dealing with," Sandy continued, ignoring BJ. "First, we have BJ, better known as Super-klutz, and then we have Billy, the super-jerk."

Sandy abruptly turned around and left.

"What was that all about?" I whispered, watching her as she hastened back to the counter in a huff. "She sure doesn't seem to like you guys very much."

"That's just her way of showing how much she adores us," BJ said unconvincingly. "But she's probably still sore about Billy's stupid alarm fiasco."

"It wasn't my fault! No one warned me," Billy countered. "And, anyway, it was you who knocked over the coke display and broke half a dozen bottles that spilled all over the floor."

"I think she was even more upset with you," BJ re-joined. "Because *you* knocked over her cosmetic display."

"See what I mean, girls," Sandy said, suddenly reappearing and with a big grin on her face.

"Not really," Kathleen replied. We looked at each other in puzzlement.

"They're just being modest," Sandy began as she pulled over a stool and sat down at the end of our booth, while Billy and BJ rolled their eyes and looked away.

Sandy continued, "Shortly after Billy first started working here, BJ was hanging around waiting for his shift to end. We'd just got in a new shipment of supplies, and Dad had asked Billy to put some of the boxes on the shelves under the counter below the cash register. I'm sure that Dad mentioned to Billy that he only needed to put one or two boxes of each item on the shelves and take the rest to the storeroom. Anyway, Billy, oh so diligently, tried to fit them all in the space available, so he began jamming the boxes in tightly, but he had no idea there was a silent alarm button underneath the register. It sends a signal directly to the police station in case of an attempted robbery, and when the police came charging in the front door with guns drawn, they assumed that BJ and Billy were thieves! The 2 B's panicked, and Billy had an asthma fit, and you've already heard what happened and–"

"Oh, my God," I interrupted.

Sandy laughed and continued, "The cops told Billy that the alarm was for emergencies only, and Mama politely reminded them that the last time there was a real emergency, it took them fifteen minutes to get here, but this time they made it in two. She asked if she could expect that level of service from now on, as she thanked them for coming. Then she turned to Billy and suggested that we owe the two fine gentlemen a fresh coffee. Billy got the coffee while Mama brought out the mop and handed it to BJ."

She looked at me and Kathleen.

"Consider yourself warned, ladies."

With that, Sandy slipped off her stool and headed back to the counter, leaving us trying not to laugh at BJ and Billy, who looked pretty mortified.

BJ cleared his throat, "It usually takes weeks for people to discover I'm a klutz. Does this mean you won't ask me to the dance in February?"

That's when I noticed that he had really cute dimples. We didn't stay much longer, but before we left, I gave him my phone number and he called me numerous times over the next few weeks.

Chapter 2
The Sadie Hawkins/Valentines Dance

After Christmas, Kathleen introduced me to Amanda. She was looking for more Melrose students to join her dance committee, so I volunteered. I was tasked with finding a band, so I asked BJ's friend Terry Mitchell if their band would be interested. When he agreed, I explained that it was a Sadie Hawkins dance. The band, in need of a name, selected *the Shmoos*, inspired by one of Al Capp's most popular cartoon characters. The Shmoo character is shaped like an amorphous bowling pin with two stubby legs, friendly eyes, and a few sparse whiskers. This should not be confused with the iconic Winnipeg Schmoo Cake, which tastes much better than it looks and is even more tasty than a Shmoo.

As Valentine's Day approached, it was shaping up to be a very busy weekend, because, on the same weekend, a hockey camp was being organized by Victor Lean. He was a celebrity sports writer and well-known as a hockey advocate for underprivileged kids. 'Uncle' Vic, as some called him, was a good friend of my father's, who agreed to help with the hockey camp and be a referee.

Dad had explained to me that the government opened a Residential Indian School on Academy Road in the old Children's Home, and they wanted Uncle Vic to help their kids learn how to play hockey. I asked what a residential school was, and he explained it was a school where kids live as well as study.

"You mean like one of those fancy boarding schools for rich kids?" I asked.

"Not for rich kids," Dad replied. "It's for Indian kids whose families live in small, isolated communities, far away from any existing schools."

"You mean like kids who live on farms or something?" I asked.

"Sort of, but for kids who live in even more remote communities," Dad replied. "The kids at this school have never had an opportunity to learn how to play hockey, so we're going to run a hockey camp and introduce them to Canada's favorite game."

I asked Billy and BJ if they would help with the dance since hockey camp didn't start until Saturday. On the weekend before the dance, we met at the school to help the Shmoos prepare some decorations for the stage. Terry and his band members, Leonard, Vincent, and Charlie, asked if we knew how to make paper mache, as they wanted to build some life-sized Shmoo figures to put on the stage. Our art teacher allowed us to use the art studio as long as we didn't touch any of the projects.

In the morning, Charlie brought two large bags of flour and Vincent hauled in a huge stack of newspapers. Leonard brought a box of balloons to use as forms for the Shmoos, along with a roll of duct tape to hold them together. We had an empty ten-gallon paint pail to mix up the flour and water, although none of us really knew what we were doing.

All I knew was that we had to mix up flour and water paste to soak the newspaper strips in so that we could cover the balloon forms. Kathleen agreed to mix up the paste, and Charlie advised that we should use mineral water to make it stronger.

"Who told you that?" Kathleen asked suspiciously.

"My grandmother," Charlie replied confidently.

"Where would we find some mineral water?" Kathleen asked.

"I don't know," he replied. "Look around; there may be some in the cupboards."

Vincent soon called out that he'd found some paint, which we would likely need anyway.

Then, he shouted, "Wait a minute! Is this it?" he asked, holding up a large metal can.

"What does it say on the can?" Billy asked.

"Mineral Spirits," Vincent replied, proudly holding up the can.

"Maybe that's what she told me," Charlie answered. "I know it was mineral something."

Vincent brought us the can of mineral spirits, and while we began making the paste, Leonard and Charlie tore up strips of paper, and Billy and BJ blew up balloons,

There wasn't really a lot of mineral spirits in the can, so Charlie suggested that we save it for last so the finishing strips would be stronger.

For some strange reason, that seemed to make sense. Kathleen poured some of the mineral spirits into the large paint pail, but then she jumped right back.

"Phew, that really stinks!" she squealed. "It's making my eyes sting. Are you sure about this stuff, Charlie?"

"Does it look like water?"

"It looks like water, but it sure smells awful," Kathleen replied, holding her nose as Charlie came over to see for himself.

"Oh," he stated knowingly as he checked the contents in the paint pail.

"The smell is just because of these are old paint pails, that's all. Just put the lid on until we need it for the final layer."

Charlie went back to tearing up strips of paper. I didn't know Charlie at all before that day, but I soon learned never to trust anything he said. Once the balloons were blown up, they were taped together to make the rough forms of three Shmoos. The big one was almost six feet tall while the smaller ones were about five feet and four feet. This way, we could create a family cluster of Shmoos.

After lunch, we added another layer using just the flour and water mixture and then Charlie brought over the mineral spirits pail. As soon as he removed the lid, we all pinched our noses and stepped back once again.

I conveniently glanced down at my watch and announced, "Oh! Look at the time. I'm afraid I have to go. I promised Mom I'd be home to help with dinner. We're having company."

That statement was mostly true, except that my uncle wasn't really 'company.' Kathleen picked up on my cue and let the boys know that it was time for her to leave, too.

Charlie asked, "What about the final layer?'

Kathleen quickly replied, "You can do it, boys. After all, these are your Shmoos."

Although I couldn't make it on Sunday, Kathleen helped to paint the Shmoos.

"How'd they smell?" I asked curiously.

"Pretty bad at first," she replied. "But once we finished painting them white, they just smelled like paint, so it wasn't quite as strong."

"Did you paint them all white?" I asked.

"At first," Kathleen replied. "But someone had to paint the eyes and whiskers and those boys were hopeless."

"So, you did all the finishing?"

"Of course, but I convinced them to let me paint some colorful clothes on, the big one."

"What kind of clothes?"

"Just some red shorts with yellow suspenders," she said, laughing. "It looks a bit weird, but I think that's rather appropriate, don't you?"

"Absolutely," I agreed. "Have you heard them play yet?"

"No, but BJ says they're not too bad. I'm sure it'll be fun."

We arrived early for the dance so we could help the Shmoos set up their display. Kathleen, and I brought the Shmoo figures to the stage while the boys set up the instruments, amplifiers, and mics. Our Shmoos were a lot lighter than I expected, so we had no trouble moving them around.

"Where do you want us to put them?" Kathleen asked.

Charlie responded with his arms waving, "Just put them down for a second until we sort out all the wires. Once we plug in the amp, you can cover the cords with the Shmoos to hide them."

"Okay!" Kathleen yelled back and turned, shaking her head.

As Kathleen picked up one of the extension cords, she asked Charlie, "Are you sure these things are safe? They look a bit ratty."

"Gosh, where'd you get them?" I asked. "They look like they were pulled out of the garbage."

"Don't worry, they're just fine," he responded, sounding a little too overconfident, "I got them from the garage."

They didn't look like any extension cords I'd ever seen, since they seemed to be wrapped with a frayed cloth fabric.

"Do you think they know what they're doing?" Kathleen whispered to me.

"Probably not," I replied. "But let's get this over with so we can find out."

With the delicate touch of a demolition expert, Kathleen slowly plugged the cords into the electrical outlet. I think we all behaved as if we were expecting it to explode, but much to our surprise, nothing happened. When Charlie turned the amps on, they actually worked. With a big sigh of relief, we carefully placed the Shmoos on top of the cords to hide them from view and got ready for the dance.

The evening finally got rolling when the Shmoos started to play. While they certainly weren't great, they were definitely loud. Charlie was a very animated drummer who, surprisingly, managed to maintain a solid beat. This was fortunate since Terry and Vincent weren't particularly good singers. Vincent was reasonably proficient on bass, but Terry's guitar skills were limited strictly to rhythm. However, for a group that had only been practicing for a few weeks, they managed to play a few acceptable songs.

Kathleen disappeared for a while, joining a group of East St. Paul high school kids who'd come with one of her classmates. I went over to talk to her when the tall, red-haired guy sitting beside her grabbed me and pulled me down on his knee, trying to kiss me in front of everyone.

As I pushed away from him and stood up, he pretended to be offended and said, "Oh, c'mon baby, you know you really want to."

I ran back to my table, mortified and furious, not stopping to look back. BJ asked what the matter was, but before I answered, the chaos began. I glanced at the stage to see the Shmoos smoking. I don't mean the Shmoo band was smoking cigarettes. No, I mean our amorphous Shmoo characters were leaking smoke. Then they burst into flames, and the balloons started popping. Many of the kids cheered and clapped, thinking this was all part of the act.

The cheering and clapping quickly switched to screaming and yelling when the sprinkler system went off. Fortunately, the sprinklers didn't go off in the hallway, so that was a dry refuge area, which quickly filled with a mob of soaking wet students. The fire trucks and police soon arrived. As might well be imagined, it was mass chaos for almost an hour, with students running in every direction, looking for their coats, boots, and whatever they'd dropped while trying to get out of the gym and trying to find some way to get dry.

We never did hear the rest of *the Shmoos* repertoire as they were banned from performing again by the fire department. That's when I learned from a fireman that mineral spirits are used as a paint thinner, are highly flammable, and should never, ever be confused with mineral water. They also confirmed that the fire was caused by Charlie's faulty wires.

Chapter 3
The Party

After the confusion following the accidental pyrotechnics show, I finally connected with Kathleen in the corridor. She said she was invited to a party in East St. Paul, and she'd call me tomorrow.

Then, the tall, red-haired kid showed up again, wrapped his big ape arms around her, and, looking straight at me, said, "C'mon Kath, we're leaving. There's no room for her in the car."

I thought this was very unlike her, to just run off like that, and so I asked BJ and Billy if they knew any of those students she was with. BJ mentioned that he'd seen them before but couldn't remember exactly when or where.

Then Billy interrupted quite suddenly, "I remember now!"

"Remember what?" I asked, mystified.

"The streetcar!" he stated excitedly. "The tall kid with the red hair!"

"What streetcar? What are you talking about?" I asked.

"Oh. Yeah, the cat!" BJ replied, remembering something.

I just stood there bemused while Billy and BJ reminisced about some strange incident that happened on a streetcar a few years ago, and all I could understand was that it involved a cat and a box. I was feeling left out of the conversation, deserted by my best friend, and suddenly very tired after helping with the clean-up, so I asked BJ to take me home. His Mom picked us up, and when she dropped me off, I really looked forward to crawling into bed.

My parents were still at a party, and the house was really quiet with just Angel and me, as Sharon was staying over at a friend's place. I quickly got ready for bed, grabbed my book, and settled in for a quick read and a welcome sleep. Angel placed her wet nose on the edge of my bed, pleading to be allowed up. I knew Mom wouldn't approve, but those beautiful eyes. She snuggled up beside me, and I turned the light on to read, but quickly drifted off to sleep.

I had barely closed my eyes when I heard the doorbell. Angel barked as I quickly glanced at the clock. It wasn't even midnight. The only thing I could think of was that Mom had forgotten her key. Angel jumped down beside me as I grabbed my robe and slippers and rushed down the stairs.

The porch light was still on, so when I reached the bottom of the stairs, with Angel barking beside me, I glanced through the window beside the door. My heart almost stopped when I saw a uniformed policeman. Assuming the worst—that my parents had been in some kind of accident—I yanked the door open. What I saw next was even more of a shock.

In front of the tall, handsome policeman was a small figure wrapped in a heavy blanket. I nearly cried out in shock when I realized the figure was Kathleen. She was dwarfed beneath the blanket and looked lost in a huge pair of rubber boots that came up past her knees.

Angel stopped barking immediately. I didn't even notice that it was snowing until the officer cleared his throat, which made me close my gaping mouth and remember my manners.

"Come in, come in," I mumbled as I stepped aside from the doorway and grabbed Angel's collar to pull her out of the way.

As they made their way inside, the officer said, "I'm Constable Amundson. Are you Kathleen's sister, Carolyn Riley?"

I glanced at Kathleen, who gave me a pleading look, and I immediately understood.

"Yes, I am, officer," I lied politely. "What happened to my sister? Did she forget her keys again?"

"I found her standing at a bus stop in East St. Paul, looking almost frozen," Constable Amundson said softly. "She had no hat or gloves and was wearing high-heel shoes, which is a poor choice for a snowy evening."

"Oh, my god, Kathleen!" I blurted out. "What happened?"

"She seemed unaware that the bus service out there stopped at ten o'clock," he answered, glancing around the room. "Can I speak to your parents, please?"

"Uh! Oh!" I muttered, fumbling for the right words. "I'm, I'm sorry… they aren't home yet."

"Well," he said, his tone full of concern. "First of all, I think we need to get this young lady into some warm, comfortable clothes. I'll help her out of these boots if you can get her some slippers and a warm housecoat?"

"Right away," I replied as I raced upstairs with Angel in hot pursuit.

On my way up the stairs, I heard Constable Amundson call out, "Could you also bring some identification, please, as your sister seems to have lost hers."

"Okay," I shouted back.

I grabbed Mom's woolly housecoat and my fluffy rabbit slippers, which Angel tugged away from me. I started toward the stairs when I remembered the Constable's request for some identification. Angel headed downstairs with the slippers while I picked up my school bag and was back downstairs in a flash.

Constable Amundson had lifted Kathleen out of the rubber boots and was guiding her over to the Chesterfield in the living room. He then removed an enormous pair of woolen socks from her feet and, without taking his eyes off her, he patted Angel softly, pulled the slippers from her mouth with no resistance, and placed them gently on Kathleen's red, swollen feet, all while Angel licked his hand. He then took away the blanket, helped her on with the housecoat, and tucked a pillow behind her back as he encouraged her to lie down.

"I think a nice warm bath might be what you need, along with a hot drink," he said, glancing at me.

"I'll get them ready for her, officer," I said.

"Did you bring some identification for me?" he asked gently.

"Sure," I responded as I picked up my bag.

"How old are you, Carolyn?" he asked.

"Fourteen," I replied as I fumbled through my bag.

"And your sister?" he asked suspiciously.

"She's fifteen."

He scanned the room, looking at all the photos on the wall, shelves, and on the mantel. He stopped to pay special attention to a picture of Kathleen and me at my birthday party a few months ago and then turned his attention back to me.

"Could I please see your ID and then I'll leave your sister in your capable hands until your parents get home."

I didn't have much in the way of ID, but I did have my school notebooks and my report card. He seemed to be okay with what I showed him and then he handed me a police business card with a phone number on it and his name written on the back, Constable Egil Amundson.

"Could you please give this card to your parents," he said. "And ask them to call the station in the morning to let us know how your sister is feeling."

"Certainly, officer," I replied politely, "And thank you for bringing her home."

"You're very welcome, Carolyn. And you, young lady," he said, speaking softly to Kathleen, "Just remember, you're much too young to be drinking alcohol."

With that surprising advice, he picked up the boots, socks, and blanket and stood by the door, gently patting Angel.

"Good night, girls. And, Carolyn, please take good care of your sister."

As soon as he left, I turned to Kathleen and started to speak, "What the...?"

That was as far as I got when it hit home, that my frightened best friend looked a complete wreck, with tears streaming down her face, her makeup a total mess, and she was still shivering. I quietly asked her what happened, and she simply said she didn't want to talk about it.

I sat down beside her and gave her a big hug. Angel rested her snout on Kathleen's knee, and I patted her gently to show my appreciation. We just stayed still for a few minutes until her shivering subsided.

Then she looked up at me and asked, "Can I stay here tonight?"

"Of course, you can," I said reassuringly. "But it's really late, so I'd better phone your mom right away. She's probably worried sick about you."

Her Mom seemed more relieved than angry about getting my call. I apologized for forgetting to phone earlier, and she said it was okay because it was dark, snowing, and cold, and she didn't want Kathleen walking home so late anyway.

"The bath should be ready," I said softly as I guided her upstairs.

I helped her into the bath and left her soaking while I went to get some hot chocolate and prepare the bed. Since I only had a single bed, I pulled out the air mattress and put it on the floor beside the bed, but I sensed something was really troubling Kathleen and decided it would be better if we just squeezed in together in one bed, with the hope she might tell me what happened.

When she finished her bath, I brought extra towels to make sure she stayed warm, gave her one of my extra nighties, and led her to bed. I placed her drink beside her while I went back down to the kitchen to leave a note for Mom and let her know that Kathleen was staying over.

When I got back to the bedroom, she hadn't even touched her drink but had crawled right into bed and was fast asleep with Angel snuggled up beside her. I never had a chance to ask her anything, so I blew up the air mattress on the floor beside my bed.

It was a long night, and I kept waking up to check on her. She was out for the count and was still sound asleep when I woke up. Angel jumped off the bed when I got up, but even that didn't awaken her.

Mom was in a good mood making breakfast because she had won twice at Rummoli. I warned her that Kathleen might be a bit groggy as she had a bit of a rough night. I helped Mom with breakfast by setting the table and when it was about ready, I went back upstairs to see if Kathleen was awake. Her eyes were open, but she was just lying there, focused on the ceiling.

I gave her a cheerful greeting, "Rise and shine, sleepyhead, breakfast is ready."

She glanced at me without a word, but as I was letting the air out of the mattress, I noticed that her eyes were still red. I shoved the mattress into the closet, rushed over to the bed, sat down beside her, and put my arm around her.

"Would you like to have breakfast in bed?" I asked.

She nodded slowly and said, "I'm sorry to be such a nuisance."

"It's no problem. Actually, it'll be fun," I said, doing my best upbeat voice.

Back in the kitchen, I dished out breakfast and put it on a tray. Mom looked at me and smiled, which was her nod of approval.

"Bon Appetit," she said, without even turning around while I hurried carefully up the stairs with Angel on my heels.

Kathleen didn't have much of an appetite, which was a bonus for Angel, but I was glad to see her eat something at least. She finally broke the awkward silence, knowing that I was anxious to learn what had happened and what she had done with her boots, hat, and ID.

"I'm so sorry, Carolyn," she said with a tearful sniff. "I appreciate everything you've done for me, I really do, but I just can't talk about last night…at least not yet."

That was all I could coax out of her. When I finished my breakfast, and Angel finished Kathleen's, she said she had to go home and try to recover her stuff. I didn't know where she thought her stuff might be, and she still didn't want to talk about it.

I loaned her a warm coat and some boots. She muttered thanks, but she looked totally preoccupied as she headed out the door.

I called after her to remind her about going to the hockey camp to see the boys play, and she just glanced back at me, shrugged, and said, "Maybe."

I went back upstairs to get showered, and I dressed warmly to watch some hockey, even though I wasn't much of a hockey fan. I was just about ready when I heard the front doorbell and wondered if Kathleen had decided to join us. As I started downstairs, I heard a man's voice speaking to Mom at the front door. My heart stopped when I recognized the gentle voice of Constable Amundson.

The next thing I heard was Mom's stern voice calling for me, "Carolyn, could you come down here, please?"

I wanted to just hide somewhere because, of course, I never told Mom about last night, and I hadn't given her Constable Amundson's card either. I nervously descended the stairs, and the first thing I saw was Mom and Constable Amundson, his hat in his hand, staring at me from the front entrance.

"Do you have something you want to tell me, young lady?" Mom demanded.

Whenever she called me a young lady, I knew I was in big trouble.

Constable Amundson greeted me with a big smile.

"Good morning, Carolyn. I was just asking your mom how your sister was feeling this morning."

"Yes, Carolyn, how is your sister, Kathleen?" Mom asked with a disapproving look.

"Much better, thank you," I replied, smiling back.

"Could you please come down here, young lady, and explain why Constable Amundson thinks Kathleen is your sister?"

"Oh, no," I thought, as she used the 'young lady' expression again. I couldn't hide, and I had nowhere to run.

Angel was sitting happily beside Constable Amundson, who was gently petting her.

"She doesn't usually take to strangers," I smiled awkwardly, trying to ease the tension.

"Oh, I grew up with border collies on our family farm. Maybe that's why. What's her name?"

"Angel," I replied softly.

"Hi Angel," he replied, giving her ears a good rub.

All I could do was take a deep breath and go down to face the music.

"I'm really sorry, Mom, but I promised Kathleen I wouldn't say anything," I said as I finally reached the bottom step.

Constable Amundson smiled up at me with a gentle and almost forgiving look and said, "It's all right, Carolyn. And your loyalty to your friend is very commendable. But please remember that we all have the same objective here, which is Kathleen's best interest. Right?"

"I guess so," I replied, embarrassed, as I slowly crossed the floor.

"I'm sure your mother would agree with me," he said, "That if something ever happened to you, she'd want to know all about it so she could make sure you were properly cared for."

"I suppose so," I replied, staring at my slippers.

Angel sensed my discomfort and left her post with Constable Amundson, rushed to my side, and licked my hand to comfort me.

"You have a loyal friend as well," he observed with a smile. "Did Kathleen tell you anything at all about what happened?"

I shook my head and said, "She just said she didn't want to talk about it."

Constable Amundson turned to my Mom and asked if she could provide him with Kathleen's address and phone number. He then asked Mom if he could have a word with her in private.

Mom looked at me and asked, "Carolyn, could you please write down Kathleen's address and phone number and bring some coffee into the living room for the Constable?"

As I was writing down Kathleen's address and getting the coffee ready, I was desperately trying to hear what Constable Amundson was saying to Mom, but his voice was too soft. I whispered to Angel to go spy on them for me, but she was more interested in the biscuits I was putting out. I didn't want to interrupt, so I waited for a lull in the conversation to bring the coffee in.

"Coffee Constable?" I asked as I set the tray on the coffee table, along with Kathleen's address and phone number.

"Just a half cup, please, Carolyn," he replied, "I really need to talk to Kathleen's parents as soon as possible."

I poured the coffee and handed Constable Amundson the address, but he barely had two sips before he got up to leave.

"Thank you both, and please, Mrs. Reilly, don't be too hard on Carolyn; she was just trying to be a good friend."

He then turned to me and smiled at me, "Kathleen is very fortunate to have a friend like you, Carolyn, and she's going to need a lot of support over the next little while."

Once he was ready to leave, he thanked us for all our assistance and gently closed the door behind him. Mom headed right for the kitchen wall phone to call Kathleen's Mom while I just stood there for the longest time, wondering what Constable Amundson meant.

I desperately wanted to talk to Kathleen, but I had to wait until Mom got off the phone. Angel sat beside me on the bottom step of the stairs as I waited.

Finally, Mom put the phone back on the receiver and saw me sitting there in kind of a daze.

"Can we talk?" she asked in her soft voice to let me know she wasn't upset, but her face showed grave concern.

"Would you like some coffee, dear?" she asked as I followed her to the kitchen table.

I thought her question a bit strange since she'd always told me that I couldn't drink coffee until I became an adult. At that moment, I certainly didn't feel like an adult.

"I was supposed to call Kathleen about going over to watch the hockey game," I said.

"That can wait, dear," Mom said with a sigh. "We really need to talk. Let's just sit and have that coffee."

"Okay, I guess... Does coffee help when you're feeling stressed?" I asked.

"Well. It helps me."

As I sat down, she said, "This won't take long, and I know you're anxious to see Kathleen."

She filled a cup on the table and passed it to me, along with the cream and sugar. It felt really weird being served coffee by my mother.

She just sat there looking at me for several long seconds before she smiled, took a deep breath, and asked, "Now tell me truthfully, Carolyn, what did Kathleen say about what happened last night?"

"Honestly, Mom, she wouldn't tell me anything," I stated firmly. "She just kept saying she couldn't talk about it."

"It's okay, sweetie," she said softly. "It's just that after my discussion with Constable Amundson, I realized that you and your friends are quickly becoming young ladies… and I… that is, as your mother, I probably should have had this discussion with you earlier."

"Like when I got my training bra?" I asked curiously.

"No, dear, it's a bit more complicated than that," she smiled awkwardly.

"Are you talking about the birds and bees talk, that we never had?" I asked. I sat up a little straighter. "Because I already know all about that stuff."

"Stuff?" Mom asked. "Just where did you learn about that stuff?"

"From the nurse at school," I answered. "She explained the facts of life to us in one of our occasional health Q and A sessions."

"Really?" Mom said slowly, as she stared at me for a few more seconds, and with a very curious look.

Then she simply said, "Good, that means you'll understand what Constable Amundson meant when I tell you he thinks that Kathleen may have been taken advantage of by those boys in East St. Paul after they plied her with liquor."

"Seriously?" I asked loudly.

I almost knocked my coffee over in shock. I didn't really understand what she meant, but I knew it was bad.

"Constable Amundson seems to think so, but he's only speculating based on his experience and on Kathleen's behavior," Mom replied. "So, you see, honey, if Kathleen has confided in you, we must tell her mother and the police so they can help her."

"Well, she just kept saying that she doesn't want to talk about it," I said. "But if she does, I'll let you know."

"You have to promise me, sweetheart," Mom stated firmly. "For Kathleen's sake, okay?"

"Okay, Mom," I promised, anxiously trying to end this awkward discussion. "Now, can I call Kathleen?"

"Okay, but you haven't even touched your coffee," she said, smiling at me.

"I love the smell, but I don't really like the taste very much, even if I add sugar," I said as I quickly got up and headed to the telephone.

"You've had coffee before?" Mom asked with surprise.

"At Amanda's place," I answered as I reached for the wall phone. I picked up the receiver while Mom just sat there looking at me. It made me feel uneasy. I felt worse when Mrs. Melnyk answered and told me that Kathleen had gone back to bed and wouldn't be going anywhere today. After I hung up, I turned around and saw that Mom was still sitting there staring at her coffee cup. I went back to the table and sat down again.

"Are you okay, Mom?" I asked.

"Just very concerned for Kathleen and her mother, sweetie. Now you run along while I make something special to take over to the Melnyk's."

Chapter 4
Hockey Camp

I walked over to the hockey rink, anxious to talk to BJ about what Mom had said about Kathleen being 'taken advantage of.' When I got there, I saw a slew of boys skating around in circles in the middle of the rink. Then I saw my father in his referee's shirt. He blew his whistle, and the kids turned around and changed directions. They were doing practice drills. I wasn't interested in watching them practice, and as I stood there wondering what to do, I heard my name called. I turned around and saw Amanda standing there with Rachael Neuman.

"Hi, Amanda and… Rachael, what brings you here?"

"David forgot his toque and gloves," Rachael replied.

"Is David playing hockey?" I asked with surprise.

"No," she replied. "But he's in a skating program that Vic Lean runs for special kids, so Vic is letting him practice skating with the players when they do their drills."

"That's wonderful," I replied, "I didn't know you two knew each other."

"Rachael's mom's the head nurse at the hospital where I volunteer as a candy striper," Amanda said.

Rachael winked, "David was pretty excited when Vic told him that Billy and BJ were playing,"

"Are you here to watch the game?"

"Perhaps, if they ever start playing," I replied.

"Right," Rachael smiled knowingly. "Let's go inside and get some free hot chocolate."

We made our way over to the snack shack on the other side of the rink. The shack looked like a stretched wooden garage. It wasn't well insulated, but at least it was warmer inside than outside. It was heated by an old, black, pot-bellied wood stove that stood in the middle of the room. It had a canteen at one end and washrooms on either side. A row of windows with benches below ran the entire length of each outside wall. There was another row of benches down the center of the room on either side of the stove. Free hot chocolates were sitting on the canteen counter, so I grabbed two, handed them to Amanda and Rachael, and picked one up for myself. The shack was almost empty, and since all the boys were on the ice, we had our choice of seats. We weaved our way toward the far end of the shack, carefully navigating our way over boots and coats strewn all over the room until we finally reached a bench by the stove. We yanked off our coats and sat down and chatted for a while before Rachael advised that she had some errands to run and bid us adieu with a fancy wave.

"What's the matter with Kathleen?" Amanda asked as we waved goodbye back to Rachael.

"She had a rough night, but she's improving," I said.

"What kind of a rough night?" she asked, looking concerned.

"After the dance ended so abruptly, she went to some stupid party in East St. Paul,"

"What happened?"

"That's the problem; she won't tell me."

"Why not?"

I explained what had happened and how Kathleen ended up at my place.

"Did the police have any idea what happened," she asked.

"Constable Amundson seems to think she may have been 'taken advantage of' by those boys."

"Oh, my god! Are you serious?" she asked. "That's horrible."

I must have had the blankest look on my face as she peered at me like I'd just popped up from nowhere.

"Carolyn. Don't you think that's horrible?" she whispered.

I stuttered a bit and murmured, "I guess."

She stared at me again and finally said, "You don't know what that means, do you?"

I looked down at my lap, embarrassed, and shook my head. She slid down the bench to be right next to me and put her arm around me.

"Of course, you don't. How could you? Didn't Kathleen tell you anything at all?"

"Not yet," I replied softly.

"Look, Carolyn," she spoke slowly and softly. "If what the Constable thinks happened is true, this is extremely serious. It means that Kathleen could have been, well, physically violated."

"What do you mean?" I asked.

"Didn't the nurse teach you anything about, you know," She dropped her voice to a whisper and spelled out, "S. E. X.?"

"What? No."

"Okay," she murmured. "It's very important for you to find out as much as you can from Kathleen. She must remember something. If she does, please call me right away. Okay?"

"Okay," I replied. "Promise?"

"I promise, Amanda." I smiled and thanked her for listening.

Just then, the young hockey players stampeded into the shack.

"I think that's my exit cue," Amanda gave me a big hug. "Don't forget to call me!"

BJ and Billy followed behind a group of other players. When they spotted me, they stumbled toward me, laughing, joking, and tripping over all the boots on the floor.

"What happened?" I asked, staring at BJ's black eye.

Billy grinned, "Hockey. Sometimes it can get a bit rough."

"A bit rough?" I asked, with emphasis on the word 'bit.'

"You look like you've been hit by a truck."

"Oh… you mean this?" BJ smiled, pointing at his eye.

"Okay, now let's have the real story," I said, mustering up a bossy tone.

BJ and Billy looked at each other, trying to figure out who was going to tell what happened. I guess BJ won because Billy finally rolled his eyes and started.

"Okay, well," Billy began. "Introductions started out fine, and Uncle Vic was pretty clear on what the agenda would be for the weekend. However, some of the kids seemed a bit surprised to learn that nearly half of the players were from two Indian residential schools.”

“What’s a residential school anyway?” I asked, just then recalling the conversation with my dad, which we’d never really finished.

“A school for Indian kids, ’cause they don’t have any schools on the reserves,” BJ replied.

“From Dusty’s description,” Billy explained. “It sounds similar to boarding schools where students stay in residence and attend classes in the same building. One of these schools is in River Heights on Academy Road. The other is in Brandon. They’re swell kids, but some of the East St. Paul kids weren’t quite ready for them, so it got a bit awkward.”

“Okay,” I said. “So now tell me what happened.”

“One of the East St. Paul kids made some really stupid remark,” Billy said as he sat down on the bench, “I didn’t hear it clearly, but it sounded like he was telling them not to confuse their hockey sticks with long tomahawks, or something like that…”

“That’s when Billy’s big friend Dusty took offense and threatened to show him how to really use a tomahawk,” BJ added, shaking his head. “Then it went from bad to worse.”

“Well, you didn’t help much, BJ,” Billy quipped, “Jumping in and trying to break up the fight only made it worse.”

“I was just trying to pull Dusty off Rocky,” BJ replied with a snort. “Unfortunately, that gave Dusty a clear shot at my eye. It’s a good thing Billy was there to break it up.”

“Billy?” I asked, perplexed.

“Billy saved the day with his gold letters,” BJ clarified.

I scowled. My mood wasn’t the best that day.

“What are you talking about anyway?”

“Okay, okay,” Billy said, speaking slowly, showing me his hockey stick. “These gold letters are the ones that I used to put my name on my stick.”

“So what?” I asked.

“Dusty was billeted at Mrs. Gregg’s house,” Billy replied, “And I got to meet him on Thursday night when they first arrived. Later that evening, I was taping up my hockey stick and brought out my gold stick-on letters to put my name on my stick. Dusty thought this was really neat and asked if I could put his name on his stick, so I put DUSTY THE BEAR on his stick."

"That's his real name?" I asked.

"Not exactly," BJ replied, "Dustin is his school name. He wanted to use Mastimakwa, which is his Cree name, but the school wouldn't allow him to, so they changed it to Dustin."

"It's Mistahi-maskwa," Billy corrected him, "Which means 'Big Bear,' I think."

"How could you possibly remember that?" BJ asked.

"He wrote it down for me," Billy replied, pulling out a piece of paper. "And when the fight broke out, I simply reminded him what Uncle Vic said about fighting."

"Dusty dropped his fists immediately," BJ added. "And, just like that, the fight with Rocky was over."

"That's when Uncle Vic came in," Billy said.

"The room went dead silent," BJ jumped in again. "And then Uncle Vic said, 'Listen, boys, hockey is a sport, and sportsmanship behavior means no fighting, despite what you sometimes see at hockey games. This weekend, you're here to learn to play hockey, not fight, and you'll either learn to play by the rules, or you won't play.'"

"While most eyes were glued to the floor," Billy said, "Uncle Vic took a deep breath and asked if the boys wanted to play hockey or go home. And that's when BJ reached out his hand to Dusty, who grasped it right back, gave him a big hug, and apologized for the black eye."

"Huh, and now you're all best buddies?" I asked.

"All except Rocky," Billy noted.

"Who's Rocky?" I asked.

"The tall red-haired kid from East St. Paul, the one who's still sore at BJ for breaking up the fight," Billy replied.

"The kid from the streetcar," BJ added as he and Billy laughed at some private joke.

"Who won the hockey game?" I asked to change the subject.

"No one," BJ answered. "We spent the morning just practicing. We don't actually start playing any games until tomorrow."

I gave a half-hearted smile and stood up, "Okay, I'll see you tomorrow. I'm going to check on Kathleen."

Chapter 5
Chocolate Therapy

"Don't take your coat off Carolyn," Mom called out as I closed the door, "I need you to take this casserole over to the Melnyk's before it gets cold."

"Ok," I shouted back, thinking to myself, what good timing.

"Take Angel with you," Mom added. "She needs a walk."

While I got Angel ready, Mom wrapped up the casserole in a towel and carefully placed it in a cloth shopping bag before I headed out the door, with Angel bounding along beside me.

It was freezing, so I ran the last half block to warm up a bit. Angel stayed right at my heels.

Mrs. Melnyk greeted me with a big smile, "Your mother called and told me she made something. She's always so thoughtful."

"It's right here," I said, handing her the shopping bag.

"Thank you, Carolyn," she said, taking the bag. "Now come inside and take your boots and coats off while I turn the oven on."

Angel barked, and Mrs. Melnyk asked, "Is that Angel with you?"

"Oh, I was just taking her for a walk."

"You can bring her in and leave her downstairs with a bowl of water," she said. "If you have time to say hello to Kathleen, I know she'd love to see you."

I thanked her, pulled off my boots, and led Angel downstairs. I admit I was anxious about seeing Kathleen. I was beginning to understand that terrible things happen to ordinary people.

"Thanks a ton, Mrs. Melnyk," I said as I scrambled back up the stairs, "How's Kathleen?"

"Still a bit down." Mrs. Melnyk sighed. "But seeing you should cheer her up. Have a seat by the electric fireplace and get warmed up while I get some hot chocolate ready."

I didn't have the heart to tell her I had already drunk enough hot chocolate to last a month. Mrs. Melnyk brought me a tray with two steaming cups of hot chocolate and a plate of warm cookies. I carefully climbed the stairs to Kathleen's room, where I found her still in her dressing gown, looking like something the cat had dragged in.

"Kathleen? Is that really you?" I gasped.

"Come in," she said softly.

"You look like..." I saw the tears in her eyes, and I couldn't finish the sentence.

Clearly, she'd been crying a lot since she left my place this morning.

I set everything on the desk and grabbed a cookie as I turned around to give her a big hug, "OK, Kat...time for chocolate therapy."

I sat on the edge of the bed beside her. A smile slowly materialized on her face. She pushed back her messy red hair.

"So...?" I asked.

"I still can't talk about it..." she muttered, staring down at her hot chocolate.

"You have to confide in someone, Kathleen. And I am your very best friend, aren't I?"

The silence was deafening, as neither of us knew what to say next.

"I feel like such an idiot," Kathleen finally whispered slowly, shaking her head.

"It's not your fault," I replied, sliding my cup on the desk so I could put my arm around her.

Oh, we just sat there for the longest time, with her staring down at the full cup of hot chocolate in her lap. After a while, she began to open up a little.

"Rocky said there was supposed to be a party, but there was no party," she began. "There were just the boys. And another high school couple."

"Who were these boys?" I asked after some hesitation.

I was trying to coax some information out of her, but I was scared I was asking too much.

She didn't answer, so I asked, "Were they all from East St. Paul?

Again, she didn't answer, so I mentioned that I thought I recognized the red-headed kid as a player on the East St. Paul basketball team.

"That was Rocky," Kathleen admitted.

She chewed her lip, "And he had the car, so he drove us to the house, but I hardly saw him once we got there."

After what seemed like a forever of silence, she resumed, "The other girl brought me a drink and told me it was mostly Coke. I asked who else was coming, and she said that the others would show up soon. I looked around. I remember there were some chips on the coffee table, and that's it. I asked the girl where all the food was. I told her that Rocky said there'd be lots of people, tons of food, and great music, but I didn't hear any music either, just the TV in the living room. She said that we were just a bit early because the dance was cut short. Then she went and got me another drink."

Kathleen took a shuddery breath and began again, "I told her I wasn't thirsty, but she just handed it to me and told me she'd get me something to eat. I was feeling really uncomfortable just standing there, so I plunked down on the nearest chair and finished my drink, thinking it might calm me down, but it didn't. Not at all. She handed me the chips and asked if I wanted a refill. I told her I didn't want anymore, but she insisted. Then Rocky came in and put some music on, and he asked if I'd dance with him while we waited for the others to show up. The other boys were still sitting in the living room watching TV, and no one else was dancing. I was feeling so uncomfortable by then. I mean, it was weird, but for some reason, I felt woozy and stupid. Anyway, I thought maybe dancing would help. He put a slow song on, and we shuffled around the room, and he was, like, squeezing me and pressing really close to me. I wanted to sink through the floor…or disappear. Finally, the stupid song ended and I pushed him away and sat down again, but he grabbed my hand and said, "C'mon Kath, lighten up. The night's young. We're just starting to get warmed up.'"

She clenched her fists as she remembered it all.

"What did you say?" I asked as gently as I could.

"I said I was tired, and I picked up my drink, and he said he'd get me a fresh drink, and he let go of my hand, thank god, and I stood right up, but the room spun round and round. I was so dizzy! So, I sat down again. My head was spinning, and I felt like I was gonna puke, so I asked the girl where the bathroom was. She told me it was just up the stairs to the right."

"What was in those drinks," I said.

"Mostly Coke, she said! I don't know, but I almost didn't make it to the bathroom before I threw up."

"That's horrible, Kathleen. Did anyone try to help you?"

"I don't really remember what happened after that. It was supposed to be a big party with lots of people."

"It's ok. It's ok. You don't have to talk if it upsets you."

Kathleen finally took a sip of her hot chocolate and sat in silence while the radiator hissed. I could hear her mother clattering in the kitchen downstairs. Had she told her mother all this? I almost couldn't bear to hear the rest, but I squeezed her hand in encouragement anyway.

"The girl came up and helped me into the bedroom next door," Kathleen began again. "But I remember that I'd barely got on the bed when I had to race back to the bathroom. She stayed with me until I finished, helped me back to the bed, and put the covers over me. I think I must have passed out for a while because I didn't remember anything until I woke up. I felt really cold because the covers were on the floor. And I… I didn't have my underwear on. Where are they? I remember thinking. I stumbled to the bathroom, thinking I had left them there. And, oh, I had such a splitting headache. I was terrified by then; I was shaking. I found my underwear hanging on the towel rack. They were damp. How'd they get there? I couldn't remember a damn thing. I panicked and looked around all frantic for the rest of my things."

"Oh, my god!" I said, stunned.

She continued, speaking in a rush now, "All I could think of was getting out of there as fast as I could. I found my shoes, but I couldn't find my purse. I rushed downstairs, and my head was just pounding, I found my coat by the front door, but I couldn't find my boots. That's when I heard the girl ask me what I was doing. I didn't even answer her. I just ripped open the door and ran down the driveway towards Henderson Highway. The driveway seemed like the longest driveway ever, but somehow, I managed to get to the end, running all the way. My feet were freezing, my hands were cold, but the worst was the pounding in my head."

"You poor thing," I whispered, holding her tighter. "How did that nice Constable Amundson find you?

"All I knew was that if I turned right, I'd be heading back toward East Kildonan, so that's what I did," she sobbed.

"Just cry if you want, Kath, it's OK," I said, trying to put on my best motherly face, but I wasn't her mother and I wasn't helping, so I shut up and just held tight to my best friend. Helpless.

Kathleen's mom must have heard or sensed something because she called up to ask us if everything was all right.

I shuffled toward the door and lied, "Everything's fine, Mrs. Melnyk," I called down.

"Would you like to stay for dinner, Carolyn?"

"Thanks, Mrs. M, but I gotta get Angel home," I replied.

I quietly closed the door and sat back down beside Kathleen.

She resumed, "I ran toward East Kildonan for about a minute or two, but I was so cold I couldn't think straight. I spotted a bus stop sign under a streetlight, and I remember dashing toward it. When I got there, my head was pounding even harder, and I thought I might puke again. Then I remembered that I had no money because I couldn't find my purse, so I started to panic, but instead, I threw up in a snowbank."

We just sat there in silence again.

"Anyway," she said, "I realized the only way I could get home was to hitchhike, so I stuck out my thumb, even though it was freezing. There weren't many cars on the road, and I was really getting worried when I noticed a car slowing down on the other side of the highway. The driver made a U-turn in the middle of the road and pulled up beside me. He reached over and rolled down the window and asked me what I was doing out here at this time of night. I was a little frightened, so I told him that I was just waiting for a bus. He could see I was freezing, so he reached over and opened the passenger door. He told me to get in the car to warm up while he got me a blanket from the trunk."

"What did you do?" I asked.

"I stood there petrified," Kathleen replied. "But I couldn't figure out if it was from the cold or if I was scared of that guy. But when he came around the car with a blanket, I saw his uniform and his police badge. I calmed down a bit when he put the blanket around me. He was really kind. He told me that the buses stopped running at ten, and then he helped me into the front seat and told me he'd get me home as quickly as he could."

"Why didn't you give him your real name?" I asked.

"I just knew I couldn't face Mom if she knew a policeman brought me home. I remembered that your parents were out and just hoped that you were home, so when he asked for my name and address, I told him it was Kathleen Reilly and gave him your address. We didn't talk a lot on the way, but I learned he was off duty on his way home when he spotted me. Then, when he told me his name was Constable Amundson, I glanced up at him to get a good look. Then I just wanted to jump out of the car."

"Why?" I asked, astonished.

"It was Egil. Egil Amundson. I hadn't seen him since before the flood. "Wow. You actually know him?"

"I knew him slightly when I lived in The House, but I was pretty sure he hadn't recognized me. My head was pounding, and I couldn't think straight."

"But how on earth do you know him?"

"From the Amundson farm where Billy used to live. The family used to visit Billy at The House, and I'd play with Egil's sister Bridget. I had no idea he had become a cop."

She paused, and once more, we sat in silence. She smiled for the first time that day.

"You know. I think his dog Tess is Angel's mother."

"Really?" I asked, relieved that the silence was broken and that she was smiling.

"That's probably why Angel was so good with him at my place," I said with a smile of my own.

She looked at me and whispered, "I'm really feeling tired."

"Oh, of course, of course," I said. "And anyway, I have to get Angel home."

We traded hugs once more before I went downstairs. I thanked Mrs. Melnyk for the treats as I left, and Angel led me home in the cold and dark.

Chapter 6
The Big Game

When I got home, I realized that now I had a little more information from Kathleen than I had before, but I also had a problem. I had promised both Mom and Amanda that I'd tell them as soon as I learned anything, but who should I tell first? I decided to tell Mom as soon as I got home, but I gave her the abridged version, leaving out a few minor details. Although she seemed pleased that I had kept my promise, she said there wasn't really enough new information to bother calling Constable Amundson.

After dinner, I phoned Amanda, and she agreed to meet me before the 'big' game on Sunday. She was already there, standing by the boards when I arrived, and I quickly filled her in on everything that I'd learned.

"Thanks for telling me, Carolyn. Based on what you just told me, I think Constable Amundson is probably right."

"So now what?" I asked.

"Do you think she'd talk to the police?" Amanda asked.

I shook my head, "No. No way. Especially not to Constable Amundson because she knows him."

After I explained how Kathleen knew Egil, Amanda sighed and tapped her fingernails on the boards, "I expect that the police would probably want her to be checked out by a doctor, and I suspect she wouldn't want that either."

"I'm sure you're right. But what can we do?"

"Do you think she'd talk to me?"

"I can ask her," I offered.

"Please do that. Now let's hit the canteen and see if they've anything warm to drink."

With drinks in hand, we returned to the rink and prepared for a boring game.

"Thanks for staying, Amanda; I don't think I could watch this by myself."

"Don't you like hockey?"

"Not much. My Dad tried to get me interested after my little brother passed away. I really tried hard to learn the game because it meant so much to him, but I really didn't get it. Must be a 'guy' thing."

"I didn't know you had a brother."

"Yeah. His name was Brendan. He was born with a heart condition. We lost him three years ago. He was only five."

"I lost a brother, too. Six years ago. He was killed in Korea."

We looked at each other for a few seconds, realizing that we shared a similar tragic experience in our lives.

"My dad had so looked forward to taking his little boy to watch the Monarch's hockey games and teach him how to skate," I sighed. "He had once played for the Monarchs himself, and now, with just us two daughters, I guess he figures he'll never have a son to follow in his footsteps."

Just then, the players started to fill the rink. We spotted Billy. He was wearing a white sweater; BJ was wearing red.

Billy was a surprisingly fast skater, and he was pretty agile with his stick. His only real handicap was his small size, compared to players like BJ and Dusty. BJ mentioned that he was playing defense, which didn't require quite as much agility but, it did require the ability to skate backwards, which BJ hadn't quite mastered yet.

"Who's that other big guy on Billy's team?" Amanda asked.

"That's Dusty. See the gold letters on his stick."

My Dad soon appeared and got the game started. Those many Monarch games he'd taken me to, pointing out all the plays and players and positions and explaining all the rules, meant I knew what a good hockey game was when I saw one. This wasn't it.

Except for BJ's accidental goal and the one that BJ's team scored on themselves; it was a miracle that any goals were scored at all. After the first period ended, Amanda suggested we go back to the canteen for a refill. As soon as we picked up our drinks, I turned around and saw Billy standing right behind me. Dusty was beside him, and he greeted us with a huge grin, showing off his newly broken front tooth.

"Hi, guys," Billy smiled. "Meet Dusty."

"Did you have another encounter with your red-haired friend?" I asked

"No," Billy replied. "He didn't show up today, but it's a reminder not to try to catch a puck with your teeth."

"Now I look like a real hockey player," Dusty added, still grinning.

"How do you like the game so far?" Billy asked.

"Well, it's an interesting way to play hockey, and so generous of your opponents to give you a free goal."

"We're going for 'the most generous' award," BJ added, sneaking up behind us and giving me a big hug.

"Did you like BJ's amazing goal?" Billy asked.

"You mean the one that started with a pass from you behind your own net to Dusty, who tried to pass the puck forward and bounced it off BJ's skate right into your net? That goal?" I asked, eyes wide and all innocent.

The guys looked at each other in astonishment.

"That's the one," BJ acknowledged proudly. "It was a legitimate goal."

"I thought it might have been the other one," Amanda commented. "Where you flipped the puck and hit one of your teammates, and it bounced into your own net. That tied the game, right?"

"BJ's very generous that way," Billy said. "I think he's really trying for the most valuable player award for both teams."

The last two periods were much like the first, except there were no more goals until the game was almost over. That was not only a surprising goal but quite amazing, with credit going to an unexpected player.

The commonly reoccurring scramble around the net was in progress at the white end when the puck suddenly got loose. Billy picked it up and he found himself on a break-away down the right side toward the red net. Several red players were right behind him, with Dusty desperately trying to hold them back. Billy's only chance was a very tough angle shot at the net, but the goalie was ready for him. Then Billy suddenly had one of his asthma attacks and couldn't control the puck, so he flipped it back to Dusty, who, by some miracle, actually connected with the puck and fired a slap shot into the open top-left side of the net.

With the white team up by one goal, and only a minute left to play, it would have taken a miracle for the red team to even tie it up. It ended with the white team taking the gold.

All the white players, who were not already on the ice, clambered off the bench to congratulate Dusty and each other for their glorious victory, tripping over each other and falling down in their haste to join in the celebration. The red team joined in with a little less enthusiasm, but when they saw Uncle Vic step out onto the ice, they appeared to remember their sportsmanship lessons and began shaking hands and patting their opponents on the back.

Dad was stuck on the ice, trying to avoid the chaos, but he managed to skate around the mayhem over to the boards in front of us, shaking his head with a big smile.

"The end of the game was actually quite exciting," I declared.

"And quite surprising," Dad said. "I can drop you girls at home as soon as we hand out the medals."

"You have medals?" Amanda asked.

"Not really," Dad said a bit sheepishly.

"They're chocolate coins covered in gold foil and hung on a ribbon."

"Least you can eat them after," Dad said, then he looked at me. "Can you get yourself home ok?"

"Sure, Amanda said she'd give me a ride."

As I sat in Amanda's car on the way home, I thought about the worried way she looked at me then and about poor Kathleen. I was learning that, as a girl, getting home safely was an everyday triumph.

Chapter 7
Uncle Walter

On Monday, I was looking forward to a calm day at school after that busy weekend. Kathleen didn't show up at school for a full week, and although I talked to her on the phone every day, she wasn't up to having visitors.

Over the next few months, I spent a little more time with Kathleen, but she was never her old jovial self again. I tried to think of ways to cheer her up but with little success. She just kept everything bottled up inside and wouldn't let anyone in. The only thing she had any interest in was volleyball, and she would spike that ball as if to drive it into the ground.

Then, early in June, I heard she'd fainted during volleyball practice on Thursday and was taken to the hospital. I raced home right after school to phone her and was surprised to find Dad home early. What was even more surprising was finding him in the kitchen, making supper.

"Where's Mom?" I asked uneasily.

"She's at the Melnyk's," he replied.

"Dad. What's happened?"

Dad looked at me very strangely as he said, "Maybe you should sit down, dear."

"I'm not a kid anymore," I said, but I sat down anyway.

"I'm not even sure that I should be telling this," Dad began. "But I think you're old enough to understand, and Kathleen is your best friend."

"Is she…is she ok?" I asked, feeling sick to my stomach.

"Promise me you won't talk to anyone about this," Dad said.

"I'm not a gabby mouth," I said.

And then the bombshell exploded.

"Kathleen is going to have a baby," he said.

Dad's words hung there while their significance sank into my brain.

"She's… she's pregnant?" I finally asked.

"Yes…yes, that is the correct term," Dad replied.

He cleared his throat and stacked some plates.

"When did you find out?" I asked.

"The school nurse called Helen when Kathleen fainted during volleyball practice and told her that she suspected Kathleen might be pregnant, so they took her to the hospital."

"So that explains why there are so many different rumors flying around," Dad squinted at me.

"What kind of rumors?" he asked in his serious tone.

"Well, one of the kids said that Kathleen had been expelled for being 'knocked up,' but no one seems to know for sure."

"I had no idea that the school grapevine was so efficient," Dad commented.

"You mean it's true, she's being expelled for being pregnant?" I asked.

Dad sighed and sat down opposite me, "Not exactly, but there's probably no real need for her to return to school now, as it's almost the end of the year anyway."

"Doesn't she need to finish the year to pass?" I asked.

"The board has agreed to grant her a grade eight certificate based on her good grades."

"It still sounds like she's being expelled," I said, crossing my arms and glaring at him. "And I think it's really unfair."

"Well, Carolyn, perhaps you could consider it as an exemption instead of being expelled?"

"Who said that?" I asked.

"As I recall, it was how the principal phrased it."

"When were you talking to the principal?" I asked.

"Your mother and I were at the Melnyk's this afternoon when he arrived."

"Why were you both at the Melnyk's on a Friday afternoon anyway?"

"Well," Dad explained, "Kathleen's mom was still pretty upset this morning, so your mom went over to see what she could do. When she learned that the principal was coming to see them, she needed Stan to be there, so, of course, your mom phoned me at work."

"Because it's your week to drive?" I asked, remembering that Dad and Mr. Melnyk shared driving to work on alternate weeks.

"Of course," he said. "I brought Stan home, and your mom was still there, so Helen asked us to stay. When the principal arrived, he apologized profusely throughout the discussion and kept reminding Helen and Stan that they had to think of Kathleen and how awkward and difficult it would be for her."

"Is that all he said?" I asked. "Didn't he give her any choices or options?"

"This is not really the school's problem, Carolyn," Dad explained. "This is a private matter that Kathleen's family has to deal with."

"So, what are her choices?" I asked again.

Dad looked rattled, "Maybe we should wait until your mom gets home," he suggested as he got up abruptly and went back to the stove, "I promised I'd get dinner started, and I expect she'll be home any minute. Could you set the table, please?"

Dad was saved from further discussion by Mom opening the back door.

"Just in time, Sheila, dinner is almost ready," Dad called out. "How are the Melnyk's doing?"

"It's been a pretty rough day," Mom sighed. "I helped Helen with dinner, but Kathleen wouldn't come down from her room."

"Was Walter still there?" Dad asked.

"He was sitting at the dinner table when I left. Honestly, I just don't understand why he was so adamant about his position being the only solution."

"He clearly has his opinion," Dad said.

Mom glanced at me and lowered her voice as she spoke to Dad, but I could still hear them.

"He knows how upset Helen is about the subject of termination, yet he kept pressuring them to consider it."

"What do you mean?" I piped up.

"Oh, it's nothing, dear," Mom said, then added, "And please don't eavesdrop on adults' conversations."

The silence that followed was unnerving. I finished setting the table. Dinner was awkwardly quiet; it was clear that my parents were all talked out. After dinner, I stayed in the kitchen to help Mom clean up and then worked up the nerve to ask her how Kathleen was.

"She's still upset, dear," she said. "Which is completely understandable. And being so stressed themselves, her parents are finding it tough to give her the support she needs."

"I understand that, Mom," I said, "But I don't understand why you seem so irritated with her Uncle Walter, and I still don't know what 'options' you're talking about. She's my best friend, I should know!"

Mom sighed, "Well, dear, her Uncle Walter kept insisting that the best option for Kathleen was to terminate the pregnancy if she wanted to have any kind of future."

"You mean an... an abortion?" I asked.

She seemed stunned at my question, "Carolyn. Where did you learn that word?"

"At school, and I know it's illegal," I replied timidly now; after all, I had just stepped into a new arena with no armor or clue what I was doing.

"At school?" she asked, puzzled.

"In our health session," I explained. "Remember I told you about the school nurse?"

"The same one who told you all about that 'stuff'?" Mom asked.

"It's actually part of our Social Studies program," I explained, "The school nurse holds a question-and-answer session with us occasionally."

"What kind of a question started a discussion on abortion?"

"It started with the nurse explaining Planned Parenthood when someone asked the question."

"What did the nurse say?"

"Not much, really, except that abortion was illegal."

"I certainly hope you didn't ask that question."

"No, but some kids were discussing it afterward, and I just listened."

"You're right about one thing, dear," Mom confirmed. "Abortion is illegal, and it's also immoral according to the teachings of the Catholic Church."

"So why would Uncle Walter even suggest it?" I asked.

"That's something we don't understand either, but it doesn't matter because I'm sure they won't consider that option anyway."

"What are the other options?" I asked.

"Adoption is probably the most practical alternative," Mom said.

"But then Kathleen would never see her baby again, right?" I asked.

"Oh! I almost forgot," Mom said, suddenly changing the subject, "Kathleen's mom asked if you could pick up her things from school on Monday."

"Sure," I replied, realizing that this conversation was over.

Monday came quickly. At school, I was distraught listening to all the nasty gossip that was circulating around me. Although I still thought the school's decision was unfair, I had to admit that it was probably better for Kathleen not to have to listen to any of the gossip.

Dad loaned me one of his hiking backpacks to load up all of Kathleen's things, and I went straight to her place after I cleaned out her locker.

I arrived to find Kathleen coming slowly down the stairs, her face grave. But when she saw me, she smiled, and her steps quickened. She stopped halfway down and gestured for me to come up.

I followed her up to her room and dumped the backpack on the floor. Then we sat on the bed, and I got a closer look at her eyes. It was obvious that she'd been crying again. I gave her a big hug, that started up a new flow of tears.

"I can't even imagine what you are going through," I said, crying myself now.

"I'm scared…really scared!" she sniffled, trying to subdue her tears.

"What are you so scared about?" I asked.

"They're going to murder my baby!"

I drew back and stared at her in horror, "What? Wait! Who? Who's going to murder your baby?"

"My Uncle Walter and … and my Dad," she sputtered out between sobs. "I heard him say I should have my pregnancy terminated!"

"Are you sure that's what he meant?"

"He called it a miscarriage, but I know what that means. It's murder!" Kathleen said, as she pounded her fists on the carpet.

Then she pulled up the upper part of her nighty to show me her belly. It was already getting rounder.

"There's a baby inside here. I can feel him moving sometimes. And I'm his mother. It's my responsibility to protect my baby."

Kathleen took my hand and placed it on her tummy so I could feel the baby moving. We sat there for a minute, and then I looked up at her. I felt something move. A tiny foot? A hand?

"You see," Kathleen said, staring lovingly at her tummy. "There's a little person in there who must be protected."

"No one's going to murder your baby, Kathleen!" I said firmly.

"Uncle Walter told my parents that it had to be done very soon to be called a miscarriage," she said bitterly.

"How soon?"

"I'm not sure, but I think, I think in the next few weeks."

"You don't know that for sure, though, do you?"

"I just need somewhere to hide for a little while," she said as if she hadn't heard me.

"But what are you going to do about the baby when it arrives?" I asked.

She looked at me like I'd lost my mind, "I'm going to keep him, of course!"

"But how? How can you look after a baby all by yourself? You don't have a husband. Or any money. Or a place of your own. Or a job. Or anything."

"I'll find a way. I will."

"But how?" I was feeling desperate. "Billy does it, so why can't I?"

"He doesn't have a baby to care for," I reminded her.

She sat there staring at her belly, shaking her head.

"I'm going to have to get home for dinner now," I said, feeling very uncomfortable.

I visited her every night after supper that week, and every evening, the discussion ended with her concern about what Uncle Walter said. On Friday, I went there directly after school as I'd promised BJ that I'd go to their lacrosse game in the evening. When I told Kathleen I had to leave to go to see the Shamrock's play, she just looked at me.

"Why are they playing lacrosse anyway?" she asked,

"Apparently, it's our national game," I explained.

"I thought it was hockey," she replied.

"Billy told me that lacrosse has been our national game for about a hundred years."

"Well, don't tell my dad," she cautioned me. "He thinks it's hockey."

I smiled, "Mine, too. Look, I better get moving. I don't suppose you'd like to join me?"

"I don't think so. But wish them luck."

At the game in Elmwood, Dusty introduced me to his girlfriend Nadie, and I guess I misheard her name because I called her Nadine. Then she explained that they actually called her Nadine at school because they wouldn't allow her to use her proper Cree name, Nadie, which means wise. At first, she seemed very withdrawn and quiet, but when I told her that Nadie was a very pretty name, she opened up a little. As we got to know each other better, she confided in me about her difficult past.

I learned that she was still living at the residential school on Academy Road because she wanted to finish high school and go to nursing school. She explained that life at the school was extremely difficult but that she was prepared to stick it out so she could have a future.

When I got home after the game, I was feeling really tired and so I went straight to bed. I didn't sleep well though, thinking of Kathleen's dilemma, and to add to my sleepless night, my mind wandered back and forth between Kathleen and my conversation with Nadie.

It was a good thing the Shamrocks won because I needed something positive to think about. I got up late and dragged myself out of bed with my head full of concern for both Kathleen and Nadie, just as the phone rang.

I rushed to the phone and grabbed the receiver. I didn't even have a chance to say hello before my ear was flooded with Kathleen's frantic crying.

"Carolyn … Carolyn, I need to see you right away!" she pleaded.

"Oh, no, what's wrong?" I asked.

"I can't talk now," she whispered. "Just get here as soon as you can … please?"

"Ok, all right," I replied, but hesitantly. What was going on? I wondered. What was I getting myself into?

I gulped my breakfast down and told Mom that Kathleen needed to see me. Mom encouraged me to help Kathleen as much as I could, so I hurried to her place and found her waiting for me, anxious to go for a walk.

"What's going on?" I asked as she started to sniff and sob again and then reached into her pocket and pulled out an envelope.

"My Uncle Walter dropped by last night when Mom and Dad were out to leave a note for my dad," she said as she stopped to open the envelope. "It's the name of a doctor with an appointment date at his office!"

"Can I see?" I asked.

"Here!" she said, frantically holding the envelope. "This is the doctor that Uncle Walter was talking about."

"You mean the one who terminates pregnancies?" I asked.

"Who else could it be? He didn't even bother to seal the envelope."

I took the envelope from her shaking hand and slid the note out. The note simply had a printed name and address at the top – Arthur J. Kernaghan MD, Orthopedic Surgeon, 546 Academy Rd. with a handwritten scrawl below that read Tuesday, June 25th at 4:30 PM.

"It doesn't mention anything about you," I pointed out to her.

"Of course not! It's supposed to be a secret. I know what a Pediatrician is, and I think that Orthopedic means just some kind of Pediatric procedure."

I was speechless.

"If I only had somewhere to hide for a while," she murmured quietly. "Could I hide out at your place – maybe in the basement?"

"There's no place to hide downstairs. Come on now, Kathleen, I'm sure you've got this all wrong."

She stamped her foot, "No! I'm not wrong! I'm not!"

"I just think you're overreacting," I replied, rather primly I admit now. "And, anyway, I don't know of any place where you can hide."

"Fine! If you can't help me, I know somewhere."

With that, she headed off in a huff, leaving me standing there riddled with confusion. I wanted desperately to tell her that this was really a bad idea, but after seeing the note I wasn't sure. I debated running after her, but I didn't.

Chapter 8
Return To The House

Monday came and went without a word from Kathleen. I saw BJ and Billy at school, but I didn't want to talk about anything, so I told them I wasn't feeling well and went home right after school.

When I got home, I found Mom and Mrs. Melnyk sitting at the kitchen table. Mrs. Melnyk was dabbing her eyes and wringing a napkin. I don't think I'd ever seen a grownup so upset.

"Gosh, what's the matter?" I asked.

"It's Kathleen! She's run away!" Mrs. Melnyk cried.

"What? Why?" I asked, trying to sound surprised.

"Her parents are sick with worry," Mom sighed, looking sadly at Mrs. Melnyk.

"Why ever would she do such a thing? Why?" Mrs. Melnyk muttered to herself.

Mom looked at me, "Carolyn. Do you know anything about this?"

"I honestly have no clue where she is, Mom," I answered truthfully.

"I haven't even talked to her since Saturday."

"Did she say anything?" Mom asked.

"She was still pretty upset about something that she heard her Uncle Walter say," I answered.

Mrs. Melnyk's eyes darted to me, "What did my Kathleen hear? What?"

"Something about termination," I replied slowly, trying to avoid saying the wrong thing.

"She must have heard everything then," Mrs. Melnyk said, burying her face in her hands.

Somehow, I mustered the courage to say, "Kathleen told me that she heard that Uncle Walter wanted to murder her baby."

"She said what?" Mom asked, befuddled.

"She said: Uncle Walter wants to murder my baby!" I cried.

"Those were her exact words," Mrs. Melnyk began to cry and kept mumbling. "It's all my fault."

Mom composed herself and asked me to set the table because Mr. Melnyk had had gone to pick up Dad, and they'd be here soon. She explained that Mr. Melnyk had to leave work early to come home and meet with the police, so now he had to go back to get Dad since this was his week to drive.

"Why were the police here?" I asked.

"Because Kathleen is missing," Mom replied sharply.

"They had to report it. Now, please set the table while I get dinner ready."

Mrs. Melnyk pulled herself together and joined Mom in the kitchen just as Dad and Mr. Melnyk arrived, and I was sent upstairs to pry the comics away from Sharron and herd her downstairs. Mr. and Mrs. Melnyk had had a brief private discussion in the front room, while Mom and Dad had a similar meeting in their bedroom, so dinner was fairly quiet.

I couldn't stand the silence and all the tension, so I hurried through my dinner, anxious to meet BJ at the lacrosse game. I excused myself before everyone else was finished. All Mom asked of me was that if I learned anything from my friends, to be sure to tell her as soon as I got home.

I felt a huge relief as soon as I made it through the door. I'd been so afraid of being grilled by both Kathleen's parents and mine, that I could hardly breathe all through dinner. I couldn't wait to get out of the house.

When I got there, BJ and Dusty were standing inside the rink talking to Nadie, who was outside the boards. I hurried to join them and asked if they'd seen Kathleen.

"No. Why?" BJ asked.

"She's run away!"

"Who's run away?" I heard Billy ask as he joined us.

"Kathleen," BJ said.

"Why?" Billy asked.

I started to explain, but Billy suddenly said, "I've gotta go. See you guys later."

He disappeared without any explanation. We all looked at each other, wondering what that was all about. Just then, the referee blew his whistle to start the game. I sat with Nadie in the stands and explained what was going on with Kathleen. She was a very good listener. After I brought her up to date, she asked me how I was doing. I lied and said I was fine, and she just patted my hand and softly said, *right*, knowing I wasn't.

"Kathleen will be just fine, I'm sure," Nadie said.

"Thanks, Nadie," I paused, then said, "I know it's none of my business, but are you and Dusty… uh… you know?"

"Good friends?" she asked, raising her eyebrows.

"Y-yes," I stammered, "That's it… good friends."

"Good friends, yes," she confirmed.

"But not *really* good friends. At least not yet."

"But you'd like to be, right?" I asked, feeling bold.

"Someday," she said with a smile.

"How long have you known each other?"

"I was friends with his sister at school back when my brothers and I were moved to Brandon."

I looked at her in surprise.

"Dusty has a sister?"

"Yes," Nadie sighed.

"But she's still in Brandon."

I still had a lot more questions, but the game had started, and I knew that I wanted to watch it. I was finding it tough to concentrate on lacrosse, thinking of Kathleen, but when suddenly BJ scored a goal, I snapped back to the here and now. Lacrosse wasn't as fast as hockey, but there was still a lot of action, and it was surprisingly more interesting than I expected. The Shamrocks won four to three, so it was a close game.

After the game, we went to the clubhouse. Dusty came out first, and he and Nadie said goodnight as I joined. There was no sign of Billy.

"Did you like the game?" BJ asked.

"I liked it when you scored," I said with a shy smile.

"Me too," he laughed, and then he walked me home.

I was dreading being grilled again, that was until BJ reminded me that none of us actually knew anything.

Mom and Dad were reading in the living room, so I poked my head in and said, "I still have no idea where Kathleen could be."

I couldn't deal with any more questions, so I went straight to my room. My cozy bed was a welcome relief from a stressful day.

At school in the morning, I ran into Billy in the hallway, and before I could ask why he didn't stay for the game, he told me that he was skipping school that afternoon.

"Skipping? Why? That's not like you."

"Tell you later," he said as he rushed away at the sound of the bell.

The next day, when I got home after school, the first thing Mom asked me was if I knew where Billy was.

"I haven't seen Billy since yesterday," I told her "Why?"

"The police want to talk to him," Mom said.

I nearly dropped my books on the floor.

"The police? What about?"

"They think he might know where Kathleen is," Mom answered.

Just then, the phone rang. I answered it. On the other end, BJ quietly urged me to come over as quickly as possible.

I asked him why he was whispering, but he just repeated, "Come over, quick as you can."

I told Mom I was just going to see BJ, nodding dutifully when she reminded me not to be late for dinner.

I peddled there as fast as I could. I was barely off my bike when BJ stepped out of the garage door and said, "Let's go."

"Go where?"

"For a walk," he answered quietly.

"Away from my big-eared sisters."

"So, what's the big secret?" I asked as we started walking.

"Kathleen's not at The House anymore," he replied.

"And Billy's waiting for us in the playground over at Angus MacKay."

"House? What house?" I asked.

Oh, it was a confusing evening.

"Assiniboine House," BJ replied.

"Where we all lived when we were little kids."

"What? I thought it was demolished!"

BJ shook his head, rueful, "Nope. Just condemned."

"What was she doing there?"

"Hiding," BJ replied.

When we reached the playground, we found Billy sitting on the merry-go-round all by himself.

We joined him, and all whirled around while Billy explained that after I told him about Kathleen running away, he knew exactly where she had gone.

"I raced straight home," Billy began, "To get a flashlight and some food and water. That's when Dusty asked me if he could help."

"Why was Dusty at your place?" I asked.

"The police dropped him off there after they arrested him."

I put my foot down and stopped the merry-go-round.

"What? Why did the police arrest Dusty for heaven's sake?"

"Some girls from school had reported seeing Kathleen walking down Linden with Dusty and me," Billy said.

"The cops thought Dusty kidnapped Kathleen, and they think I helped him."

"Why would they think that?" I asked.

"Because he's an Indian," BJ replied, his face hard.

Billy continued with his explanation, "So, Dusty and I went to the house, and we wandered around, calling out her name and telling her that we'd wait in the furnace room if she wanted to talk. We made ourselves comfortable and waited for only a few minutes before a flashlight blinded us."

Billy went on to say how, when the light turned away their eyes refocused to see Kathleen standing in the doorway checking the rest of the room. She wanted to make sure they were alone. Then she came in, sat on the floor, and broke into tears. Billy said he brought out some food and water and tried to calm her down, and after a long discussion, she agreed to accompany them back to Mrs. Gregg's house.

"Oh, please tell me that is where she is now?" I asked hopefully.

Billy shook his head, "Nope."

I scowled at him, Why won't you tell me, for heaven's sake?"

"It's just, well, I don't know exactly," he said.

"What do you mean? What are you talking about? You have to tell me. Her parents are frantic and—"

Billy put up his hands to stop me from going on.

"But I do know that she's in good hands,"

"Arhg! You're so exasperating," I said.

I got up from the merry-go-round and paced back and forth.

"Calm down, Carolyn," BJ said, coming up and putting his arm around me, "Kathleen's safe and she wants to come home."

"She does? Really? Then we have to tell her parents right away!"

"Hang on. Not just yet," Billy demanded.

"Kathleen wants her parents to promise that they won't make her terminate the baby or even make her give it up for adoption."

"This is ridiculous!" I shouted.

"Not so loud," Billy whispered.

I dropped my voice, "We can't hide from the police."

"You don't have to," Billy said softly.

"Just me. And just long enough until I get her parents to promise."

"Why can't we do that right now?" I demanded.

"We need witnesses," Billy explained.

"When then?"

I was feeling so anxious by this time. My head was spinning.

"Saturday morning," Billy confirmed.

"At the Melnyk's place."

"What time?" I asked.

"And who do you want as witnesses?"

"Egil would be good," Billy answered with a smile.

"And you two and your parents, if they want to be there too."

"What time?" I asked, staring at him.

He looked small as ever but somehow bigger, too.

"Nine in the morning," Billy said.

"That gives you tomorrow to make the arrangements."

"Why me?" I asked.

"Because Kathleen's parents trust you, and you're her best friend," Billy reminded me.

"If I can't arrange it, where can we contact you," I asked.

"Don't worry. I'll be there at nine, and if I see a police car, I'll come to the door."

"Why are you making this so complicated, Billy?" I asked.

"Because," Billy explained slowly, "The only person who knows where Kathleen is not available until Saturday morning."

"Where is he?" I asked.

"Did I say it was a '*he*'?" Billy asked smugly.

"I thought you said Sam would take care of her?" BJ now asked.

"I said Sam *knew* someone," Billy replied.

I threw up my hands in exasperation, "I gotta go. It's dinner time."

I said goodnight and headed back to my place, feeling very frustrated.

As soon as I got home, I told Mom and Dad what conditions Billy wanted. Mom was shocked.

Dad said that if he told Stan about Billy's ultimatum, Stan would probably throttle him.

I said, "That's probably why Billy wants the police to be there."

Dad just rolled his eyes and said, "Okay, let's get hold of the Melnyk's and get this sorted out. At least we know that Kathleen is safe."

The one good thing to come out of Billy's stupid plan was that Mrs. Melnyk invited everyone for breakfast at eight o'clock, and her breakfasts were famous.

It was a short walk to the Melnyk's place, and I left early on Saturday morning with my parents and my sister so Mom could help out with breakfast. BJ rode over on his bike and got there just after eight. My stomach was in knots. It felt like this whole thing was turning into a circus.

When we arrived, Mr. Melnyk pulled Dad away, ignoring us kids completely, while Mom headed straight into the kitchen with Mrs. Melnyk.

"Morning, Mike," he greeted Dad.

"Thanks for coming. Can I get you a coffee?"

Mr. Melnyk emerged from the kitchen in a flash with two coffees and said, "Let's sit in the living room."

Sharron and I joined Mrs. Melnyk in the kitchen, but we could easily hear Mr. Melnyk's booming voice.

"Jesus! What's with that kid, Mike?" he asked Dad, his voice popping with anger.

"I feel like I'm being blackmailed or something. Where did he get this stupid notion that we'd do anything to hurt Kathleen or her baby anyway?"

I knew I shouldn't have interrupted, but I couldn't help myself, so I peeked my head into the living room.

"From... from Uncle Walter," I said timidly.

"What?" he boomed as he turned to see who spoke.

"From... Uncle Walter's note," I replied, even more sheepishly than before.

"What note?" he yelled.

That drew Mrs. Melnyk out of the kitchen to see what the fuss was.

"The note to you that Uncle Walter left with Kathleen," I said, staring at my feet.

"I never saw any note! Did you see a note, Helen?" he yelled, spotting her standing in the doorway.

"No, I did not," Mrs. Melnyk said, "Now stop yelling Stan. You're scaring the living daylights out of poor Carolyn."

Mrs. Melnyk turned to me and smiled tenderly, and in a quiet voice, she asked, "Did you see the note, sweetie?"

"Kathleen showed it to me," I said, trying not to tremble.

"It had a doctor's name and address printed at the top with a handwritten note that said Tuesday 4:30 pm."

"What? What?" Mr. Melnyk sputtered.

"Calm down, Stan," Mrs. Melnyk said, glaring at her husband.

Then, turning back to me, she asked gently, "Do you know why she didn't give it to her father?"

"She thought it was an appointment for her to have her pregnancy terminated," I mumbled, my eyes focused on my shoes.

"Do you remember the name of the doctor?" Mrs. Melnyk asked.

"It was an Irish name on Academy Road somewhere, I think," I replied, trembling now.

"Kernaghan?" Stan asked loudly.

"I… I think so," I replied.

"I don't believe this," Mr. Melnyk sighed, putting his hands on his head, "Where'd she get this preposterous notion?"

"I'm afraid she overheard all of Walter's ramblings, Stan," Mrs. Melnyk said, guiding her husband to his favorite living-room chair.

"Why would she think we agreed to his absurd suggestions?" he asked as he sat down.

"Maybe because you never told Walter to shut up," Mrs. Melnyk answered.

"What was that note all about anyway?"

"Walter was making arrangements for me to see a sports medicine specialist friend of his," Mr. Melnyk replied.

"He's a knee specialist for crying out loud."

"Why do you need a knee specialist?" Dad asked.

"Too much Hopak dancing when he was young," Mrs. Melnyk replied.

"What's that?" I asked, once again forgetting my mother's advice that girls should be seen and not heard.

"Ukrainian dancing," Mrs. Melnyk answered with a smile.

"And he was quite good, I might add."

She smiled at her husband, breaking the tension.

I must admit that I had a hard time imagining Mr. Melnyk as a young Ukrainian dancer. Except for the mustache, nothing else seemed to fit.

Mrs. Melnyk's enormous breakfast buffet was soon ready. As fabulous as this breakfast was, I just wasn't interested in eating. I was worried about Kathleen, Nadie, and now Billy and there were still so many unanswered questions. There was no sign of Billy, and I was beginning to wonder if he'd even show up. Then the front doorbell rang. As I was the only one not sitting down, I offered to get it.

There were two policemen standing at the door. To my surprise, I recognized one of them.

"Constable Amundson?"

He took his police hat off and nodded.

"And how are you, Carolyn? Ah, this is my partner, Sergeant Don Bell."

"Come in," I said, opening the door wider.

As the police officers came in, they exposed two familiar figures standing behind them: Billy and Dusty.

"Billy!" I cried.

"So, you're here with a police escort?"

"It's safer," he replied, flashing his big grin.

"And, besides, I had to go to the police station to get Dusty out of jail."

"Come in, please," Mrs. Melnyk said, greeting the police with a warm smile and coaxing them into the dining room, "Please come in and join us for some breakfast."

"Thanks, Mrs. Melnyk," Sergeant Bell said, tucking his hat under his arm.

"But we've already had breakfast."

"Not like this, I'll bet," I motioned toward the dining room buffet.

It was covered with Mrs. Melnyk's marvelous breakfast spread.

The policemen stared at the buffet in disbelief.

"You wouldn't want to insult. Melnyk's cooking, would you?"

I asked as I guided them into the dining room.

When Mr. Melnyk spotted Billy, he charged over and, pointing his finger at Billy's chest, he demanded, "Okay, young man, you tell us where Kathleen is right now."

"As soon as you promise not to harm her baby!" Billy said, standing his ground, much to Mr. Melnyk's surprise.

"What's your problem, kid? No one's going harm her baby, so just tell us where she is or, so help me, I'll throttle you right here in front of these policemen."

"Stan," Mrs. Melnyk pleaded.

"For heaven's sake, just say you promise. I want Kathleen home now."

"Okay, okay, I promise," Mr. Melnyk said grudgingly.

"But first, just tell me, why are you doing this?"

Billy looked to me, then to Mrs. Melnyk, "Because Kathleen insisted that I make sure you promise before I tell you 'cause she said you never break a promise."

"Oh," Mr. Melnyk said, turning to Mrs. Melnyk, "Let's talk in the living room."

"Why *are* you doing this, Billy?" Mrs. Melnyk, eyeing him with suspicion.

"Are you the father?" Mr. Melnyk asked curtly.

"What? No, no, I'm not," he said, turning pale.

"I swear it."

"Then why?" Mrs. Melnyk asked again.

"Because Kathleen is my friend, and she asked me to, and because I can relate to her situation," he answered softly.

"Why's that, Billy?" Dad asked.

"Because my mother was in a similar predicament when my maternal grandmother didn't want her to have me."

He looked around, embarrassed.

"Good thing my paternal grandparents wanted her to have me. Otherwise, I wouldn't be here today."

"Well, kid," Mr. Melnyk said sternly.

"At this very moment, I'm thinking that the world might be a better place with fewer people like you."

"Stan!" Mrs. Melnyk, "That's a horrid thing to say."

Then, turning to Billy, she pleaded, "Please, Billy, where is she?"

"I don't personally know exactly—" Billy began.

"What is this?" Mr. Melnyk cut in, his face red from shouting.

"But I know who does," Billy quickly added, "Sam Grady."

"Sam Grady?" Sergeant Bell asked.

"Shall we talk to him then," Constable Amundson asked.

"He's right outside," Billy replied, "Sitting in the Salvation Army van. I'll go get him."

"I think I know where Kathleen is," Sergeant Bell smiled, as if thinking on something intently.

"Where? Where? Please tell us," Mrs. Melnyk said, wringing her hands in anxiety.

"The Church Home for Girls," he replied.

"It's in East St. Paul, about twenty minutes from here."

"Why there?" Mrs. Melnyk asked.

"It'd be the most logical place," Constable Amundson replied in support of his partner.

"And Mr. Grady is quite familiar with it."

Just then, Sam and Billy entered the house, and Billy introduced Sam to Mr. and Mrs. Melnyk.

"Let me guess, Sam?" Constable Edmundson asked, "The Church Home for Girls?"

Sam just nodded.

"What exactly is this Church Home for Girls?" Mrs. Melnyk asked, her face desperate now.

"It's a home for unwed mothers, Mrs. Melnyk," Sam replied.

"Is that where she is?" Mr. Melnyk asked.

"She is indeed," Sam replied.

"And being very well taken care of, for sure."

"If you like?" Sergeant Bell asked, "Constable Amundson and I know the folks there, so we'd be happy to take you right now."

"You two just go," Mom shooed the Melnyk's toward the door.

"We'll take care of everything here."

"But none of you have even touched your breakfast," Mrs. Melnyk said, glancing sadly at her remarkable array of sausages, bacon, and other interesting creations arranged so perfectly on the table.

Her omelets were to die for, as were her pastries.

"Don't worry, Mrs. Melnyk," I told her.

"There are some big appetites here."

Chapter 9
Mr. Melnyk's Surprise

Through the summer and well into October, I visited Kathleen as often as possible, with Angel joining us for long walks. I kept her up to date about what was happening at school, but by September, she had lost interest in school and had, instead, become focused on becoming a mother.

Sometimes, Kathleen would reminisce about her time at the house. I was thrilled when she told me that her parents had taken heed of what Billy's grandparents had done and had agreed to officially adopt her baby.

By the middle of October, I began to see less and less of Kathleen as she prepared for the birth.

The big day happened on November 17th. It was a boy, just as Kathleen had predicted.

After she came home from the hospital, she invited Billy, Dusty, BJ, and me over to see her baby. In the living room, we found Kathleen claiming her dad's favorite chair and lovingly cradling her precious little treasure. He was a beautiful, healthy, nine-pound baby with a head of strawberry blonde hair.

"Come in and meet your new nephew, Brendan," she beamed.

"Brendan?" I asked.

"Of course," Kathleen replied, "Since your parents are his godparents, we named him Brendan after your little brother. His middle names are Michael, after your dad, and William, after Billy."

"Really?" Billy asked.

"And your father agreed to that? I thought he was still pretty angry with me?"

"Not anymore," came the sound of Mr. Melnyk's familiar voice from behind us.

"And Stan has a surprise for you, Billy," I heard my father say as they both entered the living room.

Dad was carrying his guitar case, and he placed it down beside Mr. Melnyk's chair.

"Are you going to serenade your godson, Dad?" I asked curiously as I looked down at his guitar.

"No," he laughed, "That's Stan's."

"Mr. Melnyk's?" Billy asked.

"Not for long, Billy," Mr. Melnyk replied with a playful smile, "I believe I owe you an apology, young man."

"After what I did?" Billy asked.

"No, Billy," Mr. Melnyk replied.

Kathleen handed Brendan to me and hurried to stand beside him.

"It's because of what *you* did."

"I only did what Kathleen asked me to do," Billy replied sheepishly.

"Exactly," Mr. Melnyk said with a smile.

"After Kathleen explained, I realized how very lucky she is to have friends like you."

"Thanks so much, Daddy," Kathleen said as she kissed him on the cheek.

"A short while back, Billy, I made some regrettable remarks to you," Mr. Melnyk said.

"Hmm, I don't recall any, sir," Billy replied, tapping his chin as if in deep thought.

Mr. Melnyk grinned, "I can't remember exactly either, Billy, and I don't really want to."

That's when Dad picked up the guitar case and handed it to Mr. Melnyk, who took it and held it out for Billy.

Mr. Melnyk handed the case to Billy.

"Of course, since I never make mistakes, it wasn't really my fault. As usual, that responsibility lies with my brother Walter, who has a long history of getting me into trouble, but I sincerely hope that, in some small way, this may make amends for his mistake."

Billy, still confused, placed the case gently on the floor and opened it to reveal a beautiful guitar.

"Wow!" Billy cried as his eyes welled up.

"It's a Martin classical guitar."

I sniffled and laughed at the same time.

"It's so wonderful to have such good friends," Kathleen smiled, "And I hope those are happy tears."

The End.

Book 5
The Cameras

By Billy Johnson

Chapter 1
Changing Places

The prospects for finding work as a teenage wannabe detective were pretty dismal, so I took whatever I could get to pay for room and board. Fortunately, there were plenty of opportunities for clearing driveways in Winnipeg after a spring snowfall.

I had just finished shoveling the driveway at the Page residence when it began to snow like the dickens again. I watched bleakly as the snowflakes slowly blanketed my clean driveway; I probably looked as miserable as I was feeling, which may be why Mrs. Page took pity on me and asked me to come inside and warm up.

I was happy to accept the invitation, and she seemed pleased to have someone to talk to. She asked me a lot of questions, and I decided to share my pitiable life story, right up to my current situation of living in Mrs. Gregg's basement while completing grade eleven. Mrs. Page was kind enough to invite me to stay for dinner, during which she relayed my doleful situation to her husband. Their daughter, Amanda, confirmed my story.

I first met Amanda at school a few years before, and even though I was three years her junior, she seemed to enjoy our discussions on common interests as much as I did. She was not only crazy attractive but also smart as a whip, which, combined with our age difference, left me miles out of her league. Nevertheless, we had a curious connection.

When Amanda arrived home late after dinner, coffee was served in the living room. That's when I learned that my being here was not as accidental as I'd thought. Amanda explained that they had an extra bedroom in the basement that'd once been her older brother Leonard's room. He had been killed in the Korean War seven years earlier, and since then, Mrs. Page had been keeping the room frozen in time, exactly as it had been when Leonard left. Amanda described it as a mausoleum.

Following some heart-wrenching discussions, her parents decided it was time to make use of that room for a good cause, and, by some miracle, Amanda convinced them to deem me worthy of being such a cause.

After most appreciatively accepting her most generous offer of free room and board, Mrs. Page asked if I'd like to see the room.

It was perfect, but I had one question, "Would it be possible for me to have my own key to the house?"

"Of course," Mrs. Page said. "Why would you even ask?"

"Well, Mrs. Gregg wouldn't allow me to have a key, and she locked the door at ten o'clock every night."

"How'd you get in when you were late?" Mr. Page asked.

"I didn't," I answered.

"I stayed at BJ's place. But I only made that mistake once."

It was a large room with a long window, a large bed with a side table, a dresser, a desk and chair set, and a closet full of Leonard's old clothes. It was neat and tidy. And it was perfect. But with all the personal pictures and other things in the room, it looked to me as though someone was still living there.

"We can have it ready for you by the end of March," Mr. Page said.

By some curious coincidence my friend Dusty called me from Dauphin the very next day to ask if I knew somewhere, he could stay during lacrosse season. Having already paid my rent for April, I asked Mrs. Gregg if Dusty could have my room.

Mrs. Gregg, who was a Major with the Salvation Army, said he could stay all summer for free if he was willing to volunteer some spare time at the Salvation Army to help Sam Grady deliver Easter Baskets. BJ and Carolyn offered to help me move, so on a moving day, I packed up my stuff in one duffle bag, and we headed off to my new home in BJ's Mom's car.

"Is this all you got?" Carolyn asked.

I threw my bag in the back seat, "It's everything I need."

"So, you don't really need our help then?" BJ asked.

"No, but I really appreciate the ride," I replied.

"And since Kathleen and Brendan are visiting with Amanda, I thought you might like to have a visit."

"Will you be in Leonard's old room?" Carolyn asked as we got in the car.

"I will," Billy said. "And I'll have my very own bathroom."

"Are you sure Amanda's good with this?" Carolyn asked. "She idolized Leonard."

"Don't worry. She's just fine with it," I replied.

"It was her idea, and she's quite relieved, because the basement is a bit depressing with all his stuff still there."

When we got there, Carolyn joined Amanda and Kathleen in the rec room downstairs, where little Brendan was playing on the floor. While the girls were all fusing over Brendan, BJ followed me into my new room and dumped my bag on the floor. The room was warm and cozy, but it looked almost barren compared to when I first saw it. Mrs. Page showed me where everything was, then pointed to the downstairs fridge and told us to help ourselves with refreshments.

After a short visit, BJ and Carolyn drove Kathleen and Brendan home, and I began setting up my room. I was just starting to unpack when Amanda came in with coffee and freshly baked muffins. They smelled like heaven.

She grinned, "Fresh from the oven. A warm welcome from Mom."

"Thanks, Amanda, it's so good to be here, really. It's the best. And I understand I have you to thank for all this."

She flopped down in a chair, "I only made the suggestion. You did all the rest."

"What? I don't recall doing anything."

"You endured my parents' interrogation, didn't you?"

"That wasn't difficult; they're nice as pie," I grinned.

"Now I understand where you get your good nature from."

"Apparently, you don't know me very well," she said and chuckled.

"Maybe not yet, but I hope to change that."

She just smiled. Boy, she sure was extra pretty when she smiled.

"Looks like you and Kathleen have become good friends."

"Well, when I told her I planned to specialize in pediatric medicine, we started talking and realized we had a lot of things in common."

"And she's very easy to talk to," I replied.

"She told me all about you," she said and gave me a wink.

"Uh, oh," I replied, just as her mother called us for dinner.

Chapter 2
Easter Baskets

Lacrosse practices were all in the evenings, so when Dusty arrived, he was available to help Sam deliver Easter baskets during the day. On the Thursday before Easter, I had no classes, so I offered to help them. Because of his arthritis, Sam appreciated me joining them so he could just drive the Sally Ann van and not have to get in and out at each stop.

We finished most of the deliveries shortly after lunch, and the last four baskets were all in the same apartment building. Two were on the first floor; the other two were on the second floor but in opposite wings of the building. We each took one wing, delivered the first-floor baskets, and then headed to the respective stairs at the far end to get up to the second floor and deliver the last two baskets. I made my first deliveries quickly to some very grateful families. As I glanced down the long corridor on the second floor, I noticed Dusty standing in the hall, apparently waiting for someone to answer the door, so I walked down to join him. He appeared to be listening at the door as I came up.

"No one home?" I asked.

"I rang the bell, but no one answered," Dusty said. "But I can hear voices inside."

I knocked hard on the door.

Finally, this big guy pulled the door open and yelled, "What-a yuh want?"

"I have an Easter Basket for the Klassen family," Dusty replied politely.

The man growled, "Beat it, kid."

He sounded drunk and smelled of beer. Just as he was about to close the door, a lady reached around from behind him and stopped him.

"What are you doing, George? That's for the kids for Easter."

"We don't need no handouts from some dumb Indian," he yelled as he pushed her away.

Then, while Dusty was still standing there holding the basket, the man pushed him and yelled, "I told you to get lost."

The lady reached her hand around again to reach for the basket and as Dusty handed it to her, the man pushed him again, forcing him to drop it. Dusty stepped back but didn't fall down. Then the man lunged toward him with his arm pulled back, ready to throw a punch, but Dusty pulled his right arm up as fast as he could and caught the man right on the jaw. The man went flying backward and landed on his back.

It all happened in a flash. I just stood there in shock.

The lady knelt down beside the man, crying out, "George, George."

Then we heard voices behind us as some of the neighbors appeared in the hall to see what was going on. With George flat on his back and the hamper on the floor, they came to their own conclusions.

One man said, "That kid's trying to steal the basket!"

Another said, "Let's grab him!"

Another lady cried, "I'm calling the cops."

"Wait, wait," I cut in. "We're from the Salvation Army, delivering Easter baskets for the family."

One man pushed me out of the way as another man grabbed Dusty from behind, pulling him backward onto the floor. Then, two guys jerked him back on his feet again, wrenching his arm, while another man grabbed hold of me. They held us both tight while the lady kept crying and trying to revive George. Meanwhile, her four children, who all looked to be under the age of ten, discovered the basket on the floor and tore it open. They were laughing as they pulled everything out, having a wonderful time examining all the contents. That's when we heard loud footsteps clambering up the stairs. The man holding me jerked me around to see who it was. Two police officers marched towards us.

With everyone telling them something different at the same time, one officer knelt down beside George to see what he could do, and the other approached us.

"Caught him stealing that Easter basket there," the man holding Dusty said.

"And he punched out George over there," another said, pointing to George lying on the floor.

I protested to the officer and told him we were just delivering Easter baskets for the Salvation Army when that man attacked Dusty. The police officer told the two men to loosen their grip on us, and then he gently took hold of my arm and began asking questions. The sound of more footsteps quickly scrambling up the stairs distracted everyone as two more police officers arrived. Then I heard one of them call my name, and I looked over.

"Egil?" I called, gratefully recognizing a familiar face.

Then Sam appeared, puffing behind them as he reached the top step.

"You know this kid, Corporal?" the officer holding me asked as he loosened his hold on me.

"They're delivering Easter baskets," Egil said. "Let them go."

"Thanks, Constable Amundson," Dusty said, rubbing the back of his head.

"It's Corporal now," Sam corrected him, still breathing hard.

"Got a promotion he did."

When Egil calmed everyone down, he noticed that Dusty was bleeding on the back of his head, so he asked the officer who was holding him to get him to a hospital.

"Are you okay, Sam?" I asked. "That was a lot of steps to climb."

"It was indeed," Sam confirmed, still catching his breath.

"It's funny that I was just sitting in the van, waiting for you two, when these police officers raced into the building. I didn't follow them at first, as it was none of my business. Then I noticed the one with Corporal stripes from the second car and recognized Egil right off, so I followed him inside."

Egil joined us and suggested we go home now, "We'll take good care of Dusty, and I'll see that he gets a ride home from the hospital."

The police quickly took control of the situation, and Sam drove me home.

Chapter 3
The Circus

When I called Dusty the next morning to see how he was feeling, he said Mrs. Gregg was taking care of him, so I knew he was in good hands. The only downside of my sudden good fortune was having to hand in my notice to the pharmacy and to my customers, who'd been so good to me. By mid-week, I'd talked to all my customers except Mr. Curtis, who lived just down from Mrs. Gregg's place.

I waited until Tuesday after supper to visit him to be sure he was home. When I explained to him why I couldn't cut his grass anymore, he looked so disappointed.

"I'm really glad for you, Billy, but I'll be sorry to lose your services," he said, shaking his head.

"I could see if my friend Dusty would do it. He's living in my old room at Mrs. Gregg's, and I know he's looking for work."

"I'd like to talk to him then," Mr. Curtis said.

"I'll bring him over later," I said.

He smiled a bit sadly, "Well, I'll be home all evening."

When I got to Mrs. Gregg's, Dusty didn't appear any worse the wear after his ordeal, and we were laughing about it when Sam joined us.

"Have you told Mr. Curtis yet?" he asked. "You know Dave's already had two hernias, so it's difficult for him to do yard work."

"He didn't mention that," I said. "I was just about to ask Dusty if he wanted to work for Mr. Curtis."

"Dave's a good man to know if you're looking for summer work," Sam continued. "He's the manager of Eaton's' Annex, you know?"

"What's that?" Dusty asked.

"It's that one-story space at the back of the main store," Sam explained. "It was recently converted into a sales area for outdoor sports and recreation equipment."

"I know that place," I said. "I was in there recently when I was looking at bicycles, and it has all kinds of neat camping stuff and boats and hiking gear."

"It does indeed," Sam confirmed. "And Dave mentioned that Eaton's was looking for summer staff to help with furniture deliveries."

"Mr. Curtis is home right now," I said. "Dusty, you want to meet him?"

"Okay, sounds great," he replied with his usual enthusiasm.

Our visit with Mr. Curtis turned out to be a boon for both of us. Dusty agreed to do whatever shoveling and grass-cutting Mr. Curtis needed. Mr. Curtis said he could also get a job at Eaton delivering furniture.

As for me, Mr. Curtis said that when school finished, if I wanted a full-time summer job, I could work in the warehouse. When I mentioned this to Mr. Page, he thought it'd be a good idea because Eaton's employees got great discounts on merchandise—like the bicycle I was dying to get.

Dusty started work at Eaton's on the following Monday. I didn't see him until Saturday when he and I trekked through the melting snow to BJ's place to see his new bike.

When we arrived, we saw Dr. Neuman's Jaguar in the driveway. As we entered the house, we saw Dr. Neuman standing in the front hall talking to BJ's dad and wearing his colorful Shriner outfit with a red hat that reminded me of an upside-down pail.

"Do you boys like the circus?" Dr. Neuman asked.

"Don't know," I said. "I've never been."

"You can go for free if you volunteer," Dr. Neuman smiled.

When he talked about the circus, he was very persuasive, and before we knew it, BJ and I were convinced to volunteer. We agreed to sell programs and maybe even be part of the show. Dusty politely declined; he already had a full load of commitments.

"When does the circus start?" I asked.

I wasn't a little kid anymore, but I admit the idea of a circus made me feel like one.

"Mid-May," Dr. Neuman replied. "And don't forget to watch the parade."

"Wouldn't miss it!" I replied. "I've never seen a parade either."

BJ really had his heart set on being one of those kids who gets packed into a Volkswagen and climbs out dressed as clowns. Sadly, for him, when he went to apply, he was too big. They only had room for smaller kids. BJ tried to explain to Dusty why he wanted to do this, but Dusty didn't get it.

"Anyway," Dusty replied. "I don't have time to go to the circus, but I'll go to the parade with you."

"Great," BJ replied. "Now, who's up for some ping pong?"

On the next Saturday, BJ asked us to stop by the drugstore to show us his new bike. When we arrived, he and Carolyn were already sitting at the counter with Kathleen, Rachael Neuman, and Amanda, who was crouched by the stroller admiring little Brendan.

"Dusty," I said, introducing him to Rachael. "This is David's sister."

"David, who's football you lost?" Dusty grinned.

I nodded and quickly changed the subject as we all stepped out of the drugstore and gathered around to see BJ's new pride and joy.

"Do we get a chance to test it out?" Dusty asked.

"Jeez, can you even ride a bike?" BJ asked with a teasing grin.

But Dusty scowled at him, "I've been practicing on Billy's old bike. I can do it."

"Give us a demonstration then, Dusty," I said.

BJ glared at me but reluctantly nodded his agreement.

Dusty got on the bike and started peddling. He wobbled a bit but was doing pretty good, that is until a blue Meteor came screeching around the corner, nearly knocking him off the bike. Good thing he planted his foot on the ground, and the bike didn't clatter to the pavement.

The driver yelled out as he slammed on the brakes, "Where'd you steal the bike, Chief?"

I stormed right up to him.

"He didn't steal it," I called out.

"Mind your own business, jackass," he shouted at me,

"The owner is right over there," I replied, pointing to BJ.

But BJ didn't say anything.

The driver turned back to Dusty and yelled, "You should learn to ride before you kill someone you stupid jerk."

The auburn-haired girl in the passenger seat leaned over and said, "C'mon, let's go, Rocky. He's just a dumb Indian kid."

As the Meteor sped away, I reached Dusty and grabbed the bike to steady him while he stared at the receding blue car.

"C'mon Dusty. Just ignore those clowns."

"Didn't you see who that was?" Dusty asked, gripping the handlebars in anger.

"Who?" I asked as we strolled back to the drugstore.

"That lousy Rocky from hockey camp," he muttered indignantly.

"Couldn't be. Rocky has red hair."

"Not anymore," Dusty sighed. "I saw him in Eaton's the other day."

"Doing what?" I asked.

"I think he works in the Annex, where the bikes are."

BJ took hold of his bike, and we returned to the drugstore as Sandy stepped out to see what we were doing.

"Are you going to order something or what?" she asked, looking at us sullenly.

"Just as soon as I get a picture of everyone with BJ's new bike," I replied.

"Why don't you get in the picture, too, Sandy?"

"Why don't you, Billy?" Sandy said authoritatively. "Where's your camera?"

"Here," I replied, handing her my camera.

"What's this supposed to be?" she asked, grabbing the camera from me and looking at it curiously.

"Just what it looks like, a miniature camera. Just aim and push the button."

Sandy held up the tiny camera, "Where'd you get it from, a box of Cracker Jacks?"

I tried not to look offended, "No, now just take the picture so we can all go back inside."

Sandy finally found the button and took the picture. We returned inside and sat at a booth where everyone had a chance to examine my miniature camera.

Comments like, "It's so cute," "That's tiny," and "That's got to be a joke," circulated around the booth while Sandy took our orders.

"Where did you get this thing?" BJ asked.

"Eaton's Annex," I replied.

"They have all kinds of neat stuff like tiny transistor radios, binoculars, flashlights, telescopes, all so small you can hide them in your backpack."

BJ was pouting, likely in disappointment that the conversation had shifted away from his new bike, so he changed the subject by asking, "Is anyone going to the circus?"

"My dad's a Shriner," Rachael said. "So, I have to take David."

"We're volunteering this year," BJ replied. "So maybe we'll see you there?"

"Doing what?" Rachael asked.

"Billy and I are selling programs," he answered half-heartedly.

"When are you going, Rachael?" I asked.

"Sunday afternoon. Carolyn will be there, and Kathleen is bringing Brendan. He's going to love it."

"BJ will be joining us."

Carolyn smiled at him, "Just as soon as he's sold all his programs right?"

"Of course," BJ replied and grinned whole-heartedly.

"Good, you can both sit with us then," Rachael suggested. "I know David would love to see you."

"Is anyone going to the parade on Saturday afternoon?" BJ asked.

Dusty and I acknowledged that we were, but the others all had plans.

On Saturday afternoon, Dusty got off early to see the parade as Eaton was a major sponsor. We took the bus downtown. There'd been warnings about a rash of bicycle thefts, and BJ didn't want to risk getting his new bike nicked.

While we were trying to find a good viewing spot to watch the parade near Vimy Ridge Park, we spotted a couple of kids on their bikes and watched them to see where they were going to leave them. They went south on Home Street and turned down a back lane that led to a parking lot full of bikes, but there was no attendant.

We peered over a long hedge on the side of the lot and noticed dozens of bikes, all locked to a chain link fence on the other side of the lot. We were curious to check out some of the really fancy ones, but as we started to go around the hedge to enter the lot, we noticed two men in grey uniforms approaching the lot from the other side. They looked like security guards, so we returned to watch from behind the hedge.

"I wonder why they're carrying garden shears," I said.

"Those aren't garden shears," BJ said, dropping his head back down. "They're wire-strap cutters. I've used them on my dad's construction site."

Then Dusty poked his head over the top of the hedge and said, "Now they seem to be checking the bikes for something."

We all peered over the hedge just in time to witness the men with those wire-strap cutters select two bikes each and quickly cut their locks off. The other two, who were obviously keeping watch, ran over to help, and all four of them each took a bike and rode out of the parking lot, back to the lane, and then west toward Arlington.

"C'mon," I called out as I raced down the lane.

"We can't catch them," BJ protested, reluctantly following me.

"What's the point?" Dusty shouted, following us both. "They're bigger than us, and they got weapons."

"Hurry," I encouraged them. "Let's just see where they're going."

When we reached Arlington Street, we looked to the left just in time to see the four men riding their bikes over to the back of a white moving van that was parked on the other side of the street. With the back open, a tall man with a white cap reached down to take one of the bikes. I pulled out my tiny camera and started snapping pictures.

Then, the second man handed his bike up to the tall man in the back of the van while the first man jumped up beside him. As the other two men on the ground were passing their bikes up to the two men in the back of the van, I handed my mini binoculars to BJ and a tiny telescope to Dusty and quickly returned to taking pictures with my camera.

"What's this for?" BJ asked, confused.

"Binoculars," I hissed. "To read the license plate."

"What's mine?" Dusty asked, equally perplexed.

"A telescope," I answered sharply, continuing to take pictures.

"It's smaller than your stupid camera," he protested as he fumbled around trying to make it work.

"Mine's even smaller," BJ grumbled. "I can't see anything."

"Focus," I said as I took another picture.

BJ and Dusty fiddled with their spy equipment, and somehow, Dusty figured out how to focus his telescope.

Meanwhile, the two men on the ground climbed into the back of the van while the tall man jumped down, pulled down the back door, and disappeared around the passenger side of the van.

I was only able to take a couple of more pictures before the van pulled out into the traffic and sped away.

"5-4-6," Dusty read out as he peered through his telescope.

"They got away," BJ yelled out.

We all just stood there staring at the truck as it disappeared from view.

"Now what?" Dusty asked.

"We could report this to the police," I suggested.

"Don't be ridiculous," BJ said.

"We didn't see their faces anyway," Dusty added.

BJ sighed with relief, "Good thing I didn't bring my bike."

"Well, let's go watch the parade," Dusty suggested.

"Good idea," BJ agreed as they both handed their miniature devices back to me, grumbling something about how useless they were.

When we walked back down the lane, we noticed a police car parked at the entrance to the parking lot. A police officer was standing by the car talking to a man who kept pointing to where the bicycles were.

"Should we tell them?" I asked.

"Why bother?" BJ said. "We'll miss the parade.

"They won't listen anyway," Dusty agreed.

"I can at least try," I said as I walked over to the police car.

"Find a good spot, and I'll be with you in a minute."

BJ and Dusty shrugged and took off to find a good viewing spot.

When I joined them a few minutes later, they'd found a clear spot behind three kids sitting on the curb. I arrived just in time to see the Shriners riding their tiny motorcycles, so I started taking pictures right away.

"What happened?" Dusty asked.

"Nothing," I grumbled as I put a new role of film in my camera. "You were right, they weren't interested."

BJ chuckled, "I told you."

"I even told them I'd taken some pictures, but when I showed them my camera, they just laughed," I admit I was feeling pretty grouchy about the whole thing.

BJ's dad drove us to the circus on Sunday along with BJ's two little sisters, Ellen and Maria.

They were really good kids, and BJ now considered himself an expert big brother. However, when he was selling programs, he soon learned otherwise.

When we arrived, we checked in and picked up our float, aprons, programs, coloring books, and crayons. BJ decided to get a drink, even though we'd been told not to eat or drink while selling programs. He went off to his allocated place to sell programs while I headed in the other direction to my spot. It didn't take long before all my programs were gone, so I went to where BJ was stationed.

Just as I was approaching, I saw BJ selling a program and handing some change to a young lady with long auburn hair, who quickly handed it to a little girl standing beside her. They left, but about a minute later, the little girl returned and started pulling on BJ's sleeve.

"Where are my crayons?" she demanded.

BJ was holding his drink in his left hand, trying to make change for a young man to whom he'd just sold a program. She tugged on his left arm again while I stood watching, trying not to laugh.

"That's five cents for the crayons," BJ told her politely, still trying to find the right change for the young man with his free hand.

"My sister paid you already," she complained.

She kept grabbing at his left arm, so he raised it higher to a point where she couldn't quite reach it. BJ finally found the right change and handed it to the young man. The man stepped back and enjoyed BJ's dilemma. As BJ tried to explain that her sister hadn't paid, she jumped up and pulled so hard on his left arm that his drink tipped over and spilled all over her as BJ watched in horror. I bent over laughing, and then... the screaming started. The young man started laughing, and it seemed like everyone was staring at the little girl, wondering what BJ had done to make her scream like that.

A Shriner quickly appeared on the scene and asked, "What's going on here?"

He snatched the empty cup from BJ's hand and reminded him that he wasn't supposed to be drinking while he was selling programs.

The young man stopped laughing long enough to say, "It wasn't his fault; that little brat just pulled his arm down and made the drink spill all over her."

The girl's screaming suddenly switched to a chant, "I want my crayons. I want my crayons," until her big sister appeared from nowhere, accompanied by a tall, brown-haired man with Buddy Holly glasses.

Despite the glasses, I recognized him as Rocky, the driver of the blue Meteor.

"C'mon, Valery," he yelled. "We're going to miss the show."

"I want my crayons," the little girl chanted again.

Another Shriner joined the fray. He astutely yanked a box of crayons from BJ's apron and handed it to the little girl, creating a magical moment of silence.

"You tried to cheat me?" Valery yelled at BJ as her little sister snatched the crayons from the Shriner, turned to BJ, and kicked him squarely in the shins.

"Serves you right, Jackass," Rocky yelled at BJ as he, Valery, and her sister scurried away.

This only made the young man laugh louder, I noticed with surprise that the Shriner was Dr. Neuman. He put his hand gently on BJ's shoulder and knelt down to examine his leg.

As I rushed over to help, I managed with some difficulty to stifle my laugh long enough to steady BJ's dangling foot so Dr. Neuman could examine it properly.

BJ looked down at me, then glanced over to see his sisters coming to his rescue, "Aren't you glad you don't have any sisters like that," Maria smiled, looking up at him.

This made BJ smile, and I let out my own chuckle.

Dr. Neuman completed his assessment, "There's nothing broken, BJ, but you're going to have a nasty bruise for a while," Dr. Neuman said, looking up and smiling as BJ gently lowered his foot.

"Do you girls have programs?" Dr. Neuman asked Ellen.

"Not yet," she replied.

"Here you go," he smiled, relieving BJ of his last two programs and handing them to his sisters. "Don't forget your coloring books and crayons."

Dr. Neuman took two boxes from BJ's apron and handed them to the girls and then he took BJ's apron.

"I'll cash in for you, BJ," Dr. Neuman said with a smile. "And you, too, Billy," as he reached for my apron also.

"Are you going to sit with us too, Billy?" Ellen asked.

"David has saved you a seat beside him," Rachael added as she and Carolyn joined us.

We all took our seats and thoroughly enjoyed the show without any further incidents, especially David and Brendan.

So that was a circus. Clowns on bikes, and even a lion. It was amazing. I'll take my own kids one day, I vowed. I wouldn't make them wait until they were sixteen, either. I'd give them everything they wanted.

Chapter 4
The Heist

When school finished at the end of June, I started working at Eaton's. The job itself was interesting and the people I worked with were all nice as pie, except for one – and he was my supervisor. Mr. Curtis introduced him to me as Rob Cross, but I recognized him straight away: Rocky, the kid from hockey camp and the driver of the blue meteor. He'd dyed his hair brown and was now wearing Buddy Holly glasses, but it was him alright. Fortunately, he didn't seem to remember me, and I didn't refresh his memory. As the new person on his team, I spent more time fetching coffee for him than doing my job, but I didn't complain after seeing how he treated another employee, whose name was Neil. He was just a year older than me and a bit taller with dark hair. We got on famously as the only two stock boys.

On Tuesday, after the long weekend, Rob told Neil to get him some coffee, but when Neil returned with a hot brimming cup, Rob spun around and knocked the cup out of his hand. I was standing right there and couldn't believe my eyes.

"Watch it, jackass," Rob shouted at Neil. "Now, you owe me a fresh coffee. Give the money to your idiot friend here so he can get me another one."

Neil fumbled around nervously, pulled out some change from his pocket, and handed it to me.

"Be quick about it, jerk," Rob yelled at me as I scurried away as fast as I could.

When I returned with the coffee, I stood back a few feet while handing Rob his coffee so he wouldn't do the same thing to me. He didn't even look up. He just told me to put it down and beat it, so I headed back to the mezzanine where Neil was finishing mopping up.

"Hey, Neil, what's Rob looking for?"

"He said he was doing inventory, which is weird because we just did inventory a few weeks ago," Neil replied.

"There seems to be a lot of strange things going on here," I said.

Neil wrung the mop in the bucket, "That's for sure. You remember that load of stationary shipment that arrived this morning?"

"Are those the ones that Larry lifted up to the mezzanine with the forklift?" I asked.

He frowned and nodded, "Yup. Rob told me that we gotta put the boxes on the upper shelves first thing in the morning."

"Why?" I asked. "There's tons of room on the lower shelves, and those boxes are really heavy."

"How the heck would I know?" Neil answered and mopped even harder.

"So, how do we get them up there?" I asked.

"We lift them," Neil shrugged.

We began lifting the boxes as soon as we got to work on Wednesday morning. Just as I was lifting my third box, labeled Order Forms, I heard some steps behind me. Then something knocked into me. I lurched forward, dropped the box, and crashed onto my side. Papers spewed all over the place. I scrambled around, grabbing papers, and that's when I saw Rob glaring down at me.

"What are you doing lying down on the job, you lazy doofus!" he bellowed at me. "On your feet, jackass, and get this mess cleaned up pronto."

To my surprise, as I was getting up, I saw him collecting some papers off the floor.

I was shocked that he was helping clean up the mess, but not for long, because as soon as Neil helped me to my feet, I turned around to see Rob heading back downstairs, yelling, "It better be cleaned up when I get back!"

On Saturday afternoon, Mr. Curtis approached me and asked if I could lock the man door by the loading dock for him when I finished work. He had to leave early to take his mother to the hospital, he explained. He asked me to drop the key off at his home on Sunday. Dusty didn't work on Saturday, but he wanted to see the boats and the tent trailer, so he dropped by before closing time and was looking around when I joined him.

"Time to go home, Dusty!" I grinned at him. "We're closing up."

"I've only seen some of the stuff," Dusty protested. "And I really wanted to have a good look at everything."

"Me too," I replied.

"Haven't you already seen everything?" he asked.

"Yeah, but I want to take some pictures of the boats and the tent trailers before they're gone."

"You can always take pictures next week," Dusty shrugged.

"No, I can't. They're being picked up tomorrow, I replied."

He eyed me, "But tomorrow is Sunday, and the store is closed, right?"

"I know, but I heard Rob tell Larry and Dick that they'd have to come in on Sunday afternoon to help load a moving van for a big order being shipped up north somewhere," I explained.

"Rob told them that the movers would pay them each ten bucks to help out."

"How do you know that they were picking up the boats and the tent trailer?" he asked.

"Larry told me," I muttered. "And he also told me that when he asked Rob if he needed Neil or me to help as well, Rob just said, those knuckleheads are useless."

When Dusty and I arrived on Sunday morning, we walked up the steps leading to the man door beside the loading dock. The door had no handle on it, just a cylinder lock with a hole for the key. I inserted the key, pulled the door open, and we entered beside the loading area.

There were no windows, so it was pretty dark except for the emergency lights. I turned on the lights by the door, and we began wandering through the boat section. I had my camera out and was taking some pictures when we heard a truck engine at the loading dock.

"I better turn out the lights," I whispered to Dusty as I rushed over to the light switch.

We listened at the door and heard voices outside, so I led Dusty over to the stairs. Our eyes soon adjusted to the dim emergency lighting as we raced up to the mezzanine.

"What the heck? They aren't supposed to be here until afternoon," I whispered again.

We hid behind some boxes, and soon enough, the lights snapped on again. Then the overhead loading dock door opened, and we saw the taillight of a white moving van backing up to the dock.

"There's Rob, Larry, and Dick standing by the truck," I whispered as we watched them open the back door of the van.

A man in a grey uniform and white cap came around the van and up the stairs to the loading dock as four other men in grey uniforms spilled from the back of the van. The man with the white cap then handed some papers to Rob. Rob then passed some to Dick and the rest to Larry.

Larry and Dick each escorted two of the men in uniforms to different parts of the room, while Rob and the man with the white cap were looking at some papers.

"I'm going to take some more pictures," I whispered, getting my camera out. "Before they load everything onto the moving van."

I was snapping pictures while they loaded the van with canoes, boats, tents, sleeping bags, and even some bicycles. Then, they started to pull the trailer that held the Chris-Craft boat with the two outboard motors. I noticed Dusty staring hard at the four men as they loaded it onto the van.

"You know, Billy," he observed.

"That van looks just like the one that the bicycle thieves used, and those men? They're wearing the exact same grey uniforms. See," he pointed.

"There's a ton of white vans around," I noted. "And a lot of movers wear grey uniforms."

"I suppose you're right," Dusty said.

"But it's curious, isn't it? Especially since the first three numbers on the license plate are 546. Same as that other van."

"The numbers you saw through your telescope?"

I asked as I turned around to take a picture. In doing so, I accidentally pushed the box I was leaning on. It moved slightly with a scraping sound. Dusty and I froze.

"What the hell was that?" we heard Rob shout.

He pointed towards the mezzanine where we were, "It came from up there. Larry, go check it out."

Larry dropped his box and raced up the stairs. Dusty and I looked around for someplace to hide, but all we could do was lie down behind some boxes and hope for the best. My heart was thumping at the sound of Larry stomping up the steps. I felt a hacking cough coming on, and it took everything I had to suppress it.

Just then, we heard the whir of…wings?

I risked a peek out. Seems like Larry's stomping had disturbed some nesting sparrows and now they were flying across the room below the ceiling.

Larry stopped his search.

"It's just some stupid birds," he shouted and tromped back downstairs.

I breathed a sigh of relief and winced as I felt another cough coming on that made me choke back.

I made a small noise, but it could not be heard above the sound of the birds. I hated the way the coughing took over sometimes, like my own lungs wanted to sabotage me.

"Let's finish up and get out of here," Rob called to the man with the white cap. "Give them their ten bucks and make sure all the papers are signed."

All the men rushed around, and soon, the back of the van was being closed with four of the uniformed men in the back. The other man went around to the passenger side of the van while Rob closed the back of the van and the loading dock door. He left with Larry and Dick through the entrance into the main store at the north end. Suddenly it was dark again.

Once the sound of the truck died away and silence filled the room, I gave into my coughing and wheezing as we slowly retraced our footsteps downstairs and left through the man door, which I quickly locked behind us. On the bus ride home, we didn't talk much, worrying about what we'd just witnessed.

When we reached Mrs. Gregg's place, we found Sam sipping coffee on the porch. He asked us to grab a pop and join him. He could see we were flustered about something, and before we knew it, we'd opened up about everything, including the bicycles at the parade and what we'd just witnessed at the Annex. I showed him my camera. Sam suggested that I go to the police, but Dusty objected, saying it'd be a waste of time.

Sam considered that and then said, "Let me drop your film off to get developed tomorrow."

I trusted Sam wholeheartedly, so I gave him my camera and all the exposed film I had.

After work on Tuesday afternoon, I dropped by Mrs. Gregg's to see Sam and was surprised to find a police car parked in front of Mr. Curtis' house. A policeman stood by the car, talking to Sam, who called me over as soon as he spotted me. I recognized the officer as Sergeant Bell.

He gave me a quick smile, "Good to see you, Billy."

"You too. What's happening?"

"Sam and Dusty filled us in on your busy weekend," Sergeant Bell said.

"We were almost ready to arrest Mr. Curtis until Sam showed us the pictures you took. Now, it appears that Mr. Curtis may be innocent, but we need your assistance to help us get to the bottom of this."

"Your pictures are on the table inside Mr. Curtis' house," Sam said as he handed me back my camera.

Once inside the house, I saw that Mr. Curtis was at a desk writing something while Corporal Egil Amundson sat on the couch talking to Mrs. Curtis and gently patting her hand. He glanced at me as we came in and gave me his easy-going smile.

"Billy! Over here."

"Take a look at those pictures," Egil said as we gathered around the dining room table where the photos were spread out.

I showed Egil my camera.

He grinned, "You were always one to find the most interesting things."

"It takes real photographs," I said with a smile.

"Apparently," he said and winked, and then began examining them with a magnifying glass. "And it looks like you captured the license plate of both white vans."

"Are they the same?" I asked.

"They are," Egil confirmed. "And we've determined that the van was stolen, so now we're sure that both robberies were committed by the same gang."

"So, it was a robbery at Eaton's?" I asked.

"It was," Egil verified. "And your pictures are going to help us find out who they are."

"We just have a few questions, Billy," Sergeant Bell interrupted, handing me a piece of paper.

"Do you recognize this form?"

"Yup. It's an order form, just like the ones in the box I dropped."

"Like the ones Mr. Kross picked up off the floor?" he asked.

"Yes. Is that important?"

"Very important," Mr. Curtis said. "When the accounting staff checked the contents in the box of forms this morning, there were nineteen forms missing. The police thought I'd removed them, so you can see why this is so important."

"Also," Sergeant Bell added, "The numbers on the forms presented to Rob's team were the same as the missing forms, and they all appeared to have been signed by Mr. Curtis. However, Mr. Curtis assured us that he didn't sign any of them, which is why we're taking his handwriting sample for comparative analysis."

He turned to Egil, "Okay, Egil. I think we've got everything for today. Time to get back to the station."

"Thanks for everything," Mr. Curtis smiled. "I really appreciate your help."

And he sure looked relieved. Getting suspected of a crime you didn't commit must be pretty tough, I thought.

"If you're available tomorrow, Billy," Egil added. "I'd like to bring you and Dusty to the station to look through our photo registry."

"You bet," I replied. "But we never saw any of them up close."

"By tomorrow," Sergeant Bell said. "We'll have blow-ups of their faces, and we hope you may help to recognize some of them."

"Just like on Dragnet," I said and grinned.

Egil laughed, "Not quite. We'll talk tomorrow. Right now, I think we've detained you all long enough."

The next day, when Egil picked us up, he asked if we'd mind being fingerprinted as they were checking for fingerprints on the stolen forms.

"I thought you couldn't get fingerprints off of paper," I remarked.

Egil nodded, "It's more difficult, but it's not impossible."

He drove us to the East Kildonan Safety Division Headquarters, where the police and fire departments were now operating as one combined department. All I remember about the building was that it was intimidating as all get out. We entered through the back door, so I didn't see much, and we were quickly escorted into a room with a long table in the middle. On the table were piles of large black and white photos and a stack of photo albums.

Egil asked us to sit down, and then Sergeant Bell entered, saying, "Thanks for coming in, boys."

Egil set a handful of enlarged photos of faces in front of each of us as Sergeant Bell explained what we had to do.

"Take a good look at the photos to see if you recognize any of the men and compare them to the photos in the books on the table to see if any of them match."

For the next ten minutes or more, we scanned our books, one page at a time, glancing back and forth from the book to the photographs. Then Dusty broke the silence.

"I know this guy for sure," he declared as he pointed to a picture in his book. "It's Rocky."

"That's Rupert Krosky, sir," Egil said, looking over Dusty's shoulder as Sergeant Bell joined him.

"Not anymore," I challenged, as I checked the picture carefully. "He's now Rob Kross, my supervisor. In this picture, he's got longer, lighter hair and no glasses, but it's definitely him."

"Good eye, boys," Egil said.

"Egil," Sergeant Bell asked, "Could you please get his file and check to see if Mr. Curtis is still here."

"Right, sir," Egil replied as he left the room.

Sergeant Bell reached over to the other photos on the table, picked one up, and studied it carefully. He brought it back to compare it to the book.

"Is this Rob now?" he asked, showing us the picture.

"Yes, sir," we replied in unison.

As Egil returned, looking at the file, he said, "Charged with grand theft as a minor, sir. He served six months in reform school."

"Thanks, Egil."

We continued looking for about twenty more minutes, and Dusty found a picture that looked very similar to the photo of the man with the white cap we had seen on Sunday. Egil came around to have a look.

"Kazimir Vesely," Egil said.

"Interesting, I thought he was in prison," Sergeant Bell mused. "Kaz is an old friend of ours."

"I'll get his file, too, sir," Egil said.

When Egil returned with the file, Mr. Curtis was right behind him. "He was released over a year ago, sir," Egil said.

Sergeant Bell came around to have a closer look at the picture.

"And here," Egil added as he handed the file to Sergeant Bell. "Have a look at who his cellmate was."

"Ken the Pen Ochesky!" Sergeant Bell read out and shook his head.

"Who's he?" I asked.

"A notorious forger," Sergeant Bell replied.

Then he glanced at Mr. Curtis and asked, "Didn't you tell us that Rob got his job because he had excellent references?"

"Yes, sir, the personnel office showed them to me before they hired him," Mr. Curtis said. "But I don't recall specifically who they were from."

"Were they all in writing?" Sergeant Bell asked.

Mr. Curtis considered this, then said, "Yes, they were. Definitely."

"Would they still be on file?"

"They should be; I can check first thing tomorrow," Mr. Curtis said.

"Well, gentlemen," Sergeant Bell said, looking very pleased, "I think we've made significant progress here. Let's call it a day. But before you leave, I must remind you that this is still an ongoing investigation, and everything you've seen and heard here is strictly confidential."

"Does that mean it's a secret?" Dusty asked.

"Top secret," Egil said, his face serious. "Do not discuss this with anyone."

"Don't even chat with each other about it," Sergeant Bell added.

"In case anyone hears you. Walls have ears and all that."

"Can we talk on the phone?" I asked.

"Not even on the phone," Sergeant Bell said, shaking his head slowly.

I felt dumb then and vowed to myself to be silent as a tomb.

"I can take Billy and BJ home if we're done," Mr. Curtis offered.

Sergeant Bell thanked us all, and we rode home, with Dusty and me glancing now and then at each other, bursting with excitement. We were on a case. We were helping catch the bad guys. It was a good feeling.

Chapter 5
The Album

We didn't hear anything from the police for over a week, and, of course, we had to keep mum about it. With lacrosse sucking up all of BJ's and Dusty's spare time, we didn't see much of each other until the following Saturday afternoon when I was visiting Dusty and BJ at Mrs. Gregg's. While we were sitting on the front porch catching up, we heard Mr. Curtis' familiar voice.

"Good afternoon, folks," he said, smiling as he stepped onto the porch.

"I have a little something for our heroes. One for Billy and one for Dusty," Mr. Curtis then handed each of us an envelope.

I opened my envelope and found a thank-you card with a twenty-five-dollar Eaton gift certificate. Dusty checked his envelope to find the same.

I beamed, "Wow, that's terrific! Thanks very much, Mr. Curtis."

"Yes. Thank you, sir," Dusty said with a shy grin.

Mr. Curtis eased down in a porch chair, "You're very welcome, boys. I'm very grateful for your help in clearing my name. And, by the way, you can tell them now, Billy?"

"Tell us what?" BJ asked.

I grinned, "Rob hasn't been at work for the past few days."

"And he won't be coming back either," Mr. Curtis stated firmly.

"Rob was in cahoots with a professional gang of thieves, and now the whole gang is in the remand center waiting for their court hearing."

Dusty shuffled nervously, "Does Rob know that we fingered them?"

"I don't think there's any reason to worry," Mr. Curtis said.

"Is Rupert his real name?" BJ asked.

"Rupert Robert Krosky," Mr. Curtis confirmed as he turned and waved goodbye.

BJ asked what we were going to do with our surprise windfalls.

"With this, I'll have enough to buy a new three-speed Raleigh bike," I said.

"I'm hoping to get a really good camera," Dusty said. "so I can guide the Audubon ladies around the park."

"What the heck are Audubon ladies?" BJ asked.

"Members of the Audubon Society," Dusty replied, looking proud he knew something that BJ didn't.

"They're bird watchers," Dusty grinned.

"Why'd they want you to guide them around a park?" BJ asked.

Dusty crossed his arms and leaned against the porch rail, "So, I can show them places where they can get good shots of rare birds, of course."

"Isn't shooting rare birds illegal?" BJ asked. "I thought you didn't like killing animals."

Dusty laughed, "They shoot them with cameras."

"Oh!" BJ said, looking reassured.

"Last season, my uncle asked me to help him guide hunters and fishermen around Dauphin Lake near Riding Mountain National Park," Dusty explained.

"This one group of hunters were staying in some of the cabins in the park, and they brought their wives with them."

BJ scratched his head, "What? Their wives went hunting with them?"

Dusty punched him lightly in the shoulder. Seemed like he was enjoying having BJ on the back foot for once.

"Not to hunt or fish, but to watch birds and take pictures. Anyway, when we went to pick them up, they asked my uncle some questions about where to find birds I'd never even heard of. My uncle suggested they might find some at Lake Audy and I told them I saw a bald eagle nest near there."

"What? There are bald eagles here?" BJ asked.

"Yup, now you know. I didn't know where all the birds were, but I knew the park well enough to show them around, so they offered to pay me to guide them."

I'd been inspecting my gift card over and over while they talked, but now I looked up, "So, now you want to join them?"

Dusty grinned, "Nope, I just want to earn money guiding them around, and I like the idea of not having to watch them killing anything. I'd also like to learn how to take pictures of birds and animals, like the ones in the National Geographic magazines."

After BJ left, I stuck around to chat with Dusty.

"You didn't seem too excited about the gift card," I said. "And what do you mean by you 'were' hoping to get a good camera? Have you changed your mind?"

Dusty sighed, "No. It's just that I'll never be able to save enough."

"I know that the new Nikon F you like might be outa reach," I replied. "But there are lots of good cameras at good prices. And, hey, Sam and I were talking about pooling some money to get you a Christmas present to help you out."

Dusty just smiled sadly, "Thanks, that's real kind, but I haven't saved a nickel yet."

"Why not? You're making good money, and you hardly spend anything."

He looked at me, "You don't understand. It's my mom. The doctor thinks she's got some kind of sleeping disorder. Anyway, she's off of work a lot and the restaurant doesn't pay for sick leave, so she's barely making enough for rent and food."

"Jeez, that's rough," I said softly, "What are the doctors doing for her?"

"I'm not sure, but she said it's chronic or acute or something, and all I know is she's sick a lot, and she doesn't seem to be getting better."

"Ah… so you're sending her most of your paycheck, right?"

"Yeah. And my uncle hurt his back in a boating accident last spring, so he's okay as a fishing guide but not as a hunting guide because he can't carry anything heavy or walk too far."

"So, he's not making much money either, is that it?'

"Pretty much. He wants me to come home and help him during hunting season."

"No wonder you're so glum."

Dusty shrugged, and we watched a few cars pass by the porch; then he asked, "So, you have enough for your bike now."

I waved my envelope, "With this, I got more than enough."

He peeled some paint off the porch rail, "I, well, I don't suppose you'd care to trade my certificate for cash?"

He looked at me with such despair.

I went over and patted his shoulder, "To send to your mom?"

Dusty just nodded, and, of course, I agreed. I hated to leave him like this, but I had to get home, so I asked to see Sam before I left. Dusty peeked in the door and advised that Sam was still asleep in the front room chair, so I said I'd drop around on Sunday to see him on my day off.

Late Sunday morning, I arrived at Mrs. Gregg's and found the door locked. I rang the bell, but there was no answer. Just as I was leaving, a taxi pulled up and stopped in front of the house.

"Perfect timing, Billy," I heard Mrs. Gregg call out.

"You're just in time to help get Sam out of the cab. As she opened the front passenger door, the cab driver got out and opened the trunk. He pulled something out and opened it up, and, to my surprise, it was a fold-up wheelchair."

"Oh, no, what happened?" I asked.

"Help me get Sam out, please," Mrs. Gregg pleaded as the driver brought the wheelchair over.

She and I helped Sam as the driver held the wheelchair. The driver then helped us get him up the stairs to the house. She then paid the driver while I pushed Sam to his room and asked him what the heck happened.

"Dicky ticker," Sam said.

"A what?" I asked.

"He collapsed last night with a headache," Mrs. Gregg said as she began making up the bed. "So I took him to the hospital. They phoned after breakfast to tell me I could bring him home."

Then, I noticed that Sam was wearing his dressing gown over his pajamas. We helped him up, and Mrs. Gregg wrestled off his dressing gown while I eased him into his bed. Mrs. Gregg fluffed up his pillows so he could sit up, and once he was comfortable, she made some tea.

"Thanks, Billy," Sam said. "It's you I want to talk to."

"I think you'd better rest," I replied.

"Been resting all night. Got summut fer yuh. It's in the bottom drawer," he said, pointing to the dresser.

"Bring it over."

I opened the bottom drawer and saw a thick photo album.

"This album?" I asked.

"That's it. It's a stamp album. Do you like stamps, Billy?"

"Never thought about it much," I replied, as I brought it over to him, and he placed it on his lap.

"I heard you and Dusty talking the other night, and I'd like to help him get a good camera. This might help."

"How?" I asked.

He smiled and angled the light onto the album, "Thar's a few valuable old stamps in there, and you could sell them to help Dusty get a good camera."

"Really? But don't you want them?"

He shook his head, "It was the only thing I had of my dad's, but I've never really been interested in stamps. Time for it to serve some useful purpose, don't you think?"

"Gosh, how much do you think they're worth?"

He held out the album, "Don't know. Just take it and find out, but don't tell Dusty."

"Are you sure?" I asked,

"Positive!" Sam smiled.

Just then, Mrs. Gregg showed up with a cup of tea, "I'm sure that this old codger needs a good cup of tea and some rest."

I took the hint, tucked the album under my arm, thanked Sam, and said I'd check in on him tomorrow. After dinner, I relayed everything to Amanda and showed her Sam's album. She said her dad collected stamps, so we showed him the album. He took it to his office to examine it carefully while Amanda and I went downstairs with our tea to discuss both Sam and Dusty's situations.

About an hour later, Mr. Page came downstairs, grinning ear to ear.

"Did Sam really give this to you, Billy?" he asked.

I nodded vigorously, "Yes, he did."

"Well, if you don't want it. I'd like to buy it and add it to my collection."

"What do you think it's worth, Dad?" Amanda asked.

"Probably about two or three hundred. I can take it in tomorrow to get a written appraisal, and I'll pay Sam whatever it's worth. Sound good?"

I looked back and forth from Amanda to Mr. Page. I was busting a gut with excitement. Two to three hundred bucks!

"That'd be great, Mr. Page, just great."

Two days later, when Mr. Page came home, he handed me a big envelope with the assessment and the money: $356.25. I'd never seen so much money in one place in my life and could barely speak.

"Thank you, Daddy," Amanda said,as she gave him a peck on the cheek.

I added my heartfelt thanks and assured him that this was more than enough to buy Dusty a Nikon F camera along with some film and other photo accessories. I took the envelope to Sam, and he gave it back to me with instructions for me to visit the camera shop as soon as possible. BJ and I each added about twenty dollars to give me a budget of over four hundred dollars.

On the weekend, I purchased everything we needed. Even though it was still August, we got into the Christmas spirit, and Carolyn wrapped a beautiful Christmas hamper for Dusty to take to Dauphin.

On Thursday, I dropped by to check on Sam, and Dusty asked, "What'd you get at the camera shop this weekend? A Nikon F?"

"No," I laughed, "Just a bigger camera. Were you in the camera shop?"

"Nope. I just saw you go in while I was coming home on the bus," he said.

"Too bad I missed you," I said, relieved that he hadn't seen the size of the package I came out with.

Dusty shrugged and then grinned, "Well, come on in. Sam's waiting for you. It's your turn to entertain him."

Sam seemed in good spirits, but he looked pale and seemed low on energy. We played some cribbage, and I went home worrying about him and then had tea with Amanda. Talking to her always made me feel better.

Who knows, maybe one day, when I'm older, taller, and smarter, she might look at me differently.

Chapter 6
The Escape

I was still feeling in good spirits until Friday when I read in the paper that Rupert Krosky had escaped custody. The article said that he'd come down with a serious illness that required him to be transferred to hospital under close guard. In the middle of the night, he overpowered his orderly, took off the orderly's clothes and badge, and then brazenly strolled out of the room, right past a police officer who was posted at his door. They didn't even realize he was gone for over an hour.

I wasn't feeling too concerned until Egil drove up in his squad car that Saturday. I invited Egil in, introduced him to Amanda, and went to the kitchen to make some coffee.

"So, you're the Corporal Egil Amundson Billy's talked so much about," I heard Amanda say.

"Don't believe everything Billy says," Egil replied.

"I don't," Amanda replied, "But I do believe Kathleen."

I couldn't quite make out what they were saying after that, but I heard Amanda laugh as I brought the coffee in.

"Egil tells me you were a real handful when you were little, Billy," Amanda said with a grin.

"He was and still is, which is the reason I'm here," Egil replied.

"What did you do this time?" Amanda smiled.

"He's not in any trouble, but he may be in danger," Egil began. "It seems that our friend Rupert is quite a vindictive fellow. He bragged that he'd get Billy if it was the last thing he ever did."

"Just me?" I asked.

"By name, yes," Egil answered with an official nod. "But we can't assume anything."

"Jeez, we thought he'd be trying to get as far away from here as possible," I said.

Egil stirred his coffee, "That'd probably be a wise move, but he seems unpredictable."

"What are you two talking about?" Amanda asked, confused.

Egil patiently explained about Dusty and I being witnesses to the Eaton's heist.

Amanda glared at me, "You never told me about this?"

"He wasn't allowed to," Egil cut in before I could sputter a response.

"Now, just be careful and watchful, Billy. Don't go out at night on your own and check the street to see if there are any suspicious vehicles around, especially any parked with someone sitting inside."

Amanda leaned forward and asked, "Do you think Rupert could be violent?"

"He has no official record of violence," Egil replied.

"He has, however, been involved in a number of skirmishes, and apparently, he has a short fuse."

I looked around the room nervously; suddenly, everything seemed ominous, "Should I stay home from work?"

Egil shook his head and put his coffee down, "I don't think that will be necessary. We're just taking precautions; that's why we're just alerting you and Dusty. In the meantime, don't go anywhere unless it's absolutely necessary. We'll keep you informed of any new developments."

Amanda thanked him, and, as Egil left, he smiled at her and handed her his card, "Please call me anytime."

I smiled at Amanda when Egil left and mockingly repeated, "Please call me anytime."

"Just when were you planning on telling us about this, Billy?" Amanda asked, arms crossed.

I shrugged and cleaned up the coffee cups, so I didn't have to see her glaring at me.

Next week, I didn't hear from Dusty until Friday night, when he called to let me know he'd seen a blue Mercury parked outside Mrs. Gregg's place and thought it might be Rupert.

"Was anyone sitting in the car?" I asked.

"Nope, I don't think so," he replied, "Okay, okay, I'll be over right away."

When I arrived at Mrs. Gregg's, the Mercury was gone, so I went downstairs to Dusty's room. We were hanging out at his desk when we were startled by sharp, popping sounds coming from the backyard.

"Holy! What's that?" Dusty cried out, jumping up.

"Firecrackers?" I supposed as I peered out the window in Dusty's room. "But, shoot, it's the wrong time of year."

We ran upstairs and found Sam in the kitchen.

"Sounded like a BB gun," he said.

I noticed then that a small window in the kitchen was all cracked, and some shards had fallen inside the room. Dusty and I rushed over to the back door with Sam close behind us. Sam turned out the kitchen lights so we couldn't be seen.

It was fully dark by this time, inside and out, so I grabbed the large flashlight that Mrs. Gregg kept on the hook by the door. Just as Sam reached around us and turned on the back porch light, he peered through the small window in the door but couldn't see anything. He opened the door. As he pushed on the screen door, a black figure sprung out from beside the door and grabbed him around the neck. Another black figure tore open the screen door and reached around to help his pal. They couldn't see us standing behind Sam because the lights were off inside the house, so the second assailant was caught off-guard when I bashed him on the head with the flashlight.

As he crumpled to the ground, the first assailant glanced up to see what was going on and was pretty surprised when Dusty punched him squarely in the face. He slumped beside his friend on the ground, and I dropped the battered flashlight, grabbed hold of Sam, and yanked him inside. Dusty locked the door, turned off the outside light and we helped Sam into the kitchen just as Mrs. Gregg came in to see what all the commotion was about.

She wasted no time in phoning the police. When she came back to check on Sam, Dusty and I were helping him onto a chair. He was holding onto an old cloth, which fell from his hand on the kitchen floor, mumbling one word, chloroform. Then he slouched down in his chair.

A few minutes later, two police officers showed up and checked around outside the back door.

Shortly after this, Egil arrived and asked us some questions.

"I recognized the first guy," Dusty said. "Just before Billy hit him with the flashlight."

"Who was it?" Egil asked.

"Rupert," he replied. "For sure."

"How hard did you hit him?" Egil asked me.

I grinned, "I broke the flashlight. Why'd he use a BB gun and not a real gun?"

"It looks like they were trying to lure you out of the house so they could kidnap you," Egil replied, holding up the pillowcase he'd picked up by the back door.

"What was the pillowcase for?" Sam asked, who'd revived and was straightening up and looking better by the minute.

"My guess is that while Rupert was holding the cloth soaked in chloroform over your mouth, the other assailant was planning to put this pillowcase over your head."

"Why on earth would they want to kidnap Sam?" Mrs. Gregg asked, hands on her hips.

She was not impressed with all the hullabaloo, as she called it.

"I suspect they were looking for Billy, Mrs. Gregg," Egil replied politely.

"But Billy doesn't live here anymore," Mrs. Gregg said.

"They probably didn't know that," Egil replied.

"But they must have known I used to live here," I mused.

"But how?"

"Rupert's girlfriend, Valery Graham, worked in Eaton's personnel department," Egil said.

"And I remember now that when Mr. Curtis showed us your files, Eaton's had both of you listed as living here."

"Did she get fired?" Dusty asked.

"No, she quit," Egil continued. "She didn't show up after the robbery, and she vacated her apartment without paying her rent."

I felt so bad all this happened at Mrs. Gregg's house, and I tried to help with the broken glass.

"Don't yuh be worrying about that," Sam said. "You did the right thing by helping catch those thieves, and sometimes the right thing has repercussions."

Chapter 7
The Chase

The following Monday was a special day because that's when I picked up my new bike. I gave my old bike to Dusty, and even though it had no gears, he could make it go faster than I ever could. On Saturday, I was riding up Linden St. on my way to see if Dusty wanted to go for a bike ride when I spotted the blue Mercury. It was parked just up the street from Mrs. Gregg's place. Sitting at the wheel was none other than Valery Graham, the girlfriend of our old nemesis, Rocky.

I suggested to Dusty that we call Egil, but he told me to check if the car was still there before we called. I checked, and it was gone, so we decided it was safe to go for a ride. On our way home, we were riding down Leighton towards Kildonan Drive when the blue Mercury pulled out behind us from Woodall Street. Instead of turning left on Kildonan Drive, I indicated to Dusty to follow me as I turned right and went up Mossdale. The Mercury also turned right, so I became concerned.

Dusty said, "Maybe we should call Egil."

"It's closer to the phone from the Page's place," I replied, "And I don't think Rocky and Valery know where I live now."

We peddled as fast as we could to the Page's and got off our bikes at the back of their driveway.

I accidentally dropped my bag, and I was bending down to grab it when I heard a car backfire, followed by a loud bang on the garage door.

I peered down the end of the driveway to the street. I saw a motorcycle and someone pointing a gun right at me. Dusty saw him, too, and we scrambled on our hands and knees behind the house just as a second shot rang out, with the bullet hitting the ground about a foot away from Dusty.

Then we heard footsteps running towards us. My first thought was to run, but I knew I couldn't outrun a bullet. I started wheezing to catch my breath, so

I looked around, and right beside me, I noticed the rake leaning against the wall and a hose lying on the ground. Before I could even move, Dusty grabbed the rake and stood close to the corner of the house. I managed to grab hold of the hose and we waited until the footsteps were really close to the corner. Dusty stepped out on the driveway and swung the rake hard into the chest of the approaching attacker. He fell backward, and his gun skidded across the driveway. It was Rocky. I turned the hose full on both him and the gun, pushing the gun into the grass.

My heart was beating so fast I could hardly think. I started breathing heavily and grabbed my bag as we both jumped on our bikes to get away from Rocky before he could get back on his feet. We rode toward the path that runs along the river, forgetting that the path only goes about two hundred yards before it stops. I was wondering what to do when we heard a motorcycle starting up behind us. Then, I knew exactly what to do. I panicked.

As we were running out on the pathway, Dusty glanced into the Landry's backyard. They had four kids, and all their bikes were sprawled chaotically across the backyard.

"Let's park our bikes here and find somewhere to hide," he called to me.

As we hid our bikes in plain sight by throwing them down amongst the other bikes, I remembered that there was a dock down by the river. I guided Dusty to the dock, and we quickly tucked ourselves under the small space between the dock and the water's edge. There was a short bush to hide behind, and so we just sat there and waited while I tried to catch my breath and stop wheezing.

We heard the motorcycle stop abruptly at the end of the path and then spin around.

A familiar voice called out, "They must have cut through that yard."

As the motorcycle began heading back along the path, we heard Mr. Landry yell out, "What do you think you're doing there?"

His wife's voice followed, "Your supper's getting cold, Al."

Then I heard, "Stupid kids," as the door slammed shut.

We swiftly crawled out from under the dock and snuck into the Landry's yard. Apparently, he hadn't noticed two extra bikes in the yard, so we snatched up ours and, with stealth, made our way quietly up their driveway back to Kildonan Drive. We glanced down toward the Page's place and saw the blue Mercury still parked in front, but no sign of Rocky or his motorcycle. So, we dashed across the street with our bikes and up the driveway of the house on the other side. I knew it would take us to the back lane that went up alongside Angus McKay School, where we stopped for a moment.

"We need someplace to hide," Dusty said anxiously.

"The House!" I said, "We need to get to the House as fast as we can."

We veered our bikes off the lane and onto the grass to cut across to the Greene Avenue back lane and make our way to Woodvale Street. We cut through yards, under laundry lines, and through many back gates to stay mainly on back lanes as we wound our way toward the Redwood bridge, all the time checking in our mirrors for any sign of Rocky. We needed to stay off Main Street, so we crossed over the bridge and as soon as we spotted the golden boy on top of the legislature building, I knew where we were, so we headed south toward the Assiniboine River.

Unfortunately, Dusty caught a glimpse of Rocky's motorcycle in his mirror, so when we passed St. Mary Ave, we took a right to get out of sight and kept going until we reached the Granite Curling Club. We found a path around the back of the building that went along the river, so we found a spot to rest where we could watch the cars crossing over the bridge. I was so relieved for a chance to rest, get my aspirator out, and stop my wheezing.

Dusty soon spotted both of them heading south across the bridge and we decided it was our time to be the followers, thinking they wouldn't be looking for us in their rear-view mirrors. We safely made it over the bridge and stayed on Osborne until we found a phone booth at a service station.

We carefully hid our bikes at the back, out of sight, so I could phone the police. Egil was not there, and neither was Sergeant Bell, so I left a message. I panicked again when I spotted the blue Mercury, so I quickly turned my back to the street and phoned BJ in desperation. While still wheezing and out of breath, I explained to BJ what was happening.

"Are you okay?" he asked, "Where the heck are you?"

"We're at a service station on, on … Osborne Street," I whispered between wheezing and taking deep breaths.

"I can hardly hear you," he said.

"What's going on?

He's got a-a real gun," I whispered, wheezing loudly.

"What are you talking about, and what are you doing on Osborne Street?" BJ asked, confused.

"Tell me–"

"Rocky is after us," Dusty interrupted, taking the receiver from me.

"We have to hide someplace where they can't find us. Oh, oh, I see the blue Mercury. Gotta run. Call Egil, please!"

"Dusty? Dusty?" we heard as he hung up the receiver.

"I don't think she saw me," I whispered, "But Valery just pulled up for gas, and Rocky stopped beside her on his motorcycle."

We quickly ducked out of the booth, hoping we weren't spotted, and then poked our heads around the corner to see what was happening. The attendant filled up the car while they stood there talking. Valery paid for the gas and got in the car while Rupert mounted his bike. They left, heading back north on Osborne. We waited until they were gone and went into the station to get some pop, snacks, and a flashlight.

We got back on our bikes and headed south on Osborne as fast as we could. We kept glancing back, thinking we were home free because they had gone north. But they suddenly reappeared about six blocks behind us. We turned right at the next intersection, heading towards Lord Roberts School, but before we reached the school, Rocky once again appeared behind us. We cut through a yard on the left side of the road to get to the back lane so we could continue west until we reached Daly Street.

We both knew this area like the back of our hands, so Dusty suggested we split up and meet at The House. I raced down Daly and turned right onto Jubilee, but before I could reach Churchill Drive, Rupert appeared again like a bad penny. I decided to push on to the Elm Park Bridge because turning onto Churchill Drive would have led them to the now-abandoned Assiniboine House. I quickly zipped into the parking lot at the new drive-in ice cream stand on the corner, dumped my bike beside some other bikes, and found cover in the bushes behind the stand.

I calmed down with my aspirator and tried to control my wheezing and catch my breath. As usual, the narrow old trestle bridge was quite busy, just as I'd hoped. When Rocky's motorbike rounded the corner from Jubilee, he headed straight over the narrow bridge, weaving in and out around cars and bicycles along the way. The ice cream stand was buzzing with people, so I wasn't really noticed.

Just as I was feeling safe, I spotted the blue Mercury turn off Jubilee, and, much to my surprise, Valery didn't go across the bridge.

Instead, she turned into the drive-in and parked. Now, I felt trapped.

Wondering what she was doing, I stepped back into the bushes to watch. She got out of the car and walked over to the stand to join the order line. Now what, I thought?

Some kids with ice creams in hand walked over to their bikes, which were near mine. I saw my chance, reversed my jacket inside out so it was now black, and scurried over to my bike. I walked my bike behind the other kids to distract attention from myself. As soon as I reached the road, I hopped back on my bike, raced back to Jubilee, and turned right. I didn't have time to check to see if Valery had noticed me or not, so I could only hope she hadn't seen me.

I quickly reached Churchill Drive with a burst of speed and turned right. Before I knew it, there she stood, Assiniboine House, her red brick now covered in vines. She was derelict but a welcome sight. I zipped around the back, wheezing all the way. Dusty was already there, opening the garden shed. We pushed our bikes inside, closed the door, and raced over to the coal chute. Dusty opened the chute doors and quickly slid down. With my bag in my hand, I sat at the top of the chute, as I had done so many years ago, and pulled the flaps closed as I slid down behind him.

In an instant, we were safe in the basement. I used my flashlight to find our way to the wardrobe room, where I found my old hockey stick, and we settled down in my favorite hiding place, in the closet behind a rack of old clothes.

The air had a moldy, stale odor, but it was quiet and peaceful for a while. As my heart rate slowed to normal, I finally caught my breath and my wheezing settled down.

Our rest time didn't last very long before we heard some sounds outside, followed by a clanging at the front entrance, which was fortunately still chain-locked. Then I heard footsteps approaching the wardroom, and I saw a light through the crack in the door.

My heart stopped, and I started to wheeze again until we heard a familiar voice call out softly, "Billy! It's BJ! Are you in there!"

I opened the door and shone my flashlight on BJ.

"How did you find us?" I asked, coughing and wheezing.

"Before you guys hung up on me, Dusty said you had to find a place to hide," BJ said, "So where else would you be?"

"Did you phone the police?" Dusty asked.

"I did, but I also phoned Sam to see if he could get a hold of Egil."

"How did you get here?" I asked as I crawled from the closet.

"On my bike." BJ grinned. "The first thing I did was check the garden shed, and I saw your bikes."

"Sure, glad you're here!" Dusty said.

"Hey, what's with the hockey stick?" BJ asked.

Just then, we heard footsteps at the east entrance.

"C'mon, this way," I said.

I led them to the east side of the building and told them to look for some brooms or long sticks.

"They've got guns," Dusty reminded me. "Sticks won't help much."

"Unless you know how to use them," I said with a grim smile.

The rattling of the doors at the east end suddenly stopped, and we heard footsteps running away.

"Are they leaving?" Dusty whispered.

"Maybe they're just checking all the doors," I suggested.

Soon, we heard noises at the west door, which apparently wasn't chain-locked. The footsteps upstairs were getting closer to our end of the building, so I slowly started tapping my hockey stick lightly on the ceiling, mimicking the sound of footsteps.

From up above, we heard a woman's voice faintly call out, "I hear footsteps over there."

Then we heard their footsteps running overhead to where we were. I quickly led Dusty and BJ down a corridor to the south and when we reached the end, I noticed that Dusty had a broom and BJ had found an old mop, so they both started tapping the ceiling, mimicking footsteps.

"This way," we heard a man's voice say, followed by more running footsteps upstairs.

We ran around the basement repeating this for several minutes, always keeping a few steps ahead of them. My fear lessened a bit as I found myself enjoying this strange game. Before we knew it, we were back in the furnace room.

"Okay, you guys," I said. "Up the chute and get our bikes out. I'm going to lure them downstairs and see if I can get them lost in our old rabbit warren. Then I'll follow you up the chute after I lock the furnace door so they can't follow us."

BJ and Dusty quietly scurried up the ladder beside the chute while I led our 'friends' upstairs on another short goose chase. Then I pushed over some old shelving to lead them downstairs and ran back.

I went to the furnace room, locked the door behind me, and was clambering up the ladder when I caught my arm on a nail at the top of the ladder. Damn, I'd done the exact same thing years ago, but there was no time to do anything about it. My bike was waiting for me as I clambered from the coal chute, and we all quickly rode out to Churchill Drive.

As BJ was cycling west, away from The House, I noticed Dusty heading toward the blue car and the motorcycle, motioning with his arm to follow him. Seeing him pull out his knife, I understood. I followed him on my bike, and pulled out mine, too, before joining BJ. We glanced back to see two figures running out of The House toward the car and the motorcycle. Dusty and I stopped to watch while BJ kept going until he noticed a police car heading straight toward him from the west end of Churchill Drive.

He quickly pulled over to the side of the road and turned around when the motorcycle started up.

As the motorcycle swerved away, it flipped over on its side, and as the Mercury pulled away, it gave out a loud flopping sound as it, too, came to an abrupt stop.

Another police car appeared from the east with its lights flashing, and, despite my wheezing and coughing, I stood there, enjoying the scene as it unfolded with two police cars converging on Rocky and Valery. Dusty and I stood there, laughing with relief.

"What's so funny?" BJ asked.

I couldn't speak for laughing and hacking, so I pulled out my army pocket knife, opened the blade, and waved it in the air. BJ joined in the laughter, finally realizing that Dusty and I had just slashed their tires. We walked our bikes slowly toward the police cars as a familiar figure appeared before us. It was Sam walking over with Egil following behind him.

"Was sure yuh . . . just had to be here . . . somewhere," he struggled to say like he was out of breath.

"Got your message."

Sam leaned forward and put his hands on his knees just as Sergeant Bell joined them.

"I thought you were going to stay home, Sam," Sergeant Bell said as he placed his arm on Sam's shoulder.

"You shouldn't be exerting yourself."

"Can't … breathe," Sam wheezed.

"You sound like me," I smiled.

Sergeant Bell called out, "Medical kit, please," as Egil assisted him.

Two constables raced over to help. One was carrying a medical kit; the other had a blanket and other things. The blanket was laid out on the ground and Sam was carefully eased down on it, which allowed the officer with the kit to check him over. After a few seconds, he declared that we needed an ambulance, and the other officer hurried back to his car to make the call.

Sergeant Bell stood up and asked Egil to take care of Sam while he took over supervising the arrest of Rocky and Valery.

Dusty, BJ, and I stayed focused on Sam, but I glanced over just in time to see Rocky and Valery being maneuvered into a police vehicle. Then Egil noticed the blood on my arm, and I told him what happened. As Egil bandaged up my arm, an ambulance arrived, and we watched solemnly as they took Sam away with the siren blaring.

As we stood there, staring at the receding lights, my wheezing and coughing began again.

Gripping my aspirator, I struggled with mixed emotions of dread for our good friend Sam and relief at the demise of Rocky and Valery. It was like being cold and hot at the same time.

Egil ushered me over to a cruiser and suggested that I sit inside to calm down.

"Just leave your bicycles here, boys," Egil said to BJ and Dusty, "We'll drop them off tomorrow when we pick you up. Get in the car with Billy, and I'll take you home."

Egil arrived shortly after breakfast on Sunday, and we were chauffeured to the station to give our detailed statements. On the way, Egil let us know that Sam was in intensive care at the hospital, and they were trying to stabilize him. He had suffered another more serious stroke in the night. The thought of Sam suffering like that set me off, and I started wheezing again, so I pulled out my aspirator once more and said nothing all the way to the station.

I couldn't concentrate on what happened on Saturday because I was so distraught about Sam.

Fortunately, Dusty had an excellent memory and gave an accurate account of the events. When Egil drove me home, I was already feeling a bit shaky, but when I saw the look on Amanda's face as we walked in the door, I felt even worse. I knew instantly what it meant.

"No!" I cried as she hugged me tight.

"I'm so sorry, Billy," Amanda sniffed, with tears in her eyes.

"When?" Egil asked tenderly.

"About twenty minutes ago," Amanda replied softly.

"Mrs. Gregg called. She was with him at the hospital, but he never regained consciousness."

"C'mon, Billy, I'll take you into the living room," Egil said, gently steering me.

Amanda looked over at me, "I think he'd be more comfortable downstairs. I'll make some tea."

Amanda was right. She knew that I thought of the downstairs rec room as my own personal living room, what with its comfy Chesterfield and black-and-white TV. I was still shaking, and I wanted desperately to cry, but I couldn't. Egil helped me ease down on the Chesterfield and sat with me until Amanda came down with the tea and set it on the coffee table. After a quick tea break, Egil got up and apologized for having to leave but promised to call back later. Then Amanda stepped over to the bar and chose a brown liquor bottle to put on the tray, along with a set of shot glasses.

We sat together in silence, slowly finishing our tea, until she put her cup down and reached for the bottle on the tray.

"What's that?" I asked.

"Drambuie," she replied, pouring some in a shot glass.

"It helps calm me down when I get stressed. Would you like to try some?"

"If it helps," I replied, setting my cup on the table.

Amanda poured us each a shot, and we sat back on the Chesterfield. I finished mine in one gulp. I felt a warm shiver all the way down, but the aftertaste was lovely. I took a deep breath and noticed Amanda looking at me curiously.

"It's better if you just sip it," she advised as she demonstrated a proper sip.

She refilled my glass, and I sat back and tried again. As I relaxed, it began to take effect and made me feel all warm inside. When we finished, I leaned back, and she put her arm around me to comfort me. This time, she gently drew my head toward her and nestled it into her shoulder. I felt so comfortable I couldn't move. I had just lost one friend and was about to lose another— Dusty was moving back to Dauphin soon.

My thoughts shifted from Sam to Dusty. I felt good about the present we got him, and it looked wonderful after Carolyn wrapped it so beautifully, but I wouldn't be there to see him open it.

I had to be content with imagining the look on his face when he opened the box and saw the camera.

As my mind calmed down, I realized how fast it had been racing since this morning, what with all that had happened. I was now feeling so comfy that I didn't want to move, but I also had a powerful urge to double-check to see if it really was Amanda's arm around me and not just a dream.

I glanced up to see her smiling down at me. Her smile was so beautiful, and she looked so inviting that I couldn't resist it. I gently kissed her on the lips. I regretted it right away, thinking it was wrong and expecting her to turn away. But she didn't. She kissed me back as she pulled my head back into her shoulder. We stayed in that position until I drifted off, wondering if this was what heaven felt like.

The next thing I remembered was the delightful smell of coffee. I opened my eyes slowly and realized that this was not my bed. I glanced around to realize I was still on the sofa, and as my eyes focused, I saw Amanda sitting on the chair beside me with a coffee in her hand and looking at me with that lovely smile on her beautiful face.

"How are you feeling, sleepyhead?" Amanda asked softly. "Would you like some coffee?

I stared at the coffee in her hand and wondered again if yesterday had all been a dream. Then I noticed the bandage on my arm and knew it was real.

"You must be hungry," Amanda said, ending my trance.

"Why don't I fix you some lunch while you get yourself cleaned up."

As I stood up slowly, Amanda disappeared upstairs, and I glanced down at the coffee table. The Drambuie bottle and some shot glasses were still on the tray. My mind returned to Sam, so I poured myself a shot, lifted up my glass, and said to myself, "Farewell, my old friend."

The tears began to flow freely. They were not happy tears.

The End

Book 6
The Play

By Amanda Amundson (née Page)

Chapter 1
Leonard's Room

When my parents offered to let Billy Johnson move into my brother Leonard's old room at the end of March in 1960, I found him to be a far more complex and intelligent young man than I had expected for a seventeen-year-old grade 11 student. I began my summer job at the Shriners Hospital for Crippled Children right after my finals in April, and I was working the evening shift throughout May and early June, so I only saw Billy at breakfast unless I slept in and missed him altogether.

Our occasional breakfast discussions covered a variety of common interests, including books, music, theatre, and games, but as infrequent as they were, what I looked forward to most was the oxymoron word game, where we each had to think of an oxymoron for a selected topic.

Both my parents had cars, but my mother disliked driving, so I had the use of her car whenever I needed it. Billy, on the other hand, had his bicycle and seemed quite content to use it or take the bus to get around. Sometimes, he ran errands for Mom on his bike because he didn't have a driver's license, so Mom asked if I could teach him to drive and even offered to pay for his license.

Once he passed his learner's test, I began teaching him and, as soon as he was proficient enough not to need much advice, we resumed our discussions on interesting oxymorons. He got his license before the end of the school year, so we continued our discussions at breakfast.

One Sunday in late June, I slept in because I had worked late the night before. Usually, on Sundays, I accompanied Mom on our weekly walk to John Black United Church—where we were both members of the choir. I would have slept longer, but Misty, my beautiful golden cocker spaniel, had other plans. It was time for her walk, and I knew she wouldn't leave me alone if I had breakfast first, so before getting showered and dressed, I looked out the window to check the weather. I noticed Billy cutting the grass with a hand mower. He was wearing shorts and no shirt, so I knew it was warm enough to go without a jacket.

Watching him pushing the mower around, I observed that he was slim but not skinny, fit but not muscular. Indeed, he was filling out nicely and growing out of his boyish looks. I pictured him transforming into a rather handsome young man someday, especially with his curly blond locks.

Misty demanded my attention again, so I turned away from the window, thinking: Yes - he's kind of cute but too young.

I was holding Misty's leash in my hand as I stepped out the door, but she slipped past me before I could catch her and charged out straight for Billy. At the sound of her bark, Billy stopped and knelt down to greet her. She dashed toward him, pounced on him, knocking him over sideways and licking his face. Somehow, he managed to reach into his pocket to bring out an offering. As she gobbled his treat, her paw became entangled in the chain he wore around his neck, and Billy began to choke from the strain. I swiftly reached down to untangle Misty's paw and save poor Billy from being strangled.

Misty didn't even notice me releasing her leg, as she was totally focused on finishing all the treats offered to her. Once she was detached from the chain, Billy managed to sit up and began wiggling Misty's head from side to side, speaking softly to her while still coughing and wheezing.

"Are you OKAY?" I asked.

"I'm fine, Amanda. It's just my asthma."

"What did you give her?" I asked.

"Doggie biscuits."

He smiled without taking his eyes off Misty.

"You keep dog biscuits in your pockets?"

"Just for Misty."

He grinned up at me, and I noticed something dangling on the end of his neck chain.

Pointing to it, I asked, "What is that?"

"It's a ship's wheel," he said, showing it to me.

I smirked, "Oh, so you're the captain of a ship?"

He chuckled at that, "Nope! Just my soul."

"What's that supposed to mean?"

"Do you know the poem Invictus by William Ernest Henley?"

"Hmm, no, but I do like poetry."

"The last lines are, *I am the master of my fate, I am the captain of my soul.*"

"And that means …?"

"To me…well, it symbolizes that I my responsible for how I deal with whatever happens to me in life, be it fair or unfair," he replied as he gently removed Misty from his chest and brushed the grass off his arms.

"And just how do you do that?"

He grinned, "When life seems unfair, I try to suck it up and move on. But…when it is fair, I soak it up…like I'm doing right now, living here with you and your parents."

His response caught me off guard, so I just looked down at him.

Seeing me hesitate, he clarified further, "Take the loss of your brother, for example. I'm sure that didn't seem fair, did it?"

"No, it didn't," I replied slowly.

"Everyone experiences loss or disappointment that seems unfair." He continued, "But some people deal with it and move on, and others don't."

I had no answer for that either, so when I glanced back down and noticed the hand mower, I quickly changed the subject.

"You do know that Dad has a power mower sitting in the garage doing nothing?"

"I do! He told me I could use it anytime I wanted, but Misty didn't like it, and the hand mower cuts the grass cleaner. Besides, it's noisy, and your mom mentioned that you were still sleeping."

"Really?" I was skeptical and intrigued by how a high school kid could have such mature reasoning.

He gently picked Misty up as he got up and handed her to me, "She's ready."

"Thanks," I said as I slipped Misty's leash on and set her back on the ground.

"Say thank you to Billy."

Misty ignored my command as she dragged me away while I attempted to wave goodbye to Billy. My mind focused back on the day at hand, and I realized that I'd forgotten all about our youth group meeting to select our Christmas play project; the meeting was starting right after church. I cut Misty's walk short so I could have some breakfast before leaving. Misty ran around looking for Billy, but he was nowhere in sight.

I was only a few minutes late for our meeting, but by the time I arrived, they'd already selected a play—A Christmas Carol by Charles Dickens. As that was my favorite Christmas story, I was delighted, but I didn't know there was a play version. Carolyn told me that Dickens himself used to perform a one-man play version of his book, and she had found a copy of a script based on the 1951 movie version.

When I came down for breakfast on the following Sunday, I found Billy showing Mom a duffel bag he had found in his closet. I recognized it right away. It was Leonard's badminton equipment bag. Mom was reminiscing as she carefully checked each item.

"You remind me of my grandmother when she used to think about my dad," Billy said softly, "She had that same faraway look in her eyes."

"What was your father like?" Mom asked.

"He died in the war before I was born," Billy replied. "But even though I was really little, I can still remember her telling me about him. That seemed to make her feel better, and I loved to hear her stories."

"What about your mother?" I asked as I joined them with my coffee in hand.

"I never knew my mother at all. I just had my grandparents," he replied solemnly.

"So, you were raised by your grandparents?" Mom asked.

"Only until I was five, that's when they died in a car accident," he replied.

"What was Leonard like?"

"I didn't want him to join the army," Mom began, placing the badminton bag on the floor, because of our horrifying experiences during the air raids in London and—"

"That was awful," I interrupted.

"But you were so young, dear," Mom sighed.

"I still remember us rushing to the shelter every time the sirens screamed," I countered. "And I remember how worried you were because Dad was a warden and stayed outside until the last minute."

"Somehow, he always made it inside just after the bombing started," Mom added.

"But I can still see the anxiety on your face waiting for him to join us," I said. "That I do remember."

Mom sighed, "That was a very difficult time for us, especially after my cousin's house was hit by one of those horrid flying things."

Billy moved next to her and held her hand. They sat there in silence while I got Mom a fresh cup of coffee, and then she began again.

"I thought we'd left that all behind us when the war ended," she said, shaking her head.

"To lose Leonard, to such a senseless war that had nothing to do with us at all has been a nightmare. Sometimes, the world seems to be a very unjust place."

"The world is indifferent to justice," Billy replied sadly and handed her a tissue. "Maintaining balance seems to be the only thing nature cares about."

"We're going to be late for church, Mom," I said, trying to change the subject.

Mom asked Billy if he would like to join us. He confessed that he hadn't been to a church since his grandparent's funeral, so I was quite surprised when he agreed. I invited him to join our theatre planning group after church, and he told me that Carolyn had already asked him and that he and BJ had agreed to work on the sets and props.

I looked at him in surprise, "Really? I didn't know you were interested in theatre."

He shrugged and grinned, "Not in acting because of my asthma, but I'm happy to help with sets and props."

"As long as they don't catch on fire, like your Shmoos," I reminded him and we had a good chuckle at that.

On the way to church, he opened up about some of his own experiences. He certainly was no stranger to loss and challenges in his own young life. I was quite impressed by his sensitivity to the difficulties that my mother was experiencing. I think she appreciated having someone new to share her stories of Leonard with, and I know I really appreciated the special effort he made to spend time with her.

For the next few weeks, I spent my spare time working with the committee, planning for our play, finding volunteers, casting parts and securing a venue. I had a lot on my mind, and although I had many discussions with Billy, I realized I had no idea what he did with his time every day until one Saturday in late August when I returned home to find a police car in the driveway.

As soon as I came through the door, I noticed a rather handsome police officer sitting in the living room. Billy introduced him to me as his almost big brother, Corporal Egil Amundson, and then he went to make us some tea. Kathleen had already filled me in on some of Billy's early life at Assiniboine House and on the Amundson farm, so at least I knew a little about him. She had also explained how Constable Amundson had rescued her on that fateful night after the Valentine's dance, but, gosh, she never mentioned how good-looking he was.

I patted my hair, "Please excuse me, Corporal. But what does 'almost' big brother mean?"

He grinned, "Babysitter mostly, and please call me Egil."

He quickly filled me in on some of the history and challenges he experienced with Billy and his brother Ingar when they were under his care, which made me laugh. When Billy returned with the tea, Egil clarified the reason for his visit, and that's when I first learned about Billy witnessing the Eaton's heist. Now, it seemed that the perpetrator of the crime had escaped and was looking to harm Billy.

I remember reading all about the heist in the paper over a month ago, but it was a bit of a shock to find out that Billy had been a witness and had never mentioned a single word about it. After Egil left, I asked Billy to tell us about it, but he just shrugged it off and said the police told him he couldn't discuss it with anyone.

As the Labour Day weekend approached, I finished my last shift at the hospital and was looking forward to starting my final year of pre-med at the University of Manitoba. On a warm and sunny Saturday, I left after breakfast to spend the day with Kathleen and Brendan at Assiniboine Park while Billy took his new bike out for a ride with Dusty.

Kathleen and I had a lovely day wandering through the park with Brendan running everywhere, but I think his favorite part of the day was when we got him some ice cream at the pavilion. He managed to eat almost as much as he spilled on himself, but he had such a good time. When I got home, feeling quite relaxed, I was once again surprised to find a police car in the driveway again and immediately wondered: "Now what?"

I soon learned from Egil that Billy's day was significantly less peaceful than mine, as he explained the details of how Dusty and Billy were chased all over town by the perpetrator of the heist. Billy was sitting in the living room, listening attentively while using his aspirator between coughs.

"Are you feeling all right, Billy?" I asked when Egil finished his narration. "You sound terrible."

Slowly removing the aspirator from his mouth, he replied, "It's just asthma."

"Are you sure it's just asthma?" Mom asked. "Shouldn't we take you to see a doctor?"

I agreed and asked him when he had last seen a doctor.

"You were there," Billy replied, looking up at Egil, "I think I was five."

"You remember that?" Egil asked.

Billy smiled, "I remember being in the hospital for a while."

"Over two weeks," Egil confirmed, "Suffering from hypothermia and a serious case of pneumonia."

"And…you haven't seen a doctor since then?" I asked, shocked.

"How do you know it's just asthma?"

Billy shrugged, "Sandy's dad said it probably was. He's the pharmacist who gave me my aspirator."

"But he's not a doctor. Did you tell him what happened to you?"

"No," he replied meekly.

I shook my head, "I'll make an appointment for you as soon as possible."

Unfortunately, Billy's old friend Sam Grady passed away the very next day, and Billy took it really hard. Egil helped him downstairs, and I tried to console him. When Egil left, I sat with Billy on the couch until he fell asleep with his head on my shoulder. Just as his head slid down onto my chest, Mom came downstairs and saw us sitting like that.

"What are you doing?" she asked.

"I was just consoling, Billy," I replied. "He's had such a rough day."

"Really?" she asked suspiciously, looking down at the Drambuie bottle. "Is that what you were doing?"

"Mother," I hissed.

"Amanda! For heaven's sake, he's still a child."

"He's sleeping like one," I replied, looking down at him.

She threw up her hands and instructed me with a strange look.

"Well, don't wake him up. Just settle him down comfortably on the couch while I get his pillow and some blankets. Let him sleep right there tonight."

Once Billy was settled in, I scurried upstairs to bed, feeling like a reprimanded child.

In the aftermath, I'd been so concerned about Billy and emotionally distracted by my own feelings that I forgot to make an appointment for him to see a doctor.

Chapter 2
Adversity

On the way home from Sam's funeral, Billy's heart was racing, and his coughing was quite hoarse. As soon as we got home, I called Dr. Duncan at the Shriner's Hospital. I explained the situation, and he agreed to meet us in an hour. He asked if there was anyone who had direct knowledge of what happened twelve years ago. I called Egil, and he quickly offered to join us.

Dr. Duncan conducted a basic physical examination and arranged for a series of tests, starting with simple blood tests. He then asked us into his office. After questioning Egil about Billy's ordeal with the iceberg and his stay in the Winnipeg General Hospital with pneumonia back in March '48. Dr. Duncan took the time to explain that adult-onset lung disorders often have their origin in childhood, which is why it was so important to learn more about Billy's early life. He said he'd check to see if there was still a file on his case and arranged for some X-rays to see if there was any evidence of damaged lungs. Before we departed, he said he'd let us know when and where we needed to take Billy for further testing and advised me not to let him drive by himself to these appointments. Thus, I became Billy's personal chauffeur.

I was quite impressed with Billy's composure in the face of this new adversity and as we were driving to his first appointment, I started up a discussion on the subject. I already knew about his previous misfortunes, but otherwise he seemed to be an average young man; that is, in every way except one: his intuitive reaction to adversity.

He claimed he'd never heard of the famous Greek philosopher, Epictetus, who is credited with saying; *It's not what happens to you but how you react to it.* Yet, he seemed to instinctively understand the importance of dealing with adversity by letting go of the negative conditions as soon as possible. He seemed to appreciate that holding onto negative conditions such as grief, retribution, envy, and animosity can become all-consuming and hinder him from moving forward with his life.

I wondered where he could possibly have learned how to do that. I knew he was a voracious reader, and one can learn so much from books, but I also believed that real wisdom comes from experience. His wisdom could hardly have come from the preferred literature of his peers: comic books. So, I asked him where he learned this.

He shrugged, "Living in foster care with so many different dysfunctional people can teach you many survival skills."

Then he asked how I'd dealt with the loss of my brother, and we digressed into a rather lengthy debate about loss in general. We discussed the impact of different types of loss in a person's life, beginning with the loss of someone close to you and the problem of dealing with grief.

Following a discussion on other types of loss, such as loss of memory, hair, weight, track of time, losing a game, and every other type of loss we could think of, but there were three general types of loss that resonated with us both. In addition to grief, there was the loss of trust, which I added to the list, and the loss of identity, which was Billy's suggestion.

This led to our favorite word game, which was looking at related oxymorons. By a curious coincidence, the word oxymoron itself is an oxymoron, originating from the contradictory Greek root words, 'oxys' (meaning sharp or keen) and 'moron' (meaning foolish).

The next day, we tried to think of a new oxymoron that dealt with a personal loss in some way. Even though many of them weren't true oxymorons, we enjoyed the challenge. Today the internet can give you a list of oxymorons in a snap, but back then we had to think of our own. It was far more challenging. And a lot more fun.

Chapter 3
Good Grief

I soon received a call from Dr. Duncan asking to discuss the x-ray results. He spoke seriously and deliberately, explaining that when young children contract a severe disease like pneumonia while their lungs are still developing, the lung's structure and function may be adversely affected with an increased risk of subsequent chronic lung disease. In simpler terms, he explained that it may be more serious than asthma or chronic bronchitis.

"What does that mean for me?" Billy asked.

Dr. Duncan sighed, "More tests, I'm afraid, Billy."

"Good grief, is that all?" Billy asked.

"It's not funny, Billy," I said.

We thanked Dr. Duncan and took our leave.

The next day, we discussed Peanuts, by Charles M. Schultz, which was clearly Billy's favorite comic strip. Charles Shultz once said that Charlie Brown, must be the one who suffers because he is a caricature of the average person. Most of us are much more acquainted with losing than winning.

The expression good grief, which is so often associated with Charlie Brown, is, according to Merriam-Webster's dictionary, used to express surprise or annoyance. As such, the phrase does not actually incorporate the normal meaning of either of the two words. Billy argued that, regardless of whether good grief is an oxymoron or not, it seemed appropriate for our discussion.

"Is that your oxymoron for today, Billy?" I asked.

"It is," he said and smiled.

"Why that one?"

He shrugged, "Charlie Brown always uses it."

"But what specific type of personal loss is it associated with?"

"What's the major cause of grief?" he asked to test me.

"Loss of a loved one?"

"Okay. Do you think there really is such a thing as grief that is good?" he asked.

"I can't think of one," I replied.

"Me neither, but I believe there is a type of grief that's bad."

"What's that?" I asked.

"It's the kind your mother has."

"What do you mean by that?"

"Well," he began, "It's her grief for Leonard… she's letting it fill the void in her heart when that void could be filled and healed with loving memories of Leonard instead."

"Where did you learn that kind of wisdom?" I asked, astonished.

He smiled in remembrance, "Mrs. Amundson explained that to me when my grandparents died."

"But you were only five!" I replied. "How can you remember that?"

He chuckled, "Easy. She reminded me just last summer when she told me that Patch had passed away."

"Who's Patch?" I asked.

"He was my dog when I lived with them."

"I'm sorry," I replied, "I know how I'd feel if I lost Misty."

"She also told me that grief is like a pole that props you up when you're first faced with loss," he expounded, "But if you chain yourself to that grief pole, you may be trapped in a life of despair until you finally let go."

"That sounds very profound," I said. "Egil's Momma is an extraordinary lady."

I'm not a psychiatrist, so I can't speak authoritatively on the workings of the mind, but I observed that when Billy asked my mother about Leonard, which he did a lot, she seemed to come alive again, especially when she laughed at the funny things she remembered or the clever things he'd done. Sometimes, she relived a precious memory in a certain part of the house or the yard, and perhaps it was just my imagination, but when she talked about all the good times, she did not seem so consumed with despondency.

It took some time, but it seemed to me that it brought Leonard back into her life during those discussions, and, in so doing, I got some of my old mom back. Perhaps that is what letting go means. I would sometimes catch my dad watching her while she recalled these stories, and he simply smiled as he listened. I think he got his wife back too.

Chapter 4
Bittersweet

After weeks of more testing, we returned to Dr. Duncan's office. This time, he was even more serious and explained that scarring of the air sacs in the lungs, which showed up on Billy's x-rays, can lead to interstitial lung disease or pulmonary hypertension. This can make it more difficult for oxygen to pass into the bloodstream, increasing the blood pressure in the lungs.

"Does that mean more testing?" Billy asked dourly.

"I'm afraid so, Billy," Dr. Duncan replied. "Sorry, but this time, we'll need a pulmonary function test, a diffusing capacity test of the lungs, a bronchoscopy, and a lung biopsy."

"Well, to quote Albert Einstein: the more I learn, the more I realize how much I don't know," Billy pondered out loud.

"Did Einstein really say that?" I asked.

"That, and much more," Billy replied. "Most of which I don't really understand."

"What's important to understand now is that this process is complicated," I said, "Which requires patience."

"It's paradoxical, is what it is," he replied.

Dr. Duncan glanced up at us from his desk, looked at us curiously, and said he would provide us with a list of dates and locations for each of these tests as soon as possible. We thanked him and left quietly.

In the car, I asked Billy why he thought it was paradoxical.

"Because," he began, "If I keep learning how much more there is that I don't know, then the amount of what I don't know keeps increasing at a greater rate than the amount of knowledge that I've actually accumulated. This means that the more I learn, the less I know. Hence the paradox, as the increase in accumulated knowledge continues to decrease, the ratio of what I know versus what I don't know is in a never-ending, downward spiral."

I sensed that this curious response was triggered more by his frustration at the lack of progress on his problem than as a serious philosophical opinion.

"Look, Billy, I'm really sorry," I said softly. "I know this must be very disheartening for you, but Dr. Duncan and his team are doing everything humanly possible for you."

"I do understand that, really," he replied, "But I have the feeling that I'm just going around in circles."

"Perhaps it's not really a paradox at all," I proposed, trying to shift him away from this negative mood.

"It seems to me that 'more is less' is an oxymoron rather than a paradox."

"It could be," he smiled, "But I think 'less is more' is a better oxymoron.

"Is that your oxymoron for today?" I asked as I turned onto Portage Avenue.

"Nope, because I can't think of a connection to a personal loss. I guess that means it's your turn."

"Bittersweet," I replied at once.

"That's a good one. What type of loss is that associated with?"

"Loss of trust," I replied confidently.

"So, what do you know about the loss of trust?" Billy asked.

"In high school," I began, "I had a boyfriend and I really liked him but, as you know, there aren't many secrets in high school. One day I learned that he'd being seeing my former best friend behind my back."

"That's awful. What happened?"

"They got married," I said.

"So, are you still bitter?"

I shrugged, "Not anymore."

"How was the wedding?" he asked with a grin.

"I wasn't invited, smarty pants."

"And how did you deal with your bitterness?"

"Not very well at first," I confessed, "Especially since I felt like I'd been betrayed twice."

"That sounds like it was a tough time for you. I've never actually experienced that kind of betrayal, so it's hard for me to relate to it."

"Never?" I asked.

"The closest thing I ever experienced was when I had to leave the Amundson's farm. I felt betrayed, but not by the Amundson's."

"Who betrayed you then?"

He thought about that for a moment.

"I'm not really sure. I suppose it was the lady from Children's Aid because she said I couldn't stay there anymore."

"Why ever not?"

Billy sighed and looked out the car window as we passed Eaton's. He seemed focused on the building and was silent till we passed it.

"That's the hard part for me. I still don't understand why. They said it had something to do with the size of the house and the number of children that the Amundson's already had, but that never made much sense to me."

"At least you're not bitter with the Amundson's."

"You're right. They were the sweet part for me."

I nodded, "You're fortunate because you hold no bitterness for the ones you care for."

He shifted to look at me more closely, "So, what was the sweet part for you?"

"My relationships with both of them were sweet at the beginning, but then, after the loss of trust, I only knew bitterness and resentment. However, memories of the good times gave me hope for the future, that I'll have more good memories, ones that won't be tarnished by bitterness."

"Are you still bitter now?"

"Not much, but my memories are still bittersweet."

"How did you overcome your adversity?" he asked.

I laughed, "I'm working on it, but I'll know when I find the right man."

He smiled, "Sounds positive."

Chapter 5
Alone Together

Billy completed all his tests by the end of October, and we returned to Dr. Duncan's office once again. There had been a noticeable change in his health, including an increase in his coughing attacks, a decrease in his energy levels, and even occasional fainting spells.

The tenor of the meeting was serious and very distressing. Dr. Duncan was accompanied by a colleague–a specialist in chronic lung diseases. It was a long session, and they attempted to focus more on general explanations than on complex technical details. The result was that they weren't absolutely certain what was causing Billy's condition but guessed it to be a combination of chronic obstructive pulmonary disease and interstitial lung disease.

When I asked what the prognosis was, their answers were somewhat vague, and I couldn't figure out whether they really didn't know or simply didn't want to say. My own interpretation was that the prognosis was not very positive, something I was not inclined to share with either Billy or my parents. We drove home in solemn silence.

At breakfast, Billy smiled as he sat down, "I must have learned a lot yesterday because I'm aware of so much more that I don't know today."

"You seem to be in a curiously sunny mood," I replied.

"It's my turn," he said, "And I choose 'Loss of Identity.'"

"What possibly made you think of that?" I asked.

"Dusty called today," I said.

"Oh, how's he doing, and how's his mother?" I asked.

"He says they are doing okay," he replied, "But he hasn't opened his Christmas hamper yet, and he won't until Christmas Day."

"Something to look forward to," I replied.

"It started me thinking about his life at the Brandon Residential School," he said.

I looked at him, puzzled, "A residential school?"

"You know," he replied. "Like a boarding school for Indian kids."

"I don't think I've ever heard of them."

"Very few people seem to know anything about them."

"Are there many?"

"Too many," he said, "According to Dusty."

"Are they on the reservations?"

"Some, I suppose," he replied, "But Brandon is not on a reservation."

"What's that got to do with loss of identity?"

"When Dusty was eight," Billy explained.

"Some people from the government showed up at their home on the reservation, and he and his sister were taken away to a school in Brandon, operated by the United Church."

"Gosh, why would they do that?" I asked.

"They told him that he needed a proper education. They said there wasn't a large enough population near the reservation to build a school, and they didn't have enough teachers."

"Why couldn't they just bus the kids?" I asked. "Like they do in rural areas around Winnipeg."

"I'm not sure, but I know it was difficult for Dusty, his sister, and his mother," Billy replied solemnly. "In fact, it was very traumatic for them because the government people only spoke English, which made it hard to understand what was going on."

"But didn't his mother speak English?" I asked, feeling a bit uneducated now.

"Not much," he sighed, "And Dusty and his sister didn't speak any English at all, so it was a good thing that his uncle was there to translate."

"And they just took them away?" I asked.

Billy snapped his fingers, "Just like that. He said his uncle was forced to pack their bags while he and his sister sat with their mother. His mother cried through the whole ordeal."

"That's horrible," I said. "Really horrible."

"And when he finally got to the school," Billy added. "They changed his name to Dustin, and he wasn't allowed to speak Cree at all."

"How did he communicate then?" I asked.

"He told me that all the kids simply had to learn English, or else the teachers would beat them."

"No, I can't believe that any church-run school would do that," I said, still stunned. "Especially the United Church. Are you sure he was telling the truth?"

"Oh, I'm pretty sure. He showed me a few scars."

"Well, I've never heard of such a thing," I said

"Most white people haven't," Billy said sadly. "And if they do, they don't seem to care."

"But I've never read or heard anything about them. Nothing." I replied.

I was feeling defensive but also more and more outraged.

"Dusty's uncle told him it was part of the government's plan," Billy continued. "Apparently, his uncle had attended a residential school when he was young, but he ran away and never returned."

"This sounds like a horror story. What government plan was he talking about?"

"I don't know what it was called, but it was started a long time ago, and all the schools are run by Christian churches," Billy explained.

"That can't be right," I protested.

"Look it up," he challenged me.

I was really upset about where this discussion was going, and I remember the feeling of relief when Mom reminded us that it was getting late.

He gave me a tired smile. "We'll pick this up later then. Have a good day."

While driving to university, my head spun with a mixture of confusion and guilt. Could Billy really be right about these schools? After my second class, I had a spare, so I went to the library to see what I could learn about residential schools. I found a thesis on the subject and took it to a table read because it could not be checked out.

I sat there by myself, thumbing through this thesis, and it corroborated much of what Billy had said, specifically that the program was real. I copied down the following passage from the document, but in my haste, I neglected to note the author's name or the title of the thesis.

"In Canada, the Indian residential school system is a network of mandatory boarding schools for Indigenous peoples. The network is funded by the Canadian government's Department of Indian Affairs and administered by Christian churches. The school system is created for the purpose of removing Indigenous children from the influence of their own culture and assimilating them into the dominant Canadian culture. By the 1930s, about thirty percent of Indigenous children were believed to be attending residential schools."

I took my notes to the Students Union Building to meet some fellow students for lunch, and I broached the subject with them. I shared my notes, and most admitted that they had never heard of this program. They were often doubtful of anything I had to say, being one of only three females enrolled in pre-med. Two said they were vaguely aware of it but didn't know much about it. Most of them felt that it sounded like a reasonable concept to provide a good education for kids who lived in remote locations, but when I told them about Dusty's perspective, they were quite skeptical. I was just beginning to feel a little relieved that I wasn't the only one who never heard of this until my good friend Simon Cohen weighed in on the discussion.

"You know Hitler managed to keep most of Germany and the rest of the world in ignorance about his concentration camps during the war," Simon pointed out thoughtfully. "Out of sight, out of mind... you know."

We all just looked at each other for a few seconds and then Simon shrugged and said, "Just saying."

We changed the subject and went back to finishing lunch. The next morning at breakfast, Billy asked if I wanted to finish the discussion.

"Which part?" I asked. "The schools or the loss of identity."

"Okay. Seems like you still have doubts about the schools, so let's just talk about loss of identity."

"Okay," I agreed, feeling relieved.

Let's just suppose," Billy considered, "That you had amnesia and that you'd forgotten your language and your name. Wouldn't you feel some sense of loss of identity?"

"That'd be a horrible sensation," I granted.

Billy nodded and drank some coffee, "And you'd probably feel alone, right?"

"Probably," I toyed with my egg. "So, where are you going with this?"

"It's all about knowing who we are," he declared.

"Do you know who you are?" I asked.

"Nope. At least not yet. Do you?"

He grinned and then chomped his toast.

I sighed, "I think so."

Billy pushed his plate aside, "When I was really little, I always believed that before I was born, I was somewhere else. Not physically, of course, but somewhere with just my thoughts."

"You mean, like, with your soul?" I asked.

"Maybe. I'm not sure, but I'd wake up every morning and think: I'm the only one in the world who is me. I'd go to bed being me and wake up again, still being me, and I wondered if everyone thinks they're unique that way?"

I cradled my coffee cup, then said, "I do sometimes. And I'm sure most people do, but they don't dwell on it."

"You're probably right, but it's different for Dusty because he knew who he was before he was taken away, and now, well, now, he doesn't."

"He's still the same person inside. Don't you think?"

Billy shook his head and leaned his elbows on the table.

"Not really. I think he's caught between being a Cree Indian and a white Canadian person. Must be pretty confusing because now I think he feels he's neither."

"I suppose it is confusing," I said, and then I told him about my discussion with my classmates and Simon's comment about 'out of sight, out of mind.'"

"I think your friend's right," Billy replied. "We may all live together in a commonplace, but many people don't feel like they're part of a real community, so they feel, well, all alone."

"I concede," I replied and gave a mock bow. "I think I'm done with oxymorons for now."

The interesting thing was that you could tell Billy anything, and he wouldn't judge you. How many people in the world are like that?

Chapter 6
Melanie

Between tests and treatments, Billy spent a lot of time at the hospital. I often dropped him off early on my way to university, but he never seemed to mind being early or waiting late for me to pick him up, mostly because he always carried his backpack full of books and really enjoyed reading to the sick kids. They loved this, as well as all the stories he would tell them. In mid-November, I came to pick him up and found him sitting on a chair in the middle of the ward with about a dozen youngsters, either seated around him or sitting in wheelchairs. As I watched him, I heard a familiar voice from behind me.

"Amanda?"

"Mrs. Neuman!" I replied, greeting her with a big hug.

"Looking for Billy?" she asked.

"I'm his chauffeur," I explained, and we chatted while I waited for him to finish his story.

"These kids sure relate to him," Mrs. Neuman noted. "Probably because he's still a wide-eyed kid at heart."

"What's he reading now?" I asked.

"A Christmas Carol," Mrs. Neuman replied. "And he does all the parts in different voices. He's very entertaining."

"Isn't he just?" I smiled.

"Did he tell you about our Christmas play?"

She clapped her hands, "Yes! And I ordered four tickets. I know David will just love it!"

Billy noticed me waiting for him and waved. A few minutes later, he loaded his backpack and came over to us.

"Thanks for letting me stay, Mrs. Neuman. Give my best to David."

"Happy to have you around, Billy," Mrs. Neuman smiled.

"So, this where you worked as a candy striper?" he asked me.

"And where Mrs. Neuman had the challenge of managing us," I said, smiling at her.

Mrs. Neuman laughed. "You were all wonderful. Like little princesses."

"My lady," Billy said and bowed to me.

"Time to take Prince Charming home, my dear," Mrs. Neuman said as she patted me on the shoulder and waved to Billy. "Take care of him, Amanda."

"Can I drive?" he asked, "My test was hours ago, and they didn't give me any meds or shots."

"Best not to take any chances."

Driving up Maryland, Billy told me all about the kids and how brave they all were. Then he went quiet as we waited for the light to change at Portage. I asked him what was wrong.

"Melanie Skoffer was one of the kids in the hospital today," he said dolefully. "She has a broken arm."

"Who is she?" I asked.

"Do you remember me telling you about the last Easter Baskets we delivered?"

"Oh, yes, when Dusty hit that drunk guy?" I asked.

"Yeah." He looked out the car window, silent for a moment.

"That drunk guy was Melanie's Dad, Mike Skoffer," he began again when we passed The Bay, "And I remember seeing Melanie standing in the doorway as we all tussled and seeing that she had bruises on her face and arms. I think that brute's beating her."

"Couldn't it have just been an accident?" I asked.

He fiddled with the lock on the car door all the way to Main Street.

"I know the signs. I lived with a foster father who was abusive."

I turned onto Main Street and glanced at him, "You mean your foster father abused his foster kids?"

"No, just one kid and it was his own daughter. I remember hearing a loud argument upstairs one night, but Eric and I were too scared to leave our basement room to find out what was happening."

"Who's Eric?"

"He was another foster kid. We shared a room. He was a year older than me."

"So, what happened?"

"I was only eleven at the time, and when we heard pounding on the front door and different voices. Eric and I crept out of our room to listen. We soon figured out that it was the police. When things calmed down upstairs, we expected someone to come down and check on us, so we scurried back to our beds, but no one came. Not until the morning, anyway, when we came upstairs in the morning, we found two people from the Children's Aid Society in the kitchen making breakfast for us. After breakfast, they helped us pack up our things because we were being moved to a different foster home. We didn't see our foster parents before we left, and we were both taken to different homes, so I never saw Eric again either."

Billy paused and studied the rain hitting the windshield until we reached the new Disraeli bridge.

He sighed and continued. "No one ever told us anything about what had happened, and it was weeks before I even heard a rumor about our foster father's arrest. After that, I read the paper carefully every day for weeks before I finally found a small court case article with only sketchy information about what had happened."

"So, what really happened?" I asked.

My parents had only ever been kind to me, and this was all a kind of horrible revelation.

"I found the name of the Free Press court reporter," he began. "And phoned her to tell her about my foster care experience with that family. She asked me a few questions, and a few days later, someone from the Children's Aid Society showed up with a lawyer to ask me more questions about certain behaviors of the father. That's how I learned about the signs of abusive behavior, including the behavior of the victims."

"Gosh, did they ask you to testify in court?" I asked.

He shook his head and grinned wryly, "No, I think I was too young to be reliable."

"Have you talked to anyone else about Melanie and your suspicions?" I asked.

"Egil, but he said he couldn't do anything unless Melanie spoke up, but I know she won't as long as she's with her father."

"Did you ask her about her arm today?"

"I did, and she mumbled something about slipping on some ice, then I asked her if her father broke her arm, and she nodded, just a little, but it was a nod."

"Oh, dear, this is awful. But I don't see what we can do about it."

"Well, we have to do something," I stated emphatically.

"It's not our responsibility."

He grimaced and began wheezing again, "Maybe not yours, but I feel it's mine."

"So, what are you going to do?"

He bit his lip as we finally turned up the driveway. He got out slowly, his lungs still wheezing.

"I don't know yet. Nothing at the moment. Her father was there to pick her up when we were leaving."

After that, he didn't mention Melanie again for some time, but I knew she weighed on his mind because his sunny mood dimmed for several days.

Chapter 7
The Rise And Fall Of Ebenezer Scrooge

Over the next few weeks, I remained concerned about Billy, but I also had to focus on my studies and memorize my lines for our Christmas play. I had the part of Mrs. Cratchit; Billy was playing the Ghost of Christmas Past and was dressed up as the Grim Reaper. This worked out great for him because he had no lines, and he didn't have to be on stage until the end of the play. If he happened to wheeze a bit, people just thought it was part of his character.

Billy was a true champ when it came to searching out costumes and props, mostly because of his connection with the Salvation Army. He also found a used electric garage door opener to lift and lower Scrooge's four-poster bed, which we also used for the gravestone scene near the end of the play. The set he designed was ingenious. It was an eight-foot-square platform with a bedpost fastened in each of the four corners. The wires were connected from the top of the posters to the pulleys fixed to the roof trusses, which were then connected to the garage door opener. Hollow cardboard tubes, decorated like trees, were also connected by separate wires with manual pulleys so they could be dropped down over each poster for the graveyard scene when the platform was on the ground.

Near the end of the play, when Scrooge was kneeling at the headstone and lamenting his fate, the plan was to turn the lights down. The trees would be manually pulled up to reveal the posters, and the bed curtains would be lowered while Mr. Scrooge continued with his lamenting monologue but hidden from the audience. Then, the platform would be raised up about two feet by the garage door opener, and since the headstone was only just a piece of cloth that covered the headboard, it could be easily removed by Scrooge.

Once the scene was magically transformed from the graveyard scene to the bedroom scene, the lights would come back up, revealing Scrooge pulling back the bed curtains to discover that he was in his own bed and not really dead.

That was the plan, and it actually worked when we tested it at the Miles Macdonell gymnasium where we were performing the play.

When one of the 'urchin' kids dropped out, BJ volunteered his sister Maria to fill in, and since BJ was in charge of props, he brought her along for her first rehearsal. I was straight away enchanted by her smile, and I took her under my wing, introducing her to all the cast, crew, and our director, Rev. Dawson.

"Welcome," Rev. Dawson smiled, taking Maria's hand, "Have you ever been in a play before?"

"No, but I've seen one at Rainbow Stage," Maria replied proudly.

Rev. Dawson called the rest of the cast together to introduce our new member and advised that we start with the street urchin scenes so we could let the kids get home early. Except for Maria, the other kids were quite shy, but Rev. Dawson and the rest of the cast were so patient and supportive that they soon gained the kids' confidence, which got them even more excited to be part of our magical production.

Maria was especially interested in all the sets and props. And BJ was only too happy to explain everything to her before she went home. She was fascinated by Billy's platform design when BJ demonstrated how it could be lifted up and lowered down. He made a point of telling her not to touch anything without permission.

Dress rehearsal went surprisingly well, and we all felt we were ready for opening night on Saturday. Opening night went off without a hitch, and as we approached our final performance, a Matinee on Christmas Eve, we were feeling quite confident, especially since we'd received a wonderful press review, and our attendance numbers were much higher than expected.

Due to his numerous tests, by early December Billy had to stop working at Eaton's. However, he was happy to drive Mrs. Gregg to the Salvation Army College every morning, using the Sally Ann bus. Then he would spend the rest of the morning delivering Christmas hampers. Since he had the use of the bus, after he finished his deliveries, he dropped in to visit the kids at the hospital almost every day.

Billy left before I did each morning and I found myself missing our breakfast discussions, but I still did all the driving to and from Miles Mac for our performances every night. On our way to our second-last performance, Billy seemed quite downcast again, I so asked him what was bothering him.

"Melanie is coming to the hospital tomorrow morning to have her cast removed," he told me. "And I just wish there was something I could do."

"What time will she be there?"

"She told me her father is coming to pick her up around eleven o'clock. I was thinking of dropping in to see her after my deliveries in the morning."

"Just don't do anything foolish," I reminded him.

He just laughed, which always worried me.

When I came downstairs for breakfast the next morning, Billy had already left to make his deliveries. Mom said he'd meet me at the theatre since he had the use of the bus for the day. When I got to Miles Mac, Billy was already there, sitting in the front row beside a little, dark-haired girl, who I guessed to be about nine or ten years old. I went over to see them, and, to my surprise, he introduced her as Melanie.

"I'll be right back, Melanie," Billy said, patting her hand and grabbing mine as he led me backstage.

"What are you up to?" I whispered urgently. "Are her parents here?"

"Listen, Amanda, don't worry. There's a good reason and a real reason."

I crossed my arms. "It better be very, very good."

"The good reason is… she really wants to see the show."

He smiled and then added, "But the real reason is that she is willing to talk to Egil."

"Did you get permission for her to be here?" I asked.

"Her parents weren't there, but I have her permission," he responded slowly, "And that's all I need."

"No, it's not," I said (oh, he could be so stubborn, that Billy).

"How did you get her here anyway?"

"In the bus?" he answered, eyeing me cautiously.

I stared at him, stunned, "You mean you abducted her? That's simply outrageous and completely irresponsible."

Billy threw up his hands, "She just really wants to see the show, Amanda. And it's Christmas."

"You could go to jail for this!"

He sighed, "That's a risk I'm willing to take if her father comes with me."

"Oh, Billy, you don't even know her."

"That's where you're wrong. I know Melanie and many kids just like her."

"I've got to get in costume," I said scornfully, and as I turned around to stomp off to the classroom that was used as a dressing area, I saw a familiar, handsome face – Egil's.

"Are you all right, Amanda?" Egil asked. "You seem a bit flustered."

I was flustered, but I tried to compose myself. "I…I'm just concerned for little Melanie."

"Melanie will be just fine, Amanda," he replied kindly. "That's why I'm here early. But is it Melanie, you're really worried about?"

"I-I- I don't know what you mean," I stammered.

He smiled, "It's okay, Amanda. I love him too, you know. And we're all worried about him."

I felt like my every emotion was on display. I was anxious to escape. As I attempted to step around him, he gently touched me on the arm, not trying to stop me, but simply to get my attention before I left.

"If you want to talk, Amanda. Please call me any time," He smiled at me.

I smiled back. I couldn't help it.

"Thank you, Egil. I…I will."

I patted his hand and left.

The play was about to start, and I was determined to be professional about all this and not let it affect my performance. I took a deep breath, refocused, got into costume, did my makeup, and returned backstage to check the audience to see if Melanie was still sitting there. That's when I caught Albert Reimer, the actor who was playing Scrooge, staring at me.

"Are you okay, Amanda?" he asked. "You look like you've seen a ghost."

"What?" I asked, startled, "Oh, well, it is a ghost story, right?"

"Right, just getting into character then?"

"Exactly," I smiled as I returned to my dressing room to check my makeup.

I felt sick, but I remembered my breathing exercises, so I took deep breaths until I heard the five- minute call. The play was soon underway, and I concentrated only on the show and on my part, so I was ready whenever I had to go on. When I made my first entrance, I noticed Egil sitting beside Melanie. Somehow that calmed me down a bit.

The remainder of our performance was on track, right up to the part where the Grim Reaper showed Scrooge his own grave. Scrooge was kneeling down on the platform in front of the headstone, pleading with the Ghost. When the lights dimmed, I heard the bed curtains being lowered down and assumed that Scrooge was doing exactly what he did every night in the dark.

I heard the operator use the garage door to raise the platform and then saw him step away to manually raise the trees that covered the bedposts. Then I heard the garage door again and turned to see the operator returning to the control station.

Unbeknownst to any of us, Maria had taken her turn with the button and when the operator returned, I heard him whisper to Maria: "Don't touch that button."

Too late!

Scrooge pulled the curtains back right on cue, but just as he started his lines again, he glanced down over the side of the bed. Laughter filtered up from the audience as Scrooge stared down at the audience.

Simultaneously, I realized that the bed had been raised to a height of five feet above the stage. Billy, the Grim Reaper, who was exiting the stage, whirled around and rushed towards Scrooge at the side of the bed. He backed up toward Scrooge and silently motioned to him to climb on his back.

Scrooge quickly understood and, as flustered as he was, managed to climb onto Billy's back. However, as Billy crouched down to lower him to the stage, he began to cough, and Scrooge lost his grip, slowly slipping off Billy's back, much to the amusement of the audience.

Maria, who was watching from the wings, came running out on stage to help.

"Don't worry, Mr. Scrooge," she called, as Scrooge propped himself up on one arm, "I'll help you."

"Thank you, thank you," he replied, trying to get up with Maria's assistance.

Billy, still holding the scythe in one hand, offered his other hand to Mr. Scrooge and pulled him up. Remaining in silent character, except for his wheezing (which only added to his eerie performance), Billy pointed with his scythe to the window. The audience was now roaring with laughter.

Maria grabbed Scrooge's sleeve, dragged him to the window, and said quite clearly, "It's time for you to talk to the window, Mr. Scrooge."

Albert Reimer was a seasoned veteran who quickly and professionally recovered his composure.

"Quite right, my dear," he replied, back in character as Scrooge. "Could you please find my slippers for me?"

The audience was clearly enjoying this version of the play. Scrooge called out to the imaginary little boy through the window and delivered the rest of his lines without a hitch. Maria returned with his slippers, and he thanked her repeatedly while placing the slippers on his hands and clapping them together. He then began dancing around the room just as he had rehearsed the part. He gently picked up Maria and waltzed off the stage with her waving to the audience. The audience roared with approval.

When the play ended, and we'd all completed our bows, Albert took both Maria's and Billy's hands and led them to the front of center stage, where the men bowed, and Maria curtsied.

The audience gave them a standing ovation. I was so proud of Maria and quite pleased with myself that I'd taught her how to curtsey!

Once the final curtain came down and the audience began to leave the gymnasium, the backstage became a beehive of activity with people packing props, dismantling sets, taking down lights, and collecting whatever needed to be loaded in the truck. I just headed straight out on stage where Egil and Billy were standing with Melanie.

"What's happening?" I asked as three ladies approached us from the wings.

One of them rushed to Melanie and held her tightly. It was clear she'd been crying. The other two ladies looked more official and stood back while Egil crouched down to speak with Melanie.

"These two ladies with your mother are from the Children's Aid Society," he explained.

"I'm so sorry, sweetheart," Melanie's mother said, teary-eyed. "It's all my fault."

"No, it's not," Egil replied softly, taking a gentle hold of the mother's hand.

He then turned to Melanie, "These ladies are here to help you and your mom. Is that okay with you?"

Melanie just nodded her head and hung on to her mother. Her mother gently took hold of her hand, and they all left the stage. I stood there, still in shock.

"I suppose you want me to explain what happened?" Billy asked me sheepishly.

I stared at him. I was so awash in mixed and conflicting emotions that I couldn't speak.

"Is Melanie okay?" I finally managed to ask.

He smiled, "Just perfect."

"No."

He looked at me curiously, "No?"

"I don't want an explanation as long as everything is really okay; I prefer what happened to remain a mystery," I smiled. "Like some kind of Christmas miracle."

He just smiled at me, and that smile is burned forever into my memory, that wondrous, open, beaming smile of Billy Johnson's.

That was Billy's last Christmas Eve, but I know it was also his favorite, and whenever I think about it, happy tears fill my eyes.

Chapter 8
The Memorial

The funeral service for William Frederick Johnson was held at John Black Memorial Church on Saturday, March 8th, 1961, shortly after his eighteenth birthday. The church was packed with standing room only. Suffice it to say there were no happy tears that day.

Following the services, Kathleen invited both Egil and me to join her, BJ, Carolyn, and Dusty in a short visit to Churchill Drive to witness her beloved prison, Assiniboine House, being demolished.

The End

Epilogue

On Christmas Eve, 2011, the children's party was a resounding success, with a magnificent array of delicacies from Melnyk's Bakery and Catering. Presents for all the kids from Santa, AKA BJ MacDonald, were distributed by his charming elves, followed by the appearance of a humorously inept magician.

The opening ceremonies, on the other hand, were serene and mercifully brief, lacking both a formal ribbon-cutting ceremony and the traditional lengthy speeches. However, it did take Mr. MacDonald some time to introduce and personally thank all the guests.

Everyone seemed to enjoy the escorted tours of the impressive new facilities that boasted a full gymnasium, an exercise room, a swimming pool, a multi-purpose room, a computer equipped learning lab, meeting spaces, private counselling rooms and what would prove to be the most popular amenity - a full cafeteria.

Most guests had read the six stories, so they were familiar with Billy's life and sad passing.

However, having received the last book only a week before Christmas, his death came as a bit of a shock to several of the grandchildren, who voiced their displeasure that they had not been forewarned. One of BJ's granddaughters had fully expected to meet Billy at the opening ceremonies, which further exacerbating her disappointment. Yet another felt like she'd lost a good friend, and now she was grieving for someone she'd never actually met.

Mr. MacDonald's speech focused primarily on the name of the facility. In response to a common question as to why the large sign over the front entrance read Billy's Place and not the official name on the plaque, which is The William F. Johnson Youth Centre, BJ explained that when they were young foster kids, they never had a real home of their own.

"Other kids would often say things like, 'Let's go to Terry's place.' But Billy never had his own place, so he could never say, 'Let's go to my place.' And we could never say, 'Let's go to Billy's place.' But now, fifty years on, we can. We are so delighted to finally be able to welcome you all to Billy's Place."

Perhaps the highlight of the evening, which was also the end of the evening, was when BJ introduced his four-year-old granddaughter, Chelsea. He crouched down as she ran straight to him, gave him a big hug, and thanked him for her present, not fooled for a second who was wearing that Santa suit. BJ gently lifted her on a chair in front of the microphone and asked if she had something to say to these wonderful people. She softly wished everyone a 'very Merry Christmas to all and many happy tears.'

Then BJ gave her a big hug and gently set her back down on the stage. She ran straight toward her father, then suddenly stopped, turned to the audience, curtsied, and continued her race toward open arms.

The Very End.